ENCIZO LOADED ANOTHER BOLT

Upon seeing his comrade pitch to the ground, the second terrorist dropped into a crouch and fanned his AK-47 over the horizon, while his free hand scrambled for his cell phone. Encizo triggered the crossbow. An instant later the gunner froze as a bolt jutted from his ribs.

The little Cuban checked his watch: 9:07 p.m.

Right on time.

"Two down, Cal," he whispered into his throat mike. "Your status?"

A moment passed without reply. Then another.

"Cal? Cal?" Encizo whispered again, this time more urgently. The only thing that filled the silence was the plummeting sensation in his stomach. Before he could utter another word, gunshots rang out across the compound.

D1115241

DON PENDLETON'S

STONY

AMERICA'S ULTRA-COVERT INTELLIGENCE AGENCY

MAN®

PROMISE
TO DEFEND

A GOLD EAGLE BOOK FROM

W🌐RLDWIDE®

TORONTO • NEW YORK • LONDON
AMSTERDAM • PARIS • SYDNEY • HAMBURG
STOCKHOLM • ATHENS • TOKYO • MILAN
MADRID • WARSAW • BUDAPEST • AUCKLAND

First edition October 2005

ISBN 0-373-61963-4

PROMISE TO DEFEND

Special thanks and acknowledgment to
Tim Tresslar for his contribution to this work.

Printed in U.S.A.

PROMISE
TO DEFEND

To my wife, Robbie, my parents, Dennis and Anita,
and my brother, Tony, without whom there'd
be no writing career for yours truly.
And to O. C. Hayden, who sang like an angel
long before he was called to join them.

CHAPTER ONE

Washington, D.C.

His face a stony mask, hands clasped behind his back, David Campbell stood at the window of the safehouse's third-floor library, staring at the nation's capital. Although he saw the endless rows of stately marble buildings, the throngs of people, the carpet of lights, they barely registered with him. Other things occupied his mind.

The same landscape, but consumed.

Consumed with fire.

Unspeakable carnage.

Squeezing his eyes shut, Campbell tried to banish the images, but found they only returned with a greater vigor. So be it, he thought. He was a man of vision, a man chosen to lead the nation, hell, the world, to greater things. And men of vision suffered. If that was his price, his burden, he'd shoulder it, like the good soldier his father had trained him to be.

Both his father and grandfather had been great men, laying the groundwork for all that would transpire during the next few days. Not that they ever would have envisioned it unfolding as it would, a hellstorm of blood and fire sure to shake the country to its very core. They'd been good men. No, great men. But they never could have envisioned the current circumstances that drove Campbell to do what he was about to do.

There'd be fire, but it'd be a cleansing fire, a rebirth, something that in a dozen years would be celebrated as ushering in a new era for the country. That he had been called upon to marshal such forces and channel them into this pursuit was humbling, indeed. Campbell considered himself a simple man, like his forebears. Not stupid, but simple. A man who saw things in black and white. And he knew, like the Campbell men before him, he'd do the right thing just as they would have done, were they here to see the complexities he faced in his solemn family duty.

A door opened from behind Campbell, and he whirled to greet the visitor. A thick man, his lumpy head shaved clean, entered, stood at attention, waiting for permission to speak.

Jonas Barrins was Campbell's most trusted confidant. Like Campbell, he was dressed in crisp khakis, a black turtleneck and steel-toed boots. A 9 mm Beretta rode on the man's left hip, the handgun's butt jutting forward in a cross-draw position, also just like Campbell.

Other than their mode of dress and their armament, however, the two men differed greatly. Campbell towered six inches over his lieutenant. His body, conditioned by hours of exercise, dwarfed the other man's slender frame. His steel-gray eyes, wide and intelligent, bore into Barrins's piggish brown eyes that never seemed to blink.

"At ease, Jonas," Campbell said, his voice little more than a hoarse whisper.

"Control is waiting."

"For permission?"

"Yes."

"Then all, I assume, is ready."

"Just a word from you."

"You realize what I'm about to do, don't you, Jonas? The world I'm about to create? Are the men ready to do this? To take so many lives?"

"We're ready to follow your lead. To do as you ask."

Pleased, Campbell gave his comrade a tight smile. In the next instant, the visions—the fire, the screams, the corpses—erupted in his head. He shook them away vigorously. If Barrins caught the behavior, his impenetrable expression gave no indication. Instead he stared at Campbell like a dog awaiting another command.

"You know why I do this, Jonas," Campbell said. "You of all people understand."

"Sir?"

"What will happen tomorrow, I mean. I don't want to do this. But this country, my country, leaves me no choice. I cannot sit by while it destroys itself, chasing third-world savages as a greater danger grows elsewhere. What I will do, I will do for America. The world, really. It can be no other way."

"It can be no other way," Barrins echoed. "You can't second-guess what needs to be done. Or let it trouble you."

Campbell nodded. "You're a good soldier and a good friend, Jonas. Please. Sit," he said, gesturing. "We must rest now, because during the next few days, we'll be busy doing our sacred work. Our country has grown soft. It's forgotten its purpose. We aren't here to spread democracy to the world, but to defend only our own. We worry about the Arabs when we could crush them, turn their region into a smoking hole. We ignore the Communists while they grow stronger."

Even seated, Barrins kept his back ramrod-straight. "It's insane," he agreed. "Your father would agree, if he were still here."

Campbell's voice grew icy. "Do not speak of my father. Or his death."

A nervous tic pulled at the corner of Barrins's mouth. "I'm sorry. I didn't mean—"

"What you meant is immaterial. My father is gone. I'm trying to honor his legacy. Only I may speak of him."

"Of course."

"They talked of him as though he were crazy, a mad dog to be put down. He tried to warn them, but they wouldn't listen. He tried to tell them that the Communists remained a threat, despite the end of the cold war."

"But they wouldn't listen."

"No," Campbell said. "They wouldn't listen." Campbell shook his head, felt the anger churn in his gut as he recalled his father's efforts to sway the government, the President, all to no avail. Swallowing hard, he chased away the memory with a dismissive gesture. "He did his best, and that's all a man can do. You smoke, Jonas. Please have a cigarette."

"You don't mind?"

"Be my guest."

Campbell watched as the other man produced a cigarette and torched the end with a flame from his lighter. Barrins made a show of turning his head to the left, blowing the smoke from the corner of his mouth so it didn't stray close to his companion. Campbell suppressed a smile. The little kiss-ass was always so eager to please, so reluctant to make waves with Campbell or his father before him.

"I thought you didn't like smoke," Barrins said.

"I can make an exception, for a friend," Campbell stated. "Especially one so close to the end."

Barrins raised a fist to his mouth and coughed, expelling tendrils of white smoke from his mouth and nostrils. He raised his eyes at Campbell, even as he tried to clear his throat and lungs. "Sir?" he managed to choke out.

Campbell leaned back in his chair and pinned the other man with his gaze, letting an uncomfortable pause hang between them for several seconds before replying. "Please, Jonas," he said. "We both know my father's death was no accident."

"Of course not, sir. He was assassinated—"

Without thinking Campbell swept an arm across his desktop, clearing it of its contents. The sudden movement caused Barrins to start.

"I told you not to speak of him," Campbell shouted. "Or his death."

"Of course," Barrins said, a tremor audible in his voice.

Campbell watched as Barrins ground out his cigarette and settled his forearm on the armrest, bringing his fingertips closer to the pistol's butt. Before it all was over, Campbell knew he'd make a play for his gun. It didn't matter. He had the bastard dead to rights. He could've killed him before, but he wanted to drag it out. Toy with the little troll before taking him out.

"You've been with us how long now, Jonas? Ten years?"

"Twelve. I've been with you twelve years. I joined shortly before—" he caught himself, nearly choking on the words "—I mean, before the change," he said, referring to the elder Campbell's death.

Campbell leaned back in his chair, not letting his eyes drift from Barrins's.

"The President asked that we bring you aboard, as a personal favor to him. From my father's standpoint, that was good enough. My father trusted the Man. He trusted you. Implicitly, I might add. I trusted you, too, after he died. It was the way I honored his memory."

"Thank—"

Campbell silenced him with a gesture. "Let me finish. What my father created, what his father created before him, is vital to national security. The Cadre is the only thing that stands between anarchy and the government's continued operation, should the country suffer a decapitating strike."

"I understand."

"I don't think you do. Many in Washington consider us a cold war relic. They believe I've overstepped my bounds, selling arms to raise money and assassinating those I deem a threat to national security. The President wants to pull the plug on the entire operation. Do you know why this operation has succeeded since 1954?"

"Because—"

"Because of loyalty. Unlike other covert programs, we've built in a certain level of loyalty—security, if you will—by keeping this a multigenerational project. Most of the men and women working for the Cadre are third or fourth generation. They've been raised from their youth, trained in warfare, politics, medicine, agriculture, to step in and take over the country should something happen.

"We're what the media likes to call a 'shadow government.' And we maintained security by keeping to ourselves, never bringing aboard outsiders. We often went into the real world, worked at companies, fought in wars, lived in regular society, but we always came back. This system always worked. We remained a secret to all but a handful of legislators and administration officials."

Barrins squirmed in his chair. Sweat glistened on his forehead.

"Where are you going with all this?" he blurted, his voice taut.

Campbell smiled. "Where? Where, indeed? As you know, I file reports with the President. I let him know where things are. I don't tell him about the illegal weapons sales. I don't tell him when I kill a high-ranking Chinese or North Korean official. Yet he knows these things and it puzzles me. So much so, in fact, that I had to sit back and think. I had to ask myself, 'Who had the most to gain from betraying me?'"

Barrins's piggish eyes began darting right, left, looking everywhere but at Campbell.

"After that, I took it a step further. My father was assassinated, I believe, by the very government we serve. And if that same government infiltrated the Cadre with a rogue agent, what might that person do. Kill me, perhaps?"

"Surely you don't think…" Barrins protested.

"I don't think," Campbell said. "I know."

He mashed a button under his desk with a boot-clad toe.

The door behind Barrins opened and a man entered the room.

His hand dwarfed the SIG-Sauer P220 he carried. Barrins clawed for his weapon. He emitted a small whimper as he realized he'd never complete the move.

The bigger man's handgun cracked twice, the bullets drilling through the seat's backrest and into Barrins. His body seized up and he gagged. Blood frothed at his lips as they worked soundlessly.

"You see, Barrins," Campbell continued, as though the words still registered with the dying man. "I looked at two things, ability and motive. You had access to the most critical intelligence. I fed you some of it as a test. The rest you stole with good, old-fashioned tradecraft, particularly hacking into our most secure servers and drilling your subordinates for information. Your motive? Well, you're a kiss-ass, a weak-willed kiss-ass and you couldn't help but please the President. I'm sure money changed hands, too. But I think that was secondary."

Barrins shifted around in his chair. Struggling fingers grasped his Beretta's grip. The SIG-Sauer cracked once more and a bullet cored into Barrins, shattering his spine before exiting his stomach and lodging itself into Campbell's armored desk.

Campbell shook his head, made a clucking noise with his tongue. "Poor, misguided bastard," he said. "He just didn't understand who he was fucking with." With a gesture, he beckoned the shooter to step from the shadows and enter the library. "Ellis?"

The big man took a couple more steps into the room, holstering the side arm as he did.

"Sir?"

"Let the others know. This betrayal changes nothing. Nothing. Soon it will be a different world. I don't care what it takes to create it, we will have a different world. Let everyone know that."

"Gladly," Ellis White said.

Mexico

CONCLUDING HIS PRAYERS, Hassan Salih stuffed his weathered copy of the Koran into his pocket, then checked his wristwatch. A smile tugged at the corners of his lips. It was time.

He rose to his feet. Dusting off the seat of his pants with his right hand, he hefted his canvas duffel bag and slung its carrying strap over his shoulder. After spending hours crammed inside the sweltering tunnel, breathing the dust-laden air as they sat in stony silence, the sudden burst of movement grabbed the attention of the others. They all turned to regard him.

He met their expectant gazes and said, "Come, brothers. It is time to perform God's work."

Still silent, the others stood, shouldering their gear bags as they rose. Turning, Salih started down the narrow passage, which was carved into the desert floor. From what he'd been told, the tunnel had been dug by a Mexican drug cartel and used for transporting narcotics into America and cash south of the U.S. border.

This night it was to be used to smuggle something much deadlier. He and his fellow warriors had come to the United States looking to draw blood from the Americans. As with many of the men accompanying him, Salih was young, just twenty-six years old. He'd graduated from university in Riyadh four years earlier, armed with a degree in Islamic studies but sentenced to a life of state-sponsored welfare. Humiliation and rage seemed to be his most constant companions as he'd searched for meaningful work, but to no avail. With nothing but time on his hands, he'd spent his days in religious schools, studying the Koran, deepening his faith, speaking with others who shared his anger and frustration over the circumstances he and his brothers faced.

Part of the blame, he knew, lay with his own country's

government. The royal family was as addicted to Western money as America was to his homeland's oil. The Saudi rulers encouraged immigrants—men and women from Pakistan and other Muslim nations—to take jobs that rightfully should go to the Saudis.

But it was America that propped up the royal family, supporting it with weapons and money, even as the Saudi people continued sinking into an ever-deeper quagmire of humiliation and rage. Meanwhile, the royal family with its palaces, private jets and portfolios of American stocks ignored the rage simmering all around it. It continued to do business with a country that sold weapons to the Israelis, which in turn, used them to hunt and murder other Muslims in the West Bank and Gaza Strip.

Fortunately a few true believers within the government still understood the plight of the Arab people. They had been more than happy to give him the money he needed to travel to training camps in Afghanistan where he'd learned to shoot and fight. God had blessed him, placing him in Afghanistan as the United States had brought in its damnable weapons to overthrow the Taliban. Salih had watched several of his friends die under the onslaught of machine-gun fire and so-called daisy cutter bombs unleashed from America's flying warships. Though a piece of him died each time a comrade fell, he'd held on to the anger, using it to fuel his battle against the Americans.

When it became apparent that Afghanistan was largely a lost cause, he'd traveled to Waziristan, the territory along the Afghanistan-Pakistan border. From there he'd traveled to Iraq, only too eager to engage the enemy again. In Afghanistan, he'd found himself in the unfortunate position of battling against warriors from the Northern Alliance. But in Iraq, he'd been blessed to engage the real enemy, the Americans, face-to-face. Using a rocket-propelled grenade, his aim guided by God, he'd downed a Black Hawk helicopter, killing five American soldiers. His rejoicing had come to an abrupt end when, a few days later, he'd taken a bullet in the chest, forcing him to be smuggled out of the country and into a Syrian hospital for treatment. After that, he'd heard that his name and face had become known to the Americans, forcing him to abandon the Iraqi conflict to avoid arrest. It wasn't that he feared death. Quite the contrary; he feared being taken alive, where he could potentially be co-opted into helping the Americans and potentially destroying all he held dear. Unwilling to let that happen, he'd moved to Paris.

During his time in Europe, he'd prayed many times a day for the chance to exact revenge on the Americans in their own land. During his time in France, he'd been approached by recruiters from the Arm of God, a group of like-minded warriors ready to exact revenge on the West for its transgressions in the Middle East. Once he'd agreed to join, things had moved quickly for him and the other recruits. There'd been more training in Somalia, not just weapons and assassination techniques, but lessons on American culture and speech training to nearly eliminate what Westerners would consider an accent.

Since he'd joined the group, he'd found a seemingly endless stream of money and weapons. For that, he considered himself truly fortunate, a humble warrior handed a once-in-a-lifetime chance.

He would repay God for the opportunity by killing as many Americans as possible and facing his own death with pride, courage.

He walked the next half mile or so keenly aware of the excitement buzzing in his stomach as he anticipated the upcoming events. As he moved, he cast the flashlight's white beam over the narrow passage. He heard the steady, plodding footsteps of his fellow warriors and the occasional frenzied scratching of a rodent scurrying away. The light hit a wall, indicating the tunnel's end. To his left, he saw a ladder that led into a small farmhouse on the American side of the border.

Reaching the ladder, he extinguished the light, shoved it into the back pocket of his blue jeans and grabbed for the first rung.

At the top of the ladder was a trapdoor fitted with two locks. When the top of his head came within a few inches of the door, he reached inside the breast pocket of his shirt, felt around until he located a pair of keys. Slipping one key into the lock farthest from him, he gave it a twist, but left it in the keyhole. Following the same procedure with the second lock, he felt his breath hang in his throat as he turned the key. According to his contact in Mexico, a biker named Ed Stephens, the door was fitted with an explosive charge set to detonate if the locks weren't opened in a certain order and the keys left in place. Grasping the handle, he gingerly pushed the door open and breathed a sigh of relief when it came free without incident.

Within minutes he had exited the tunnel. His comrade, Jamal Hejazi, a short man with unkempt hair and narrow shoulders, stood at his side.

"We should look around," Salih said, "while the others unload the equipment."

Hejazi nodded.

Filling his hands with a Glock 17 and his flashlight, Hejazi a few steps behind, Salih exited the room and crept down the hallway. A sharp noise from outside the house brought him to a halt. He shot a questioning glance to Hejazi, who nodded in reply. Salih extinguished the flashlight beam, slipped into a room to his left and peered through a dust-laden window. A dark, bulky vehicle stood near the front porch. He couldn't identify the brand of vehicle, but he immediately recognized the logo on the driver's-side door: U.S. Border Patrol.

His grip tightening on the pistol, he whirled toward Hejazi, but found him gone. Salih swore under his breath and trailed after his friend. As he stepped into the hallway, he heard the front door come open, squeaking on rusted hinges. Flashlights immediately pierced the darkness, sweeping over the walls. He caught Hejazi's shadow up ahead, flattened against a wall, his handgun held next to his ear, muzzle pointing skyward.

Hejazi gave him a look and Salih shook his head, held up his hand. Edging along the wall, he tried to bridge the gap between the two men, even as a pair of shadows overtook a nearby wall.

"U.S. Border Patrol," a female voice said. "We saw the vehicles out front. I want you to step out here and show yourselves. Now."

Salih felt fear and anger roiling within. Their contact had told them that he'd leave a pair of vans at the house for transportation. The Border Patrol agents had spotted them and decided to investigate. Had they called for backup? And, if so, when would it arrive? The notion that they'd come this far only to fail was intolerable to Salih. That a woman—*a woman*—had interfered and was shouting orders only increased the sting. They needed to act, to go down fighting, if necessary. But go down as men.

Apparently, Hejazi felt the same way.

The small man rounded the corner, his weapon rising as the flashlight beams illuminated his chest and face. The officers, their voices taut with fear, shouted for him to halt his advance. But he didn't. The pistol cracked twice and Salih saw one of the shadows fall. A microsecond later bullets hammered into Hejazi's chest and stomach, launching him into a backward march that ended when he collided with a wall. Unable to take another step, his limbs became rubbery and he crumpled to the floor.

Salih, Glock held high, his heartbeat thundering in his ears, approached his old friend.

"Officer down, damn it," he heard the Border Patrol agent saying from the other room. The agent's shadow loomed larger as he approached Hejazi's corpse. "Where the hell's my backup?"

Despite the vengeful rage boiling within, Salih forced himself to think clearly. They needed to get out of here before more agents arrived and they ended up making a last stand here in the desert.

The officer came into view, his handgun leveled in front of him. His eyes widened as he saw Salih. The muzzle tracked toward Salih, but he already had the American in his sights. The Glock's report echoed throughout the corridor as a pair of 9 mm slugs caught the Border Patrol agent's head, killing him instantly.

By the time the American folded to the ground, Salih's fellow warriors had flocked to his side or gathered around Hejazi, checking in vain for signs of life. He didn't wait for them to pronounce what he already knew in his heart.

"Take his body to the van," Salih ordered. "We have no time to waste. For today, we must go, hide. But tomorrow the Americans will pay for his death and many others a thousand times over."

CHAPTER TWO

Stony Man Farm, Virginia

With Stony Man Mountain situated to his left, Rosario "The Politician" Blancanales stood outside the farmhouse, black eyes peering over a coffee cup's rim, drinking in the milky orange-red line of predawn light cresting the Blue Ridge Mountains' peaks.

Awake since 3:00 a.m., the Able Team warrior finally had surrendered to his insomnia, showering, dressing and adjourning outside to watch the sunrise, beating it by a good fifteen minutes. Sleep rarely eluded Blancanales. A trained soldier, he usually could will himself to doze, if only for a few minutes, despite time zone shifts, adrenaline rushes or anticipated danger. In the field, sleeping, like staying alert, was a survival skill one mastered as part of a larger repertoire of skills, both practical and deadly.

But between missions, burdened with time to think and remember, Blancanales occasionally found himself in his present circumstances: wide awake, mind littered with bits of wreckage from his past. Sometimes the ghosts just wouldn't go away.

Scowling, he watched a smoky-gray blanket of fog rise above the acres of hardwoods and conifers that surrounded Stony Man Farm, the nation's ultrasecret intelligence and counterterrorism operation. Pressing the coffee cup to his lips, he slurped it, trying at once to cool and consume it.

A voice sounded from behind. "Didn't realize you were into sunrises."

Blancanales turned to see Hermann "Gadgets" Schwarz, Able Team's electronics genius. Schwarz, a man of medium height and build, leaned against the farmhouse, arms crossed over his chest. Blancanales flashed his most disarming grin. "If you'd gotten here a minute later, I might have started writing poetry," he said.

"Or yodeling."

"God forbid. I leave the loud, unearthly sounds to Ironman," Blancanales said, referencing Carl Lyons, Able Team's third and final member.

"Good choice."

"How'd you find me?"

Schwarz held up the coffee, made a face. "I figured either you or a hog farmer cooked up this swill. I didn't see you in the house, so I figured you might be outside."

"You need something?"

Schwarz shook his head. "Nah, just nosing around. I was already up. Up all night, in fact. I got caught up in hot-rodding my laptop. I added more memory, upgraded the wireless fidelity capabilities, added some dandy new encryption software."

"Have my eyes glazed over yet?" Blancanales asked, grinning.

Schwarz arched his upper lip in mock disdain. "Savage. My great genius cannot be appreciated by one such as you."

"Right." Blancanales swallowed more coffee.

"So you dodged me long enough. What the hell are you doing out here?"

"Not sleeping."

"And not answering my questions."

Blancanales opened his mouth to reply, but a vibration on his left hip cut him off. In almost synchronized movements, he and Gadgets unhooked their pagers from their belts, brought them closer to their faces and studied the liquid-crystal displays.

"War Room," Blancanales said.

"Not good," Schwarz replied. "Not at this hour."

Blancanales nodded his agreement. A tickle of excitement passed through his stomach, followed by a sense of relief. Just what he needed—a little action to distract him. He gestured toward the house. With a nod, Schwarz pivoted on his heel and started for the front door. Blancanales fell into step behind him.

ENTERING THE WAR ROOM, Blancanales swept his gaze over its occupants, smiled at them. Barbara Price, Stony Man Farm's mission controller, Aaron "The Bear" Kurtzman, chief of Stony Man's cybernetics team and Lyons were seated at the oval-shaped table. Price, her honey-blond hair pulled back in a ponytail, skin bare of makeup, and Kurtzman, thick body settled in his wheelchair, big hands wrapped around a steaming mug of coffee, returned Blancanales's smile. Lyons looked up from his coffee long enough to nod at his teammates before returning his attention to the mug's swirling contents.

Hal Brognola stood at the head of the table, arms crossed over his chest. His white cotton dress shirt was open at the collar, the sleeves rolled up to the middle of his forearms. An unlit cigar jutted from between the big Fed's lips.

"Nice breakfast, Chief," Blancanales said as he dropped into a chair.

"Beats your coffee," Brognola shot back.

"Oh, Lord," Blancanales said. "Hal's tossing out jokes. Isn't that a sign of the apacolypse?"

"Could be in this case," Brognola said.

"Okay, you've got our attention," Lyons said. "Elaborate."

Plucking the cigar from his mouth, Brognola studied it for a moment as he collected his thoughts. When he spoke, his voice sounded weary. "Within the past few hours, the country took a double-barreled gut shot. Both home and abroad. I have Phoenix Force working things overseas. I need you folks to defuse the homeland threat."

"Which is?" Schwarz asked.

"Nothing short of mass murder," Brognola said. He turned and looked at Price. "Barb?" She pressed a button on her laptop and an image of middle-aged man with black hair and a dark complexion came into view on the wall screen.

"Name's Abdul Rashid," Brognola said. "He heads a lovefest called Arm of God. As far as terror groups go, it's fairly new, surfacing a year ago. But it seems well connected and well funded. And, as of this morning, it moved to the top of our must-hit list."

"How so?" Blancanales said.

"Some of Rashid's men seized our embassy in Liberia

this morning," Brognola said. "They have a couple dozen hostages, including a handful of Marines working security at the facility. From what we've gathered, Rashid's not there."

"Casualties?" Blancanales asked.

"Six dead. All Marines. They went down defending the place."

"How could this happen?" Schwarz asked, his face flushing with anger. "I mean, a dozen Marines in a walled compound ought to be able to kick serious ass. I take it these guys didn't just scale the walls and storm the building."

Brognola nodded. "Right. Initial reports indicate that someone lobbed a live hand grenade over the wall. When it exploded, some of the Marines went to investigate, while the rest tried to secure the embassy."

"Divide and conquer," Schwarz stated.

"Precisely," Brognola said. "At least two Marines were shot inside the embassy, even as the others were going outside to investigate the blast. And the terrorists didn't need to scale the wall. The gate was open, a dead guard lying next to it. The smart money says that someone inside the embassy either opened the door or at least left a key under the mat, so to speak. The State Department security guys are checking the staffers again, looking for possible traitors. But if they didn't find them during the initial screening, they probably won't now, either. Our cyberteam is doing likewise, but again, I'm not too hopeful."

"I beg your pardon?" Kurtzman asked.

"Sorry, Bear, but my guess is that, if it was an inside job, then that person covered his or her tracks pretty well. Embassy security hasn't exactly been lax since the World

Trade Center attacks. These creeps probably coerced someone into helping, someone without previous ties to the group, making them harder to trace."

Kurtzman nodded. "Makes sense. Just the same, we'll keep bird-dogging this thing, in case someone else missed something."

"I'd expect no less. I sent Phoenix Force to handle the embassy seizure. The group was already in Africa, fresh off another mission, and I could have them there within a matter of hours. And, according to our intel, Rashid is hanging his hat somewhere in Africa. So we'll likely send Phoenix in to take him out, once they free the embassy."

"So you got us out of bed why? To tell us that Phoenix Force will be late for dinner?" Lyons said.

Brognola gave Lyons and the others a weary smile. "I wish. Unfortunately we have trouble here on the home front, too. That's why I'm depriving all of you—especially you, Carl—of your much-needed beauty sleep. From your standpoints, the African situation is necessary background for what needs handled in the United States. Barb will explain."

"The point, finally," Lyons muttered. Draining his mug, he stalked over to the coffee machine to refill it.

In the meantime Brognola fell into his chair, chomped on his cigar while Price got to her feet. Price hit a button on her laptop and a new picture flashed on the projection screen on the far wall. As everyone took a moment to study the image, she wordlessly handed out mission packets to Able Team.

Flipping through the file folder, Blancanales came across a photo of a man sprawled on his back, his uniform shirt darkened by blood. Most of his head had been torn away, apparently by a bullet. Blancanales recognized a U.S. Border Patrol insignia on the guy's shoulder patch. In a second photo, he saw a woman patrol agent, her throat savaged by a bullet, curled up on a floor. Her pistol lay several inches from her fingers.

Blancanales held up the pictures. "Where did this happen?"

"California-Mexico border," Price said. "Near Tijuana, Mexico. The exact location is listed in the mission packet. The woman's name was Jennifer Drew. She was thirty-two and been with the patrol for six years. Single mother, two little girls. Going to law school in the evenings. According to her records, she wanted to be a prosecutor when she got out of law school."

"Damn," Blancanales said. "What about the guy?"

"Jon Copper. Joined the patrol three months before. No immediate family. He'd just been discharged, honorably, of course, from the Marine Corps. Served one tour in Iraq where he earned commendations for bravery and a purple heart. The bad news is that the killers were gone before backup arrived."

"The good news?" Gadgets asked.

"Apparently either Drew or Copper nailed one of these bastards before they could escape. Investigators found blood at the scene, splattered on a wall, pooled on the floor. They were able to collect that, some hair samples and other forensic evidence. Not to mention shell casings from the killers' guns."

"That stuff tell us anything?"

"Surprisingly, yes. The shell casings had been wiped clean of any prints. But the blood and hair yielded some DNA evidence that helped us identify one of the shooters. His name is Jamal Hejazi."

"Or was," Schwarz replied. "Hopefully, anyway."

"Most likely. Judging by the amount of blood, bone fragments and other physical evidence at the scene, this guy should be riding a horse through Sleepy Hollow, carrying a pumpkin under his arm. We're still waiting on the rest of the forensics reports to come in, but we're guessing that Hejazi was wounded by the Border Patrol agents and one of his own people 'retired' him with a bullet to the head."

"Why do that?"

Price shrugged. "Probably didn't want to risk taking him to a doctor or hospital."

"Makes sense."

"What do we know about Hejazi?" Blancanales interjected.

Price leafed through the file's contents until she found what she was looking for. "He was a Saudi national. About ten years ago, he lived in the United States on a student visa. He was studying medicine. During that time, he came up on rape charges."

"Charges he hotly denied, I'm sure," Lyons said.

"Of course. The court forced him to submit DNA evidence. They swabbed him for saliva and matched the DNA with stuff collected at the hospital's E.R."

"Surprise," Lyons said, his voice indicating anything but.

"Once that information went to the grand jury, Hejazi decided to leave the country. Without the court's permission, of course. He went to Sudan."

"Double surprise," Lyons said wearily. As a police officer, he'd seen the same script played out to the letter too many times.

"I guess the victim's family had some money, too. They hired a bounty hunter to chase after him and drag him back to the United States. He went underground until the family's money ran out. Once he learned he was off the bull's-eye, he crawled out from under his rock and decided he wanted to fight the Great Satan. Judging by his record, he's otherwise pretty unremarkable."

"Hey, give the guy his props," Blancanales said. "He is an international fugitive, after all."

Price smiled. "I won't grace that with a response. Obviously our big concern here is that a known terrorist snuck into the United States. He's dead. But we know for a fact that he didn't come alone. Before they entered the house, Drew told her dispatcher that a pair of vans was parked outside the house. She also radioed in the numbers for the license plates, both of which were stolen. By the time their backup arrived, both vans were gone."

"So we have a couple of carloads of terrorists touring the West Coast," Blancanales stated.

"And, while we can assume they're here to launch an attack," Brognola said, "we have no other specifics. That's where you guys come in. I want you to beat the bushes, find out what these bastards are up to. We're expecting a big bang. We just don't know when, where or how. Your mission packet contains plenty of background on these guys. And we have a couple of contacts for you to look up, including one in San Diego. There's a plane waiting on the landing strip. While we've been talking, a team of black-suits has been loading it full of weapons and equipment, all your usual favorites. I want you guys in the air and ready to hit the West Coast within an hour. The Man is worried. So am I. We need you to hunt these guys down and to find out what they're up to. He's also been very explicit as to how you deal with them once you accomplish those tasks."

"Exercise our full diplomatic authority?" Blancanales queried.

Brognola nodded. "Exactly. Kill them."

CHAPTER THREE

Monrovia, Liberia

David McCarter navigated the van through the throngs of soldiers, bystanders and journalists gathered two blocks from the American embassy.

The van bore the symbol of a humanitarian organization, an effort by Phoenix Force to disguise its approach. If his opponents were smart enough to seize a well-guarded embassy, McCarter figured they also were smart enough to station observers among the crowds gathered outside the perimeter. Wheeling the panel van to the curb, he brought it within thirty yards of a rug store that had been evacuated and converted into a command center. The embassy lay straight ahead, its top floors visible over the security fence. At least one terrorist was visible from the rooftop, watching the approaching vehicle through a pair of binoculars.

"Ever get the feeling you're being watched?" asked Gary Manning, who was riding shotgun.

"Hope the bastard gets a good look," McCarter said. "Pretty soon, one of us is going to be the last thing he sees."

Shifting the van into park, McCarter and Manning disembarked. Motion in a second-story window caught the Briton's attention. Glancing up, he saw a figure fill the embassy window, watching his every movement. Two more sentries, brandishing AK-47s, faces swathed in brightly colored scarves, also were visible through the bars of the security fence surrounding the embassy compound. The brazenness didn't surprise McCarter. He knew the terrorists assumed they'd be safe so long as they had hostages. Their threat had been clear: for every terrorist harmed, two hostages die.

He averted his gaze and proceeded to the back of the panel van.

As he moved, he took in the burned-out or bullet-pocked buildings, leftovers from a civil war that lasted nearly a decade and killed hundreds of thousands of Liberians. Rounding the rear of the van, he saw the other three members of Phoenix Force—Calvin James, Rafael Encizo and T. J. Hawkins—disembarking, carrying with them coolers and insulated boxes used for transporting food. Stony Man pilot Jack Grimaldi had remained at a nearby airfield, ready to provide air support, if necessary.

McCarter grabbed one of the boxes, lifted it. He felt a hand clap him on the shoulder as he came to his full height.

"'Bout time you decided to join the working people," Hawkins drawled.

"I'll be happy to do just that, mate," McCarter said. "If I ever find them."

Laughing, Hawkins hefted a cooler and started to walk away from the van.

A pair of U.S. Marines stepped into their path, their M-4 rifles held in easy reach. McCarter and his crew had already been through two other checkpoints, and the Briton was starting to lose his patience with all the security hoops being forced upon him.

"Halt and identify," the first Marine ordered.

McCarter set his cooler at his feet. Fingering an ID card bearing his picture and fake credentials suspended by a small chain around his neck, McCarter held it up for the soldier to inspect. "Rick Cornett," he said, using an alias supplied by Stony Man Farm. "Your man should have alerted you to my arrival."

The soldier studied the ID for another moment. He nodded over his shoulder. "Mr. Colvin's expecting you. He'll see you immediately. I'll show you inside."

"Bloody decent of him," McCarter growled.

Stepping inside the shop, the Phoenix Force warriors stripped away their white coveralls, revealing black combat suits. Opening the coolers and insulated food bags, they emptied their contents—weapons and equipment—onto the floor, each man arranging his gear in a neat pile. Five Marines donned the coveralls and hats. In about five minutes, they'd load up in the van and leave, their faces hopefully obscured by the hats and the coming dusk.

McCarter and the others readied their weapons. The Briton heard footsteps moving in clipped cadence approaching from behind. Glancing over his shoulder, he saw a slender man, about five feet eight inches, his white hair trimmed close to his pinkish skin and flat on top, moving toward them. He halted about ten feet away and scrutinized each member of Phoenix Force with a hard gaze, saving McCarter for last. Scowling, he crossed his arms over his chest and stared at the Phoenix Force leader.

"So you're the hot-shit commandos the White House made us wait for," he said. "God, give me strength."

"He just did, mate," McCarter said, "in spades. You got a name?"

"Colvin. Steve Colvin."

"You're State Department?"

Colvin nodded. "Diplomatic Security Service. And you're Justice Department."

"Rick Cornett," McCarter said, using his alias. He didn't bother to introduce the other men. He didn't plan to start a long-term relationship with Colvin.

"You with the FBI? Hostage Rescue Team maybe?"

"No."

"Delta Force?"

"No."

"Care to elaborate?"

"No."

His cheeks reddening, Colvin glowered at McCarter for a stretched second. Despite his rising impatience, the Briton didn't avert his own gaze. Colvin reached into his breast pocket, extracted a crumpled pack of cigarettes and tapped one into his palm. Replacing the pack, he lit the smoke with a disposable lighter, inhaled deeply and gestured with a nod at the space behind him.

"All right, Cornett," the State Department man said, "why don't you drag your Limey butt over here and I'll brief you."

He turned and headed toward a table topped with a pair of laptops and three satellite telephones.

McCarter glanced at Manning, who grinned. "'Limey butt?'" Manning asked. "Not very diplomatic for the State Department, eh?"

"He's sizing me up," McCarter said. "It obviously hurts his professional pride a little to have Washington send in outsiders to handle this mission. Probably wants to see whether we're up for the job."

"Think we passed his test?"

"I couldn't care less," McCarter said.

Manning shot him a grin and they fell into step behind the State Department man, following him to a makeshift briefing area set up in the rear of the store. A table topped by laptops, architect's drawings and scattered papers sat in the middle of the converted storeroom. Three technicians, two women and a man, all dressed in civilian clothes, were positioned around the table, working at computers.

"Lynn," Colvin said, "show us the layout."

A thirtysomething brunette nodded. She tapped a few keys and moments later an architect's drawing of the embassy filled the screen. McCarter noted several X's situated at various points on the image. A small laser pointer in his grip, Colvin rested the device's red dot on a large rectangular room.

"This is the first-floor lobby," he said. "According to early security camera images, there were at least eight shooters in this area. Unfortunately the latter information is dated. Within thirty minutes of taking the embassy, they'd shut down the surveillance feeds to our satellites. Doing so creates a closed system. They can monitor every inch of the place, but we can't see a damn thing. We can still track people by their body heat, but we can't tell whether they're the good guys or the bad guys."

"What about the second floor?" Encizo asked.

Colvin nodded at the computer operator, who with a few

keystrokes, changed the picture again. "Flyovers indicate a great deal of body heat here. And it'd make the most sense for them to keep hostages here. They can herd them into rooms, most of which have no windows, for security reasons, making it easier to guard the prisoners."

"What are your negotiators telling you?" McCarter asked. "What do these blokes want?"

"Typical terrorist crap—release certain members of their group, cut U.S. aid to Israel, withdraw troops from the Middle East."

"In other words, the impossible," McCarter said.

"You got it. Frankly, I think they're stalling. These guys may be fanatics, but they aren't stupid. They have to know we don't negotiate with terrorists. Especially in today's climate. I don't understand what their endgame is here."

"Probably doesn't matter at this point," McCarter said. "The only endgame I envision for these bastards is to go horizontally. How many hostages do we have inside?"

"About fifty, including the six Marines killed during the initial fighting. When they seized the place, they let a lot of the locals go. Some of the staff was out of the compound, doing other things."

"The locals tell you anything?"

"Depending on who you believe, they have anywhere between two dozen and thirty fighters in there. We've had U2s winging over the compound all day, snapping off surveillance photos. Near as we can tell there's between a half dozen and ten terrorists patrolling the grounds or stationed on the rooftops at any given moment, just daring us to take them out. According to the people who got away, everyone else was herded into the main building."

"What other ways are there into the building?" asked James, the lanky former Navy SEAL.

Colvin's associate changed the screen again. A split-screen image pictured the embassy's rooftop in one frame and a boarded-up hotel in the other. McCarter remembered seeing the hotel as they'd approached the embassy. His face must have betrayed his curiosity because Colvin immediately jumped in to explain.

"Liberia was a damn mess for years," he said. "A corrupt government, a civil war, drug-crazed rebels. At the same time, al Qaeda has hammered embassies on this continent and has more than its share of followers running around. Place is a security man's nightmare."

"Only more so today," James said, running the tip of his index finger along his pencil-thin mustache.

"Sure. Compound that with other events like the attacks on the WTC and the takeover of our Tehran embassy in the 1970s, and you know the State Department's been waiting on something like this to happen for years. We didn't necessarily expect it here in particular, but we did expect it."

"The point?" McCarter asked.

"The point is that we have more entrances into the embassy than we let on. The thinking was that we needed a way to get our people out of here in case of an emergency, an escape hatch, if you will. To do that, we built a tunnel that connects the embassy to this burned-out hotel."

"Get out," James said. "You're saying there's actually a secret tunnel leading into the embassy?"

"Of sorts. But it's secure as hell. It stretches about three hundred yards, with battleship-steel doors every seventy-five yards or so. It also has a boatload of cameras, motion detectors and other protective measures installed. We designed it to get people out, but also to sneak commandos in."

"Any way they could know about it?" McCarter asked.

"Only an idiot would guarantee that it's foolproof."

"Then that's the way we'll go, at least some of us. I want to hit these SOBs from more than one direction. So I'll need at least two volunteers."

MAJID JASIM CURLED his fingers under the edge of his ski mask and peeled it away from his face, discarding it with a careless toss. He noticed a few of the hostages, all bound by ropes but not blindfolded, sneak looks at him, maybe memorizing his features in case they were rescued. Or just to satisfy their own morbid curiosity, a look at their executioner, perhaps. He allowed himself a smile. Let them look.

He mopped his forehead with his handkerchief, replaced it in his pocket and unconsciously smoothed the hairs of his mustache with the thumb and forefinger, raked back his thick black hair with the fingers of the same hand. At five feet ten inches, he had a wiry build of a welterweight boxer and the ramrod posture of a soldier. He'd been both for many years, but that was before he'd lost everything and been forced to change professions.

Scowling, he gripped his weapons belt with both hands and hitched it higher up on his hips. He rested his right hand on the worn grip of the Heckler & Koch VP70 pistol, one of the few things he still possessed from his former life. He'd been a commander in Saddam Hussein's fedayeen army, had lived comfortably with the government salary and an endless supply of money, food and sex extorted from civilians. He'd provided a good life for his family. But all that changed after the Americans invaded the country and Baghdad fell. He'd stood and fought, both during the invasion and as an insurgent in the ensuing occupation. He'd pretended it had been out of a sense of nationalism, a conviction that the infidels wouldn't sully his homeland with their damned occupation. In reality, though, he just had hoped to wear the Americans out, make them go home. As that possibility had become increasingly distant, he'd fled the country and journeyed to Syria where it had been all too easy to parlay his military talents into mercenary work.

That's how he'd met the American, David Campbell. The man had sought him out, wanting him to help pull off an impossible mission. And when it had come time to discuss price, Campbell had—how did the Americans say it?—made him an offer he couldn't refuse. So he hadn't.

The sound of footsteps pulled him from his thoughts. He looked and saw another man, face wrapped in a scarf, approaching. He held an AK-47 by its pistol grip, let the muzzle point at the floor. Although the wrap obscured most of his features, Jasim could see the man's furrowed brow, his narrowed eyes, all telegraphing his concern.

The man—Tariq Hammud, who Jasim considered his closest adviser—kept his voice barely above a whisper, addressing him in Arabic.

"Sir, you expose your features to these people. Is that wise?"

"Is it wise to ask such a question?" Jasim countered.

"I mean no disrespect. But I was told we must keep our identities secret. At least, that's what the American said. Has all that now changed?"

"Have I said it's changed?"

"No."

"Do you take orders from me, or from the American? Are you now a loyal subject of the infidel?"

The creases in Hammud's brow deepened and his voice took on a cold edge. "Of course not."

"But you suppose that I am a loyal subject of the American and should follow his orders to the letter. Am I understanding this correctly? Or perhaps that I should behave like a woman and cover my face in public. Is that it?"

"Never," Hammud said, his voice rising in volume. "To suggest such a thing would be an insult."

"My point exactly. We are agreed, then, that I may expose my face as I choose, rather than when given permission?"

"Of course. I was in error to suggest otherwise."

Jasim suppressed a smile as he watched the other man squirm. "Did you come only to harass me about this?"

Hammud shook his head. "No, we found Fisher. He wants to speak with you."

"He has news?"

"He says so."

"We'll see. Have we secured the grounds? Nightfall is only a few hours away. We will be at our most vulnerable."

"We're taking the necessary precautions."

"Fine. Tell Fisher I will meet in him the library."

"I'll have him taken there."

Jasim grabbed the suitcase that stood next to his ankle. He strode past the hostages, making a point to meet their gazes as he passed. As expected, most of them looked away. However, he caught one man, a Marine dressed in camouflage fatigue pants and matching T-shirt, glowering at him as he walked by. His hands were bound behind his back, his legs tied at the ankles, his boots removed and discarded.

The Arab halted and stared into the American's pale blue eyes, held his gaze for several seconds. Another Marine, secured in a similar fashion, was situated several feet away.

"What are you looking at?" Jasim asked.

"You killed my sergeant, you piece of shit," the Marine replied.

"Tom, let it go," the second Marine warned.

Jasim smiled. "You should listen to your comrade. He has the right idea."

Color spread through the first Marine's neck and inflamed his cheeks.

"Kiss my ass," Tom said.

With lightning-quick movements, Jasim fisted the VP70 and aimed the weapon at the second Marine, the one who'd uttered the warning. Jasim stroked the handgun's trigger, unleashing a 3-shot burst that reduced the man's skull to a crimson spray. The remaining Marine's eyes bulged with anger and shock, while other hostages gasped or screamed.

"You son of a bitch." Despite his bonds, Tom struggled to come to his feet. Jasim watched the man's struggle with amusement.

Jasim swept the gun around the room. Hostages screamed and flinched, some were paralyzed with fear while others balled themselves up to form smaller targets.

"I made it clear from the beginning that heroics would cost lives. Resistance would cost lives. That includes your incessant yammering. For every ill word you speak, someone dies. So choose each word carefully."

The Marine's face beamed pure hatred. The Marine's lips had tightened into a bloodless line and his skin had turned an angry scarlet. After a long pause, Jasim said, "Nothing else to say? Good."

Holstering his weapon, he spun on his heel and started for the library, whistling as he went.

A few minutes later he stood in the library, smoking a cigarette. The door handle rattled, grabbing Jasim's attention. Turning, he saw a slender, pale man with unkempt hair enter, escorted by a pair of Jasim's men.

Jasim gestured toward a nearby chair. "Mr. Fisher, sit."

Fisher did so. Lacing his fingers together, he set his hands on his knees and studied his thumbnails while Jasim looked down at him. Fisher, a low-level embassy worker, had been feeding Jasim and the others intelligence on the embassy for months. From what Jasim understood, the American had been frequenting underage prostitutes in Monrovia's slums. When confronted with photographs and promises of cash, Fisher had been all too happy to betray his own country.

"You killed somebody else," Fisher said.

"You have an issue with that?"

Fisher shrugged his narrow shoulders. "I have no issue with anything."

"Good," Jasim said. "You had something you wanted to tell me."

"One of the women, Barb Kendall, she's CIA."

Jasim felt his gut twist into a knot. Heat radiated from his face. "Why am I just now learning this?" he asked.

Fisher tensed visibly, anticipating a blow. "I just found out. I overheard her discussing it with the ambassador. I always thought she was a public-information officer. I guess that was a cover."

"I will deal with her. Anything else?"

"She says that there's a tunnel, a way out of here. Which means, a way in."

Jasim scowled. "This tunnel, where is it?"

Another shrug. "I asked, but she wouldn't say. I didn't want to force the issue. I figured she'd get suspicious. I did all right, right?"

Jasim looked at the guards. "Return him to his cell. And bring me Kendall. I want to speak with her. We need to find this entrance before it creates a problem for us."

MCCARTER HELD his sound-suppressed Heckler & Koch MP-5 at hip level as he moved through the concrete corridor leading to the embassy. Like his fellow commandos—Manning and Hawkins—he scanned his surroundings through night-vision goggles, which bathed the area in pale green. The DSS agents had extinguished all tunnel lights, an effort to give McCarter and the others an advantage should their approach be discovered.

"Crawling through tunnels like a bunch of bleedin' rats," he groused. "I can't believe we flew halfway around the world for this."

"Three minutes without a complaint," Manning whispered. "I think that's an all-time record for you."

"Feel free to kiss my arse," McCarter said. "How much farther?"

"Another 150 yards or so," the big Canadian said. "Then we hit the third door. Two more after that and—bang— we're in the basement."

BARBARA KENDALL FELT fear gnaw at her insides as the guards led her up the embassy steps to the second floor.

They had untied her feet, but had left her hands secured be-hind her back. The captor to her right dug his fingers hard into her bicep, causing white lancets of pain to emanate from the area. She ground her teeth, suppressing a pained yelp.

"Watch it, asshole," she said in flawless Arabic.

The terrorist raised an open hand, ready to strike her. The guard on her left, a short, barrel-chested man, yanked her toward him. "Stop it," he said to the other man. "We do not strike this one without Jasim's approval."

Hesitating, anger still flaring in his eyes, the first man finally let his hand drop. "You'll die before this all ends," he said.

We do not strike this one without Jasim's approval.

Her captor's words troubled her. Considering the abuse being heaped on the other hostages, why not strike her? And why was she being summoned in the first place? In the best-case scenario, they wanted her, as the public-in-formation officer to communicate with the outside world, perhaps to put an American voice to their demands. But, a dyed-in-the-wool cynic, Kendall put little stock in best-case scenarios. Did they know that she also was an intel-ligence agent? The possibility chilled her to the core, but she knew she couldn't dismiss it. If so, she could face tor-ture, or even death, she thought, suppressing a shuddering.

Arriving at the library door, they stopped. Her heart hammered against her chest as she waited. The guard who'd nearly hit her took out his aggressions on the door, striking it hard with his knuckles. A heartbeat later she heard someone call for them to enter. She heard the me-tallic click of a handle, the almost-imperceptible squeak of the door swinging on its hinges, then a hard shove to the middle of her back stole her breath and sent her stumbling into a room.

She scanned the library and saw three hardmen positioned throughout the vast area. A fourth man, seated to her right, cleared his throat and she turned toward him. The Arab wore a pistol on his hip and he had an AK-47 propped against a table within easy reach.

"The tunnel," he said, "where is it?"

A cold rivulet of fear coursed down her spine. He knew, she thought. How the hell? She tried to keep her face impassive, then gave him a confused smile. "What? What are you talking about?"

His features hardened. "The tunnel leading out of the embassy. I know of it. I have people searching the grounds even as we speak. It's only a matter of time before we find it. It will only help you to help us."

"I don't know what you're talking about," she said, letting her voice sound uncertain, confused.

"You are an agent of the CIA."

In spite of herself, Kendall tensed. Her mind raced as she tried to figure out how he knew this and how she should respond. Other than the ambassador, no one else knew of her role here. She'd played her part to the hilt, or so she'd thought. Did he really know something or was this a game the bastard playing?

She laughed nervously. "CIA? I'm with the State Department. I'm a public-information officer. I write press releases and talk to reporters. I have nothing to do with the Central Intelligence Agency."

"I hear otherwise."

"You've heard wrong. Ask anyone here. They'll tell you otherwise."

"Excellent idea," he said. The man looked past her. Nodding at one of the men behind her, he said, "Go get the ambassador."

She spent several minutes standing in front of the terrorist, his gaze cold and unreadable, pushing against her like an unseen force. Relief washed over her momentarily when the door flung open, grabbing the seated man's attention. The sense of relief immediately dissolved when Ambassador Bruce Hughes tumbled through the doorway, shoved forward by one of his captors. A sick feeling twisted at Kendall's gut as she watched the man, hands tied behind his back, struggle to come to his feet. A tall man with long hair and a patchy beard rewarded Hughes for his efforts by striking him repeatedly in the kidneys and spine with a rifle butt. Kendall winced in sympathetic pain as she watched the red-faced man struggle to regain his breath. Kendall felt anger burn hot through her skin as she witnessed the cruelty.

"What the hell do you want?" Hughes asked.

"What do you know of this woman?" Jasim asked.

Hughes's eyes rolled up at Kendall, caught her gaze. She felt an urge to look away from his reddened, pained expression. But she tightened her lips into a bloodless line and forced herself to hold his gaze.

"She's our PIO," Hughes said. "Didn't she tell you that?"

"What she told me and what I believe are two different things," Jasim said. Fisting his side arm, he raised it and leveled it at Hughes. Kendall opened her mouth, but the weapon cracked once, the sound causing her words to catch in her throat. A 9 mm round drilled into the floor next to the ambassador's face. A moment later the stench of human excrement filled the room.

"The ambassador seems to have fallen for your lie," Jasim said through clenched teeth. "I'm not so stupid. Are you CIA or not? Give me the wrong answer and I'll kill him. Then I move on to the next hostage."

Kendall felt her resolve drain away. She looked downcast. "Yes, I'm CIA."

"And there's a tunnel leading into the embassy. Is that correct? Look at me."

Kendall felt anger and frustration constrict her throat. She looked at Jasim, saw the stony expression on his face. She knew at that moment there'd be no negotiating with this son of a bitch. His next words only verified it.

"For every minute that passes without a satisfactory answer, I will kill a hostage, starting with the ambassador."

"Yes," she said, her voice barely audible, "there's a tunnel."

Jasim holstered his weapon and leaned back in his chair. He looked at the two terrorists flanking Kendall and barked orders to them in Arabic. She understood every word.

"I want that door found and wired with explosives. I want anyone coming through it killed."

"As you wish," one of the men said as he grabbed Kendall by the arm and spun her around.

CLAD HEAD-TO-TOE in black, Rafael Encizo crept through the blackness of the alley, a crossbow held steady and sure in his grip.

His nose unconsciously wrinkled against the stench of rancid meat and vegetables emanating from a nearby trash can. Dropping into a crouch, he set the crossbow at his feet, rolled up his sleeve and checked the illuminated dial of his diving watch. It was 9:05 p.m. He rolled his sleeve back down, obscuring the watch. Another sixty seconds and things would get very interesting indeed.

Grabbing his crossbow, he remained in a crouch, but moved to the alley's mouth. The stifling heat barely registered with him. He was accustomed to such temperatures and, in fact, found them more comfortable than the cool evenings that sometimes prevailed in Virginia at Stony Man Farm.

He returned his attention to the problem at hand. Peering around the edge of the building, he stared at the embassy grounds and saw a pair of men, each carrying an AK-47, walking the grounds.

He felt a new rush of anger as he watched them swagger through the compound, faces obscured by scarves. They walked in the open, apparently unafraid, while they held innocent people inside, terrorizing them and the free world as they held the hostages.

Calvin James's voice sounded in his earpiece.

"Rafe?"

"Go."

"I'm in position. You?"

"Affirmative."

"Fifteen seconds until they cut the power."

"Then it all goes by the numbers, my friend."

"Swift and silent."

"Damn straight."

The radio went silent. Encizo waited another moment until streetlights and the large halogen spotlights illuminating the embassy winked out, plunging the compound into darkness. When they did, he slid his NVGs down over his eyes, crept out from the alley and darted for the embassy grounds.

In less than a minute he came to rest a few yards from the fence, his approach obscured by the hip-high concrete walls used to stop truck and car bombers from hurtling into the compound. Chancing a look over the barrier, he peered through the gate and spotted a pair of terrorists separating from each other and sweeping the muzzles of their assault rifles over the horizon as they evaluated the power outage. Rising from behind the barrier only as much as necessary, Encizo locked the crossbow's sights on the nearer terrorist and triggered the weapon. The shaft drilled into the man's throat. Gurgling, stumbling backward, the man's weapon fell from his hands as he grabbed for the bolt protruding from his throat. A moment later life left his body and he folded in on himself.

Staying low, Encizo turned at the waist and loaded another bolt. Upon seeing his comrade suddenly pitch to the ground, the other terrorist dropped to a crouch and fanned his AK-47 over the horizon, his free hand scrambling for a cellular telephone. Encizo triggered the crossbow. An instant later the terrorist froze as a bolt jutted from his ribs, the razor-sharp tip tearing through his heart. Even as his corpse pitched toward the ground, power returned to the embassy compound, probably thanks to the emergency generators. External lights kicked back on, flooding the grounds with white as lights winked back on inside the main building.

Encizo checked his watch: 9:07 p.m.

Right on time.

"Two down, Cal," he whispered into his throat mike. "Status?"

A moment passed without reply. Another second—this one more agonized—came and went, too.

"Cal? Cal?" Encizo whispered again, this time more urgently. All that filled the silence was the plummeting sensation in his stomach. Before he could utter another word, gunshots rang out from within the compound.

CHAPTER FOUR

San Diego, California

Carl Lyons checked the load in his .357 Colt Python, then returned the revolver to shoulder leather. Scowling, he stared at the nondescript building across the street from him and watched for the black Mercedes coupe he hoped would come soon. He leaned his left shoulder against the exterior wall of a convenience store and checked his watch for the fourth time in three minutes.

"You think that son of a bitch knows?" he growled into his throat mike.

"Negative," Blancanales replied. "You're just getting impatient."

"Damn straight I am," Lyons said. "We've been waiting for forty-five minutes and the guy still hasn't shown. He's the best link we've got at this point."

"Hang loose, hombre. He'll be along."

"Maybe he knows that we're looking for him."

"You think Hal called and tipped him off?"

"All right. Point taken."

"Relax," Blancanales said. "He'll be along any minute."

They'd come looking for Abda Hakim, a Saudi Arabian who, according to classified reports from the Treasury Department, raised money for Arm of God and funneled it back to the group's overseas operations. The current site housed a fairly sophisticated money-laundering system that tapped into dozens of overseas banks. In addition, it backed into a warehouse containing stacks of counterfeit CDs, DVDs, software and video games shipped from overseas and sold in the United States.

A fairly sophisticated operation, Lyons grudgingly admitted. For a hairball. Having lost the terrorists' trail at the border, Able Team had decided that Hakim made the best point of contact for the killers once they moved into the country.

That put him at the top of Able Team's list.

Increasingly impatient, Lyons returned to his full height and brushed the brick dust from his shoulder.

As he did, three young men dressed in gang colors swaggered past, eyes boring into him, unsuccessfully trying to intimidate him. Lyons, his mouth a hard line, his eyes hidden by mirrored sunglasses, held their stares behind the shades and let his scowl deepen. The stakes of the mission in front of him and the other members of Able Team were high, and he was in no mood to indulge in a contest of wills with a pack of gang bangers. The first two either lost interest or sensed they were outclassed; the third let his hard stare linger, apparently waiting for the moment when the former L.A. cop would back down. It didn't happen.

As the final gang banger walked on, Lyons noticed

a tremor pass through the guy. He allowed himself a tight grin.

Blancanales's voice came over his earpiece. "Ironman, you still got it."

"Bet your ass I do."

Schwarz, who was watching the rear of the target building from a nearby rooftop, broke in. "Look alive. We've got Hakim's Beemer pulling in."

"Roger that," Lyons said. "He have help?"

"Right. Two, no, three hard-looking guys. Probably bodyguards."

"Probably," Lyons said. "Or walking corpses. Depends on how they want to play it. Let's move."

Lyons crossed the parking lot and waded into traffic. Irritated drivers honking their horns and shouting obscenities barely registered with him as he crossed the street. From his peripheral vision, he saw Blancanales exit a surveillance van disguised as a bakery truck and approach the office building from the right.

The men met at the building's entrance, a pair of glass doors. Lyons slid his hand inside his jacket. His fingers encircled the Colt's grip, but he left it in its holster. Driving a shoulder into the door, Lyons entered the lobby with Blancanales a step behind him. Moving in lockstep, they strode across the room. A pair of heavies, one dressed in a suit, the other in jeans and a T-shirt, lounged at what Lyons guessed was a guard station, a steel desk topped by a telephone and a sign-in sheet attached to a clipboard.

The bigger of the two men, the casually dressed guy, rounded the desk, his face a hard mask of anger. His exposed arms a mosaic of ropelike muscles, veins and stretch marks, he stepped between Lyons and the elevator.

Snapping off his shades, Lyons stepped to within a hair-breadth of the guy and locked eyes with the bigger man. The guard stank of perfumed hair gel and apparently had bathed in a mixture of anabolic steroids and cologne before work.

"You are here to see who?" the man in the suit asked.

"As I was about to explain to your lady friend here," Lyons said, "we're here to see Hakim."

"You got an appointment?" the suit asked.

"You work for Hakim?" Blancanales asked.

"I ask the questions around here," the suit replied.

"I beg to differ." Blancanales produced his fake Justice Department credentials and flashed them at the man.

Scowling, the guy studied their credentials. He reached for the telephone. "I got to call the man."

Blancanales shook his head. "Wrong. You and Mr. Anabolic here are going to cop a squat off the premises and wait until we're done with our business. *Comprende?*"

The guy stared at Blancanales for a long moment, nodded his head. "Sure, man. We can do that. Anything for the Justice Department."

"Much obliged," Blancanales said. "I trust you won't call your boss?"

"Wouldn't think of it."

Lyons heard footsteps slap against the floor behind him. Staring over the body builder's shoulder, he saw a reflection of Schwarz stepping into view, a dart pistol in his hand. The pistol whispered twice as he swept it over the two men, planting tranquilizer darts into the bigger guard's neck and the smaller man's left shoulder. Lyons watched as the big man's face contorted with anger and confusion. He slapped at his neck, trying to find the source of the pain.

Lyons drove an open-palmed strike into the man's sternum, knocking him back. The guy hit the floor. He tried to bring himself back up, but found his muscles going slack. Within moments, he'd fallen unconscious.

"So much for negotiating in good faith," Blancanales said. "How long will they be out, Gadgets?"

"Hours." Intel had it that Hakim used contract security for the building, so the team had opted for nonlethal weapons.

They dragged the men out of sight, hiding them in a vacant office. Blancanales and Schwarz took the elevator to the fourth floor, while Lyons used the stairs. According to intel provided by Stony Man Farm, Hakim occupied the entire top floor of the building, which was only accessible from a single elevator located further within the building.

The men converged on the fourth floor and fanned out. The elevator opened into a large waiting area filled with cushy chairs and potted palms. A pretty Latina sat behind the reception desk. Flashing his own Justice Department ID, Lyons jerked a thumb over his shoulder.

"Jackpot time, lady," he said. "You just got the day off. Go home."

The woman gave him a quizzical look and started to reach for the phone. Lyons put his hand on hers before she could lift the receiver.

"What do you say we do this smart? Your purse. Home. Now. Understand?"

The woman cast a glance over her shoulder at her boss's office, but nodded and began to gather her things. When she palmed her mobile phone, Lyons shook his head.

"Uh-uh," he said. "Leave the phone. You can pick it up later."

Hesitating, the woman regarded Lyons for a moment, then nodded. Clutching her purse, she came to her feet and rounded the desk, giving the men an uncertain look as she did.

Lyons lightly gripped her upper arm, stopping her. "Anyone else on this floor besides Mr. Hakim?" he asked.

She shook her head no. "He sent everyone home yesterday, telling them to take the weekend off. He asked me to come in and answer phones. He promised me double time and I figured, what the hell? I've got a baby at home, you know, and the money—"

"He have any visitors?" Lyons asked.

She paused, chewed at her lower lip and scrutinized Lyons with a lingering stare. Finally she shook her head. "This morning. A group of men. In the conference room. I heard them, but Mr. Hakim never let me see them. They were speaking a foreign language. Not Spanish. I'd know that if I heard it."

"Arabic?" Blancanales ventured.

The woman shrugged. "Could be. Mr. Hakim always speaks English around me."

"Those guys gone?" Lyons asked.

"Yeah."

"When?"

"Ten this morning. I take a break at ten-fifteen and they left just before that."

"Hakim alone?"

"Just his usual guys."

"How many?"

"He had two with him when he came in a little bit earlier. He always has the same couple of guys trailing after him every day. Says they're his cousins or some such.

They never say anything. They just skulk around the office, stone-faced, staring at everyone. I thought maybe something was going on, like Hakim was gay or something, the way these guys followed him around. But one of them started staring at me so I started to think otherwise. Is Hakim in trouble?"

Lyons nodded over his shoulder at the door. "You're not. That's all you need to know. Go."

"I'm not sure," the woman said. "Mr. Hakim asked me to stay after work. Said he had something he needed to discuss with me."

Blancanales flashed a winning smile. "My guess is he wanted to terminate your employment, so to speak."

Lyons watched the woman's expression change from confusion to grave understanding as the meaning behind Blancanales's words sank in. Swallowing hard, she grabbed her things. The click of her heels receded quickly as she distanced herself from the office.

"And they say I have no tact," Lyons groused.

Reaching inside his jacket, Lyons palmed the Colt, his most trusted weapon. Blancanales and Schwarz each produced micro-Uzis from under their jackets. Lyons knew both also carried Beretta 92s in hip holsters.

Crossing the room in quick strides, Lyons stepped up to the door leading into Hakim's network of offices. Kurtzman had supplied the team with layouts of the office space used by Hakim as well as the penthouse located on the building's top floor. According to the plans, four offices lay on the other side of the door as well as the private elevator leading to the Arab's penthouse.

With Schwarz and Lyons on either side of the door, Blancanales tried the handle and found the door locked.

The Beretta spit two subsonic rounds into the lock, shredding it. Blancanales stepped aside to avoid retaliatory fire. When none came, he cocked his leg back and drove a booted foot into the door, knocking it inward.

Lyons rounded the corner in a crouch, the Colt extended in front of him in a two-handed grip. The corridor split into two directions. Ahead lay three rooms, doors closed, two to the left, one to the right. Blancanales was right on his tail. A glance over his shoulder told him Schwarz had headed in the opposite direction to check the rooms at Lyons's back.

The blond commando edged along the wall, listening for signs of danger. He reached the door to his right first. Crouching, he passed under the pebbled glass window that took up the door's upper half. Reaching the other side, he came to his full height, grasped the doorknob and twisted. The door came free and swung inward. He tensed for a moment, waiting for a fusillade of hot lead to lance its way through the opening. When none came, he chanced a look around the doorjamb and scanned the interior.

He flashed Blancanales hand signals indicating that he wanted cover. Blancanales gave him the okay. Lyons rounded the doorjamb, sweeping the room with the Colt. The office was nondescript, outfitted with a steel desk topped by a PC, a row of brown filing cabinets, a small roller table and a four-cup coffeemaker. He checked behind the desk, the only possible hiding place, found no one there, and gave his friend the all-clear signal.

Checks of the other two rooms yielded similar results.

Schwarz rejoined his teammates, shaking his head. "Nada. You guys?"

"Same," Blancanales said. "Time to hit the penthouse?"

Lyons nodded. As the three moved for the penthouse elevator, the Able Team leader switched the Colt for the micro-Uzi he carried in a custom shoulder rig underneath the windbreaker. He stopped several paces short of the doors, a scowl creasing his features.

He turned to his comrades. "Nothing like boxing ourselves up for an easy kill," Lyons said. Before the others could reply, motion registered from the corner of Lyon's eye and he spotted a pair of thugs, each armed with submachine guns, stepping into the corridor.

In almost the same instant, the beating of chopper blades sounded in the distance, growing louder with each heartbeat.

The thugs spread out across the hallway, each man's weapon spitting long tendrils of orange-yellow flame. Bullets sizzled the air around Lyons and the others before slamming into walls. Lyons felt everything slow down around him as he came under attack. His noticed his comrades each responding, Blancanales flattening against a wall, firing his chattergun with one hand. Schwarz dropped into a crouch, his weapon chugging out an angry swath of 9 mm death as three more men poured through the door.

CHAPTER FIVE

One of the attackers lunged forward, flattened against the floor and tried to draw a bead on Lyons, who knew he was a nanosecond from death as the stream of bullets slashed toward him like a cutlass sinking in a downward stroke.

A guttural cry welling up from within, Lyons stroked the Uzi's trigger. The volley of slugs closed the gap between him and his attacker, pounding into the man, eliciting a crimson spray as the man jerked under the Uzi's onslaught.

Swinging his weapon forty-five degrees, Lyons squeezed off a second burst that ripped through another terrorist's white button-down shirt and pulped his chest. The bullets whipsawed the man until Lyons eased off the trigger and turned his attention elsewhere. The man folded to the ground in a boneless heap.

A third man, weapon at hip level, came into view, but withered quickly under relentless blasting from Blancanales, never getting off a shot.

At the same time the door of Hakim's private elevator slid open behind them, revealing another trio of hardmen.

From the corner of his eye, Lyons saw Schwarz turn to meet the threat, his Uzi up and ready. The stout weapon stuttered out a searing line of 9 mm slugs as Schwarz hosed down the elevator car's interior, cutting down the men before any could squeeze off a shot. One of the men pitched forward from the automatic door squeezing and releasing his body as it tried to close.

Lyons stared through the thick haze of gun smoke that clung to the air. He strained his ears, listening for more attackers, but heard only the roar of blood thundering through his ears and the muffled beating of helicopter rotors.

As the din of gunfire died down, he looked at Schwarz, who shot him a grin. "You think they know we're here?" the electronics genius asked.

Schwarz let his micro-Uzi fall free on its shoulder strap. Wedging himself between the corpse and the elevator door, the Able Team warrior grabbed the corpse by his belt and shirt collar and heaved him into the corridor. A moment later he again fisted the Uzi while propping open the elevator door with his hip, waiting for the others.

His teammates boarded the elevator. Schwarz punched the penthouse button and the elevator lurched to life. All three men ejected spent or partially spent magazines from their weapons and inserted fresh ones. Lyons also fisted the Colt Python.

Holstering his Uzi, Schwarz withdrew a pair of grenades from special pockets in his jacket. As the elevator came to a stop, all three men crouched low, figuring they'd face an almost-instantaneous onslaught of weapons fire when the door opened.

They were right.

The angry chatter of submachine guns sounded and weapons fire lanced through the doorway, splintering the elevator's interior, a few of the rounds ricocheting around the confined space. Schwarz armed the flash-bang grenade and rolled it into the room while Blancanales and Lyons returned fire from prone positions, their shots shredding upholstering, chewing through wood and showering the room with shredded stuffing.

The first grenade exploded, filling the room with a sudden white flash and a crack of thunder. The thugs' weapons fire became more sporadic and less focused as men fought to reorient their senses after the startling explosion.

In the meantime, Schwarz activated the second device and tossed it through the doorway. The cylindrical object skittered across the mirror-finished hardwood floors before banking off a table leg and coming to rest next to a large vase. Plumes of gray smoke poured from the grenade, shrouding the room in a seemingly impenetrable haze.

The Able Team warriors used the cover to exit the elevator, crawling on their stomachs, propelling themselves forward on their elbows.

Lyons was the first on his feet, coming up in a crouch. He glided along the wall, using it as a touchstone while he waited for the smoke to clear. The big man had walked about twenty paces when a thug spilled out of the smoke, hacking, rubbing his eyes with one hand, but searching out a target with the muzzle of his handgun. Lyons snap-aimed the Colt, squeezed off two shots, planting both into the man's center mass. The force shoved his body into a nearby hutch, shattering the etched-glass windows and showering the floor with bits of china, glass and blood.

Motion to his right caused Lyons to whirl. He spotted a second shooter drawing down on him with an automatic pistol. The big ex-cop bent at the knees, aiming the Uzi and triggering it within the span of a heartbeat. As Lyons fired, the Arab shooter triggered a quick burst of autofire that cleaved the air a foot or so above Lyons's head. In the same instant, a reply from the Able Team leader's Uzi hammered into the man's midsection. The gunner emitted a short cry of pain as the rounds drilled into him and dumped him in a heap.

The rattle of weapons fire to Lyons's right caught his attention. Whirling toward the source, he spotted Blancanales pinned down behind an overturned dining-room table. Concentrated autofire from assault rifles wielded by two of Hakim's killers shredded the wooden barrier.

The shooters were positioned at twelve and three o'clock from Blancanales's position. The Able Team commando was curled up behind the table, reloading his Uzi, as rounds from the twin AK-47s pierced the table and sizzled the air around him. Fear for his friend's safety quickly morphed into white-hot rage.

Lyons brought the Colt into target acquisition, trying to nail the guy closest to him even as he brought the Uzi around to gut the second thug trying to kill his teammate. As he did, a third man sprinted from the hallway, pistol in hand as he ran up on Blancanales to get a clear shot.

"Pol!" Lyons yelled.

As the warning escaped his lips, Lyons caught the vague impression of a lithe shape, little more than a blur, thundering toward him. A second later, someone struck him with a flying tackle. He felt air explode from his lungs as he lost his footing and tumbled over. As he went down, his senses trying to identify this latest threat, he heard gun-shots from near Blancanales's position, followed by an an-guished cry.

As THE SMOKE from his grenade began to clear, Schwarz saw a shape cross the hellground of Hakim's penthouse, apparently heading for the glass double doors that led onto the rooftop that doubled as a patio and helipad.

Uzi held at the ready, Schwarz threaded between bits of furniture savaged by the fighting and closed in on the fleeing figure, hoping to get a better look. As the door slid open, the gale-force breeze whipped up by a helicopter's rotor wash exploded through the doorway, the whining of the turbine engines overtaking the crackle of gunfire. The smoke thinned to little more than a haze and Schwarz saw Hakim silhouetted for a moment in the doorway as the man passed through it and onto the rooftop.

Schwarz proceeded for the door at a dead run, vaulting overturned chairs and coffee tables as he closed in on his quarry. At this point, the bastard was their best bet for finding the other Arm of God killers running loose in America, their best bet for preventing a possible terrorist strike, mass murder in America.

That meant escape wasn't an option for Hakim. At least not while Schwarz and the others lived. One of Hakim's killers crossed Schwarz's path, the muzzle of his pistol fast locking on Schwarz. The Able Team warrior fired from the hip, the Uzi stuttering out fire and lead that thrust the man back against a wall, body jerking until Schwarz eased off the trigger. The man slid down the length of the wall, leaving a bloody smear in his wake.

Schwarz barely acknowledged the death as he darted

through the doorway. Instantly the transition from indoor light to the brilliant San Diego sun caused him to squint for a moment as his eyes readjusted. He made out the vague impression of Hakim's silhouette as the man sprinted for the chopper. He considered firing low, raking Hakim's feet and ankles with bullets, hobbling him and ending his escape plans all at once. He dismissed the idea for the moment, at least until his eyes adjusted. He couldn't risk shooting too high and killing rather than wounding his quarry.

The men in the chopper had no so such limitations when it came to nailing Schwarz. Gunfire lanced through the air around him as he darted for the fleeing man. Someone was firing upon him from inside the helicopter. Running in a zigzag pattern, the Able Team commando covered the distance between himself and his quarry, his breath growing ragged under the stress of dodging live fire.

A bullet scorched the air next to his cheek. Ducking, he spotted the source, a man crouched in the chopper's door, a pistol in his hand. The hard guy squeezed off a second shot, but in the same instant, the hovering chopper lurched forward, throwing off his aim, causing the round to slice through the air above Schwarz's head rather than into his face. Cursing, the warrior lunged forward, landing hard against the fake grass carpeting the patio. The Uzi ground out a quick burst that stabbed into the chopper, driving the man under cover, but not striking him.

In a heartbeat, Schwarz was again up and running across the roof. Reflexively, he squinted against the rotor wash, the incessant beating of the blades tousling his hair, causing his clothes to ripple. The shooter in the helicopter came back into view, exposing a sliver of his face, a shoulder and a knee.

Not much.

But, in this case, maybe enough.

Schwarz tapped out a sustained burst from the Uzi, the shots pounding into the chopper's skin just next to the crouched shooter. The bullets rent steel, penetrating it before slamming into the terrorist. The guy's eyes widened and his mouth opened, apparently in a scream. The man's limbs went rubbery and he pitched forward, his body hanging half in, half out of the chopper, suspended by the harness. His pistol fell to the ground.

Schwarz closed in on Hakim, who, after taking a brief spill, was back on his feet and darting for the helicopter. Schwarz raked his Uzi over the ground at Hakim's feet. However the slugs caught dead air as the terrorist sprang through the door. In the same instant, the submachine gun clicked dry.

Shit. It would come down to this, Schwarz thought.

Reloading as he ran, the Able Team commando vaulted an overturned table, ducking reflexively as he closed in on the chopper with its whirling blades. Engines whining, the craft lifted off the rooftop, its skids about five feet off the ground.

Springing forward, Schwarz caught the landing skid by looping an arm around it. With his free hand he grabbed the elbow suspending him from the skid, hoping to fortify his position.

The chopper continued its ascent. Suddenly, Schwarz's world became one of deafening engine noise, nauseating fumes, buffeting winds and the steely pull of gravity. Muscles straining, burning, he freed his hand from his elbow and closed it around the skid, tried to pull himself onto it, his body held back by the rotor wash's unseen force. He kicked once, twice, unsuccessfully trying to loop his leg over the landing gear.

He chanced an upward glance. Two things registered with him, Hakim's face contorted with rage and a pistol muzzle tracking in on his head.

BLANCANALES SPOTTED a pair of hardmen pushing through the sliding doors leading from the rooftop patio and fanned out across the luxurious living room. A third man popped out from a kitchen door, molding himself around the jamb and trying to acquire Blancanales as a target. The commando dropped into a crouch and raked a punishing, waist-high burst through the room.

Blancanales's initial volley of slugs chewed through plaster, slicing and dicing the midsection of the man hiding out in the kitchen. The man uttered a strangled cry accompanied by a stuttering protest from his AK-47 as his trigger finger tightened reflexively in death.

The other two men parted and went to ground, each unloading his assault weapon at Blancanales. Bullets scorching the air around him, the Stony Man warrior pressed his attack. He swept the stammering Uzi in a horizontal line, dropping a hard rain of fiery lead on his opponents.

His weapon clicking empty, Blancanales ejected the machine pistol's clip as he dived forward. Skidding to a stop underneath a large oak table, he drove a foot into the table, tipped it onto its side, grateful for the cover as he reloaded his weapon. He heard the dull thump of bullets smacking into the furnishing, ripping its finely crafted, curved edges into a jagged line, like a mouthful of broken teeth.

He rolled onto his stomach, peered around the table's

curved edge and poked the Uzi through the opening. He caught one of the hardmen breaking cover, assault rifle snug against his hip as he closed in on Blancanales for the kill. The second shooter was firing sporadically at Blancanales's position.

He targeted another hardman delivering a blistering volley of 7.62 mm slugs from his AK-47. The commando heard glass shattering overhead, felt shards raining down upon him. He snapped off a short volley of slugs that came within a hairbreadth of slaughtering the gunner.

His combat senses crying out, Blancanales thrust himself to the right before his mind understood why. A chandelier plummeted to the floor, hitting the spot he'd just vacated. The glass light fixture struck the ground and exploded, littering the air with shards that bit into the exposed skin of his face and hands. He shut his eyes, protectively wrapping a forearm around them and riding out the assault of splintered glass.

Blancanales popped open his eyes in time to see his opponent drawing a bead on him with the AK-47. Snap-aiming, he fired the Uzi. The swarm of 9 mm slugs speared through the man's lower stomach, shoving him back as the bullets devastated his internal organs.

Ears still ringing with gunfire, Blancanales nevertheless sensed motion to his left. He spun and caught another shooter, this one armed with a sawed-off shotgun, popping up from behind a chair. Blancanales stroked the Uzi's trigger as he swept the SMG in a figure-eight pattern that lanced through the overturned furniture and drilled into the man's center mass. In a last act of resistance, the man triggered his shotgun, the weapon unleashing a thunderous blast that tore into the ceiling.

Getting cautiously to his feet, Blancanales traded the Uzi for his Beretta. The thrumming of the helicopter sounded from outside. The aircraft's noise combined with their distance from the street made it impossible to tell whether the police, sirens blaring, were descending upon the building. But he knew it was only a matter of time before the local cops hit the scene. Scanning the room, he took in the battlefield littered with corpses, shattered glass and shredded plaster. He couldn't help but mutter an oath under his breath.

Lots of carnage and no information.

From behind a couch, he heard a grunt that unmistakably belonged to Lyons.

At the same time he also noticed that Schwarz was nowhere in sight, and a cold sensation traveled down his spine. Where the hell was he?

"C'mon, lady, give me a break here," Lyons said.

First things first.

The Beretta leading the way, he rounded the couch and found Lyons tussling with a woman. She was dressed in black jeans, fashionable boots and a cranberry-colored, long-sleeved shirt. He couldn't see her face, but her glossy black hair had spilled over the floor. From her profile, he could tell she was Asian. She also was giving Lyons a pretty fair tussle. Lyons had straddled the woman at the waist. He held her wrists in his big hands, but the woman continued to struggle.

"Get your hands off me, you bastard," she yelled. Blancanales recognized the voice in an instant, felt his heart skip a beat. Shit! What was she doing here?

"Relax, lady," Lyons was saying. "You jumped me, remember?"

Shaking off his surprise, he closed in on the pair, each step intensifying the squeezing sensation on his heart. In an instant he recognized the woman from her brown eyes and full, coral-colored lips, to the fiery temper that seemed to emanate from every pore.

It was Donna Ling, a woman from his distant past. And they had a history.

WITH GRAVITY TUGGING at his feet and the punishing wind of the rotor blades smacking into him, Schwarz knew he had only one chance for survival.

He raised the Uzi and fired the weapon at Hakim, dragging it across the man's exposed knees. Hakim's eyes widened in shock and the pistol fell from his fingers as 9 mm slugs tore through flesh and bone. He stumbled forward. At the same moment the pilot gave the chopper a hard jerk, an apparent attempt to knock Schwarz from the landing gear. The sudden motion caused Hakim to pitch out the door, his face instantly morphing from shock to fear as he went forward.

Schwarz looked down, saw the distance between himself and the roof. He guessed a good twenty feet already separated him.

Hell.

Letting go of the landing gear, he watched as the rooftop rushed up to meet him.

THE PRESENCE of someone approaching from behind had caused Lyons, his face red with anger and exertion, to glance over his shoulder. When he saw Blancanales, he rolled his eyes, but his teammate barely noticed. In the same instant, Blancanales's gaze intersected with Ling's and they stared at each other. He watched as the anger and fear fueling her struggle drained away to be quickly replaced by shock, the same emotion roiling inside him.

"Let her go, Carl," Blancanales said.

"What?" Lyons shouted. "Are you crazy?"

The woman stopped struggling, whipped her head toward Blancanales. "Pol?" Ling said.

"I can explain," Blancanales said to Lyons.

"This ought to be good," Lyons fired back.

More gunfire crackled outside, followed by the sickening thud of something heavy hitting the roof. Almost immediately, the chopper's whine grew louder and the sound of the aircraft's engine more distant.

Gadgets!

Blancanales was sprinting for the door. Lyons was on his feet and following, the Colt Python gripped in his right hand.

The Able Team warriors burst through the door. Blancanales swept his gaze over the rooftop. He saw a man, Hakim, writhing on the ground, his pant legs stained dark with blood, his flesh rent by bullets. Schwarz stepped into view, his Beretta held in front of him, muzzle aimed at Hakim as he closed in on the Arab. He was shouting for the man to stay down.

The thrumming of the chopper's engine grew louder. Peering up, he saw the craft circling and coming back for another pass, its side door pulled open. A hardman cut loose with a burst from the AK-47. The volley of rounds slammed into Hakim, causing him to convulse wildly. A half-dozen geysers of blood erupted from his torso.

Schwarz dropped into a crouch and fired upward. A trio of bullets sailed through the aircraft's door, driving the man inside. The chopper grabbed altitude almost immediately and left.

"Damn!" Lyons yelled.

Able Team converged at Hakim's body. Schwarz already had moved to the terrorist's side and was examining him for a pulse. He looked up at the two men and shook his head.

"Need a séance to interrogate this guy," he said.

"Wonderful," Lyons commented. "I guess we're back at square one."

Blancanales looked over at Ling. "Maybe not."

CHAPTER SIX

James heard someone approaching from behind. Propelled by instinct, he thrust himself forward, the movement sparing him the full impact of a buttstroke to the head delivered by his attacker. A glancing blow, however, caught the back of his skull, rattling his teeth and rocking his world. Staggering forward, he went to his knees, twisted at the waist and raised his crossbow.

He caught a brief impression of his opponent—a lanky man, head and face wrapped in a black scarf, dressed in jeans, T-shirt and athletic shoes. James fired the crossbow. The bolt plunged into the man's shoulder, causing him to drop his assault rifle.

James followed up by lashing out with a blurring kick that caught the side of the man's knee, snapping it, causing him to teeter. The Phoenix Force commando surged up from the ground and dropped on the guy like a stone, his weight driving the air from the man's lungs. Fisting his combat knife, he pressed its keen edge against the man's throat and, with a deep stroke of the blade, killed the man.

Wiping the steel clean on his opponent's shirt, James

dragged the corpse into a nearby stand of bushes. He recovered his crossbow, reloaded it and continued through the embassy grounds, immersing himself in the shadows.

A cough followed by the scratch of a lighter's wheel sent a cold sensation plummeting through his belly. He halted and dropped back into a crouch. He saw an orange flicker several yards away, illuminating a terrorist's face as he lit a cigarette.

The rank amateur move surprised James. Terrorists were by no means a match for well-trained commandos, but their training and weapons had become increasingly sophisticated over the years. To see one of these men break such a basic rule caused James to feel suspicious. Was the man just undisciplined, or was he trying to call attention to himself? A distraction, perhaps? Regardless, James would assume the worst.

Encizo's voice sounded in James's earpiece. "Two down, Cal. Your status?"

He had enough distance that his quarry never would hear a whisper. He cast a glance around and began to reply. Before he could, he caught another shadow closing in from his right.

Encizo's voice, still cool, crackled again in his earpiece. "Cal? Cal?"

Powerful leg muscles coiling and uncoiling, James thrust himself forward. A glance right revealed a man closing in on him, weapon held at hip level, spitting flame and lead. The volley of shots sliced the air just above James.

Still in midair, he fired the hastily aimed crossbow. He was rewarded with a one-in-a-million shot, planting the bolt into his attacker's right eye socket. Dropping his weapon, the man covered his face with both hands and cried out in pain. Stopping in midstride he pitched backward, his foot twitching as he plummeted into death.

James's superbly conditioned body hit the ground. He launched into a roll and let the crossbow slip from his grasp. The man with the lighter began unloading a small grease gun in James's direction. The bullets struck the ground, shredding grass and kicking up bits of dirt. Still rolling, the warrior plucked his sound-suppressed Beretta from a thigh holster and squeezed off three shots. The first two went wild, missing the terrorist, but coming close enough to foul his aim. The third round made a neat hole in the man's shoulder before exploding from his back. The man stumbled backward, his injured shoulder unable to raise the rifle. The Beretta coughed twice more. Parabellum slugs drilled into the man's sternum, chewing through his heart and spine before dropping him in a boneless heap.

"Cal?"

James keyed his headset. "Go, Rafe."

"Shit, man—"

"I know. I know."

"You okay?"

"Yeah."

"What's your position?"

James told him.

"I'm on my way," Encizo said. "You get your two guys?"

"Three, man. You gotta start carrying more water here."

"Son, I was carrying water when you were still pissing in your diapers." Encizo's grin was almost audible through the line.

James stood, dusted himself off and put a full clip into the Beretta, pocketing the partially spent one. Holstering the handgun, he brought around the sound-suppressed MP-5 and set it for 3-shot bursts.

His eyes roved the terrain for other attackers. At the same time his mind roiled, particularly over the terrorists' errant gunfire. The noise had been unwanted, but unavoidable. Now the bastards inside knew a hit was coming. That brought heightened urgency to the mission.

Encizo's voice came over the com link. "Coming up on your six."

"Clear." Within moments, the two men were crouched together, next to a two-story, redbrick outbuilding.

EXITING THE TUNNEL, McCarter, Manning and Hawkins fanned out over the dimly lit room in the embassy basement. McCarter, in concert with the other two men, swept the muzzle of his MP-5 over the room, but found nothing other than computer servers, two computer workstations and a minifridge.

"Embassy Command," he whispered into his com link. "Embassy One and team are inside."

"Clear," Colvin replied.

McCarter nodded toward the door and headed for it. The other warriors fell into step behind him, spreading out in a triangular formation. McCarter knelt next to the door and let his MP-5 hang loose on the shoulder strap. He extracted a handheld device outfitted with a small television screen and a lengthy, tubular camera lens. He slid the lens through the space between the door and the floor and checked the screen. The door led into a corridor. A pair of Arabs stood in the hallway, smoking cigarettes and talking. One man carried his AK-47 on a shoulder strap, the barrel canted toward the floor. The other man had leaned his against a wall. His hand rested on his pistol.

McCarter turned to his friends and with hand signals indicated the number of opponents and their positions. The men nodded.

Pocketing the handheld camera, McCarter brought the SMG back around. For the hostages's sake, he knew that they needed to keep the element of surprise for as long as possible. They'd need a quick, quiet takedown. Resting a palm on the doorknob, he held the MP-5 ready. A glance at his comrades told him they, also, were ready to go.

McCarter surged through the doorway, the sudden motion causing the Arabs to turn toward him. The men scrambled for their weapons. But their inattention would prove fatal. The man who'd abandoned his AK-47 dropped into a crouch and scrambled for his pistol. McCarter's MP-5 chugged out a burst of 9 mm rippers that shredded the man's middle, killing him.

The gunner who'd held on to his assault rifle proved to be a livelier target. He raised the weapon to acquire a target. Manning rewarded the man's efforts by laying down a burst from the sound-suppressed MP-5. The slugs stitched the man from right hip to left shoulder, launching him back several feet. To McCarter's relief, the man didn't trigger his weapon in a death reflex.

As Manning and McCarter had fought, Hawkins had taken out the surveillance cameras with a small device he, Schwarz and Kurtzman had developed. The zapper could be aimed at a camera and destroy the fiber-optic cables by bombarding it with microwaves. A dead camera would attract attention, but not with the urgency of images of two bloodied corpses.

A quick check of the rooms in the basement revealed them to be empty. McCarter led the other men down the hall and to the stairs, which they took to the ground floor.

AS THE PHOENIX FORCE commandos stood on the stairwell, McCarter knelt next to the door leading into the first floor. He swept the camera's tubular lens again under the door, trying to determine what he and his comrades were preparing to walk into.

He saw a vision of hell.

The corpses of Marines killed during the initial raid still lay scattered throughout the lobby, in pools of blood. Spent shell casings littered the floor. A half-dozen terrorists, their heads swathed in scarves, armed with Uzis and AK-47s, walked among terrified embassy employees and other bystanders who were crouch on the floor. He saw three huddled against the wall just outside the door, and made a mental note to draw fire away from that area as soon as possible.

McCarter's stomach churned with rage. His face grim, he let the other men take a look at the viewer. Judging by their expressions, both shared his reaction.

"Embassy Two," McCarter whispered into the com link. "Status report?"

"In position," Encizo replied. "Ready to move on your command."

"Clear. Stand fast."

McCarter reached into a belt pouch and extracted a pair of flash-bang grenades. In a brief conversation, he, Manning and Hawkins etched out a quick plan to take the room.

McCarter gripped the MP-5 by its pistol grip and grabbed the door handle. Hawkins shot to his feet. Manning took a final glance at the viewer. He gestured for the other men to wait, beckoned them to look at the screen.

The Briton knelt again. He saw the terrorists yanking people from the floor, walking them to the exterior walls, positioning them in front of windows. He whispered a terse oath. A human wall. The bastards were surrounding themselves with hostages.

Damn!

A clatter sound from upstairs heralded yet another change in McCarter's plans. He whipped his head toward the noise to identify it. Hawkins, who'd been watching the stairs, wheeled toward the other two, his eyes wide.

"Grenade!" he breathed.

ENCIZO GAVE the rope one last tug. Satisfied that the grappling hook was set, he stepped to the roof's edge, crouched and waited for McCarter to give them the go.

As he waited, he swept his gaze over the rooftop, let it linger on a pair of terrorists lying together in a tangled heap, their chests glistening where blood had saturated their shirts. Encizo and James had downed the two men moments earlier and begun preparations for a two-pronged, lightning-fast insertion through the second-story windows.

James was crouched next to Encizo, his MP-5 held steady as he covered them both. Encizo flashed a thumbs-up and James grabbed his own rope. The Little Cuban reached inside his combat pouch and palmed a flash-bang grenade. The plan was relatively simple. Scale the wall, toss the stun device through the window, disorienting the terrorists and the hostages. After that, it would be basic shock and awe. The orders were explicit: grab one or two terrorists for interrogation purposes.

Everyone else went out in body bags.

Encizo could live with that.

"Been a while," James said. "You want to check in with David?"

Encizo nodded. Before he could make another move, a peal of thunder seemed to erupt from within the building. A cold sensation rolled down Encizo's spine like a rivulet of ice water. He and James exchanged quick glances. Before either man could say a word, though, they heard the muffled rattle of gunfire from within the building.

"Shit," Encizo said.

He keyed his throat mike. "Embassy One. Sitrep?"

McCarter's reply was instantaneous. "Taking fire. Proceed as planned."

Encizo and James rose as one and started for the edge of the roof. Encizo placed one foot onto the parapet and prepared to step off. Steel clanged against brick, snagging his attention. He and James looked in unison at a service door leading onto the roof and saw that it had slammed open. Three armed men spilled from the doorway, fanning into different directions, flames spitting from the muzzles of their weapons.

Bullets chewed into the rooftop at the warriors' feet, shredding the rubber roofing material. His hand moving with practiced ease, Encizo freed the Beretta from his hip holster, raised it and acquired a target. The Beretta sighed, dispatching a trio of Parabellum rounds. Encizo had a vague impression of his target being slammed back, red geysers of blood springing from his chest. In the same instant, a million fiery needles stabbed inside his chest as something slammed into him, causing his legs to go rubbery. He stumbled backward, trying desperately to regain his footing. His hands flew up to his chest defensively and he realized that he'd dropped the Beretta.

He glimpsed James's face, saw the panicked expression there as his comrade mouthed his name.

He had no time to think about it. It wasn't until he flipped over the ledge of the roof that some corner of his mind realized that he'd been hit. His body armor had stopped the bullet, but the blunt-force trauma of the hit had ripped away his breath, racked him with pain.

As he plummeted toward the ground, his hand stabbed out into space, caught hold of something hard. Steely fingers closed on the object. His other hand grabbed hold of the same object, his mind clearing enough that he realized it was a window ledge.

Encizo grunted with more pain, this time from the tearing force that accompanied his last-ditch grab. His lungs opened again. The sudden rush of air caused his eyesight to sharpen, though blood still roared in his ears as his pulse had reached a fever pitch.

Arm, shoulder and back muscles burning, Encizo, in agony, began to haul himself up, bringing his gaze in line with the window. At the same time, he kicked his right leg upward. After two unsuccessful attempts, he hooked a booted foot up over a ledge and used the extra leverage to raise himself.

A cacophony of gunshots sounded from the roof and from within the embassy. The knowledge that his comrades and the hostages were in danger injected an extra urgency to Encizo's movements.

Suddenly the window above him shattered, showering him with shards of glass. He saw a head, then the battered and bloodied form of a dead Marine flying through the opening. Even before the corpse cleared the window, gunfire lanced through it, forcing Encizo to instinctively flatten against the concrete wall, still warm from baking in the day's heat. The thump of the body hitting the ground, mixed with the cries of terrified hostages, caused his concern for his friends to be replaced by a red-hot rage for the senseless murder erupting around him.

Dangling one-handed from the ledge, the anger anesthetizing the pain in his chest and shoulders, Encizo jabbed a hand into his combat pouch and extracted a flash-bang grenade. Activating the device, he lobbed it through the window. He was already scrambling for the opening when sound and fury exploded from within the building.

Pulling himself level with the window, he looped an arm over the sill and filled his other hand with the MP-5. Hostages, now blinded, deafened and disoriented, continued to scream and fall over one another on the floor as they waited for what they believed to be a sure death.

One terrorist stepped into the open from an adjoining room. He spun toward the wall, aiming his AK-47 at the window.

And Encizo.

The commando stroked the MP-5's trigger. The subgun kicked out a storm of lead that pummeled the man's chest, opening it with less than surgical precision. Before the other terrorist got his bearings, Encizo squeezed off another burst that tore apart the man's midsection, his arms pinwheeling as he stumbled backward. Another volley felled a third fighter who was aiming his pistol at the hostages, ready to fire blind into the innocents.

He came quickly through the window and sized up the situation. Thanks to a miracle, none of the hostages had been harmed, though several still looked dazed. Encizo chalked up most of the shocked looks to the violence these people—nearly all civilians—had witnessed. He spotted a Marine leaning against a wall, straining at his bonds. Although the soldier's face had been bruised and bloodied, Encizo still could tell the man was relatively young. Crossing the room in quick steps, he slid his combat knife from its scabbard and knelt next to the young Marine.

"What's your name, son?"

"Wentworth," the young man said. "Tom Wentworth."

Encizo placed a hand on the Marine's shoulder and leaned him forward. The Phoenix Force soldier inspected the younger man's bonds, saw his captors had used plastic handcuffs.

"You seen any action, Wentworth?" Encizo sliced the blade across the plastic strips and they fell away.

The Marine brought his hands around and rubbed his chafed wrists. "You mean, before tonight?"

"Yes."

"Iraq, sir. One year."

Encizo stabbed the knife into the floor. He snatched up a discarded assault rifle and handed it to Wentworth. "Take these people to a safe room. If anyone but me tries to come through the door, drill 'em."

The young man took the weapon, checked its load even as he stood.

"What if you get killed, sir?"

Encizo shrugged. "There's a few of my teammates running around. Ask for Rick Cornett. Otherwise, improvise. Any more of these maggots running around here?"

Wentworth nodded over his shoulder. "In the library. It's the most secure room in the building. Last I saw, the leader of these guys was hanging out in there. He had Barbara Kendall, our public-information officer, with him. You want to get in there, you need an entry card."

"You have one?"

Wentworth shook his head. "Nah. They took everything." He gestured at the dead terrorists. "But I'll bet you search one of these guys you'll find one."

Encizo thanked the young man. He sifted through the pockets of three terrorists before finding a security card. The Marine, who'd busied himself freeing the other hostages, confirmed that it was, indeed, the one he wanted.

Encizo escorted the group to a nearby room, a lounge of some sort outfitted with large-screen televisions and billiard tables. He left the group inside and felt a slight bit of relief when the door locked behind him.

As he stepped back into the hallway, he saw another man standing there, surveying the damage. Calvin James. The former SWAT officer grinned at Encizo.

"You leave any for me?" he said.

"Nada, amigo. Sorry. And our friends from the roof?"

James shrugged, sliced his forefinger across his throat. "Hanging with the Grim Reaper. Once I saw you go over the side, I went a little nuts."

"I'd expect no less from an old friend."

Gunfire continued to rattle downstairs. Encizo quickly told James about the terrorists still holed up in the library. The two men hugged the wall as they proceeded toward the library. Along the way, Encizo stopped and nodded at a security camera moored to the wall. James raised his sound-suppressed MP-5 and loosed a flurry of lead that destroyed the device. The camera sparked as it disintegrated under the subgun's sustained fury.

"Nice work," Encizo said.

"I like subtlety," James said.

"Maybe that's what they'll put on our tombstones."

McCARTER DARTED from the stairwell, hit the floor and rolled, bullets chewing into the tiled floor. From the corner of his eye, he saw his comrades do likewise, each man grabbing precious distance from the impending explosion.

Thunder pealed in the stairwell, drowning out shrieks from the terrified hostages. Ripped from its moorings, the steel door hurtled across the room and smacked into a wall. Billowing orange flame tinged with black smoke shot through the doorway. The walls of the stairwell had contained most of the razor-sharp shrapnel, though a few bits of wire zipped through the air.

Pulling himself forward with his elbows, McCarter held cover behind a desk. He took a moment to size up the situation, hating what he saw. The terrorists had surrounded themselves with human shields, lining them up along a long counter that resembled a line of teller stations in a bank. His opponents continued to fire upon them even though he and the other Phoenix Force members held their fire for the hostages' sake.

These men obviously were dead-enders, ready to martyr themselves for a cause, no matter how misguided. That meant they'd kill the hostages, themselves and Phoenix Force, all to make a point.

Bloody wonderful, McCarter thought. He'd rather go

toe-to-toe with a brilliant tactician with a strong desire to live any day than a fanatic ready to fall on his sword. McCarter realized that when the enemy didn't care whether he lived or died, you lost your best bargaining chip.

"Stunners coming through," he growled into his throat mike. "T.J., do likewise and back me up."

"Clear," Hawkins said.

Pulling a flash-bang grenade from his web gear, McCarter activated the device and lobbed it over the desk, his protective cover. The motion spurred the fighters to unload their weapons in his direction, rounds drilling through the steel desk and blistering the air around him. A heartbeat later he heard the flash-bang explode, saw the brilliant white flash overtake the room. A second stunner tossed by Hawkins loosed its own senses-shattering payload.

McCarter rounded the desk, the HK held tight against him. A stunned terrorist stumbled from behind a large pillar into McCarter's path. The man covered his eyes with his hand, squeezed the weapon's trigger and swept its muzzle over the room, the bullets chipping away at marble columns and dark-wood paneling. The MP-5 coughed out a line of bullets that punched into the terrorist's stomach, the concentrated fire pulping his midsection.

Hearing more autofire, he whirled and spotted Hawkins hosing down two more terrorists with a sustained burst. At the same time, Manning was crossing the lobby in a crouch, his stocky body moving with surprising stealth.

McCarter closed in on the hostages from the opposite direction. When he reached the first—a slight, balding man, his scalp sopped with sweat—the Briton grabbed the man by his shirt collar and shoved him facedown to the ground. "Down," he yelled. He put down two more hostages in a similar fashion. In the meantime, Manning and Hawkins had reached the area and were moving hostages off the firing line, forcing them to the floor, but making them stay close to the counter for shielding.

McCarter climbed onto the counter and aimed his weapon down into the pit on the other side. Two lines of desks sat behind the counter. The terrorists closest to the impact point sat dumbfounded, their weapons out of reach. Two more were on their feet and at a rear door, trying to punch in a security code to open it.

Unlike their comrades, they apparently had decided discretion was the better part of valor.

McCarter jumped to the floor. Raising the subgun to his shoulder, he sighted in on the two men trying desperately to escape. From the corner of his eye he caught Hawkins approaching. The sudden motion caused the men to turn in unison toward the commandos. Both terrorists clawed for hardware as they whirled toward the approaching enemy.

McCarter's MP-5 dispatched his target with a squeeze of the trigger. Hawkins caught his man as the guy's pistol cleared leather, shoving him against a wall. The rattle of autofire echoed elsewhere in the lobby. McCarter wheeled around, turning in time to see Manning dispatch two more hard guys to hell with a sustained burst from his subgun.

Clouds of gray gun smoke hung heavily in the air. Dozens of bullet holes pocked walls, furniture and flooring. Blood continued to thunder in McCarter's ears and adrenaline coursed through him, sharpening his senses, setting his combat reflexes on a razor's edge.

He released the still-smoking MP-5 and rounded the counter.

"Embassy One to Two," he growled into his com link. "Status report. Now."

"We've got a rat in the hole," Encizo replied. "We're getting ready to smoke him out."

"You think it's Jasim?"

"Probably. Unless you know something I don't."

"Negative. We've got a load of downed bad guys, but no one that matches his description. You need backup?"

"Only if you've got it to give. Otherwise, Cal and I can handle this one."

McCarter raked his gaze over the lobby. He saw the hostages, many of them starting to rise as, one by one, Hawkins cut their bonds. "Give me thirty seconds," McCarter said. "I'd like to meet the bastard behind this mess."

CHAPTER SEVEN

San Diego, California

Seated in the back of their rental car, Blancanales stared at the woman next to him while she avoided his gaze by choosing instead to look at passersby on the street. Crossing her long legs at the knee, she cupped the top knee with her interlaced fingers, twitched her dangling foot to a beat pulsating in her head. She turned briefly, revealing her right profile, which had changed little in the years since he'd last seen her.

A stirring, pleasant and unsettling, passed through Blancanales as he regarded the woman. They had a shared history, and under other circumstances, running into her might be at best a melancholy experience, maybe a chance to enjoy some time with a beautiful woman.

Under other circumstances.

"What were you doing in there, Donna?" Blancanales asked.

She continued to stare out the window. "Looking for something."

Blancanales felt his face color with anger. "I need answers and I need them now. This has nothing to do with you and me."

"I don't have to tell you a thing."

Lyons, his left hand grasping the steering wheel, glanced over his shoulder. "You know this lady, Pol?"

A smile twitched at the corner of her lips. "They still call you 'Pol.' The Politician? Still smooth with the tongue, huh?"

"Darling, you don't know how much," he said, grinning.

She gave him a hard stare. "Forget it, Rosario. The patented Blancanales charm won't work with me. You and I have been down that road once. So forgive me if I don't swoon with a smile and a joke."

"C'mon, Pol," Schwarz said. "Give. Who is this woman?"

Blancanales sighed. "Her name's Donna Ling," he said. "We met back when we were in Asia. We spent some time together there and when I came home."

Schwarz's forehead creased in confusion. "I don't remember anything about that."

"She was an Associated Press reporter. You and I were running covert ops. Sleeping with reporters was strictly forbidden. I kept it to myself."

"That was the only thing he kept to himself," Ling added, scowling.

"You still a reporter?" Schwarz asked.

She nodded. *"Los Angeles Gazette."*

"She's an investigative reporter," Blancanales said. She gave him a questioning look. "I've seen your stories on the Internet. So what the hell you were doing hanging with Mr. Hakim?"

Crossing her arms over her chest, she exhaled loudly and seemed to contemplate something.

"Forget it," she said. "You want to know why I was there? Read about it in the paper. And now I want to talk to my editor."

Blancanales shook his head. "No. The last thing we need is the Fourth Estate nosing around."

"You already have it."

"Wrong," he said. "Your story—whatever story that might be—isn't going to see the light of day. Not now and maybe not ever. We're looking for answers. If you've got them, great. If not, sorry we wasted your time, but we need to move on."

"So you're going to let me go."

"Hell, no."

Rolling her eyes, she smirked. "What? Are you going to keep me a prisoner?"

"We're going to put you under protection," he said.

"Who says I need protecting?"

"I do."

"Your record on that front is wanting," she said.

"Damn it, Donna! That's not fair!"

Lyons cut the wheel into a hard right, guided the car into a nearby parking lot and shifted the gear selector into Park. Slipping off his safety belt, he turned toward the two in the backseat.

"Look, lady," he said, his face flushed. "I don't know what your issue is with Pol. Frankly, I don't care. You two want to do couple's therapy, fine. Do it on your own time. When we have time. Right now we don't have shit and lives are hanging in the balance. A lot of lives could be lost because you won't talk. Do you want to shoulder that burden or are you going to start answering some questions?"

Ling stared at Lyons. To her credit, Blancanales noticed

that the woman didn't seem at all intimidated by him, making her part of a small minority. After a few moments she sank back into the seat, moistened her lips with her tongue and sighed.

"All right," she said. "I was doing a story on the knockoff trade. You know, selling counterfeit goods. My source at customs turned me on to one of Hakim's people. The guy isn't a big player. He just fences the stuff that the major counterfeiters import. According to my source, the customs people kept him under surveillance as best as they were able. But with all the added security at our ports, some creep selling fake Britney Spears and Madonna CDs rated pretty low on their priority list."

"But not on yours," Blancanales stated.

"I figured Hakim'd be a good place to start. I'd heard of Hakim, but he's considered legitimate to the outside world. I had no idea the two men were connected."

"So you approached the guy, started asking questions and he took you to meet Hakim."

She nodded. Blancanales watched as she chewed on her lower lip. She cast her eyes down and studied the nails of her right hand.

"I take it the meeting didn't go well," Blancanales said finally.

She shook her head. "It was a trap from the word *go*. Hakim grabbed me and started hitting and yelling at me. He wanted to know everything I knew, which wasn't much." She touched a welt forming under her right eye and winced, probably as much from the memory as the pain.

Rage welled up inside Blancanales as he watched her relive the moment. He clenched his fists, the nails digging into the soft flesh of his palms as he willed himself to remain silent. A moment later she continued.

"After a while he realized I didn't know much," she said. "He handcuffed me and stuck me in one of the spare bedrooms. Told me that he'd deal with me later. I'm not a complete idiot. I knew what that meant."

"He planned to kill you."

Nodding, she hugged herself and looked down at her lap. Blancanales reached out to touch her shoulder reassuringly. She shrugged him away.

"Anyway, when I went in there, he had a whole roomful of guys. There were guns on the table and large canisters of some sort that I didn't recognize. They're planning some sort of an attack, Rosario. I saw the stuff. I think that's what freaked out Hakim as much as anything else. One of the guys stopped him from beating me, told him that they had to go. Said something about more important priorities."

"Where's the toady?" Lyons asked.

She looked at Lyons, then Blancanales. "His name is Fareed Taleb. His parents are Saudis, but he was born and raised here in California. He likes snorting coke a hell of a lot more than he does hanging at the mosque. I guess Hakim supplied him with plenty of that, too."

"You have an address?" Blancanales asked.

She gave it to him.

Lyons gave her a suspicious look. "If you were handcuffed, how'd you get free?"

"They left a guard with me. He kept gawking at me. I told him I'd rock his world if he released me."

"So?"

"He kept his end of the bargain. I kept mine. My boots may be fashionable, but they also have steel toes. They do a good job cracking the family jewels. His world was rocked."

All three men winced in unison.

"I guess I ought to be grateful that you just hit me," Lyons said.

FAREED TALEB GUIDED the black Lexus sport coupe into the driveway of his oceanfront condo and parked it. Stepping from the vehicle, he locked it remotely with the key fob, causing the vehicle to chirp and its lights to blink once. Walking along, he grazed the car's smooth surface with his fingertips and felt an almost sensual thrill pass through him.

Taleb liked things. He liked money. He cared little about how he got those things, as long as he got them.

Moving inside the house, he tossed his keys onto the bar and poured himself two fingers of Scotch whiskey, neat. Draining the glass, he poured a second. He knew his parents, both devout Muslims, would be beside themselves if they saw him drinking. He also knew he didn't care.

Glancing at the answering machine, he saw the red light blinking and scowled. Probably that little bitch from Hakim's office, the one working the front desk, he thought. He'd made the mistake a few nights ago of taking her out and showing her a good time. She'd been impressed with his car. And her eyes had bugged out when she'd seen the wad of cash he carried. The girl had liked to party, that much he knew for a damn fact. It hadn't taken much prompting to get her back here for an evening of carnal fun. Now she was calling him every day, like some weirdo stalker. Next she'd be telling him that she was pregnant.

He shuddered at the thought. If that happened, he'd

take care of it. He knew people that'd take out a pregnant woman like they were taking out the garbage. No questions asked. He'd coughed up the money for the same service before. He'd do it again.

Taleb stepped onto the deck, his Italian loafers slapping against the wooden planks. Swirling the drink in lazy circles, he stared out at the vast expanse of the Pacific Ocean, heard it crash against the beach with irritating monotony. Gulls cried overhead, and he scowled. The place would be paradise if it wasn't for all the noise, he thought. Torching a cigarette, he plopped into a nearby chair, closed his eyes and leaned back his head, listening to what he considered the melodious sounds of his own thoughts.

Hakim had looked pleased with Taleb. That was a good thing. Not that he gave two shits about Hakim's happiness in the abstract. Hell, no. But when the tightwad asshole was happy, he coughed up cash. Delivering the reporter to Hakim ought to be worth a few bucks and get her off his back at the same time. He knew what would happen to her and it was a damn shame. But business was business and he had to do his part to help keep the machine running. He made a mental note to mention the customs agent's name to Hakim, too. Crazy bastard would probably take the Fed out, too, and his family, if he had any. But to hell with it. After all, he'd made his bed when he started firing his mouth off in front of the reporter.

Grinding out the cigarette, he lit another and drank his Scotch. An image of the other men gathered in Hakim's office flashed through his mind and a shudder seized him, one violent enough to cause him to spill part of his drink on his shirt as he raised it to his lips. Damn it. He sucked down the rest of his drink, moved inside and made a third.

What the hell was the matter with him? he wondered as he returned to the deck. Sure, he knew what was coming down. He realized that the hard-eyed men in Hakim's office had journeyed halfway around the world to kill a bunch of people. So the hell what? He emptied his glass, slammed it hard on the arm of his chair. He shook his head disgustedly, massaged his temples with the forefinger and thumb of his left hand.

A knock at the door caught his attention. Rising to his feet, he slipped inside and approached the door. He halted, shuddered. What if Hakim had decided to take him out? The guy has entrusted him with information critical to national security, information that could save hundreds if not thousands of lives. What if the bastard had had second thoughts and had sent a couple of his thugs to kill him?

He tried to dismiss the thoughts racing through his head as he approached the door, but they wouldn't go away. Fear constricted his throat as he closed in on the door. He slipped his hand under his jacket and with the ball of his thumb slipped the leather thong from the hammer of his SIG-Sauer P220, making it easier to draw. He rested a sweaty palm on the door handle and peered through the peephole.

A momentary sensation of relief washed over him, followed almost instantly by rage.

He thrust the door open, startling the young Hispanic woman on the other side.

"Carmen, what the hell do you want?" he shouted.

She shrank a bit and seemed to fumble for words.

"Spit it out," he said.

"Some guys came to the office today. I thought you might want to know."

"What? Have you lost your freaking mind? Men come in the office every day. Why the hell should I care?"

"They were cops. They were from the Justice Department."

Taleb took a step back as though struck. "Justice Department? What the hell do you mean? Were they looking for me?"

"No, they were looking for Mr. Hakim. They asked if he had any visitors."

"And you told him what?"

"I told him about the guys who came in this morning."

Fucking idiot! "You tell them about me?"

"No, Fareed, I wouldn't do that. I don't want you to get in any trouble."

"I can take care of myself," he said. "Get your ass in here."

The woman's eyes narrowed in anger. Shit! Him and his big mouth. Now she might turn and walk away. Hell, she might even hunt down those jack-off Justice Department agents and drop his name. He needed her in the condo where he could get control of her, if necessary. Softening his features, he nodded over his shoulder. "Hey, sorry I blew up. Come on inside."

She regarded him suspiciously, but decided to comply. He closed the door and locked it, the dead bolt slipping into place loudly. The woman's head whipped around toward Taleb and she gave him a questioning look.

"Did they mention me? The Feds, I mean. Did they mention me?"

Carmen shook her head. "No. I told you that they just wanted to know about Hakim. And the other guys."

"And you told them what?"

"That he was in the office and so were the men. But that was all I told them, Fareed, I swear. Why are you acting so crazy? What else could I tell them?"

Taleb thought about it for a minute. "So why the hell come here and tell me this? What's in it for you?"

Placing her hand to her chest, palm down, Carmen looked surprised and hurt by the questions. Then her face darkened in anger. "I came here because I didn't want you to get into trouble, you jerk. I thought you might be in trouble and I wanted to help."

Shit, he thought, this is all I need.

Another thought occurred to him and he felt perspiration break out on his palms and in the small of his back.

"So you just wanted to help?"

"That's all. I swear."

"Bullshit. How do I know these guys didn't follow you here? You trying to bring the law down on my back? Is that it?"

The anger drained from her face, replaced by fear. He realized he was shouting and it made him feel good, powerful.

"I didn't think—"

Taleb closed in on her, grabbed her upper arms and squeezed hard. She let out a yelping cry of pain. He shoved her into the wall hard enough to make it vibrate, causing her to wince.

Taleb opened his mouth, ready to launch another verbal assault. To tell her again how stupid she was. Before he could, another sound registered with him. It was a common sound, but under the circumstances caused him to stiffen.

The rumble of a throat clearing.

Releasing his grip on Carmen, Taleb whirled toward the noise, his hand clawing for his 9 mm handgun. What he saw made his stomach plummet, caused him to abandon his desperate grab for his weapon. Three men and a woman—that damn lady reporter—stood in the open doorway leading onto his deck. One man, a Hispanic, stood in front of the others, a shotgun in his grip, the barrel pointed at Taleb.

Taleb felt his lip quiver and raised his hands in surrender.

The Hispanic man shook his head, scowled. Rage was evident in his eyes. "You obviously have some issues with the ladies, hombre," he said. "Perhaps you and I, we can work them out."

WHEN IT CAME to interrogation, Blancanales considered himself a skilled tradesman. During his career, he'd sweated, swindled or sweet-talked information from every sort of slime-bag criminal and terrorist imaginable. He could switch from engagingly warm to the coldest bastard in one second. When it came to extracting information, he had a seemingly endless arsenal of methods, some learned on the government's dime at the hands of soldiers, federal agents and spymasters. Others he'd developed himself, a mixture of an unerring gut instinct for other people and trudging the countless killing fields of his life and career.

He was good, sure.

But with the doomsday numbers plummeting, they'd opted for a more direct approach.

Call it Carl Lyons. At the moment, the scariest bastard on the planet.

The big guy was pacing the floor, his thudding footsteps

wearing a path in the hardwood floors in front of the living-room couch. His face was a mask of white-hot rage as he stared straight ahead, apparently oblivious to his teammates and Taleb.

The young Arab was seated on the couch, his sweat-soaked silk shirt plastered against his skin, making the lines of the sleeveless T-shirt underneath more pronounced. Occasionally he lifted a shaking hand to his chest and, inserting his fingers into the breast pocket, fished for cigarettes. He needn't have bothered. Lyons had already snatched them away and ground the box under a heel.

Leaning against a wood-paneled wall, Blancanales covered his mouth with his hand to obscure a smirk as he watched things unfold. Schwarz stood near the condo's back doors, ready to run interference should Taleb try to escape. At Blancanales's urging, Ling had agreed to usher the shaken young woman into a rear bedroom. He realized her help wasn't entirely altruistic. If he knew her half as well as he thought he did, she was grilling the young woman about Hakim and his organization.

Lyons gripped a sound-suppressed Beretta 92, borrowed from Blancanales because Lyons needed a quiet weapon.

"Little man, you and I are going to have words."

"My name's Fareed. You can call me Mr. Taleb."

"Is that so?" Lyons asked. "How about I call you shit-head? After all, that's what's going on your tombstone."

"Screw yourself. You aren't going to kill me."

Lyons grinned. "Keep telling yourself that. Hope you like the smell of fresh dirt."

"What the hell do you want? You guys cops? Is that it? Damn! Hakim finds out you're hassling me, he's going to be pissed. You hear me, man? Pissed."

Lyons gave a short laugh. "That's funny," he said. "You're a damn comedian, son. You know that?"

"What's so funny?" Taleb asked, his voice becoming more shrill.

"Hakim's dead."

"Bullshit."

"No, serious shit. Rotting on a slab even as we speak. Want to join him?"

"How did it happen?"

"Shot. Six times. Maybe more. I lost count after a while." Taleb looked sick. Lyons let the words sink in for a minute. "And we're not cops. That means we can kill you six different ways and keep your ears for trophies. How's that grab you?"

"Who the hell are you?"

"Walking death. Unless you want to play ball with us."

The young man scrutinized Lyons's grim visage, weighing whether the guy was telling the truth. Whether he was willing to make good on his threats. His eyes dropping to his lap, he shivered. "Okay, what do you bastards want?"

"Information. Pure and simple."

Taleb shrugged. "Sure, man. I can give you that."

"Who were the guys visiting Hakim this morning? They Arm of God?"

Taleb stiffened. "I don't know what you're talking about. Honest, you got to believe me. I don't know about any of it. I'm just a fence. Hakim doesn't tell me anything. Hell, he doesn't even care what happens to me."

Lyons's face reddened. Screaming, his right foot lashed out, collided with a coffee table, knocking it over, scattering magazines, ashtrays and Taleb's drink all over the floor.

Taleb started. "Damn!"

"You just said he'd be pissed that we're hassling you,"
Lyons replied, his voice loud and sharp. "Now he doesn't
tell you anything. Which is it, punk? You his guy or not?
You trying to play me? Huh? Are you?"

Taleb vigorously shook his head. "No way," he said.

"Do I look like someone who likes to get played, especially by a quivering little putz like you?"

Taleb raised his hands in a placating gesture. "No one's
playing you, man. Honest."

Lyons pointed the Beretta at Taleb's forehead. "So you
were lying before, but now you're being honest. So now I
should believe you. You're shooting straight with me. Is
that it? What? You think I'm stupid?"

"You're not stupid."

"Damn straight," Lyons said. "Now, who were those
pukes in Hakim's office?"

Taleb hesitated again. Lyons fired off a double tap from
the Beretta. The 9 mm parabellum rounds ripped through
fabric and wood, missing the young man by inches.

"Shit, man."

"I got no more patience," Lyons said. "We've got lives
at stake. The next rounds go into your left kneecap, then
your right. Then the groin. Then, if you're lucky, the heart.
But more likely the shoulders. You'll hurt for a long time
before you bleed to death. Understand?"

"You kill me, you got nothing," Taleb protested.

"Apparently," Lyons replied. "We already got nothing.
And you're wasting my time here. We already know a
bunch of Arm of God goons snuck in the country yesterday. We already know that Hakim's been bankrolling the
bastards. We already know that Hakim was impressed that

you double-crossed the reporter and that he included you in on the meeting."

"Yeah. Yeah. So what?"

"So give us some meat. Something to chew on, you bastard. Why are these guys here?"

"They'll kill me, man!" Taleb pleaded.

Lyons stepped toward Taleb, kept the weapon locked on the guy's forehead. "They'll never get the chance."

Blancanales smelled the distinct odor of urine and wrinkled his nose against it.

"The Freedom Center," the man said. "They're going to hit the Freedom Center."

"You mean, the big mall."

"Yeah, the big mall."

"Hit it how?"

"Sarin gas canisters. They're going to lock the doors and pump the place full of sarin gas. The mall has thousands of visitors at any one time. It's going to be a disaster. Then, when the cops and firefighters come in, they're going to set off a truckload of C-4. The explosives are laced with radioactive hospital waste that Hakim's been buying on the black market. The radiation is weak, just enough to scare people. But the gas, the explosions, man, those are going to make it a bloodbath."

"Did Hakim give them the gas?"

"Hell, no. Hakim does knockoffs, not weapons. They got it from someone else."

"Who?"

"I don't know."

"You jacking me around?"

"No way! He doesn't—he didn't have the reach for something like that. He supplied the money. He supplied the trucks. But that's it. I swear it. You gotta believe me. I have no idea where they got the gas."

"It come from within the country?"

"No."

"How'd it get here?"

"Hakim transported it in shipping containers. He greased palms at customs. He's got a guy there. Guy figured he was just letting them bring in counterfeit blue jeans. He could give a shit about that, right? So he alters the shipping records, makes it look like the stuff came from Hawaii or some such crap. It all goes through without a hitch. Dumb bastard had no idea what he was doing."

"Name," Lyons said.

Fareed gave it.

Blancanales spoke up. "Is that the same guy that turned Ling over to you?"

Taleb nodded, smiled. "Bitch asked for it," he said. "She should stick to writing about ribbon cuttings or whatever."

"What about the C-4. That an export, too?" Lyons asked.

"No, man. That's domestic. He got it from a guy named Ed Stephens. Runs a biker gang across the border, sells all kinds of nasty shit."

"You knew about all this, but you didn't say anything," Lyons said. "Why?"

Taleb shrugged, his expression perplexed. "I don't know," he said. "Hakim wanted to make me his number-two guy. We're talking big money here. He let me in on the big deal. I mean, I guess I should have felt bad for those people—"

"But you didn't. And you didn't do this for ideals, you did it for money."

Something flickered in Taleb's eyes, as though he knew where the conversation was going. He shrugged again. Shooting Lyons a grin, he tried to keep his tone light. "Come on, man? It's not like I dreamed this shit up. Hakim and the others did. It's a violent world out there right now. You can't blame me for that, now can you? I mean, am I right here or what?"

"Or what," Lyons replied.

He shifted the muzzle a few inches right, squeezed the trigger. The Beretta coughed out two slugs that ripped into Taleb's open mouth before tearing out the other side. His body convulsed for a moment before going slack.

CHAPTER EIGHT

Seated in the semi-truck's cab, Hassan Salih regarded the mall as his comrade guided the lumbering vehicle into the parking lot. A bitter taste flooded his mouth and he clenched his jaw tightly, trying to hold in check the disgust that washed over him. Cursed with an insatiable desire for things, Americans frequented malls, shopping centers and stores like the faithful in his homeland visited mosques for prayer.

That was bad enough. But they had brought their glass towers, their loose morals and their technology to Saudi Arabia even as they fed upon its oil reserves. America had infected his land—a site of holy shrines—with its damnable Western culture and its parasitic greed, eroding his people's faith and his culture's identity. For these reasons alone, Salih knew that God smiled upon him for the actions he was about to take. For these reasons alone, he felt no guilt or remorse for killing Americans, even unarmed, unsuspecting ones. An image of his wife and their two-year-old daughter flashed briefly in his mind, igniting a brief but intense pain within him. Swallowing hard, he set his jaw and forced a smile. They would miss him. But he knew they also would rejoice when they learned the manner of his death. To do anything else would disgrace his memory.

Checking the rearview mirror, he saw three carloads of men peel off from behind the truck, each heading in a different direction. He smiled. The cars contained the rest of his group. They had their own vital roles to play in the mission, and he was sure they'd succeed. The truck rumbled beneath him, filling the cab with noise as the driver mashed the accelerator. The driver, a heavyset Algerian named Riduan, navigated the lumbering vehicle along the parking lot's outer edge, bringing it to a point parallel with the department store Salih sought.

"There," Salih said, tapping a finger against the glass of the passenger's side window.

Nodding, the man whipped the steering wheel right and guided the truck between two lines of parked cars, past a set of glass doors leading into the department store, down a concrete ramp and into the loading area. Salih saw a trim young woman, strawberry-blond hair hanging to her shoulders, an infant clutched to her chest, leading a second child, a little girl, into the store by the hand. Realizing the older girl was about the same age as his daughter, he felt a pang of guilt pass through him. Immediately awash in shame, he cursed himself for his lack of faith.

Think of all the children killed in Israel by Jews wielding American gunships and fighter jets, he told himself. These infidel bastards deserve what they get. A true son of Islam would know this instinctively. His face hot with shame, he laid an open palm on his Koran, felt its familiar shape bulge through the fabric of the green coveralls he wore. He silently prayed that God would forgive this momentary lapse.

The hiss of the truck brakes pulled Salih from his musings. Riduan had circled the truck around the loading area and was preparing to back against an elevated bay door. Shifting the semi into reverse, he stepped on the accelerator and guided the vehicle to the targeted door. The door rolled up and a man came into view, gesturing with his hands for the driver to continue his approach.

Within minutes, the truck had come to a rest at the loading dock. Salih and Riduan stepped from the cab and proceeded to the dock. Salih carried a small knapsack, slung over one shoulder, felt its steely weight press against his shoulder blade.

The young man who'd opened the door, heavyset with thick jowls, descended the concrete stairs leading from the loading dock and approached them. He carried a clipboard and the oval-shaped tag on his left breast read Joe.

"You guys with Seller's Distribution?"

The Algerian nodded. "You bet."

"Thank God," Joe said. "Menswear's been screaming all day for this delivery. Guess they had a run on blue jeans over the weekend."

"It happens," the Algerian said, shrugging.

"You have a bathroom here?" Salih asked.

"Long trip, huh? Sure, man. Go back up the stairs, across the dock and through bay door number four, the one I just opened. Stairs are to your right. Follow them. Bathrooms are to your left as you exit the second-floor landing."

"Thanks."

Joe winked. "No sweat. When you gotta go, you gotta go. Am I right?"

Salih returned the smile. "Quite right."

Minutes later Salih found himself inside the storage area. Forklifts and people scurried across the concrete floor. Boxes of merchandise, stacked four or five high and wrapped in plastic, were situated throughout the bay. The occasional steady beeping of a forklift's backing signal mixed with the chatter of workers shouting orders or bantering back and forth. He wound his way through the stacked boxes, giving people friendly nods or an occasional smile. He wanted to be friendly enough to not raise suspicions without attracting unwanted attention.

As he crested the stairs, Salih glanced around, but saw that he was alone. Excitement fluttered in his stomach at the sight of the steel ladder bolted to the wall, exactly where Hakim had said it'd be. Clambering up the ladder, he withdrew a ring of keys from his pocket. Manipulating the key ring with one hand, he worked his way through the keys until he found the right one. It slid into the lock easily. With a quick turn, the lock clicked open and the door leading onto the roof popped open.

The sun was brilliant and hot, causing Salih to squint against it as he pushed through the door. Stepping onto the roof, he shut the door behind him and proceeded to a line of massive air conditioners. The big machines vibrated and hummed as they worked against the midday heat.

Salih stepped between the units. With hurried movements, he went from machine to machine, opening the control panels and shoving inside large blocks of preformed C-4 plastic explosives with detonators. He knew another team member, a sleeper agent who'd worked at the mall for months as a maintenance man, was doing the same on the main chiller units on the central roof over the food court. As he sealed up the last unit, his mobile phone vibrated, signaling an incoming call. Plucking it from his belt, he placed it to his ear and said, "Yes?"

"Done," a man said. "You?"

Salih smiled. "Done. It is time."

Switching off the phone, he slipped it back into its case, and smiled. "*Allah Akhbar,*" he said. God is great.

Soon the infidels and their cursed country would know just how much so.

LYONS FELT ACID bubbling up in his stomach as the Black Hawk chopper carried him and the other members of Able Team to the Freedom Center mall. He was on the line with Kurtzman at Stony Man Farm, catching up on the latest news, finding it all consistently bad.

"San Diego P.D.'s dispatch center has been trying to reach Freedom Center's security chief," Kurtzman said. "It's a no go. All telephone lines to the mall have been cut. He's not answering his pager or his mobile phone."

Lyons swore under his breath. "Anyone on the scene yet?"

"Three squad cars. Emergency Response Team also has been activated."

"They're going silent?"

"Roger that. They don't want to panic anyone, least of all the bad guys. But it sounds like there's already plenty of agitation to go around."

"Wonderful. "

"The P.D. was already en route when the White House started rattling its cage," Kurtzman stated. "These Arm of God clowns started locking the doors, securing them with chains, so they won't open. Everyone inside's going nuts, of course. They're all dialing 9-1-1 at the same time with their mobile phones, flooding the system."

"Sounds like there's no chance of evacuating. We have any eyewitnesses that can provide us some intel?"

"Yeah, the police got one guy who bolted through the door when everything went to hell. He said the bad guys had started herding people toward the mall's center. The shooters are crowded on the mezzanine level so they can fire down on people, if they get out of line."

"Are they wearing gas masks?"

"Not according to our witness. But the guy was running for his life. I'm sure he didn't have much time to inventory their sartorial choices."

"I want to talk to this guy, the witness, when I hit the ground."

"Forget it. When I said the guy went through the door, I meant that literally. The food court's littered with wrought-iron chairs. I guess he's a big guy. He picked one up, beat it against the safety glass to crack it. When the shots started coming, he panicked and threw himself through the glass. He's cut up pretty bad. He may not make it."

Lyons muttered an oath through clenched teeth. He shook his head in frustration and anger. "Roger that. We'll advise when we hit the ground. Should be another three minutes."

"Clear," Kurtzman said. "Before you go, the big guy wants to talk to you. Got a minute?"

"Do I have a second option?"

"Yeah, a royal ass-chewing later," Kurtzman said. "Hold the line."

A moment later Brognola's voice boomed into the earpiece.

"You guys have everything you need?" the big Fed asked.

"The flyboys brought us all the hardware we need. Bear sent us satellite and ground photos and floor plans he hacked from the county planning department's computer. You guys nail the dirty customs agent, yet?"

"FBI's sweating him even as we speak. He swears he doesn't know anything. Taleb was right. The guy thought Hakim smuggled in knockoff jeans. Guy's beside himself now that he knows the truth."

"My heart's breaking."

"Mine, too. Guess he had help faking those shipping manifests. But he's willing to roll on those folks, too. If we'd known the real source, customs would have X-rayed the container."

"What's the source?"

"From what we've gathered, it originated in China, passed through Somalia and then a few other ports before hitting the United States."

"Hell of a long trip. You think the Chinese are involved?"

"Bear's tracking that angle. They have the money and the weapons. I'm not convinced they have the motives, though. But front a terrorist attack on our soil? It doesn't play. Smart money's on Somalia, since it's a failed state."

"Point taken."

"Look, I spoke with the Man. It's your show, once you hit the ground. The SWAT team's set up a perimeter, but they'll bow to your wishes on everything. The military is flying in its bomb squad to back up San Diego's team. They'll take care of the explosives. But you three need to take care of the guys with the detonators. Otherwise, it could get bloody real quick."

"No pressure," Lyons growled.

Lyons heard a trace of a smile creep into Brognola's voice. "Is there ever? Get us a couple of live ones, Carl. These bastards brought nasty stuff into our country. I want to know their sources, who's fronting the money, the whole shooting match. And, Carl?"

"Yeah."

"We've got about a dozen jurisdictions in there. Play nice, huh?"

"Always."

"THERE IT IS."

Lyons followed the pilot's finger, which was pointing through the glass. The Freedom Center, a retail complex covering one hundred acres, sprawled in front of him. Even from this height, he saw bedlam breaking out everywhere. Military and news choppers buzzed the air over the complex. Cars jammed the roads around the facility. Police cars, fire trucks and ambulances, their lights flashing, were positioned throughout the massive parking lot surrounding the mall.

Releasing his safety belt, Lyons came to his feet and walked into the belly of the aircraft. Blancanales and Schwarz were running last-minute checks on their M-4 assault rifles, both outfitted with grenade launchers. Blancanales also would carry a pair of Beretta 93-Rs, outfitted with extended 20-round magazines, an Ithaca shotgun loaded with slugs. Schwarz wore the Berettas stowed in a dual-holster shoulder rig. Both men also carried Applegate-Fairbairn combat daggers in point-up sheaths fixed to their load-bearing harnesses, along with ammunition, garrotes, stun grenades and other weapons of war.

In the moments before they landed, Lyons performed a quick equipment check. He wore his standby Colt Python in a nylon shoulder rig. A .44-caliber Desert Eagle rested in a thigh holster while a sound-suppressed Beretta 92 rode counterweight on his right hip, the perfect tool for quieter kills. Another silent killer, a Hell's Belle Bowie knife, a heavy monster with a twelve-and-a-half-inch blade, was sheathed on his belt, the hilt positioned behind the Beretta. He also carried an Uzi.

All three men also carried an assortment of gas, flash-bang and smoke grenades, ammo, garrotes and other equipment.

The chopper set down on the parking lot. The three men disembarked from the aircraft and hit the hot asphalt at a run. The rotor wash pushed hard at the men's backs and caused the fabric of their black jumpsuits to ripple.

After they grabbed some distance from the Black Hawk, Blancanales turned to Lyons. "You talked to Hal. What did he say?"

Lyons gave the highlights of the conversation. "He told me to take someone alive."

"You? Take a prisoner? I think we're screwed," Blancanales said. "He say anything else?"

"He ordered me to play nice."

"Now I know we're screwed."

A knot of emergency workers and military officers stood about a hundred yards away. One of them—a rawboned man togged in a black SWAT suit similar to those worn by Able Team—broke away and approached the three warriors.

"Let's dispense with the bullshit, gentleman," he said. "I trust you're our saviors from the Justice Department?"

Lyons nodded.

"I'm Higgins, the SWAT commander. San Diego P.D. At last count, we had about a dozen guys in there. We're having a hard time getting an accurate count because they've lined up civilians across all the entranceways, using them as human shields."

"You got anything at all for us?" Lyons asked.

Higgins nodded. "We've got a young mother inside, she's holed up in a broom closet in the food court, talking with dispatch via her mobile phone. She's seven months pregnant. She's got her four year old with her. Needless to say, they're both scared to death, but they're being real troupers. Says she's sees about a dozen bad guys. Those numbers are suspect, of course. I mean, she can't see everywhere. These folks have gas masks hanging around their necks, so she and all the hostages know something's up. Hell, anyone who watched coverage of the Iraqi war knows what that means. She's already asked if they have poisonous gas of some sort."

"And you told her?" Blancanales asked.

"I told her to worry about keeping herself and her child alive."

"A sin of omission," Schwarz observed.

"It was the right thing to do," Higgins said, shrugging.

"Absolutely," Schwarz said. "So they have gas masks. Obviously they want to survive the gas attack."

"But that doesn't mean they're not dead-enders."

"Right," Schwarz agreed. Whipping his hat from his head, he raked his hand through his hair and furrowed his brow in deep concentration. "They may just want to be around long enough to do more damage. We all know that the gas is just part of a larger attack."

"You're thinking something, Gadgets," Lyons said. "Spit it out."

Schwarz turned to Higgins. "Once the gas starts flowing, what would you guys do?"

Higgins shrugged. "Go in. What choice do I have at that point?"

"Exactly. So you SWAT guys go busting in, trying to save these folks. The terrorists, who want to die anyway, will detonate their truckload of radioactive C-4 and mow you down as you enter the building. They lose some, sure, but they planned for that anyway. A massacre within a massacre. Hell, you guys might even get the blame for acting too rashly, even if it's the right thing. In the meantime, they go out in a blaze of glory, thousands of Americans just go out in a blaze. And the terrorists litter the place with radioactive waste besides."

Higgins exhaled loud and long. "Shit," he said.

"Well put."

BLANCANALES DRAGGED the glass-cutter blade over the display window in a circular pattern. He'd affixed a C-shaped handle with suction cups at either end to the area he was cutting. He gripped the handle with his free hand.

The sun burned hot against the black fabric of his suit. Heat collected beneath the Kevlar vest protecting his torso. Tension knotted his shoulder muscles and his stomach. He sucked in a deep breath, held it a moment and released it. The action gave him only a little relief. Blancanales sweated hostage rescues more than any other task. Killing people was easy; saving them wasn't. But it was a hell of a lot more important. He knew his comrades felt likewise.

He split his attention between the pressure he applied

to the cutter and the buzz of radio traffic passing through the borrowed police radio clipped to his belt. The radio was switched to the SWAT team's tach channel. Blancanales heard Higgins delivering terse commands to his people as he positioned them for maximum effectiveness. Higgins's people were to act as a second wave, should Able Team drop the ball. Just the notion of failing on this mission caused Blancanales's mouth to go dry. It wasn't a fear of death. Or, more specifically, his death. If he and his team-mates fell, so be it. But once they went down, the hosta-ges likely would start dying, too. That, he couldn't stomach.

Schwarz stood at his back, covering both of them.

"Looks like they cleared away the news choppers," Schwarz said. "At least that way, these guys can't watch us make our entry on CNN."

Blancanales nodded. He'd completed the cutting. He gripped the suction handle with his left hand and gave the circular piece of glass a push with his right. It came free. He pulled it from the window and set it against the wall.

He gestured for Schwarz to proceed inside.

"First floor, intimate apparel," he said, grinning.

"I'll try not to fondle the mannequins," Schwarz replied.

"If I don't, that'll be a first."

Blancanales followed his partner through the hole. Moments later they were inside the department store, wending their way between racks of clothes, weapons held at the ready.

Blancanales noted the surveillance cameras staring down at them, but paid them little heed. With a few keystrokes, Kurtzman back in Virginia had hacked into

the mall's computers and verified that the cameras were
shut down.

Someone coughed and the commandos froze. They took
cover behind the waist-high counter surrounding the cash-
ier's station. Walking in a crouch, Schwarz made his way
to the edge of the counter, peered around it. He spotted a
single guard, a swarthy, bearded man, clutching a Glock,
standing in an aisle separating the clothing department
from cosmetics. Using hand signals, he shared the information with Blancanales, who nodded his understanding.

Schwarz rounded the counter and closed in on his target. Racks of blouses, skirts and pants provided him cover.
A glance over his shoulder told him that Blancanales had
shifted into a prone firing position and was covering him.
Schwarz's breath, shallow and quiet as he closed in on the
man, warmed the knit material of the black ski mask pulled
down past his chin.

The air-conditioning kicked on with a clatter, breaking
the silence, causing Schwarz to tense momentarily.
Schwarz was grateful for the extra noise as he closed in
on the man and lined up the shot. The Beretta coughed out
a dual dose of death. The bullets plowed as one into the
man's head, ripping away large portions of the guy's skull
and showering the area with skull fragments and a crimson mist.

The terrorist's knees went rubbery and he collapsed in
on himself. His pistol slipped from his fingers and slid
across the floor.

"One down," Schwarz whispered into his com link.
Blancanales joined him a moment later.

The two men stepped onto the escalator and dropped
into crouching positions as it carried them upward. Blan-

canales raised the M-4 to his shoulder and swept it over the area above them where the escalator spilled onto the second floor. Schwarz kept his Beretta trained on the floor below, covering their backs.

Stepping from the escalator, they fanned out and headed for the door that led toward the mezzanine level. Another guard, a gas mask looped around his neck by a strap, drained Coke from a can. Tossing it aside, he opened his mouth to belch. A Parabellum round drilled into his mouth, jerking his head back violently, causing him to tumble onto his backside. Schwarz moved to the corpse, grabbed him by the collar and dragged him from sight. He came up beside Blancanales, grinning.

"Guy really should cover his mouth," he said.

"Emily Post'd be proud," Blancanales said.

Exiting the department store, they edged onto the mezzanine that ran the length of the second floor, a forty-foot-wide chasm separating the two sides. This leg of the mezzanine stretched about a hundred yards before turning sharply left, spilling into the mall's main area. Shops lined both sides of the corridor.

The commandos split, each taking one side of the mezzanine. Upbeat instrumental music wafted through the air and geysers of water splashed from fountains. Blancanales heard the clashing sound of a hostage's occasional wail, the cries of babies and children, or a terse command barked by one of the terrorists.

Blancanales, who'd traded the M-4 for his Beretta, edged along the line of display windows, the handgun poised at shoulder level. A heavyset, bearded man in green coveralls, an Uzi held in his right hand, stepped out of a smoke shop, a large cigar clamped between his teeth and three more jutting from his breast pocket. Blancanales squeezed the Beretta's trigger, unleashing a triburst that pounded into the man's chest, stopping him cold.

Blancanales sprinted for the guy. He grabbed the terrorist, dragged him back into the smoke shop, deposited the corpse behind a counter. He returned to the mezzanine, the sounds of gunshots and screams greeting him.

CHAPTER NINE

It was a damn suicide mission, and Lyons knew it.

The chopper swooped low over the mall, its third pass in the last five minutes. The craft hovered a moment and Lyons slid back the side door, tossed a rope into the air, watched as it landed on the rooftop, coiling at the end. He had just a matter of seconds to disembark from the craft and hit the roof.

His hands encased in thick leather gloves, head covered with a Kevlar helmet and a ski mask, he grabbed the rope on the chopper's port side, stepped out, the rope pinched between his boot heels. He felt heat ignite in his palms through the gloves as he slid down the rope.

Landing in a crouch, he drew his MP-5 and swept the barrel over the rooftop. A pair of goggles protected his eyes from the debris kicked up by the rotor wash. The roof was a field of mammoth heating and air-conditioning units, exhaust vents and a cinder-block structure with a door, probably service entrances to the rooftop.

Two men and a woman rappelled onto the roof just behind him. The police officers, all togged in black, fanned out across the roof, weapons held at the ready. One of the men and the woman were from San Diego's SWAT team. The other man was a member of its bomb-disposal unit, a former military man named Clark. Lyons hadn't caught the man's first name and, under the circumstances, it didn't really matter.

The beating of chopper blades grew distant. Lyons activated his throat mike. "Eagle One to Eagle Two or Three. Report."

Blancanales's voice came through the microphone. Lyons heard a slight rustle of equipment through his earpiece. It told him that Blancanales and Schwarz were on the run. "Three guys down. We have shots fired. Tell the P.D. to stand fast. Eagle Three and I are going to investigate."

"Clear. We have the rooftop."

"Situation?"

"Flyover indicates no heavies on the roof."

"Makes me suspicious."

"Right. We're sweeping for trip lines and such."

"You sticking with the original plan?"

"Damn straight."

"You think it will work?"

"Hell, no. But I don't see any other way."

Lyons almost could hear his friend's grin. "Always the optimist. Stay frosty, guy."

Lyons killed the connection. One of the police officers motioned for him. He crossed the roof and came up next to the man. The guy had opened a small service door on the unit. With a gloved finger he pointed inside the unit. Lyons looked and his heart sank. He saw packets of C-4 explosives taped to the air-conditioning units.

"The others found the same thing," the cop said. "Not a devastating amount of C-4 in and of itself. But more than enough to disable this thing, maybe even weaken the roof and cause a couple of these things to fall through."

"They wanted to destroy the exhaust system," he said. "Blast these things out of the way and it's going to be that much harder to clear the sarin gas."

"But why not just bust up the controls? Why resort to this?"

Lyons shrugged. "Just creates more pandemonium, I'd guess. Once the gas starts flowing, they know we'll flood the place. So they ignite more explosions to distract us, maybe keep us at bay a little longer. Whole place turns into an even bigger hellground than we bargained for. Can you disable these things?"

The other guy nodded. "I'm on it."

"Tell the others to stand fast, unless I give the word. Or things go to hell. Whichever comes first."

"Roger that," the cop replied.

The Able Team leader broke away from the others and darted for the edge of the roof. He stared down and saw the semi-trailer parked below, judged it to be about a twenty-foot drop. According to earlier recon by the SWAT officers, one of the terrorists had remained in the cab. He hadn't caught a sniper's bullet yet, as the cops hadn't wanted to panic the killers inside the mall. Besides, the police wanted to make sure the guy didn't have his finger on a detonator. It wouldn't do a damn bit of good to wax him if he triggered the explosives in a death reflex.

Lyons harbored similar concerns—for the moment. Once the other Able Team members started busting caps on the terrorists inside the mall, he'd be more than happy to retire this bastard early.

And circumstances might require it, too. If the terrorists had started shooting inside, the guy in the truck might be getting antsy, too, particularly if he wasn't able to communicate with his comrades inside.

Reaching inside his backpack, Lyons pulled out a grappling hook and rope. He hooked one end onto the parapet and thrust the rope over the side. It snaked down and landed on the trailer's top. Lyons scrambled down the rope, landing softly on the trailer. Stepping to the edge, he leapt from the top and onto the loading dock. He hit the concrete, grunted and folded at the knees to absorb the impact. A moment later he was up and slipping over the dock's concrete lip and onto the ground.

Edging along the rig, he felt his mouth go dry, heard his heartbeat hammering in his ears. If the driver saw him, Lyons wouldn't take a bullet; he'd be blown away by a ton of explosives.

Along with a few thousand other people.

No pressure, guy.

Lyons edged along the trailer, a sound-suppressed Beretta leading the way. He held his breath as he came within a few feet of the cab. The driver had his window down, but had left the engine running, presumably to keep the air-conditioning running. An elbow protruded from the window, resting on the sill as though the man was taking a leisurely drive in the country.

Blancanales's voice crackled in the earpiece. "Eagle One."

Lyons knew the thrumming of the diesel engine would cover his reply. "Go."

"About to drop the hammer."

"Roger," Lyons said.

He looked up, his eyes automatically lighting on the reflection in the rearview mirror. He saw someone staring back at him.

Damn!

Lyons darted forward. As he did, the man disappeared inside the cab for a moment. The terrorist's opposite arm, tipped by a Glock, poked through the window and a corner of his face came into view. Flame leaped from the Glock's barrel. The bullet cracked through the air to Lyons's left, missing his ear by several inches.

Lyons triggered his own weapon. The Beretta coughed once, a single Parabellum round drilling into the man's exposed eye socket. The hand went slack and the Glock tumbled to the ground.

Using a built-in step, Lyons climbed onto the rig. Jamming the Beretta through the window, he scanned the cab's interior and saw only the dead terrorist, who was lying on his side, blood spilling from a fist-size wound in his head. Poking his head in through the window, Lyons saw the handheld detonator, which had fallen onto the floor.

Nice, Lyons, he thought. You didn't kill everyone, but you almost did.

Popping open the door, he shoved the corpse onto the other side of the seat. Releasing the brake, Lyons began to work the clutch and jam the truck into gear. The vehicle's power plant roared underneath the hood and the truck lurched forward, Lyons grinding through the gears, coaxing more speed from the vehicle.

In the best-case scenario, the terrorists would carry only a single detonator. But Lyons and the others weren't counting on it. Instead, he just wanted to get the truck as far away from the mall as he could before anyone with a second detonator decided to push the button. Otherwise the consequences would be disastrous.

RUNNING TOWARD THE SOUNDS of pandemonium, Blancanales began to imagine the worst, but checked himself. The burst of gunfire had been brief. Perhaps it was simply an attention-getting ploy by the Arm of God terrorists. Or intimidation. Regardless, it struck Blancanales as a risky move. The gunshots were sure to reach the throng of police and soldiers outside, possibly spurring them into action prematurely. Or it could have been a matter of necessity, if one of the hostages had attempted an escape or tried to rush one of the captors.

The last notion caused a queasy feeling to seize Blancanales's gut. If innocent blood had been spilled, then he'd failed. The whole team had failed, as far as he was concerned.

Spotting another sentry standing twenty yards or so away, Blancanales froze. The man had his back to him. The warrior crept toward the man, his crepe-soled shoes barely making a sound against the tiled floor. At the last instant, a sixth sense had to have spurred the man into action. He whirled toward Blancanales, raising his weapon and opening his mouth to scream out a warning.

The Beretta chugged out a single round. The subsonic cartridge drilled into the man's mouth, exploded out the back of his neck. His body jerked back, as though suddenly yanked away by a speeding car. Blancanales held his breath, offering up a brief prayer that the man didn't trigger his weapon in a dying reflex.

The weapon remained silent.

Until it hit the floor.

The clank of metal striking against ceramic tile jarred the silence.

Blancanales muttered an oath through clenched teeth.

He broke into a run, grabbing his M-4 as he moved. As he passed the dead gunner, Blancanales heard the radio clipped to the man's belt crackle to life as his comrades, their strained voices audible at a distance, checked on his condition.

"Eagle Two to Eagle Three," he said.

"Go," Schwarz replied.

"We go. Now."

"Roger that."

Blancanales crept along the mezzanine until it opened into the broad expanse of the mall's center. A series of three domed roofs, each topped with a skylight, each with a corresponding rounded floor below, lay in front of him. Blancanales counted seven men standing on the mezzanine. Four had let their submachine guns fall on their straps as they fitted gas masks over their faces. Three more took up positions next to the railings, pointing their weapons at the crowd of hostages gathered on the floor below.

Blancanales activated the flash-bang grenade and tossed it. Schwarz simultaneously threw a similar device from his position. The grenades exploded, unleashing a peal of thunder and a blinding white flash that stopped five of the terrorists in their tracks, caused a couple to drop their gas masks. One of the men apparently had been angled away from the flash or had at least rudimentary training in fighting after exposure to a flash-bang grenade. He responded to the approaching warriors by bringing up his Uzi and firing.

Schwarz greeted the attack with one of his own. The M-4 chugged out a punishing salvo that speared through the man's flesh. Crimson geysers of blood suddenly sprang forth from his torso as the Able Team commando stitched him from hip to shoulder with the punishing burst of slugs. The man was dead before he hit the floor.

Schwarz closed in on the terrorists, triggering the subgun as he moved. Two more well-placed bursts downed two more of his opponents. A third man, still disoriented, stumbled off the line of fire, buying himself another long second of life. Schwarz corrected his aim and loosed a blistering round of fire that chewed into the man's stomach like a chainsaw ripping through a tree trunk.

Blancanales raked his own weapon in a short arc, cutting down two men. A third had regained his wits and begun returning fire with a handgun. The Able Team warrior launched himself forward, striking the floor hard. The impact jarred him, but the elbow and knee pads and his body armor protected him from serious injury. The M-4 coughed out another round of fire, spitting hot brass onto the floor and fouling the air with smoke.

The hastily aimed rounds whizzed over the terrorist's head, sparing his life but driving him to ground. Blancanales raked another salvo that sailed several inches over the floor. The wide swath of bullets found their target, chewing into the man's feet and ankles, reducing them to rent flesh, shattered bones. The man dropped to his knees, screaming. Blancanales ripped off another volley that pierced his rib cage and heart, ending his protests.

Another hardman broke away from the others.

"Pol, we got a runner!" Schwarz said.

"He's mine. Secure the hostages."

"Roger that."

Blancanales got to his feet. He caught a flash of the man's forest-green jacket before he disappeared into a nearby corridor.

Moving at a dead run, Blancanales hugged the line of stores, using them for cover. Smoke hung heavy in the air, mixing with the traces of fried foods and the last excretions of the dead, creating a nauseating, cloying stench.

He loaded a fresh clip into the M-4 as he trailed the running terrorist. Reaching the mouth of the corridor, he stopped, listened for signs of his quarry. When he heard nothing, he chanced a look around the corner.

Pulling back behind cover, Blancanales sized up the scene. The hallway was L-shaped, with signs indicating that the corridor's unseen portion led to restrooms. A circular mirror moored in a far corner clued pedestrians to walkers coming from the opposing direction. Blancanales also had spotted the toe of a boot protruding from a recessed area, a pay phone station, according to signs posted overhead.

The warrior slipped into the corridor. Going to one knee, he raised the M-4. The red dot of its sights glided over the floor until it reached the booted foot twenty yards away. Cracking once, the assault rifle hurled a single round that sliced through leather before tearing through skin and bone. The man screamed, stumbled from hiding. Blancanales adjusted his aim, shot twice more, the bullets tunneling into the man's stomach. The hardman crumpled to the ground, his weapon falling from his hands. Blancanales came up beside the writhing the man, kicked away his weapon and knelt next to him. Ripping the head scarf away from the man's face, he recognized him in an instant.

"Mr. Salih," Blancanales said. "Unfortunately for you, you're going to live. And we're going to have a nice, long chat."

CHAPTER TEN

Ellis White felt his pulse race as he watched the carnage unfold on the security video footage.

Seated at his desk, he watched as the three men—two Caucasians and a Hispanic—took out Hakim and his men with deadly efficiency. The death drama played out via a digital recording played back on the screen of a laptop, the footage downloaded from Hakim's computers after a quick hacking job by Campbell's people.

White recognized the Hispanic in an instant.

Rosario Blancanales.

Just seeing the bastard caused corrosive anger to spread throughout his belly, burning his insides. Blancanales's whereabouts had been a mystery to White for years. He knew that Blancanales had gotten mixed up with that crazy bastard—what was his name? Mack Bolan—during his one-man war on the Mafia. If White's memory served him, Blancanales had spent some time in jail. Afterward he'd gone underground and White had always assumed he'd just been glad to get away from his scrape with the Mafia with his skin still intact. After that Blancanales's whereabouts had become sketchy. Some said he'd started pulling black ops for the government; others contended that he'd undertaken mercenary work, fighting on the killing fields of South America and Africa.

White always found the latter notion ludicrous. The guy never would have fought in wars just for money. He was too damn idealistic. Hell, too soft for that kind of crap. He had been the sort of soldier who needed to believe in a cause before he'd spill blood for it. He didn't soldier just for the sake of soldiering.

If anything, White figured that Blancanales had died. Or maybe he'd returned to his East Los Angeles roots to become a social worker, perhaps changing his name to distance himself from his wet work in Southeast Asia and at home against the Mafia.

Blancanales was enough of a chump to spend his days wiping away some crackhead's tears for a paltry salary and a government pension. A wave of disgust passed over White and he dispelled it with a self-satisfied smile. No way would Blancanales put his deadly skills to use unless he believed in the mission. No way.

That's what had separated him from White almost instantly. White liked being a soldier, a fighter. The way he saw it, he'd been given the ability to kill and to do so without the remorse, the sleeplessness, the loss of appetite that dogged other men forced to take a life. So he'd use it. He had no compunctions against killing, anytime, anywhere.

Some Army shrink once had tagged him as a psychopath. If that meant that he didn't break down and cry when he reflected on all the blood he'd spilled, that he could kill anyone, anytime, anywhere, then he guessed the tag fit. He didn't care. He considered it a blessing that he could shoot a drug-crazed rebel point-blank in the forehead and experience a dizzying rush of pleasure from it. Let the shrinks with their Ivy League degrees call him a nut. He didn't care. He lived in reality. And reality was simple. There are two classes of people in the world, the weak and the strong.

He had chosen strength a long time ago. He'd watched his mother, a Dallas stripper and prostitute, be weak, willing to tolerate anything to not be alone. She'd brought home a seemingly endless parade of drunks, each one more violent than before.

The worst, a pimp named Tucker, had beaten her. Afterward, he'd threatened her with a bone-handled straight razor he carried in his right pants' pocket. When the bastard had passed out drunk, the razor's handle had protruded partially from his pocket. White could still remember slipping it from his pocket, flicking it open, dragging it across the man's Adam's apple, leaving a precise red line that immediately brimmed over with blood. Almost from the instant the cold steel had bit through Tucker's skin, his eyes had popped open, fear, shock, anger twisting his face as realization set in.

White still recalled with cold satisfaction the sense of power and invulnerability that had washed over him as he'd watched Tucker explode from the chair, one hand gripping his throat protectively, the other lashing out at the young man. It was one of the few times in his life that White recalled experiencing such joy.

He'd killed many since then. Most times it had been pleasurable, occasionally not. But he never regretted it.

He only regretted the ones who got away.

He'd watched the film three times previously and knew what was coming. Donna Ling surged on the screen, grab-

bing the big blond guy around the waist, taking him by surprise and knocking him off his feet. The woman was fiery
and tough. But she'd not withstand what he had in mind
for her.

Knuckles rapped against the reinforced steel door leading into his room. White pulled his attention from the
bloody footage, redirecting it toward his door. He reached
under the desk's lap drawer, wrapped his fingers around
the Remington 12-gauge shotgun's pistol grip, aimed it at
the door. The weapon hung from a bracket underneath the
desk, where the lap drawer should be. The double-aught
buckshot would rip easily through the balsa wood modesty
panel and gut any attackers.

"Come in," White said.

The door swung open. Richard Taylor, White's chief of
operations, entered. Of medium height and build, he wore
his sandy-brown hair trimmed over the ears and off the collar. He wore street clothes—jeans, a flannel shirt and hik-
ing boots—but carried an M-16 on a shoulder strap. A
combat pouch, presumably stuffed with additional ammunition, rode on his left hip while he carried a .40-caliber
Smith & Wesson pistol holstered under his left arm.

Taylor shut the door behind him. He moved to a chair,
stood in front of it and gave White an expectant look.
White motioned for him to take a seat.

"You sent for me?" Taylor asked.

"You looked at the security video?"

Taylor nodded. "Right. And we ran the woman's image
through a facial-recognition program. It's definitely her."

"And the man?"

"We're going to have to trust your memory on him. We
checked all the records we could find, military, CIA, even

California DMV, but we found nothing. If this guy ever existed, someone went to a lot of trouble to sweep away his tracks."

White smiled. "So the bastard has been running black ops."

"We don't know that for sure."

"The hell we don't. Who else gets his records purged? Blancanales had a distinguished military career. His missions would be classified, sure, but not his military service."

Taylor seemed to mull this. "Fair enough. Regardless of what he's been doing, he's alive, which means he can be found. The real question is, why do it? Especially right now, when we're bringing together Campbell's plans."

"I owe him."

"Simple as that. You owe him."

"I owe him big. When I was in Asia, I had a small crew of guys, a team called Dragon Claw. Just ten of us, as elite as hell. We did the serious wet work over there. We didn't just kill the bad guys, we wiped out their families, their friends. We did some serious shit."

"Government sanctioned?"

White shook his head. "Hell, no. The government chose the targets, but I took it a few steps further, acted on my own accord. I mean, to hell with rules. We were fighting a guerrilla war, taking bad hits. I figured it was time to make my own rules, and that's what I did. I wanted the VC to piss their drawers when they even heard the word 'American.'"

"And it worked?"

White shrugged. "Perfectly. We scared the crap out of those Godless little bastards and had a good time doing it."

"So what happened?"

"We hit the wrong village, killed about forty Vietnamese. No big deal. Except that we missed a couple. Blancanales's unit came along a day or two later, heard about it from the survivors and reported us to the higher-ups. Blancanales was the one who talked to the witnesses, so they flew him in for our courts-martial. I'm out in the field, trying to save that jerk's tail from these savages, and that's what he does to repay me. I paid a visit to his girlfriend years ago and got back some of my own, but Rosario and I need to have a face-to-face. Oh, yeah.

"I want him dead, but first I want to know who he's working for and why he's chasing the Arm of God. Can you do some digging for me?"

"Sure."

"This woman, her name's Donna Ling. She's a reporter and his former girlfriend. I want you to look her up. Check with her office. Toss her apartment. Have the computer guys get any background they might've missed earlier. See if Blancanales has put her under protective custody."

"Why would he?"

"Other than the fact that she pissed off a terrorist group and almost got killed?"

"Okay, I get it. Stupid question."

"Take care of it. And when you find her, let me know. I want her here."

"That means we're going to have to kill a couple of Feds."

White shrugged.

"It's going to piss Campbell off," Taylor stated. "He's the one who's bankrolling this whole thing. What about him?"

"I'll handle Campbell. You just find the woman."

Taylor nodded. "Consider it done."

CHAPTER ELEVEN

China

Wu Deng crouched amid a sea of weeds and grasses, the waist-high stalks of green and brown hiding his slight form from occasional patrols by Chinese soldiers rolling by in trucks or flying over in helicopters.

Shading his eyes with a hand, the young Uighur stared skyward, squinting through the sun's brilliance as he sought his quarry.

The SA-14 Grail shoulder-fired missile, its cylindrical shape still sheathed in a musty green blanket, rested nearby, a gift from a surprising benefactor. He checked his watch and saw the critical moment almost was upon him. Grabbing a corner of the blanket, he flicked the cover aside, revealing the weapon, the sight of it igniting an anticipatory buzz that coursed through him like an electric current.

Lifting the weapon, he raised it to his shoulder and wrapped the fingers of his right around its pistol grip. Within minutes the Chinese spacecraft would fly overhead, nosing its way toward a grassy field three miles away. The capsule's hull, heated from reentry, accompanied by its thrusters, would make it a perfect target for the launcher, which fired heat-seeking rounds.

In and of itself, the loss of life would be minimal, a fact Wu considered regrettable. But the humiliation the Chinese dogs would suffer watching the destruction of their vaunted space capsule more than made up for the meager body count.

Peering through the optical sight, he reacquainted himself with the weapon once again. He needn't have bothered. He'd spent weeks in a training camp in Afghanistan, with his fellow Xinjiang Province separatists, learning to use weapons such as this. But he wanted to leave nothing to chance. The strike was too important.

Satisfied of his readiness, he waited for the craft to soar overhead.

At first he had been suspicious of the American agents who'd agreed to supply him with the SA-14. He knew in his heart that while America occasionally scolded China for its treatment of imprisoned separatists, it had been only too happy to arrest his fellow Xinjiang warriors in Afghanistan and imprison them in Cuba. He also realized that the Americans were waging war on his fellow Muslims in other parts of the world. So he had no delusions that they were allies in the truest sense. But the Western agents had convinced him that they shared at least some common ground.

Both wanted to ground the Chinese space program permanently.

The Americans had supplied him with flight times and the projected landing area in the grasslands in southern

China. Getting this far hadn't been easy, the whole area was heavily guarded. But the Americans had supplied him and three comrades with soldiers' uniforms, an official vehicle and the paperwork necessary to infiltrate the area.

Glancing over his left shoulder, he saw a small white dot appear to the northeast. He watched it for a few seconds more, insuring that it was headed for the designated landing spot, then turned back to the weapon.

A voice buzzed out from the two-way radio in the breast pocket of his field jacket. "Soldiers are coming," the man said in Turkic. "Two carloads. What should we do?"

"Stand your ground. The target is in sight. We are too close to fail."

"We shall stall them. God is great."

"*Allah Akhbar.*"

From the corner of his eye, Wu watched as the craft passed overhead, leaving a white trail in its wake. A moment later, the craft appeared in his sights, prompting him to trigger the weapon. The launcher hurled the missile skyward. The missile locked on to the craft and began to carve out a path toward it.

Pride rushed through Wu for a moment, but almost instantly was extinguished by fear as gunshots erupted from behind him. The gunfire crackled for several seconds and he guessed that his fellow fighters were emptying their weapons, trying to hold the Chinese soldiers at bay while the missile completed its work.

Throwing the spent launcher aside, he drew the .45-caliber pistol holstered on his waist and turned to meet the oncoming challenge.

Just as quickly as it had erupted, the gunfire ceased, the silence only intensifying the fear roiling inside Wu's gut.

The sound of dried grass crunching under several pairs of feet reached his ears. Realizing confrontation lay only a heartbeat away, he weighed whether to fight or to simply vanquish himself with a bullet to the head. He'd heard many stories, horrible stories, about the human rights abuses suffered by his fellow separatists in Chinese prisons. The notion of imprisonment and torture caused his blood to run cold. But he also knew he couldn't just kill himself. Not when he had a chance to take a few of these bastards with him.

Poised on one knee, he leveled his pistol in front of him and waited for the first soldiers to appear. In the same instant, he heard a loud popping noise from behind. Turning his head, he saw a cloud of smoke and flame hovering in midair, showering the ground with sparkling bits of debris. He smiled.

Turning his eyes back to his enemy, he saw three soldiers approaching, their AK-47s held at the ready.

Bracketing one of them in his sights, he triggered the pistol. An instant later the soldier clutched his chest, collapsing to the ground. Whipping the .45-caliber pistol toward another of his opponents, he squeezed out two more shots, both of which whizzed past an approaching Chinese soldier.

Suddenly the young man felt fire rip through his stomach. The pistol cracked once more in his hand, but he again missed, this time because his vision had begun to blur. More fire lanced through his shoulder followed by the repeated stings of autofire tearing through the flesh of his calves and thighs.

The pistol dropped from his fingers. Falling onto his back, he stared skyward, gasping for air as the remaining soldiers surrounded him. He felt someone begin poking and prodding him, checking his wounds. He tried to wave them away, a last act of defiance. But they slapped away his hand. He heard voices, slow and slurred, buzzing around him as his hold on consciousness slipped away.

"He will live?"

"He will. For a while anyway."

"Good. A while is all we need."

San Diego, California

THE BLACK BUICK ROLLED into the driveway. Ling stared at the bi-level house sheathed in brick and tan vinyl siding. She made no attempt to hide her scowl. She didn't like being in protective custody, particularly when pushed into it by Rosario Blancanales.

Ling had spent the past decade as an investigative reporter. She'd won dozens of awards and worked for the country's largest newspapers and magazines, breaking stories that made other reporters shake their heads in disbelief. And she'd done so through a mixture of guts, determination and brains. Not by hiding from trouble. Or by taking orders from the federal government. But something in Blancanales's eyes, his voice, told her that he hadn't made the request lightly. She'd seen the determined look in his eyes before and knew that one way or the other she was destined for protective custody, even if it meant placing her under arrest under patently fake charges.

The driver, a U.S. Marshal named Chuck Krall, cut the engine and cast a glance into the rearview mirror. "This is the place," he said. "Home sweet home. At least for a few days."

"Lovely," she said. "I suppose I can get all the cold pizza and beer I need. All on the government dime."

"Something like that." Though she couldn't see his

mouth, the deepening of the crow's-feet at the corners of his eyes told her he was smiling.

Ling tried to open her door but found it wouldn't open from the inside, prompting her to swear under her breath. Krall chuckled. He exited the vehicle, opened her door and pocketed the keys.

"Sorry," he said. "I forgot to tell you about that. We're usually transporting federal fugitives in this car. Not reporters. It's a security measure."

"I've been in police cars before," Ling shot back. Krall's face reddened and she immediately felt embarrassed. "Sorry. I'm just a little tense."

He dismissed the apology with a shrug. "Drop it. Most people we put in the box are pretty tense."

"The box."

"This place. It's a federal safehouse. But we call it the box. Sounds a little less forbidding."

"Gee, I'm feeling better already," Ling said flatly.

Krall gently took her left arm and led her to the front door. The second marshal, a sandy-haired young man built like a tank, strode behind them. Both men had donned mirrored shades to shield their eyes from the sunlight. But Ling guessed they were scrutinizing the neighborhood much as she was. The place seemed to be all standard suburban fare: lush lawns, decorative palm trees, unremarkable houses. Cars rolled past, but didn't slow.

Krall led her into the living room and shut the door behind them. She watched as the two men wordlessly spread out, Krall drifting through the rooms on the ground floor, while the larger man, who'd introduced himself as Marc Black, disappeared upstairs. Minutes later the two men converged again at Ling's side. Krall looked at the younger man and jerked a thumb over his shoulder at the front door. "Make yourself useful and get the bags," he said.

Nodding, the young man exited the house.

"Just wanted to give the place the once-over," Krall said. "Everything looks clean. When Marc returns with your bags, I'll show you to your room. I'd carry your bags, but I know for a fact that journalists are cheap and don't tip for shit. So you're on your own in that department."

She laughed. "Fair enough." In spite of herself, she was warming to the man.

"You have free run of the house, of course. Just stay away from the windows as much as possible. And, if you see anything strange, tell us. As a rule, when people see something that strikes them as odd, their first inclination is to talk themselves out of it, come up with reasons to say nothing. In the real world, that works fine. But this isn't the real world. You can't be too paranoid in a situation like this. Understand?"

"Of course," she said.

"Your room doesn't have a working phone, for obvious reasons. If you absolutely need to use the phone you come find me. We need to control all communications going in and out of this place. That make sense?"

"Would it matter if I said it didn't?"

He shook his head. "Not a bit."

"Then it makes perfect sense."

"Good. Two more marshals—Thompkins and Fraze— are coming in another hour. Otherwise, we shouldn't be getting any company. Whenever the doorbell rings, I need you to keep out of sight until further notice—"

The second marshal returned, carrying a tattered gym bag that looked more like a small purse in his massive hands. She'd borrowed it from a female marshal, who'd also run out to buy her basic toiletries, makeup and a change of clothes. She'd had more things at her hotel room. But the Feds were leaving the room undisturbed, waiting to see whether someone tossed it for information.

The younger agent led Ling to her room, showed her inside and left her alone. She sat on the edge of the bed and sighed loudly. Her head throbbed, as did the bruises on her face and torso where Hakim had struck her. She popped two aspirin into her mouth, washed them down with some of Krall's coffee. Setting the cup on the floor, she stretched out on the bed and squeezed her eyes shut, hoping it might ease the pounding sensation behind them. It helped, but not much.

Alone, she could admit that seeing Blancanales had thrown her, reawakening feelings she'd hoped were long gone. Not romantic feelings, those had faded a long time ago. Just pain and rage.

So her impromptu reunion with Blancanales had been a surprise, but not a pleasant one. The look in his eyes had told her the feeling was mutual. They reminded each other of failure. Though he'd never admitted it, Ling knew he felt as though he'd failed her when she'd been attacked, that he felt responsible for bringing that madman into their lives, failing to protect her. And, if she was honest with herself, a part of her blamed him, too. No matter how unfair it was, that was the reality. When they'd parted, it'd been sweet relief, probably for both of them, to close that chapter of their lives.

Blancanales had been dealt one final indignity in the aftermath. White, who'd apparently fled from Los Angeles the night of the rape, headed to Tecate, Mexico, where he'd died in a car accident, burned alive inside the wrecked vehicle. Obviously, Ling never had appreciated the irony. And she knew Blancanales felt cheated out of his chance to avenge her.

Unable to slow her mind, she raised herself from the bed and retrieved her bag. Setting the bag on the bed, she unzipped it and began removing T-shirts, panties and bras, all still wrapped in plastic, and began loading them into the drawers of a small pine dresser, one of the room's few furnishings.

A loud crash sounded from downstairs, causing her to start. She headed for the door with slow, uncertain steps.

Yelling, only slightly muffled, punched through the floor.

She froze.

A moment later she heard a brief but furious exchange of gunfire. Her body went numb, save for the slamming of her heart in her chest. Biting her lip, she glanced furiously around the room, a futile effort to locate a weapon, find an exit.

Darting for the window, she peered outside. A second sedan, its engine rumbling, sat behind the marshals' Buick. A slender man, head topped with salt-and-pepper hair, stood next to the car, a hand perched conspicuously inside his jacket.

Thunder pealed twice outside her door, causing her to jerk involuntarily. Whirling toward the door, she heard labored breathing and unsteady footsteps. Something heavy thumped against the door and a hand began jiggling the knob.

Before she could react, the door opened, revealing Krall. Teetering on unsteady legs, he clutched a bloodied hand to his chest. In his other hand, smoke curled from the barrel of a pistol. Choking down a scream, Ling started for him, ready to render aid.

Before she completed her third step, his legs crumpled beneath him and he fell facedown to the floor. His body shuddered once and went still.

Her hand flew to her mouth. She knelt next to him, grabbing for a wrist, hoping to find a pulse. In the hallway, she saw shadows moving on the wall, approaching her room.

She snatched the pistol from his hand, rose to her feet and backed away from the door.

A moment later a burly man holding a shotgun rounded the doorjamb. Immediately spotting the pistol, he dropped back from the doorway.

"Drop it," he roared.

Ling aimed the weapon at the wall next to the jamb and squeezed the trigger. The pistol cracked four times before the slide locked back, indicating the weapon was empty.

Bullets punched through wallboard. An instant later the man who a moment ago had shouted orders at Ling pitched forward, body ravaged by gunfire. Her ears ringing, Ling swallowed hard as she stared at her handiwork, transfixed for a second by the bloodied corpse sprawled in the hallway.

Go! her mind screamed. Move!

She started for Krall's corpse, hoping to get a fresh clip for the pistol. Before she made it to his side, two more men, each armed with submachine guns, came into view, their weapons trained on the reporter.

"Drop it," a gunner yelled. "Down, I said."

Setting the pistol to the floor, she stood again.

"Okay. Now step away from it, nice and easy."

Ling complied. As she did, the stout, red-faced man shouting orders approached her while two more men aimed their weapons at her. Grabbing her by the arm, he spun her, shoved her facedown on the bed. Dragging her slender wrists behind her, he secured her with handcuffs. He cinched the cold steel tightly, causing it to bite into her skin.

"You're lucky. Usually, I'd gut you for this. But someone wants to see you, and I think what he has planned for you is a hell of a lot worse than anything I could do."

CHAPTER TWELVE

Stony Man Farm, Virginia

"I've never heard of the Cadre Project, sir," Hal Brognola said. The big Fed was seated at his desk in his office underneath the main farmhouse, talking with the president on a secure telephone line.

"It was on a need-to-know basis," the Man replied.

"And I didn't need to know."

"That's the way national security works. Truth be told, if it ever got to the point of activating the Cadre, Virginia and every other state surrounding the capital would have been a smoking hole."

"Along with me and my people."

"Exactly. So what good would the knowledge have done you before now?"

We'll never know, Brognola thought sourly. "So now I need to know. And I assume it's not because I'm getting promoted to vice president."

"Unfortunately, no. Things have gotten out of hand. I

need you to bring them back under control. Otherwise, we may all be screwed."

"Explain."

The president paused, clearing his throat. Brognola couldn't see him, but assumed he was collecting his thoughts. "Our government started the Cadre Project during the 1950s. Everyone was worried about the Red Menace, you know, communism."

Brognola didn't need the lesson in geopolitics, but made an encouraging noise so the president would continue.

"The administration at the time decided that we needed a mechanism in place to run the country should a nuclear strike ever destroy the capital, taking the legislative and executive branches with it. They felt the best solution was to create a parallel government with the resources necessary to step in and run the country, should the unthinkable happen."

"You mean, a shadow government?"

"We don't like to call it that. We like to call it a continuity of government plan."

"Go ahead, sir," Brognola said, popping two antacids into his mouth.

"We created the Cadre, a group of leaders and staff capable of temporarily running things while the country got its footing. Every president has known about the Cadre since its inception, but kept it a secret from the public. A lot of people get upset when they hear about the prospect of having unelected leaders take over the country, and rightfully so. But the reality is that if there ever was a nuclear war or another major terrorist strike, Washington would be ground zero. Regardless of how people feel about government, it'd be the first place they'd look to for help in a crisis. At the time, the Cadre seemed the best solution. In hindsight, I'm starting to wonder."

"Because it's not working."

"On the contrary. In some ways, it's working too well."

"You're not making sense, sir."

"I'll get to it. Just bear with me. Erik Campbell was a lead architect of the project."

"You mean Erik Campbell of the Campbell Motors family? I thought he perished in an airplane accident with his wife and small child decades ago."

"Right. A huge scandal. He'd been sleeping with a mobster's wife and a couple of young starlets, according to the newspapers. And the conjecture was that he was murdered, though it never was proved. In fact, we faked his death, with his permission. Right down to the salacious details about his sex life. He was rabidly anti-Communist, patriotic as hell and a genius. Right or wrong, he believed in the project. He'd designed it from the ground up. And he was unwilling to turn it over to someone else to run."

"So he walked away from a successful business career and went into hiding."

"Like I said, he was a patriot."

"He did okay?"

"His service was exemplary. He spoke four languages. His understanding of world affairs was almost unparalleled. His written analyses of constitutional law and American history are still required reading at many colleges."

"So he did okay."

"Better than that. Unfortunately, he also was paranoid beyond words. He worried constantly about whether someone might betray the project or try to usurp his authority. He decided that the best way to maintain secrecy was to hand-select his successors. He chose his son, James Campbell, who then selected his son, David."

"And the government went along with that."

The president's voice took on a patronizing tone. "It was the best thing for the country. It was the right decision. Otherwise, we'd never had agreed to it."

"With all due respect," Brognola said, "I'm not sure I buy that. Otherwise, we wouldn't be having this conversation. I assume David continues to run things. Or had passed it down to a son or daughter?"

"He did until a few hours ago."

Brognola felt a cold pit open in his stomach. "Sounds cryptic."

"David has taken paranoia to a new level. He's lost sight of the mission. His father knew the organization's role. It was to remain passive, unless circumstance dictated otherwise. David doesn't see it like that. He considers the group a security agency unto itself, one completely free of all oversight. Instead of just jealously guarding the secret of the Cadre, he's started exerting influence over national security."

"And that played out how?"

"His grandfather took a page from J. Edgar Hoover's book and began keeping files on political friends and foes from every walk of life. Whenever a president or a senator talked about disbanding the group, Erik would pull out something embarrassing on them and wave it in their face until they shut up. As terrible as the behavior was, it wasn't about power with him. He felt he needed to preserve the Cadre in order to preserve the country's security."

"So he was a zealot with a heart."

"He was a pain in the ass, from what I understand. But

he knew his place. David, on the other hand, has taken operations to a whole different level. Like his predecessors, he believes that communism remains the world's biggest threat. He believes the White House, the Pentagon and the Congress are worrying too much about Islamic terrorists. And he was quite vocal in his opposition. I was willing to tolerate the ideological differences, as long as he did his job. He thinks that the United States is too soft on the Chinese. He believes we're blindly allowing them to grow into an economic superpower. The next logical step, as he sees it, is that China would force communism down Western civilization's collective throat."

Brognola felt his face flush with anger. He balled up his right hand tight, felt the nails dig into the soft flesh of his palm. When he spoke, it was through clenched teeth. "With all due respect sir, if this guy's such a head case, then why in the hell is he in charge of such a vital part of our national security?"

"Frankly, because we didn't realize how truly bad it had gotten. He never made his beliefs a secret, but in mixed company, he tones down the rhetoric so as not to tip his hand. He's well educated, articulate, has the manners of a career soldier. But apparently he's been playing a much different game behind closed doors."

"How so?"

"As I said, this operation was totally black. You won't find it on any line-item budget, you won't find it in any congressional reports. The Cadre does not exist. Because of that, we had to use some…well, creative financing to make sure we kept the operation afloat."

"Don't tell me—let me guess. Campbell and his people are entrepreneurs on top of everything else."

"Campbell operates front companies, his people invest in the stock market to fund his operations."

"And we let him generate as much cash as he wanted without oversight?"

"It's expensive to run one government, Hal, let alone a second, smaller version of the executive branch. It costs hundreds of billions of dollars a year. The money had to come from somewhere. And for decades, we benefited from the whole thing. Most of Campbell's companies make dual-use products, such as electronics with commercial and defense applications. But they also operate at least two full-fledged aerospace defense companies, both of which contract with the government."

"Does this mean what I think it does? That they have access to high-tech prototype weapons?"

After a few beats the president said, "Yes, they have prototype weapons, but only a few. Most of the company's infrastructure was used to manufacture helicopters, fighter jets and tanks, all of it off the books. Unfortunately the one we find most worrisome is the Skyfire project."

"Which is?"

"A satellite system capable of launching a nuclear warhead."

"Oh," Brognola said.

"I have the treasury secretary on the other line, Hal. Can you hold?"

Before Brognola could reply, the president put him on standby. Fire ripped up from his belly, causing him to wince. He chomped on his cigar with renewed vigor as he contemplated the information he'd been given. Despite his cynicism, Brognola considered himself a patriot, a view he could back up through his decades of service and self-sacrifice to the country. And, when it came to gutting terrorist and criminal organizations, he tackled the problem with a gusto that bordered on obsession, in part because he cared so much about the warriors that operated under his command.

But when it came to cleaning up messes created by his own government, Brognola's fuse grew damn short, indeed.

Like now.

A second later the Man came back on the line. "Sorry about that," he said.

"Am I understanding this correctly?" Brognola asked. "We have a nuclear-armed zealot running loose in this country, one with ties to our own government? Can I at least assume we tried to retire this guy?"

"We did. We had a sleeper agent within the Cadre, a guy named Barrins. He retired Campbell's father. We'd asked him to do the same with Campbell, but David disappeared. After that, he went underground. He had facilities in Maryland, California and Alaska. We've seized those and arrested a number of his people. But he was nowhere to be found. And he still has his most elite troops with him."

"So it's our turn to take him out?"

"Do it, Hal. We'll send you a for-your-eyes-only electronic dossier on the man and his operations. Treasury has a few interesting tidbits that I'll send along, too. I'll leave you to handle it as you see fit. But keep me posted. I want progress reports at least every two hours. He needs to go, Hal."

"Consider him gone," Brognola replied.

LYONS LAY PRONE on a hilltop overlooking the ramshackle ranch, surveying the property through his binoculars, sizing it up for an attack. Schwarz also sized up the property while Blancanales monitored their six. All three men had traded in their black togs for civilian clothes, but still wore Kevlar vests.

A twelve-foot fence topped by razor wire hemmed in about five acres of sand and brush surrounding the main house and a couple of concrete-block outbuildings. According to information mined by the cyberteam, the actual property stretched about twenty-five acres. The three-story house in the center of the property once had been owned by an action-film star who'd since moved to Beverly Hills. But any last vestiges of luxury were gone. Years under the relentless sun had left the paint faded and blistered. Driveways and walkways were pocked and cracked. The shattered remains of burnt-sienna-colored clay shingles lay in the sand where they'd landed after sliding from the roof.

The way Lyons saw it, it wasn't that the place had fallen into disrepair because it had been abandoned, it was just the quality of the occupants that left something to be desired. With another sweep of the binoculars, he took in two of the current residents. Both men wore mirrored sunglasses, tattered blue jeans and denim jackets with the sleeves cut away, leaving frayed edges to round the circumference of bulky arms. One of the guys wore black leather chaps. A dust-laden black Jeep Cherokee stood next to the gate, looking somehow out of place.

A dozen motorcycles were parked in two rows alongside the building. A brief interrogation of Salih, the apparent ringleader, had led Able Team to this place. According to him, the current occupant was a motorcycle gang, Satan's Warriors, a group led by Ed "Crusher" Stephens. According to Salih, the gang ran weapons from this location and had provided the sarin gas and the location of the smuggling tunnel.

Lyons lowered the binoculars and turned to his comrades. "Looks like both guys are loaded for bear. Glocks in shoulder holsters, 12-gauge shotguns slung over their backs. Not to mention the Ruger Mark 9 submachine guns I saw in the SUV."

Grinning, Blancanales lowered his own binoculars. "Those come standard?"

"The guns or the leather chaps?" Schwarz asked.

Lyons interjected, "If you two girls are done kibitzing—"

"A thousand pardons," Blancanales replied. "So, our good friend, Salih, said that that there are about a dozen of these guys, give or take a couple."

Blancanales nodded. "There may also be girlfriends or children. And the girlfriends could be just as likely to bust a cap on us as their beloveds would."

"If they try," Lyons growled, "to hell with chivalry. We need to be equal-opportunity ass kickers on this one. But we also don't want to turn this into a massacre."

"Which is why you brought your little friend, right?" Schwarz said, nodding at Lyons's Smith & Wesson A-3, a 10-round automatic shotgun, capable of firing single-shot, 3-round bursts and full automatic.

"You're only as good as your equipment," Lyons said. "I'm usually damn good. This just makes me better. Remember, we take out Stephens, but first we need to ID his source for the sarin gas."

"Meaning we stick with the original plan?" Schwarz asked.

"To the letter. Give us five minutes, Gadgets. Then make a big noise."

SCHWARZ SET THE BARREL of the LAW rocket onto a boulder in front of him and bracketed the Jeep in his sights.

The countdown was nearly over. Just a few more seconds and he would trigger the launcher, igniting a firestorm.

"Ironman, sitrep," he said into his com link.

"Ready for the big bang," Lyons answered.

"Coming."

Schwarz triggered the launcher, dispatching the payload with a hiss. An instant later the round ripped through the vehicle, igniting a maelstrom of yellow and orange fire that seemed to swallow the vehicle. The hellish heat and force twisted metal, melted plastic, choked the air with black smoke.

The blast's concussion flung the bikers from ground zero, heaving them through the air like rag dolls. Glass and metal fragments shredded flesh, killing one biker immediately. The second slammed against the ground, screaming, slapping against the flames eating through his sleeveless jacket.

Schwarz shot to his feet, stripping the Beretta 93-Rs from his shoulder sling as he did.

He strode down the hill overlooking the ranch, both weapons poised in front of him. When he came into range, he raised the Beretta in his right hand and fired a round into the screaming biker, ending the man's suffering. From elsewhere within the fenced area, he heard the crackle of gunfire.

A grim smile formed on his lips. Lyons and Blancanales

obviously had found their way inside and were mixing it up with the bikers, too.

Holstering one of the Berettas, Schwarz knelt next to a fallen guard. He rolled the guy onto his back and saw a security card hanging from a rawhide strap around the man's neck. Schwarz palmed the card and whipped it over the man's head. He strode to the gate, swiped the card through the reader and waited as the gate parted. Once inside, he pocketed the card, filled the empty hand with the Beretta and continued on.

Gunfire crackled and bullets slammed into the ground at Schwarz's feet, causing plumes of dirt to erupt skyward. Schwarz scrambled, a line of bullets nipping at his heels. He glanced at the house and spotted a biker sprinting through the door. A second man poked his assault rifle through an open first-floor window and continued to spray Schwarz with suppressive fire.

Flinging himself to the ground, Schwarz snapped off a pair of 3-round bursts at the house. Slugs missed their intended target but struck the window frame, driving the shooter under cover. Schwarz turned and caught the other biker dropping into a kneeling position, taking cover behind an oil drum. The Berettas chugged through six more rounds a piece, slugs drilling through the drum's steel skin before tearing into the hidden biker. An angry scream sounded from the house, cueing the Able Team commando that he had to get off the firing line, immediately. Rolling away, he was spared a punishing volley from the remaining biker's weapon. Squeezing off multiple bursts from the Berettas, Schwarz unleashed a withering hail at the second shooter, riddling the man with 9 mm slugs, killing him.

Stepping toward the parked motorcycles, he drove his

foot into the engine of the nearest one, knocking it over.
The cycles next to it each fell after it, like a line of tipping
dominoes. Reaching into his satchel, he withdrew a small
brick of C-4, molded it around the nearest motorcycle's gas
tank, preparing it for detonation. Moving fast, he repeated
the same process with the second line of bikes.

Satisfied, he reached into a pocket and produced a detonator. A shadow fell over him, betraying someone's approach. The warrior whirled, his eyes settling on the
shotgun barrel trained on his midsection.

QUICKLY, METHODICALLY, Blancanales worked a pair of
bolt cutters, clipping through a section of fence. When it
came free, he set it aside and slipped through the hole.
Coming onto one knee, he covered himself and Lyons as
the Able Team leader slipped through the hole in the fence.

Columns of roiling black smoke climbed skyward from
the destroyed Jeep, visible over the rooftops. Autofire
crackled for a few moments before falling silent again.
Blancanales's mind drifted momentarily to Schwarz, and
he considered checking in with his friend through the com
link. Before he could, he felt a strike to his upper arm,
pitching him forward. He landed on his stomach. Lyons hit
the ground next to him, his automatic shotgun loosing an
onslaught of sound and fury. The blast caught a biker in
the stomach, flattening him like a beer can crunched un-
derfoot.

Jagged yellow muzzle-flashes erupted from within the
house. Bullets lanced into the ground, kicking up plumes
of dirt in front of the warriors. Blancanales swept the M-
16 in a long, horizontal arc, hosing down the house with
sustained autofire that splintered wood and shattered glass

windows. Lyons fired his own weapon in concert with Blancanales, the shotgun belching out a devastating swarm of double-aught buckshot. The unrelenting firestorm caused the hostile fire to wink out momentarily.

Blancanales followed up his volley of autofire with a smoke grenade from the M-203. The projectile smacked into the earth next to the house and began belching out plumes of smoke. The Able Team warriors rocketed to their feet and sprinted right, using the smoke to cover their movements. The bikers resumed fire, their bullets chewing into earth.

Blancanales and Lyons reloaded their weapons and took cover behind a large brick barbecue. The smoke dissipated, revealing a trio of bikers stepping into the open, their various assault rifles and SMGs pounding the barbecue and stacked wood next to it with relentless gunfire. Lyons darted from behind the cover, the shotgun dispatching a trio of shots with a full-throated roar. The bold move drew the bikers's fire. In the meantime, Blancanales loaded a fragmentation round into the M-203.

"Down, Ironman," he said into the com link.

Lyons flung himself aside.

Curling his upper torso around the stout brick structure, Blancanales fired the launcher. The round arced and struck the ground behind the hardmen, unleashing a maelstrom of shrapnel that dropped the three bikers.

As the reverberations from the explosion died down, Lyons and Blancanales continued moving. Climbing the stairs leading onto the front porch, Lyons slipped through the door followed by his teammate. A quick check of the first floor revealed a bullet-riddled corpse, apparently Schwarz's handiwork. Lyons gestured at the upstairs. Acknowledging him with a nod, Blancanales started for the dead man while Lyons started for the second floor.

Blancanales crossed the room, came down next to the corpse. Like the others, the guy wore a denim vest with the gang's logo emblazoned across the back. Voices from outside the house caused him to freeze.

"This is your last warning, man," a scratchy voice said. "Drop the box or it's over for you."

"Forget it," Blancanales heard Schwarz reply. "The minute this detonator goes down, you're going to take me out. You want to shoot me now, go for it. But there's a good chance that I'll hit the trigger and take you with me."

"Son of a bitch," the guy said. "I may just do it, anyway."

"Be my guest."

Blancanales surged across the room. Stopping at the window, he peered outside and saw Schwarz with his arms in the air, the detonator clutched in his left hand. If his partner was scared, Blancanales saw no outward sign of it. Schwarz's Beretta 93-R lay in the dust, where he'd apparently discarded it, perhaps as a conciliatory move to buy himself some time.

He jabbed the M-16's muzzle through the window and bracketed the biker's more-than-ample midsection in his sights. He knew that if he shot the guy while he had the shotgun trained on Schwarz, the guy might very well get off a round.

Instead, he cleared his throat, the noise catching the biker's attention. His target's torso and shotgun moving as one, the guy whirled toward Blancanales. Schwarz saw the opening and lunged right, moving himself out of the kill-zone. At the same time, Blancanales's M-16 rattled out a burst that punched into the man's solar plexus, downing him.

Schwarz climbed to his feet. He shot his friend a grateful grin and went to retrieve the discarded Beretta. Blancanales stood, walked to the door and opened it, allowing Schwarz inside.

The unmistakable boom of a shotgun erupted from above them, prompting both men to wheel around toward the noise, their guns coming up in unison. A pair of bikers, one a scrawny guy decapitated by an up-close gun blast, the second, a husky guy with a scraggly beard, the bottom of it shorn away by the same shotgun blast that opened his midsection, plummeted from the upper regions of the house and smacked hard against the ground floor.

"Couple of prisoners," Lyons said over the com link.

Schwarz studied the dead guys for a second before averting his gaze. "I think the skinny guy will talk," he replied. "Once we locate his jawbone."

"I do good work," Lyons said.

"The best."

The warriors exited the main house and continued their blitz.

The grind of motorcycle engines filled the air. Lyons and the others turned toward the sound and spotted three bikers surging from the farthest outbuilding. The bikers had arranged themselves in a diamond formation, with the point guy trying to control his bike, even as he handled the MP-5 submachine gun stuttering in his grip. The guy's spray-and-pray cut a wide swath over the Able Team warriors' heads, leaving them unharmed, but putting them on the defensive.

Lyons, who'd reloaded the A-3 before exiting the house,

surged forward, letting the big weapon churn out thunder of its own. A dual blast hit the lead biker's center mass like a mule kick, knocking him off his machine, depositing his shattered remains in the dirt. More 12-gauge rounds spewed from the weapon's superheated barrel and hammered the second biker from his perch. The bike, now minus its rider, continued carving a path toward the soldiers, forcing Lyons to dart to the side so he could avoid the careening hunk of steel.

The third biker decided to go for broke. Gunning the motorcycle's engine, he bore down on the trio. At the same time, Blancanales hosed the guy down with a sustained blast from the M-16 rifle. The guy lost control of the bike, which swerved right and crashed into the side of the house, the gas tank exploding on impact.

As the men of Able Team distanced themselves from the house, Schwarz clicked a button on the detonator. The resulting explosion ignited a blazing column of fire that shot skyward. Two motorcycles were thrown into the air. Fire and debris pummeled the house.

"Cathartic," Schwarz said.

"Keep doing it, it'll make you wet the bed," Blancanales replied.

Gunshots sounded from within the nearest of the two steel buildings. The commandos exchanged quizzical looks and closed in on the building. They positioned themselves on either side of the door, crouching in case someone decided to spray autofire through its skin. Blancanales reached up, grasped the doorknob and tried to twist it.

Locked.

"Use the shotgun," he said to Lyons. "Take it out."

Standing, Lyons did just that. Like a gale-force wind

striking paper, the shotgun's force drove the door inward, causing it to slam hard against the wall behind it.

As the smoke and noise cleared, the commandos waited a few seconds for return fire. When none came, Blancanales plucked his Smith & Wesson tactical viewer from his back. Slipping the camera through the doorway, he scanned the interior, felt his stomach lurch at what he saw.

Several men and women, most in white lab coats, all on their knees, were arranged in a circle. He saw at least two crumpled on the floor. A big man, head shaved clean, except for a walrus moustache, stood over them, a handgun in his grip, a curl of smoke rising from the muzzle. The man was staring in the direction of the shotgun blast.

"They're executing people," Blancanales said.

"Go!" Lyons replied.

Blancanales surged inside the warehouse. His moving form caught the biker's attention. The guy wheeled toward him, his pistol acquiring a target. Blancanales slipped behind a forklift, crouched and brought the assault rifle to his shoulder. Almost instantly, the 5.56 mm round ripped through to the other side of the man's head. Dropping the pistol, he staggered sideways and fell to the ground.

Able Team descended on the hostages. "Down. Stay down," Lyons ordered.

Still in shock, the people complied.

The Able Team commandos gave the structure a quick search and found no more enemies. In one corner of the building they found a concrete stairwell that descended below the structure.

"You stay here," Lyons said. "I'll go down, check this out."

Blancanales nodded. Lyons moved down the stairwell

and came to windowless steel door, one sealed shut with an elaborate retinal-scanner locking system. Lyons knew his own baby blues wouldn't trigger the system, but he had something that would. He reached into his pouch. With practiced movements, he worked the Mao bowl substance between his palms, lengthening it into a tube roughly an inch in diameter. He wrapped the explosive around the lock and fixed a remote detonator to it. He climbed back up the stairs, stopping just short of the first floor, and triggered the explosive.

The plastic explosive responded with a loud whump. A wall of smoke filled the stairwell. Returning to the basement, Lyons found that the door had bent inward and the lock was a pile of twisted metal.

Filling his hands with the Smith & Wesson, he pulled aside the door, stepped inside and found a long wall that stretched well beyond the length of the building above. What lay in front of him was a maze of concrete and steel doors. What the hell have I found? he wondered.

He spoke into his throat microphone. "Guys?"

"Go," Blancanales said.

"We've got a whole other complex down here."

"Say again?"

"There must be a dozen doorways. Check with those people, ask them what the hell they've been doing down here."

"I'm on it."

"I'm going to search down here."

"Do it. Check this out, though. We talked to one of these guys. He says he's a scientist. I guess they all are."

"Scientists? You mean, like chemists? Are they running a meth lab here or something?"

"We both know you don't need an Ivy League degree to cook meth," Blancanales replied. "There guys are nuclear scientists."

"What?"

"And aerospace engineers, propulsion experts. Everything."

Lyons muttered an oath through clenched teeth. "Pretty sophisticated shit for a bunch of bikers."

"That's just it, Carl. These guys swear this isn't a biker den. Looks like one on the surface, maybe. But there's serious scientific study going down here."

"Like what?"

"Still pressing for that."

"Press harder."

"Right.

"Let me look around. Then I'll haul ass back upstairs and we can figure this out."

"I'm going to check in with Stony Man. We need Aaron to order in some choppers so we can haul these people out of here. Plus, Hal needs to know this."

"Roger that. Give me three minutes. I'll be back upstairs."

Lyons checked two of the doors, found them both locked. He noticed a third door across the hall lay slightly ajar. Even as he started for it, his combat senses urged him away. With every other square inch of this basement locked down, he knew better than to believe in lucky breaks. But he also knew he had to at least look. They needed to find Stephens. Whether the guy was a biker, or something else, they needed to find out his source for the sarin gas, the purpose for this facility and any other pertinent intelligence that might save lives.

Standing to one side of the door, he reached over and pushed on it. It swung inward at his touch. He flattened back against the wall, his mouth dry as he waited to see whether his actions elicited gunfire from within the darkened room. When none came, he slipped inside, careful not to tarry within the doorway where his silhouette would present a target. Running his hand long the wall, he located the light switch, clicked it on. Overhead and fluorescent lights came to life, flooding the room with a whitish glow. He estimated that the room was about forty feet by fifty feet. It was filled with several computer workstations.

Lyons's brow furrowed as he studied the room's contents. Both in layout and equipment, the room reminded him more of a control center for satellites and spacecraft than anything associated with a group of gun runners. Perhaps it served as the logistics center for shipping weapons and drugs across the country and across the continent. At least on some level, Lyons found that scenario plausible, though not necessarily satisfying.

His combat senses screamed out a warning, spurring him to turn and check his six. He caught an attacker hurtling toward him, his right hand gripping a knife. A fleeting glimpse told Lyons the guy likely outweighed him by at least forty pounds. The big ex-cop took three steps back, only barely missing the blade's bite each time. The Able Team leader tried to raise the shotgun, but the giant's leg shot out in a kick that connected with the wrist of his opponent's shooting hand, causing the weapon to fall from numb fingers. The knife again rocketed for Lyons, this time flying forward in a head-on thrust. He batted aside the strike, knocking the bigger man off balance. Lyons kicked out, driving a booted foot into the guy's solar plexus. The guy's eyes bugged out and he gasped as his lungs emptied their contents. Lyons moved in to deliver another punch. The biker came forward, his bulk colliding hard. They crashed to the ground, the bigger man on top. The biker struck out wildly with the knife, the blade whispering toward Lyons's head. He whipped his head to the right. When the blade struck concrete, the man raised the knife for another strike. Lyons snatched a Colt fighting knife from its scabbard on his chest and drove the weapon forward, punching it into the other man's solar plexus and driving it up at an angle, twisted it.

A shocked look crossed the other man's features. He howled in pain, spun back. The movement elicited another scream as the knife came free. His left hand remained locked around Lyons's shooting hand, albeit with a looser grip. Rolling onto his right side, Lyons fired out his foot in a snap-kick. The toe of his boot caught the other man in the jaw, snapping his head to the side, shaking loose a spray of blood, sweat and spittle.

As the steel sliced through muscles and tendons, skittered off bone, the man's reflexes took over, forcing him to jerk back his hand. Lyons cracked the shotgun's muzzle once across the man's face, brought it back around and aimed it dead center on his adversary, who now lay on the floor, his good arm cradling the injured one against his chest. Lyons was on his feet, the Colt Python in his grip. He planned to sweat the guy for an accurate troop-strength count.

He took another step forward, then froze. The room already stank of sweat, blood. He was suddenly aware of another suffusing odor. Gasoline.

Keeping his weapon trained on the dying man in front

of him, he turned toward the door. A river of an amber liquid rolled down the floor, darkening it. More footsteps thudded in the hallway. Cursing through clenched teeth, Lyons leveled the Colt Python down the hall. A man stepped into view, a large object in his hand. Lyons tensed as he checked out the new arrival. His gray hair, thinning on top, was combed back and collected into a ponytail that rested on his shoulder like a ferret. An ugly white scar ran the length of his right cheekbone and seemed to pulse under the fluorescent lights. Lyons recognized him instantly as Ed Stephens, the biker gang's leader.

He clutched an olive-drab-colored jerrican in his left hand. Two more, their nozzles open, stood nearby.

"I can tell by the look on your face you want to splatter my brains all over the place," Stephens said, grinning. "Go for it. We both know you can't. Or won't. You fire that thing in here and the fumes will blow this whole place apart. You'll be dead. So will your teammates and those hostages upstairs."

Lyons shrugged, feigning nonchalance. "Same goes for you," he growled. "Explosions are equal-opportunity killers. The way I look at it, if I kill you, I do the world a favor."

Stephens also shrugged, his gesture more convincing. In the same motion he held up a disposable lighter in his left hand, the ball of his thumb poised to ignite it.

"Suit yourself. Me? I'm prepared to die. Can you say the same thing? No answer? Okay, well while you think about it, why don't you put down the hand cannon?"

His mind raced through his options. Lyons wasn't worried about dying; he was a fatalist and knew he'd die when the time came. Truth be told, he knew a part of him would rather perish from a battlefield wound than a heart attack suffered at a desk.

But take other, innocent people, with him?

Forget it.

Kneeling, he set the weapon on the ground.

The other man grinned. "Good choice, hero." He kept the lighter held aloft, but slipped his thumb from the striking wheel. Not much, maybe a millimeter or so away. Maybe, Lyons reasoned, this guy wasn't any more anxious than himself to burn to death. Lyons searched the other man's face, hunted for a confirmation as to whether the guy considered himself a dead-ender. As Lyons pulled his hands away from the shotgun, he saw something flicker in the other man's eyes. Was it relief? He couldn't be sure.

The guy nodded at him. "Now the other weapons." Lyons complied, laying out his three side arms and the Colt dagger in a nice, neat line.

"Now stand up," the biker said. "You and I are going to have us a little talk."

Keeping his face neutral, eyes locked on his opponent's, Lyons slowly uncoiled from the floor. If he guessed right, about five yards separated them. It would take the man barely a second to activate the lighter, the sparks possibly igniting the fume-filled air.

Unless he moved fast enough.

As if he had another, better choice.

"Freeze!"

Another voice, belonging to Blancanales, sounded in the corridor. The guy whirled around to face the other man, opened his mouth, probably to make the same threat. Would Blancanales smell the gas and know better than to shoot? There was no way to know for sure.

Instead, Lyons saw an opening, took it. He fisted the combat knife and sprang forward, keeping his body low as he darted across the floor.

Spurred by instinct, the other man sensed the movement and whirled back toward Lyons, eyes widening as the big commando crashed into him. Lyons thrust the knife into the man's forearm, forcing him to release the lighter. The Able Team leader allowed his momentum and their combined weight to carry them crashing into the wall. Before he could rip the knife from the other man's arm, the biker planted a right jab into Lyon's chin, knocking his head back and causing a supernova of white to explode from behind his eyes. The coppery taste of blood filled his mouth from where he'd bit the inside of his lower lip.

The warrior staggered back a step, caught himself and raised his hands into a fighting stance. The other guy's hand stabbed down for his belt. He fisted a dagger and began slashing it in wide sweeps at Lyons, who took several steps back, each time the knife's tip whistling within a hairbreadth of flesh. The guy was fast, strong, but sloppy. When he decided to switch from slashing strokes to a direct thrust, the move was telegraphed, clumsy. Lyons stepped off to the side and the knife passed harmlessly by. His hand snaked out. He wrapped his fingers around Stephens's wrist, squeezed it hard and yanked the guy off balance. Lyons drove the flat edge of the palm of his free hand into the shoulder joint, threw his hip into it to increase the power. Shoving Stephens forward, he pulled back hard on the arm, dislocating it even as he took control of the other man's movements. Stephens grunted in pain. Lyons held the arm in tight against his own chest, pushed hard on it, using it like a shovel handle to push the man forward.

Stephens head collided with a wall, making a dull sound, like a coconut striking sand.

Dazed, breath coming in ragged pulls, Stephens rested on all fours. Droplets of blood fell from his face, mixing into the pooled gasoline. Grabbing the guy by the collar of his vest, Lyons brought him to his feet. With a hard shove, he pushed him toward the stairwell, ready for some hardball Q&A with the guy.

CHAPTER THIRTEEN

"Oh, my God," Barbara Price said.

Staring into her computer screen, she read the few lines of text contained in the secure message Kurtzman had sent her. He'd gotten the information by hacking into the National Security Agency's central database, an easy trick for the Stony Man computer wizard. She read the brief electronic missive once more. If its contents were accurate, and she had no reason to believe otherwise, the information was, at best, stunning.

At its worst, it might herald war. Printing the message, she rose from her chair, snatched it from the printer and headed for the door. Brognola would want this information immediately.

As she stepped from her office she heard the rumble of someone clearing his throat, accompanied by the click of dress shoes against the floor. She turned and spotted Brognola heading her way. She noticed that he'd shed his suit jacket. He was in the midst of rolling his left shirtsleeve cuff up his forearm, when he looked up and spotted her. Worry creased his forehead.

"You heard?" she asked.

"China?"

"Right."

"Yeah. It's bad." He nodded toward her office. "Let's talk."

They returned to her office. Out of respect for her boss, she motioned for the seat behind the desk. Brognola shook his head. "Not my office," he said.

He fell heavily into a love seat. Rounding her desk, Price pulled away the chair and settled into it, never once taking her eyes from Brognola. Having spent most of her career in intelligence, she'd gained a dead-on ability to read people not only by what they said but by how they acted. The big Fed and her other Stony Man cohorts were some of the coolest actors under fire she'd ever seen. But right now, he looked worried, which only deepened her concern about the situation.

"You saw the news about the space capsule getting aced, right? Killed the astronaut, destroyed the craft. The perp is a separatist from the Xinjiang Province. The Chinese government's mad as hell, and I can't say as I blame them. What happened there was terrorism and murder, pure and simple."

"But what do you make of the allegations?"

"What? That American intelligence agents supplied the shoulder-fired missile? I'd like to say with certainty that it's a load of crap. My gut says so. But experience tells me that anything's possible in geopolitics and espionage. I don't think any agency director in his or her right mind would green light this kind of op. But, hell, maybe some mavericks in the Company decided they could derail China's space program by destroying a space capsule. Or at least destroy national morale and embarrass the country in front of the rest of the world."

"Seems like a bad plan."

"Since when has that ever stopped anyone?"

"Point taken."

"I mean, look at all the rogue intelligence agents we've dealt with. These people are like a bad-idea factory. The only hole in the rogue-agent theory is that no one could seriously believe that this kind of thing would stop China's space program. I mean, what do they think, that the masses will cry out for the government to cease space exploration, that the government would comply? C'mon. It'd never happen."

Price nodded. "Anyone crazy enough to speak out would end up a speed bump under the People's Liberation Army's tanks. If anything, it'd galvanize support for their government, not only at home but also in the world community. I can't see where there's any up side from our perspective for doing this.

"Or their perspective," she continued. "With all the investment we've made in their country, there'd be no benefit in driving a wedge between us. That seems to happen easily enough without contriving a crisis between us. If relations soured, they'd stand to lose a great deal, as much or more than us."

Brognola nodded. "There's always Campbell."

Price scowled. "You mean, the shadow government guy? The one you told me about earlier?"

"None other. From what the Man says, he's clashed with Campbell a number of times over our policies with China, North Korea and Cuba. The way he sees it, the last thing we ought to be doing is trading with China or letting

The Gold Eagle Reader Service™ — Here's how it works:

Accepting your 2 free books and gift places you under no obligation to buy anything. You may keep the books and gift and return the shipping statement marked "cancel." If you do not cancel, about a month later we'll send you 6 additional books and bill you just $29.94* — that's a saving of 10% off the cover price of all 6 books! And there's no extra charge for shipping! You may cancel at any time, but if you choose to continue, every other month we'll send you 6 more books, which you may either purchase at the discount price or return to us and cancel your subscription.

*Terms and prices subject to change without notice. Sales tax applicable in N.Y. Canadian residents will be charged applicable provincial taxes and GST. Credit or Debit balances in a customer's account(s) may be offset by any other outstanding balance owed by or to the customer.

NO POSTAGE
NECESSARY
IF MAILED
IN THE
UNITED STATES

BUSINESS REPLY MAIL

FIRST-CLASS MAIL   PERMIT NO. 717-003   BUFFALO, NY

POSTAGE WILL BE PAID BY ADDRESSEE

GOLD EAGLE READER SERVICE
3010 WALDEN AVE
PO BOX 1867
BUFFALO NY 14240-9952

If offer card is missing write to: Gold Eagle Reader Service, 3010 Walden Ave., P.O. Box 1867, Buffalo NY 14240-1867

Get FREE BOOKS and a FREE GIFT when you play the...

LAS VEGAS 7
GAME

Just scratch off the gold box with a coin. Then check below to see the gifts you get!

YES! I have scratched off the gold box. Please send me my **2 FREE BOOKS** and **gift for which I qualify**. I understand that I am under no obligation to purchase any books as explained on the back of this card.

366 ADL D749

166 ADL D747
(MB-05R)

FIRST NAME	LAST NAME

ADDRESS

APT.#	CITY

STATE/PROV.	ZIP/POSTAL CODE

7	7	7	**Worth TWO FREE BOOKS plus a BONUS Mystery Gift!**
🍒	🍒	🍒	**Worth TWO FREE BOOKS!**
🔔	🔔	♣	**TRY AGAIN!**

Offer limited to one per household and not valid to current Gold Eagle® subscribers. All orders subject to approval.

our companies set up shop there. According to Campbell's dossier, he went ape when the Chinese announced their space program."

Price smiled incredulously. "What, were we supposed to put sanctions on them for having a space program?"

"Actually, he advocated targeted air strikes of facilities involved in China's space program."

"You're kidding."

"Wish I were."

"He has the resources to pull this off?"

"The Man's being sketchy on details, but I have to believe so. I've had Kurtzman checking into Campbell and his family holdings. The guy's sitting on a personal fortune. Plus, the Cadre operates a series of front companies that generate enough cash to pay for all this stuff. His grandfather set it up that way. Guess the old man didn't want to be beholden to the political whims of any given administration, so he made sure the whole venture was self-sustaining."

"Sounds like junior came by his paranoia honestly, at least," Price mused. "He does seem a likely suspect, all things considered."

Brognola's mobile phone trilled once. Snatching it from its belt case, he clicked it on, put it to his ear. "Go," he said.

"I've been checking these documents from Treasury," Kurtzman said.

"And?"

"Campbell's been propping up Ed Stephens with cash. It's a hell of a lot more convoluted than that on paper, of course, but that's the bottom line. It's not too far a stretch to believe that, by extension, at least, he's paying the freight for the Arm of God."

Brognola pulled the unlit cigar from his mouth. "You heard from Able Team yet?"

"Nada."

"Phoenix Force?"

"Not since they retook the embassy. McCarter said he'd caught Jasim and planned to drill him with some questions. He'll check in with us after that."

McCARTER SHOVED Jasim through the doorway, the blow catapulting the Iraqi toward the floor. Jasim threw out his hands to break his fall, grunting as he hit the floor. His footfalls thudding heavy against the floor, McCarter followed the guy into the room, crowding him as he tried to reorient himself. Encizo entered last. Shutting the door, he leaned against it, folded his arms over his chest and watched the situation with a stony expression.

Jasim shot to his feet and eyed his captors warily. McCarter saw the guy tensing, obviously preparing to attack. An instant later Jasim's foot shot out in a front snap-kick aimed at the Briton's family jewels. Jasim's telegraphing the attack allowed his adversary to step aside, easily avoiding it. McCarter stepped forward, jabbing the guy twice in the face, bloodying his nose, forcing him to back away from the attack. Fists raised, face red as though scalded, McCarter circled the Iraqi.

"Let's go, mate," McCarter said. "You want to show me what you're made of? Do it. Otherwise sit still like a good boy and answer some questions."

McCarter watched as Jasim's eyes flicked between the commandos. Touching his fingertips under his nose, he pulled the hand back, studied the blood and let his hands drop to his sides.

"I will tell you nothing."

"Bull. Who hired you to pull this off?"

"I have nothing to say."

McCarter felt heat radiating from his face as the last of his patience burned away. Though they'd defused the immediate threat, he knew they also needed to move quickly to find Jasim's weapons supplier. If too much time elapsed, that individual or organization would pull up stakes and hide, making any intelligence Phoenix Force gathered completely useless.

He jabbed a Player's cigarette between his lips, torched the end with his lighter and began pacing the room. He inhaled deeply, exhaled and coughed.

"Damn things'll be the death of me someday," he said to Encizo.

"Someday," Encizo replied, his voice flat.

"But I've still got more breaths coming than Jasim here, would you say?"

"Without a doubt. Our friend, he's on his way out."

McCarter turned to Jasim, showed him a nasty grin. "What do you say, sport? Ready to check out on us?"

Jasim rested against a wall, trying to look as casual as a cornered man could. He shrugged, smiled. "As you say, 'bull.' You won't kill me. I have valuable information."

McCarter countered Jasim's smile with one of his own. "Interesting. I thought you knew nothing."

"I have nothing to tell. There's a difference. But I know a great deal. If you want my information, you must give me something in return."

"I stand corrected," McCarter said. The cigarette, clenched in the corner of his mouth, wagged at Jasim like an accusing finger. "But if you're not going to talk, then we're going to kill you. No prison. No lawyers. No Geneva Convention. No nothing. Just your rotting corpse fertilizing someone's flower bed."

Blowing smoke through his nostrils, McCarter snatched the cigarette from his mouth and studied it. In the meantime, Encizo filled the dead air. "It's like this. We have three other prisoners. No one of them may know everything you know, but each might know enough to help us piece together a pretty accurate picture. So, really, you're redundant. You don't want to talk? Fine. We've got others who will."

"You won't kill me," Jasim said with less conviction. "You can't."

Encizo grinned at McCarter. "Idealistic little cuss, isn't he?" Encizo reached behind his back and produced a Colt Detective's Special. With a flick of his wrist, he tossed the weapon at Jasim's feet. Instead of lunging for the weapon, Jasim backed away from it and eyed the men cautiously.

Encizo continued. "See, we did a bad job of frisking you. Shame on us. Now you've pulled out that gun and we have no choice but to blow your head off. You understand, don't you? Nothing personal. We're fighting a war, and all's fair in love and war. Is that not right, my friend?"

"Right," McCarter said. "With three prisoners, we get less paperwork than four. And my friend and I, we want to hit the beach before we head back to the States."

Sweat beaded on Jasim's forehead. His voice sounded more brittle than brash. "I'm not a fool. The gun is empty. Otherwise, why give it to me? I will not touch it."

McCarter shrugged, dropped the cigarette and extinguished it with his foot. With lightning-quick movements, he stripped the Browning Hi-Power from his shoulder holster, aimed it at Jasim's head.

"You don't have to. We'll just stick it in your hands after you're dead."

"You'll kill me."

"On the spot."

Jasim exhaled loudly and his body seemed to sag for a moment. "What do you want to know?"

"A Delta Force team found your helicopter—one of those Russian surplus jobs—at the airport. The crew was smart and gave up without much of a fight. And my lads here found a couple of canisters of what your people say is VX gas in the underground parking garage."

"So?"

"So I'm painting a picture, and an ugly one at that. You guys planned to get your money and hitch a ride out of here in your chopper. At the same time, you were going to unload a bunch of VX gas in here and kill a bunch of innocent people."

Jasim didn't flinch. "You are correct so far. I'm waiting for a question."

"Cocky little bastard, aren't you. Did you think you'd make it out of here? Are you really daft enough to believe that we'd let you fly away after you did that? That we don't have half a dozen fighter jets passing over this damn building right now?"

"I didn't plan on flying out of here. One of the embassy personnel, a man named Fisher, was going to drive me out of here. I'd hide in his car. He'd take me out later, once everything died down."

"Not much of a plan."

Jasim shrugged. "I didn't need to get far, just a few blocks away. After that, I had my own path out of the country."

"We'll want those names," McCarter said. "Where'd you get the VX?"

"Somalia. Outside Mogadishu."

Encizo looked at McCarter, grinned. "Got some bad neighbors in these parts." He turned back to Jasim. "Who in Somalia?"

"His name's Markov. Alexander Markov."

"Who?"

"He's Russian. He runs guns and diamonds out of Somalia. I picked up the goods three days ago. It was no problem to sneak them into this country. Border security is practically nonexistent here. I could bring a truckload of nuclear weapons across the border and no one ever would know. And you're wrong. He didn't sell it to me. He gave it to me for nothing."

"He stake the money for this operation here?" Encizo asked.

"Not exactly."

"Explain."

"He said the money came from a third party, though he didn't identify them."

"And you believed him?"

"Why not? Once you've handed someone lethal gas to unload in the American embassy, why lie about something as trivial as who's paying for it? You know I'm right. I can tell by your faces. Besides, he's an extremely boastful man. And a loose-lipped drunk, besides. If it had been his money, he'd have made it a point to let us know."

McCarter nodded. Silently he acknowledged that the terrorist's words made some sense. Maybe the Russian wanted to deflect blame, maybe not. It was hard to tell without a direct confrontation, which would come soon enough.

"So how much was the payday?" McCarter pressed. "We both know you're not into this for ideology. How much were your mysterious benefactors going to cough up to see you turn Liberia into a nuclear sinkhole?"

"Ten million dollars for me, another two million for each of my men."

Encizo let out a soft whistle. "That's an impressive amount of coin. Are you sure you have no idea who was coughing up the money? A pissed-off Saudi or the Iranian government or someone like that, maybe?"

Jasim shrugged.

"Where does Markov keep himself?" Encizo asked.

Jasim gave them an address, which both members of Phoenix Force committed to memory.

"How heavily fortified is the place?" Encizo asked.

"As I said, Markov is extremely boastful, very arrogant. He considers himself untouchable. He keeps only small amounts of security there. Maybe five or six men at any given time."

"Six? You're sure of that?"

The Iraqi nodded.

"Jasim," McCarter said, "you just added a few more hours to your godforsaken life. I'm sure the CIA and military intelligence will enjoy sweating more information out of you. But we'll give your regards to Markov."

McCarter bent, scooped up the Colt and returned to his full height. Encizo exited the room first, with McCarter backing out a moment later. Shutting the door, McCarter locked it. They moved out of earshot of the room.

Using a satellite connection, McCarter contacted Stony Man Farm with his headset. Kurtzman's voice buzzed in his ear, speaking through an encrypted satellite transmission. McCarter passed along the Russian's name to the cyber-whiz and asked him to run some traps on it.

"Buzz me in ten," Kurtzman said.

"Right," McCarter said.

He stared over Encizo's shoulder and watched as a pair of medics knelt next to a dead Marine. One grabbed the fallen warrior under his shoulders, while the second grasped his ankles. Picking the man up, they fitted him inside a body bag and sealed the bag. McCarter's face reddened as he watched. "Burns my guts to let that bastard live, after what happened here," he said. "I saw that Marine's face. He couldn't have been more than twenty years old, if that."

Encizo, his gaze following McCarter's own, nodded. "You did the right thing. You traded information for the man's life. This way, we can save more lives. It was our best option under the circumstances. It's the decision any of us would have made. Besides, he might know more than he told us in there. Maybe he'll spill some more information later on that'll help us. You know that as well as anyone."

"Doesn't mean I bloody like it."

"Understood."

A pair of Diplomatic Security Service agents, each dressed in black cargo pants, a tan T-shirt, combat boots and Kevlar vests, approached. Wraparound shades hid their eyes, but the downward turn of their lips told McCarter these men were ready to grab a pound of flesh from the bastards responsible.

Though he understood their rage, he knew something else.

They'd have to stand in line behind him.

The biggest of the two, a bulky guy, his blond hair visible around the edges of his black baseball hat, stepped up to the Phoenix Force warriors. He halted a foot or so away from the warriors, stared down at them. McCarter scanned the two men. He recognized neither of them from the command center and he felt his guard go up.

He scanned the credentials of the man nearest him, saw that they looked legitimate, right down to the State Department watermark. He did likewise with the second man—as equally indistinct as the first, save for a whitish, C-shaped scar etched into his skin over his eyebrow. The second agent's credentials also looked legitimate.

At ease, lad, McCarter thought. All the gunplay, the lack of sleep, has left you jumping at shadows. You're in an embassy. These guys are DSS agents. Calm down. Don't let adrenaline override logic.

"We're here to escort the prisoner to the command center, sir," the DSS agent said.

McCarter said, "I assume he's got a command performance at Langley or Guantanamo Bay."

The agent nodded, returning the grin, albeit fleetingly. "Something like that. From what I hear, they're going to grill that bastard like a Kansas City sirloin. These bastards knew every inch of the embassy. They knew guard schedules, troop strengths, the whole nine yards. Obviously our people want to know how."

McCarter nodded. "You might want to talk to a guy named Fisher. And why do I have a feeling that our friend might fall down the stairs three or four times before he gets there?"

The guy shrugged. "Accidents happen."

"He's in there," McCarter said, indicating the room with a thumb. "Give him a shove for me."

"Will do," the man replied. Reaching into his pocket, McCarter found the door key and dropped it into the agent's outstretched hand. The agent nodded his thanks, and he and his partner headed for the room holding Jasim.

McCarter turned back to Encizo. "I guess our next stop is Somalia. Let's see what our little Russian friend has to say for himself."

JASIM PACED the small room nervously, his mind racing as he worried over what might happen next.

The Americans seemed to have bought his story. And why shouldn't they? It was, after all, at least partially true. Markov had indeed provided the weapons for this ill-fated venture. Jasim really didn't know his benefactor's identity—at least not technically. But what he did know was explosive: an American, a government official, no less, had coughed up the money and weapons. Markov had confessed the American's transgression during one of his many binges. Jasim had found the irony downright delicious, but had kept the information to himself. He knew that knowledge was power. And, under his current circumstances, he knew he could use all the power he could get. He could use what he knew either to bargain with his captors for leniency or, if he could identify his benefactor, to blackmail the bastard into helping him. Either way, Jasim stood to benefit.

But the comfort that thought brought him was quickly washed away by another wave of fear. A film of sweat formed on his palms and he felt his heart pound hard in his chest. Of one thing he was certain: what he knew gave him some bargaining power with the American authorities, but it also made him a target. Someone might decide to kill him early on, defusing any danger he posed. Considering this, he felt worry again overtake him, his stomach lurching at the prospect of death.

Despite his military training and his years as a member of Saddam Hussein's Fedayeen Saddam, Jasim had faced very little in the way of mortal danger. He'd spent most of his military career drilling and training or arresting and torturing dissidents. When the Americans and British had invaded his country, he'd been among the first to trade his uniform for civilian clothes and to cheer the Americans on as they had descended upon Baghdad in their armored vehicles, tanks and Black Hawk helicopters. Not that he'd quit fighting altogether; he'd been among the insurgents killing Americans and his own people with roadside bombs and rocket-propelled grenades. He killed his own people without guilt, slaughtering them like the mindless cattle they were, both before and after Saddam's downfall.

But during all that time, he'd done what he could to avoid the specter of death that had claimed so many of his comrades. Wringing his hands, he assured himself that he'd do so again.

The sound of a key being inserted into a lock pulled him from his thoughts. Turning, he watched the doorknob twist and the door swing open. He knew what he needed to do. He'd tell his captors what little he knew. It only made sense. He was—as the Americans were so fond of saying, screwed—so he might as well give them the information up front, glean what little goodwill he could from a bad situation and put his benefactor on the defensive, making it that much harder to track down and kill Jasim. Plus, the Americans might suspect he'd know even more and, therefore, would let him live.

Without a doubt, he'd likely rot in an American prison somewhere, but at least he'd be alive.

He watched as a dour-looking man, his assault rifle held at hip level, filled the doorway. The taller of the two Americans was visible over the first guard's shoulder. The man in the doorway nodded at Jasim and motioned at the far wall with the barrel of his assault rifle.

"Up against it," the man said.

He complied, resting his forehead against the wall's smooth, cool surface. He waited as the Americans searched him for weapons. The guard grabbed Jasim's collar, spun him and stared at him a moment before pushing him toward the door.

Jasim felt his anxiety rise, his throat seemingly constricting a little more with each labored breath. He caught the gaze of the blond man who'd first entered the room, or rather, caught his own reflection in the man's sunglasses. He saw himself, hair mussed, eyes wide with fear, and swallowed hard to clear the lump of self-disgust that formed in his throat. This was no time for pride, he told himself.

"I have information," he said. "Information I didn't tell the other two men. It's of great value. For your investigation, I mean."

A smile ghosted the blond agent's lips. "Really?"

Jasim felt a small but welcome rush of relief. He forced down a smile of his own, not wanting to betray his bargaining position. "I want protection. I want to be taken away from here immediately. In exchange, I'll tell you everything I know. None of this is as it appears."

The guard gave an easy shrug. "Sure."

The guards led Jasim through the door, down the hall

and to the stairwell, flanking him the entire way. He crossed the first-floor lobby, a hellground of corpses and spent shell casings. He watched as medics gingerly hefted one of his comrades, the man's midsection ravaged by automatic gunfire, and placed his remains into a body bag. A smug smile tugged at the corners of his mouth as he spotted the corpses of two more of his men. He felt no sympathy for them, only contempt. If they'd had his guile, his status, they'd be alive right now. But they were mindless cattle, meant to be slaughtered, while he'd live another day.

The Americans led him to an elevator. The three men stepped inside the car, which carried them to an underground garage where the ambassador and a few select individuals kept their armored vehicles. Apprehension once again seized Jasim, causing his body to stiffen. The bigger man glanced at him then stared back up at the floor counter.

"We already swept the place for trip wires and found the explosives you folks left to skrag us," the man said. "It's safe."

Jasim had only a moment to relax before the elevator halted and opened into the well-lit garage. They led him across the oil-splotched concrete floor to a black Hummer with tinted windows. The shorter agent opened the rear door, igniting the dome light and illuminating the vehicle's interior.

The Iraqi immediately noticed that the back had been covered with a blue tarp. He opened his mouth to question this. Before he could, though, the blond man spun him, stuffed a cloth into his open mouth and shoved him into the big vehicle's backseat.

As realization dawned, Jasim tried to scream, but only managed muffled cries. The second guard, the one with the scar, came into view, a sound-suppressed pistol clutched in his hands. The Iraqi kicked out at the guard's hand, in a desperate bid to disarm him. The man simply stepped back, grinned, before bringing the pistol to bear once again.

"Sorry," the guy said. "But this is much bigger than you or me."

Flailing, Jasim fired off another kick, realizing in a sickening instant that he'd never complete the move. He saw the blond man's finger tighten on the trigger and an instant later his struggles ended forever.

CHAPTER FOURTEEN

Several minutes later the Phoenix Force warriors had gathered in the embassy's library. McCarter studied his people and noticed that, to the man, they looked exhausted, but determined. He wasn't surprised. Even without the several hours' jet lag, they'd done little more than fight since arriving in Africa twenty-four hours ago. Hell, they ought to be tired. He knew he was.

McCarter swigged from his can of Coke, enjoying the sweetness coating his tongue. He'd propped his feet on the desk, leaned back in his chair and rested his eyes as he waited for his call to go through on a secure satellite phone the team carried. He was considering another cigarette and maybe a sandwich when he connected with Stony Man Farm. He and Kurtzman exchanged brisk greetings before getting down to business.

"Your friend Jasim sure can pick his buddies," Kurtzman said. "This Markov sounds like something you'd scrape off the bottom of your shoe."

"Tactfully said," McCarter replied.

"Tell T.J. I'll e-mail him a mission packet to print and

distribute. But I'll give you the highlights so you can brief the guys while we wait."

"Go."

"I half expected Markov to be the run-of-the mill Russian Mafia. You know, former KGB or Soviet soldier with lots of skills and no work prospects."

"He's something more?"

"Lots more. Guy was one of the Soviet Union's most brilliant aerospace scientists. The CIA even tried to entice him into defecting to the United States during the cold war. At the time, he told us to kiss his rump. Guess the guy is a genius when it comes to satellites, or he was during the Soviet era, and a lot of people wanted to tap his expertise. He had a good thing going until he screwed it up."

"How so?"

"He's sort of a high-tech kleptomaniac," Kurtzman said, a trace of amusement in his voice. "A couple of years ago he got caught stealing Russian satellite secrets, downloading them into a series of redundant computer systems located throughout the world. When the Russians figured out that the guy was stealing them blind, they tried to arrest him, but he already was gone. And he took all the technology with him. According to a classified Defense Intelligence Agency report I hacked into, the guy also is connected with the theft of secrets related to the Predator, the Dragoneye and other UCAV and drone projects. Investigators followed the trail through a series of subordinates and found that Markov was the guy signing the checks."

McCarter sat up straight, pressing the cold soft drink can to his temple to ease a throbbing pain that had set in there. It provided only minimal relief.

"If they know all this, then why the devil's he still running around?"

"My guess is they can't find him. If his file's to be believed, then he completely dropped out of almost a year ago. You guys are the first ones to come across him in months. If he's still in the espionage business, he's at least gotten a little smarter about it."

"Doesn't sound too bleeding difficult," McCarter groused. "Were you able to run down the location we gave?"

"Right. I've sent a pile of satellite photos your way. I also arranged transportation to the airport. A jet's waiting to haul you gents to Somalia."

"We're going to need a little more than a jet," McCarter growled. "See if you can scare up some air power."

"Working on it. By the way, H.B. wants to speak with you."

"Go. I'll put him on the speaker so we all can hear him."

"Right."

The big Fed's voice boomed through the speaker. "You guys did a hell of a job out there. The Man's happy and I'm ecstatic."

"This hit the news yet?" Hawkins asked.

"Right. All the major stations have been broadcasting it. The secretary of state plans to hold a news conference later this afternoon. Along with the Department of Homeland Security."

"What's the cover story?"

"Not far from the truth. A group of commandos stormed the embassy and waxed the terrorists. The only catch is the DSS and Delta Force get the credit for the commando work. You know the drill."

Hawkins sighed. "Right. Always the bridesmaid and never the bride, that's us."

"Comes with the territory," Brognola replied. "You guys won't be very effective if you end up on the covers of *Time* and *Newsweek*. Look, I need for you folks to keep your eyes on Markov. But I also wanted to bring you up to date on some other hot spots flaring up."

"Go," McCarter said.

Brognola updated the men on Able Team's mission in San Diego. After that, he briefed them on the downed space capsule and the CIA's alleged involvement in the mishap, along with the rising tensions between the U.S. and China. "At the same time," Brognola said," we have a couple of newspapers here in the States alleging that the Chinese actually supplied the explosives and the sarin gas used in the Freedom Center mall strike. Needless to say, John Q. Public's starting to cry out for blood."

"Is there any proof of this?" Manning asked. "I mean, the Chinese involvement?"

"Not a shred," Brognola replied. "The stories attribute the allegations to unnamed government sources. The White House has flatly denied the reports. The president plans to talk about all these issues in a speech to a joint session of Congress. Unfortunately, all the denials haven't stopped these particular newspapers from reporting the story. Unfortunately, it all makes a lot more sense when you know who owns the newspapers responsible for the stories."

"And that'd be?" Manning asked.

"A man named David Campbell."

Manning shook his head. "Name means nothing to me."

"It means something to me," McCarter interjected. "If it's the same chap I'm thinking of, his family founded a conglomerate that dabbles in aerospace, energy and tele-communications. Back in the 1960s, they made a hell of a sport coupe, called it Rolling Thunder or some such. Anyway, I read a history of Campbell Motors a few years ago, and it mentioned that David walked away from the business, all of it, and left it in the hands of some trustees or something."

"It's the same guy," Brognola said. "But he hasn't been living as the idle rich." He shared the president's briefing on the Cadre. "According to the Man, Campbell has gone rogue within the last twenty-four hours. At the same time, all hell starts breaking loose and Campbell's media holdings blame it in part on the Chinese. It may be a coincidence."

"A mammoth coincidence," Manning replied.

"Right. For now, though, we need you guys to keep after Markov. If we learn anything else, we'll let you know. In the meantime, I'll get a military transport ready to haul you guys to Somalia. Try to get some rest before then."

CHAPTER FIFTEEN

Somalia

Flanked by a pair of guards, Alexander Markov stepped from the dry desert heat into the sprawling hangar at the abandoned air base. Ignoring his escorts, Markov crossed the concrete floor in quick, purposeful strides toward the pair of aircraft. Stopping at the nearest one, he ran the fingertips of his left hand along its metallic hide, enjoying the smooth feel of the radar-blocking paint that colored it.

The rocket-shaped aircraft stretched nearly two dozen feet. The unmanned craft, powered by solid fuel and boasting a thirty-five-foot wingspan, weighed fourteen thousand pounds, including its deadly payload.

One of the guards cleared his throat and Markov turned toward him. The guard had an ample middle and a nose crisscrossed with red lines, burst capillaries, likely the result of years of hard drinking. The guard motioned at the nearest rocket with the muzzle of his assault rifle, a 5.56 mm FNC made by Fabrique Nationale Herstal SA.

"These things safe?" the man asked. "With the radiation, I mean?"

"Perfectly," Markov snapped. "Now please be quiet so I can concentrate."

The guard nodded. Markov turned back to the craft and scanned it from top to bottom, feeling pride swell within as he scrutinized his handiwork. The rocket—once dubbed the X-67 by the U.S. military before they scuttled the project—flew without a pilot and could be commanded remotely by either Campbell or himself. Once the rocket exited the earth's atmosphere, it shed its payload, the Marauder satellite, placing it in orbit about two hundred miles above the earth's surface where it could circle the globe within ninety minutes. The beauty of these craft was that they didn't require a sprawling launch site like a traditional rocket. Instead, they could be launched from a converted Boeing 707 before making the final leg of the flight under their own steam.

The satellites contained inside the rockets were, of course, the greatest prize. The low-orbit craft each contained a pair of tactical nuclear missiles, each boasting about forty kilotons of power. The Marauder project had, of course, been a black project started by Campbell Aerospace and the CIA during the 1980s, without White House consent. When the sitting president had discovered the project during the 1990s, he'd ordered it stopped. As a scientist, Markov only could muster disdain for such shortsightedness, such zeal to preserve the status quo. The Marauder was a piece of art, a weapon capable of delivering a targeted strike to anywhere in the world in a matter of minutes. And do so from an unexpected source—space.

Markov considered his disdain for attachment to be a

gift; it allowed him to do what he wanted, when he wanted, without the unpleasantness of guilt or fear. In the rare instance when he craved human touch and companionship, he bought prostitutes, sometimes four or five in a week, consuming their services like a meal. With this weakness satiated, he could again focus on what mattered—his science—for weeks at a time, before his hunger once again consumed him. But whether it was science or his shameful escapades, the result always was the same, people were tools, like a laptop. The people who would die under the Marauder's onslaught were little more than lab rats. They needed to die so that he could witness the fulfillment of this great scientific achievement. Let Campbell labor to fulfill his silly need for a new world order.

For Markov it was all about seeing this wonderful new armament function. And, if it took down the world's sole remaining superpower in the process, so much the better. He'd consider it further validation of the Marauder's potency.

The phone on Markov's hip vibrated. Reluctantly he tore his gaze away from the twin aircraft, snatched the phone from his belt and placed it to his ear.

"Yes?" he said.

"I assume all's ready." The sound of David Campbell's voice caused a shudder to pass through Markov. He hated most people, but he feared the cold-voiced bastard on the other end of the line.

"Everything's capable for launch."

"Tomorrow. We need to fire them tomorrow. The president plans to address a joint session of Congress this evening. Once the Marauder satellites already in the air hit Washington, I'll step into the president's spot. By this time tomorrow I will have ordered retaliatory strikes against China. And I want these other satellites operational. We can pummel Beijing into a nuclear sinkhole. That should bring the Chinese to heel."

"What if they retaliate with their own nuclear weapons?"

"I plan to mobilize B-2 bombers and B-52 bombers tonight to take out their known launch sites. If we decapitate their government, rob them of their nuclear arms, they should fall in line. If not, we have a nuclear arsenal and I have no problems using it. I think they'll do as I say. But first, I need to know whether your satellites are ready to go."

"They will be," Markov said. "And I'd be happy to guide the Marauders myself for tonight's strike. Just to make sure it's done properly."

"Forget it," Campbell said. "This is something I must do. It's my hand that has brought us to this point. It will be my hand that performs this sacred act. That restores order to this world. Do you understand?"

"Of course," Markov said.

"In the meantime, I want you to be on guard," Campbell said.

A cold sensation traced the length of Markov's spine. "Why?"

"Our mission in Liberia failed—"

"I assumed so," Markov said. "Otherwise I'd have heard more about it."

"That it failed isn't a surprise. I expected as much."

"Then what's the problem?"

"You met directly with Jasim, didn't you?"

Markov's first instinct was to lie, but he checked himself. Campbell often knew things he shouldn't with frightening accuracy.

"Yes, I met with him."

"And somehow that seemed like a good move to you? That he'd see you face-to-face? Why not use one of your lieutenants?"

Markov's mind raced for an answer, but he came up blank. "I assumed he'd be dead, that it wouldn't matter."

"He is dead, but only because I intervened. The commandos who freed the embassy took him alive and interrogated him."

"He told them of me?"

"I can't think of a reason he wouldn't. Could you?"

"We met in Mogadishu. At my house. He doesn't know of this place. Of that much I am certain. If they looked for me, it would be in Mogadishu."

A pause filled the line. Markov assumed Campbell was contemplating this, and the notion caused a deep unease to spread through the Russian. He was all too aware of Campbell's fanaticism, his single-mindedness, and that he may have jeopardized the mission potentially could mean a quick, merciless death.

"You have people at your house?" Campbell asked. "If someone comes looking for you, I mean?"

"Yes, of course. Good people. Former Russian Special Forces and SVR. They can handle these men easily."

"Counting on the Russian military to handle this gives me little comfort," Campbell replied. "Your vaunted military men ran from Afghanistan with their tails tucked between their legs. And they continue to struggle in Chechnya. Spare me your nationalistic chest beating. The sounds you make are hollow ones."

Markov's face flushed. He ground his teeth together and held in a nasty retort. Though he wasn't nationalistic, he hated Campbell's arrogance, particularly with the other man questioning his judgment. "These are good men," Markov said. "They will do a good job."

"Fine. I want them to clean out the premises, burn the house to the ground. When the Americans arrive, I want no signs that you ever existed there."

"I will order that. And what do you want me to do in the meantime?"

"Finish any last-minute preparations for the aircraft. I want the satellites in the air and operational before the president begins his speech. He will not finish that speech. And afterward things are going to begin moving very quickly."

CHAPTER SIXTEEN

Mogadishu, Somalia

Hawkins pushed his way through the sea of people populating the market.

The former Delta Force officer hated coming back to Mogadishu—the Mog, as they'd called it back in the day. Little had changed since his last visit. With a fast, purposeful stride, he passed the squat storefronts, apartment buildings and mosques that ringed the street. Countless people speaking in unison created an almost overwhelming din that seemed to press in on Hawkins like the oppressive heat beating down upon him.

He and the other men of Phoenix Force had checked Markov's compound on the outskirts of the city and found it not only empty, but razed to the ground by fire. That the Russian's estate had been destroyed didn't surprise Hawkins all that much. The guy had to know someone would come for him, once the embassy was freed. So the question now on the minds of Hawkins and his teammates was whether Markov remained in the country. And, if so, where was he? During Phoenix Force's flight to Somalia, the cyberteam at the Farm had found a link between Markov and Ed Stephens. The two men had been passing around money and arms for years, apparently. But it had taken work by Huntington Wethers and Akira Tokaido to link the two men together by analyzing a series of covert and complicated financial transactions through a number of false accounts.

With nowhere else to look, Hawkins had agreed to enlist an old friend in the hunt for Markov.

Hawkins threaded his way through a group of men beneath an awning, hiding from the relentless sun, smoking cigarettes. A hard-looking militia man, his AK-47 cradled like a baby in his arms, went out of his way to jostle Hawkins, who whipped his head around and met the man's hard look. Despite a cold rage that passed through him, he flashed the man a smile and continued on.

He hadn't come here to fight.

Not yet, at least. And likely not with these people.

Hawkins was traveling as a freelance journalist, using the alias Tom Paddock. He wore a tan photographer's vest, the pockets overstuffed with memory cards, film canisters and batteries for the two cameras looped around his neck. In a canvas camera bag slung over the opposite shoulder, he carried more critical gear: an Uzi loaded with a 20-round magazine, spares, a smoke grenade and a .45-caliber Colt M-1911A1 loaded with alternating hollowpoint and hardball rounds.

A Beretta 92-F rode on his left hip in a cross-draw position, obscured by the vest.

The rest of Phoenix Force waited on the outskirts of the city at a makeshift base in the desert. He kept in contact with the men by using a small microphone clipped inside the collar of his vest. A device that resembled a portable digital music player was clipped to his belt. Hawkins could keep the earphones in place and even react to what he heard without arousing suspicion.

An oxcart led by a small boy passed. Hawkins side-stepped the conveyance. Sweeping his gaze over the buildings, mirrored sunglasses shielding his eyes from the sun's onslaught, he searched for the correct one. He'd come looking for one man in particular, Jama Abunawas. The African often had supplied Hawkins and other soldiers with street-level intelligence when the United States and its UN counterparts had tried to bring peace to Somalia. Abunawas continued to supply local CIA officers with intelligence regarding al Qaeda and other Islamic terrorists operating within the country. If anyone knew of a Russian selling illegal arms out of Somalia, it was Abunawas. At least Hawkins hoped so.

He reached the building, a tan, two-story structure with windows boarded over.

"Nice digs," Hawkins murmured. He skirted the front of the building, entered an alley, the hard-packed brown earth littered with animal dung and discarded papers. His nose wrinkled against the stench. He felt his heart pound against his ribs and a film of sweat cover his palms as he left behind the crowds in the open-air market. He was now out of plain sight, a dangerous place for a foreigner carrying thousands of dollars in photographic equipment.

Hawkins peered upward, scanning the rooftops that lined the alley. He saw nothing. A cold sensation—a sixth sense developed in combat—swept through him, heralding potential danger. A boot sole scratched against the dusty ground and a shadow slipped over the alley, spurring Hawkins into action. He whirled, muscles tensing for confrontation, but left the Beretta holstered, not wanting to immediately blow his cover as a journalist.

A black man, dressed in worn jeans and a button-down shirt with the sleeves torn off, stood about thirty feet from Hawkins. Heavily muscled arms were crossed over the man's chest. The butt of an automatic pistol was visible just above the waist of the man's trousers.

Hawkins exhaled loudly, flashed the other man a lopsided grin. "Lord Almighty, son, you damn near gave me a heart attack, skulking around like that."

Abunawas returned the smile and sauntered toward Hawkins, who extended his hand in greeting. "You should watch your back, my friend," Abunawas said. "Particularly if you insist on such a flimsy disguise."

"Flimsy? I'd fool my own mother in this getup."

"Having seen you shoot a rifle, I'd hope your aim with a camera is better," Abunawas replied.

"Yeah, I missed you, too," Hawkins said. He clasped the other man's outstretched hand and shook it vigorously. "You still giving them hell here in the Mog?"

The African's face turned serious and he released Hawkins's grip. "Nowhere near as much as they've given me and my people. But enough. The peace process is slow, the world patient. I have neither of these attributes, so I go on stalking the warlords. I cannot sit in a tin shack in the desert, hoping to go to America. Not when there's so much to do here."

"You always were an idealist," Hawkins said.

Abunawas shook his head. "Not an idealist, my friend. A realist. These savages killed two of my wives, my babies, because they could. They rape, kill and terrorize my people, leaving them to scratch out a meager existence. Or starve. The paths to the camps are littered with their corpses. For that reason alone, I'd sooner die with my hands around a warlord's throat than as an old man counting camels on his farm."

"Understood."

Abunawas allowed himself another grin. His lips split, exposing teeth turned brown from years of chewing khat, a plant with amphetamine qualities. "Come, my friend," the African said. "I can tell by your demeanor that you're nervous out in the open like this."

"Only when I'm seen with such poor company," Hawkins said.

A robust laugh exploded from Abunawas's lips.

"Still a bastard, aren't you? Even so, I have a gift for you."

He nodded toward the building to Hawkins's left, and started for it. The American fell in behind him, casting wary glances at either end of the alley. He trusted Abunawas, trusted him at least as much as he trusted anyone else outside Stony Man Farm. What he didn't trust was Mogadishu. Maybe it was better, safer today; maybe not. But in the Mogadishu he knew, life was cheap, weapons cheaper and people were tools used for gratification or power.

For an instant, he thought he smelled burning tires, heard the thunder of Black Hawk choppers passing overhead. During his time in Somalia, Hawkins had performed a dozen "snatch and grab" missions and assassinated several of warlord Mohammed Aidid's men. It was during one of these missions that he'd met Abunawas, a widower no longer willing to watch thugs and killers bulldoze his country. The African had shoved him from a volley of bullets as one of Aidid's men had tried to shoot him in the back. Though most of the bullets would have peppered Hawkins's body armor, he'd lost his Kevlar helmet, leaving his head an easy target. The African almost certainly had saved him from death.

The door to Abunawas's place squeaked on its hinges, dragging Hawkins from his reverie. After they slipped inside, the African shut the door behind them, locked it. Slivers of sunlight, interrupted by clouds of dust motes, poked through the cracks between the boards covering the windows. A moment later he pulled on a chain and a bare bulb came to life overhead.

"Generator," Abunawas said.

He crossed the sparsely furnished room in long strides. Bending, he grabbed a corner of a Persian-style rug, worn and dirty, and peeled it back, folding it over onto itself. Hawkins saw a rectangular seam in the worn floorboards.

"No shit," Hawkins said. "A trapdoor."

"Hardly. It's simply a cellar. It once was used for storing vegetables." He raised the door and set it softly to the floor. Hawkins noticed that about Abunawas. The man never made extraneous movement or noise.

"I assume this place is safe," Hawkins asked. "I had to go to three different locations to find you."

"Very safe. As for the precautions, I apologize. My links to the CIA are well-known here in Mogadishu. I can't move with the freedom I once did."

"How's the Company treating you?"

Rising to his full height, Abunawas turned and stepped back onto the first rung of the ladder leading into the cellar. "Much better now. With al Qaeda roaming the country, trying to establish operations, I've become quite popular with American intelligence. I have two satellite phones, a laptop and a small arsenal. And I collect a thousand dollars for each al Qaeda pelt I turn in to the station chief. I get five thousand for locating training camps."

"Not bad coin," Hawkins said.

Abunawas grinned. "A simple existence for a simple man. The dollars come in handy."

Hawkins followed the larger man down the ladder and into the cellar. As in the room above, a single exposed lightbulb illuminated the cramped quarters. Hawkins saw a man, his ebony skin slicked with sweat, seated against one wall. His breath came in tortured rasps as he gave the two men a wide-eyed look. A moment later Hawkins noted a length of fishing line looped around the man's neck, the other end tied to the pin of a grenade that was duct taped to the wall. His hands and feet also were secured with the silver tape.

Abunawas slipped a knife from its scabbard and knelt next to the man. Even in the meager light, the blade glistened menacingly in his grasp. With a quick swipe of the blade, he cut the line connecting the man to the grenade.

The man began cursing Abunawas in Somali. The big man laughed and came to his feet. Pointing at the man on the floor, he said to Hawkins, "He seems to have some strong opinions about your ancestry and mine. He's a courier for one of the local warlords. Don't let him fool you. He speaks English as well or better than me."

"You ask him anything yet?"

"Just whether he preferred a bullet to the head or being blown to small bits by a grenade. He couldn't decide, so I did it for him. Fortunately, the grenade was a dud." The prisoner, his eyes narrowed and ablaze with anger, shot Abunawas a look. The big man shrugged. When he spoke, his voice was matter-of-fact, as though sharing a weather report. "I would no sooner blow up my home on your account than I'd mate with your favorite ox."

"Alexander Markov," Hawkins said, his voice sharp. "What do you know about him?"

The man gave the soldier a hard stare and spit at him. "Fuck you," he said. "Americans killed my brother. I won't tell you anything."

Abunawas spun toward the man, his jaw set angrily. Hawkins laid a hand on his shoulder to stop him.

"Let me handle the Q&A." Hawkins fisted the Beretta. Withdrawing a sound-suppressor from his vest pocket, he threaded the device into the weapon's muzzle. He knew firing the weapon in such close quarters would deafen all three men.

"You been running packages to Markov?" Hawkins asked.

"I told you—"

His free hand snaking out, Hawkins reached down, grabbed a handful of the man's shirt and brought him to his feet. Pinning the man against the wall, he pressed the Beretta's cold steel muzzle against the man's carotid artery.

"Look," Hawkins said, "don't let the Southern accent fool you. I'm not friendly, I'm not patient, I'm not slow. If you don't want to tell me anything, I'll spray your brains all over the wall, find another guy with a bigger mouth and let him trade information for his life. What do you think of that?"

The man opened his mouth to speak. Before he could, Hawkins struck him across the chin with the butt of the Beretta, causing a loud cracking noise. The man spit out fragmented teeth and blood onto Hawkins's shirt.

"You know this jerk, Jama?"

"Yes."

"He has a family?"

"A wife and five children."

Hawkins nodded, satisfied. "So we tell the warlords that this guy gave them up, then his dies, right?"

"But I didn't—"

"Doesn't matter," Hawkins said. "It'll be your word against Abunawas's word. And you'll be dead, so you'll have a hell of a time making a case to the contrary. Least you won't be lonely in the afterlife, you'll have all your kin there, too, to keep you company. I'm sure they'll be anxious to discuss the decision you make now."

The courier pursed his lips and searched Hawkins's eyes with his own, apparently trying to gauge whether the American was bluffing.

"The Russian has a base west of the city," he said. "It was a military outpost left over from Major General Muhammad Siad Barre's regime."

"Coordinates?"

The man gave them.

"What kind of troop strength are we talking?"

"Ten, maybe twelve."

"All Russian."

The courier shook his head. "Some are Russian, some are American."

"Americans?"

The man's lips were swelling and it obviously pained him to talk. "Americans. Like you. They don't wear the uniforms, of course, but I recognize the accents, the phrases they use. There are many others there, too. All foreigners."

"Soldiers?"

"I don't know what they do. They don't carry guns. Many of them seem scared of the Americans."

"Good enough," Hawkins said. With a vicious swing, he drove the pistol butt into the man's temple. The courier's eyes rolled into the back of his head and his skinny form sagged in Hawkins's grip. The American unwound his hand and let the man slide to the floor. He sat against the wall, head lolled to one side.

He felt Abunawas's eyes boring into him from behind. He turned to the other man.

"What do you make of it?" Hawkins asked.

"It's possible. Somalia is a lawless land. If you pay the right people, they will leave you alone to do as you wish. Did you mean what you said? About killing his family?"

Hawkins shook his head. "Hell, no. I got a knot in my stomach even saying it. I just wanted to shake him up a bit."

"Fair enough. But they may soon be better off dead."

"What the hell are you talking about?"

"She will be a widow, they will be orphans. Such people do not do well in Somalia." Abunawas brought around his hand, a sound-suppressed Glock clutched in it. The weapon coughed once and the courier's head seemed to cave in on itself, as though deflated by the .40-caliber round drilling into it.

"Damn, Jama!" he said.

The African turned to him, his face grim. "The warlords want me dead or alive. This man can help them find me." He made a sweeping gesture that took in the cramped cellar. "He can lead them here. I know it's not much, by your standards, but it's really all I have. The fight is all I have. I cannot risk a betrayal. I will take some of my CIA stipend and send it to the family. It will be more than this bastard would have earned in a year. And they won't have to betray their country to get it."

Trying to ignore the rolling sensation in his stomach, Hawkins nodded. "I understand."

Abunawas clapped him on the shoulder. "Welcome to my world, as you Americans are so fond of saying."

LING AWOKE to darkness.

Her head—wrapped in cloth, eyes covered—throbbed. Reflexively, she tried to reach up to remove it from her head. She found her hands bound behind her back and the realization caused panic to surge through her. The movement ignited a searing pain in her wrists where the handcuffs had dug into flesh. Pressed between her cheek and the floor, the rough fabric scratched her skin. Fleetingly, she wondered what it was. Burlap? Maybe, it was hard to tell under the circumstances.

Listening, she heard the rumble of a car engine, felt the vehicle rock and shudder as it traveled over rough roads. Every jolt caused the pain in her skull to worsen and set her teeth on edge. She tried to straighten her legs, the muscles cramped after being stuck in the same position for an undetermined amount of time. Her feet, also tied together, clanged against something hard, metallic. The cramped quarters, the stale air, the smell of tire rubber told her she was in a car's trunk.

The driver braked, slowing the vehicle. She rolled against one of the walls of her cramped prison. A moment later, she felt it turn and begin to accelerate again, though not to the same level of speed, judging by engine noise. She took a couple more deep breaths, trying to clear her head. She had no idea how long she'd been unconscious. All she knew was that her head ached sharply and each bump seemed to awaken other tender spots in her ribs and stomach. She vaguely recalled what had happened after she'd surrendered her gun.

The men, hopped up on adrenaline and rage, had kicked and hit her for what seemed like hours, though logically she knew it had probably been a minute or two. A third man had entered, yelling for the other two to stop. The men had complied, yanking her to her feet. A moment later, a white light had exploded from behind her eyes as something struck her skull. She had sunk to her knees and everything had gone dark.

Her stomach roiled, a mixture of pain and nausea. The image of the man she killed, his body ripped apart by the gun, flashed across her mind again, only causing the nausea to worsen. He'd forced her hand, made her shoot in self-defense, but that didn't mean she felt good about taking a life. There'd only been one man she'd ever hated bad enough to kill, and he already was dead. Breathing deep of the exhaust-tinged air, she forced the nausea away. Save your conscience for later, she thought. If this band of killers has its way, guilt will be the last of your worries.

She needed to focus on the problems—and questions—at hand. Who would hunt her down and kidnap her? And why?

She thought briefly of Hakim. He was dead, but that didn't mean there wasn't a connection. After all, he likely had bosses of his own, people who were skimming from his smuggling profits. With him dead and his operation smashed, someone stood to lose money. So maybe someone wanted revenge, or to plug a potential leak in the organization. Still, Ling doubted it. Someone with those motives might exist. But would they hunt her down and plow through a couple of marshals to get to her? Not likely. And how would they have found her in the first place? She was, after all, holed up inside a government safehouse. So it more likely was someone with government connections. But, again, she could think of no one that fit that bill, either.

The car bounced again, jostling her. The accompanying pain caused her to grunt, but simultaneously seemed to clear her head. Maybe she was approaching this wrong. She thought again of the men who'd taken her captive. Clean-cut. Fit. Caucasian. In some respects, she considered the last factor to be the most troubling. None of these men resembled Hakim's thugs. That raised another question. Just who were they?

Think! she chided herself. Knowing who she faced, what they wanted, might be useless, but it also might tell her which buttons to push, providing the leverage she needed to buy herself more time. If not? She didn't want to consider that scenario. Not yet, anyway.

Her thoughts drifted back to Blancanales. Perhaps he was the link. After all, she had no idea what path he'd taken since they'd last met. Did he have enemies, ones powerful enough to snatch her from a government safehouse? She recalled the deadly efficiency with which he and his comrades had slain Hakim's men, shuddered and decided that, yes, it was entirely possible that a link between her captors and him was plausible.

The car turned twice, slowed and stopped. Gravel crunched and popped under the tires as it slowed. A moment later the transmission slid into place. The engine fell silent.

She heard car doors open, then slam shut. Footsteps

slapped against the ground, growing louder as someone rounded the rear of the car. Keys jingled. An electronic chirp registered with her, followed immediately by the click of the trunk latch. The lid sprang upward. Light filled the trunk and filtered through the weave of the bag wrapped over her head. A shadow fell over her, blocking out the light.

Fingers wrapped around her upper arm, dug into flesh. She recoiled and a yelp of surprise threatened to burst from her lips. She bit down on her lower lip to stifle it, not wanting to give her captors the satisfaction of knowing they'd hurt her.

"C'mon, lady," a rough voice said. "Someone wants to see you. Says he's got an old score to settle with you."

Somalia

A CHINOOK HELICOPTER set down twenty miles north of Mogadishu, in a clearing in a stretch of woodlands lining the bank of the Shabeelle River. Phoenix Force, armed and dressed in camouflage fatigues, exited the craft. David McCarter flashed one of the crewman a thumbs-up signal. The guy returned the gesture and disappeared inside the craft. Moments later, the growl of the big bird's engines grew louder and the craft was airborne, looping once over the commandos before buzzing south.

Phoenix Force fanned out into a ragged line and melted into the trees and brush, making its way toward Markov's air base stronghold. The mission should have been simple. March two miles through the sand and brush to Markov's hard site, knock down a few hardmen, grill the Russian about his connections to David Campbell. But, if recon photos from satellites and U2 spy plane flyovers told an accurate tale, things would be much more difficult. Rough counts indicated that at least three dozen guards populated the grounds. According to images secured by the U2, intermingled among Markov's killers were large groups of people who, according to zoom shots from satellites, carried no visible weapons, making them, at best, dubious targets. Photos also showed that the compound contained a Boeing 707 and a quartet of Black Hawk helicopters. And a pair of X-67 rockets

However, the warriors did have air support in the form of six Apache helicopters, six F-18 fighters and an E-8 reconnaissance plane capable of monitoring troop movements in a 125-mile radius.

The warriors moved swiftly, silently, one eye glued to their surroundings, the other to their GPS units to make sure they remained on track. The quiet suited McCarter just fine. As far as he was concerned, there was little left to discuss.

As the group moved within a quarter mile or so of the target, McCarter felt an anxious flutter in his gut. Prebattle jitters or a premonition? Hard to tell, he thought. He also smelled wood smoke. A bonfire? Maybe, but not likely. At last check, the temperature was around 80 degrees. So why the hell light a fire?

"Look alive, mates," he said into his headset. "We're likely to encounter sentries sometime soon."

All five men acknowledged his radio traffic, but kept moving ahead.

The closer they came to the compound, the more intense the burning smell became. McCarter strained his eyes and ears for danger. He found nothing, but knew better than to let his guard down. A combination of experience and cynicism told him that at any minute he could expect everything to fall to pieces.

Trees gave way to brush and eventually bare earth. Manning, who was walking point, stepped into a dry creek bed and, with a wave, urged the others to follow. After ten minutes of walking, he stopped, dropped into a crouch and motioned for the others to do likewise.

"Two sentries," Manning whispered into his throat mike. "Two o'clock and ten o'clock."

By this time, McCarter had spotted the two men. He'd also noticed the whine of aircraft engines in the distance, coming from the direction of the base.

"T.J., take the guy on the left. Gary, the other's yours."

He watched as Hawkins and Manning slipped past the others, hugging trees and brush for cover. A strangled cry reached his ears a moment later, followed by the heavy sound of a body hitting the ground.

"Mine's down," Hawkins said.

"Mine, too," Manning stated.

When the group reached the tree line, McCarter sized up the compound. He guessed that at least two hundred yards of cleared land stood between them and the security fences. Though the facility likely hadn't been a military base for decades, the security fence glinted brand-new in the sunlight; the Quonset huts looked freshly painted. A pair of guard towers stood on the north and south sides of the compound.

McCarter noted superheated air shimmering over the 707's idling engines. Gunshots rang out from within the complex, the hollow crackle standing in stark contrast to the din of aircraft noise. A pair of black Hummers burst through the gates.

"Someone's breaking camp," McCarter said into his earpiece. "Cal, T.J., take the runaways. J.G.?"

"This is J.G.," said Jack Grimaldi, Stony Man's pilot.

"Things are moving fast. We need air support. The big bird is preparing to fly the coop."

"Say again?"

"The 707. It's warming the engines. I don't want the damn thing to leave the ground."

"On it."

"And take out the damn towers. Just be careful. If we have hostages, I don't want to bomb them."

"Still on it."

Satisfied, McCarter and Manning forged ahead, keeping several yards between them as they closed in on the compound. Encizo, who'd been carrying an M-60, remained several yards behind watching the team's six as they advanced on the stronghold.

Gunfire erupted again from within the stronghold, this time lancing through the fence and heading toward the trio of Phoenix Force warriors. McCarter spotted a pair of hardmen positioned behind an SUV, their weapons spitting flame and lead as they tried to down the approaching commandos. Before either man could respond, thugs in the nearest tower joined in with their own chorus of raging autofire, unloading their weapons at the approaching warriors, sending them scrambling.

"Rafe, the tower!" McCarter said into his throat mike.

"On it." Sustained thunder pealed from behind McCarter as Encizo cut loose with the M-60, raking the weapon in a wide arc. A stream of 7.62 mm NATO missiles shredded the guard tower and drilled into the shooters, whipsawing them around in a grotesque display.

Seeing their comrades dispatched by the big machine gun spurred the men behind the SUV to fight harder.

Manning's voice came over the headset. "Cover me!"

"Go!" McCarter replied. At the same time the fox-faced Briton thrust himself to the ground, landing on his stomach. McCarter raised the FNC assault rifle in target acquisition and swept it in a long arc, hosing down the SUV with a spray of hot lead. Dozens of holes appeared almost instantly. A heartbeat later McCarter swept the FNC in a long arc several inches above the ground, hoping to catch at least one of the attackers in the legs. Slugs ripped through tires, flattening them, causing the vehicle to drop several inches in height as it landed on its rims.

While McCarter changed out magazines, his targets resumed fire, this time with deadly resolve. Bullets carved a ragged line in the earth just a foot in front of him, forcing him to roll off his position as he finished slamming home a fresh magazine.

Laying down another barrage of suppressive fire that drove the shooters to ground, McCarter heard Manning's M-203 launcher fire a round. It arced over the fence, striking behind the vehicle before exploding in a shower of shrapnel. Manning followed up with an incendiary round that struck near the vehicle's gas tank, igniting its contents and causing a second explosion that lifted the vehicle several feet in the air. It fell back to the earth a burning mass of rent metal.

McCarter rose into a crouch, sweeping the FNC's barrel in target acquisition. Someone burst from behind a Quonset hut and sprinted for the gate. The Briton spun toward the guy, ready to shoot. He froze. The runner was a white-haired, brown-skinned man. His hands were empty, his face etched with terror. A lanky man wielding an assault rifle stepped from behind the hut, his own weapon flaring to life. Fear gave way to shock as bullets drilled into the runner's back, transforming a last-ditch sprint into a death march.

McCarter bit off a curse and squeezed the FNC's trigger. In the same instant Manning loosed a sustained burst from his CAR-15. Their dual onslaught pounded into the shooter's chest, transforming his midsection into a bloody ruin.

The metallic screeching of brakes along with the stuttering of gunfire caught McCarter's attention. Whipping his head right, he saw that Manning and James had engaged the fleeing Hummers. Bullets from James's and Manning's concentrated fire sparked off the hoods and doors of the vehicles. One of the SUVs had smacked into the other, knocking it from the road and sending it fishtailing directly for James's position.

McCarter opened his mouth to shout a warning when something caught his attention. A rumbling sounded from within the compound, the source obscured by the smoke winding around the burning buildings. The noise, dragon-like in its ferocity, but unmistakably mechanical in origin, rose above the din of automatic-weapons fire and screams. The rotors cleared away much of the smoke as the craft climbed into the air. A door gunner swung the barrel of a mounted machine gun toward McCarter, ready to rain down death on him and his comrades.

FOR A HORRIFYING INSTANT James watched the Hummer launch into a sideways slide toward him. Its occupants unleashed a hail of autofire through gun ports mounted in the doors as the vehicle careened toward James. The warrior threw himself sideways, hit the ground hard and rolled out of the vehicle's path. Involuntarily, his eyes squeezed shut as it shot by. The vehicle careened forward several more yards before plunging into a V-shaped ravine. The front end struck a wall of dirt, bringing the vehicle to a shuddering halt.

Coming up into a crouch, James rushed for the Hummer and arrived just as the front passenger door swung open. He clutched an MP-5 subgun in his fist. A man exited the vehicle. Spotting James, he raised his weapon and fired. The man's hastily placed burst burned past James's left side. The commando responded in kind, his MP-5 chugging out a short burst that punched into the man's stomach, flattening him against the open door. When James eased off the trigger, the man slid to the ground in a boneless heap.

The Phoenix Force commando cautiously advanced on the vehicle, his MP-5 held at shoulder level. The vehicle's rear driver's-side door slapped open and another man emerged from inside. His body shielded by the armored vehicle, the man was bringing an autoloading pistol to bear on James. Firing the MP-5 with one hand, James unleashed a quick burst of suppressive fire that drove the man back into the safety of the vehicle.

More autofire rained down upon James from his left. Wheeling, he spotted two hardmen surging through the main gate, their weapons spitting out a blistering fusillade. James squeezed off a burst of suppressive fire that drove his attackers under cover. He was out in the open and keenly aware that he was on the edge of being caught in a cross fire.

He cut loose with a sweeping arc from the MP-5 that scattered his attackers, driving them to ground. Pressing the advantage, he swung the subgun's barrel into target acquisition and caught the man to his right still collecting himself after his mad dash off the firing line. The guy made eye contact with James, saw the deadly intent there, and scrambled to draw down his Uzi on the former Navy SEAL. James's subgun spoke first, dispatching a swarm of slugs that drilled into the man's head and caused his body to jerk as though connected to live electric wires. A series of blasts rent the air east of James. He thought for a moment, of his comrade, Manning, who'd disappeared from sight. He quickly dismissed the thought, knowing he had to concentrate on the situation at hand.

Acting on instinct, James coiled toward the ground a microsecond before a volley of slugs chewed through the area formerly occupied by his upper chest. A hastily placed burst of 9 mm stingers sizzled just past his opponent, who'd dropped into a tight crouch. The guy was a pro and his near-death experience did little to throw him off his stride. Rather, he held his ground, readjusted his aim, his coolness pressing James to react all the more quickly. With no margin for error, the commando emptied his magazine into the other man, the deadly impact slamming the man back and causing his weapon to discharge wildly in the air as he triggered it in a final act of defiance.

Ejecting the spent magazine from the MP-5, James snatched a fresh clip from his combat pouch and prepared to slam it home. A sudden mule kick struck between his shoulder blades, thrusting him forward and stealing his breath, knocking the fresh clip from his grip. Despite the pain searing his back, he hit the ground and rolled over.

He saw the man from the ravine standing in front of him, a smile twisting at his lips as he aimed again at the fallen commando.

James made a last desperate grab for the Glock 19 secure in his thigh holster. Before he could complete the grab, though, the man suddenly seized up as bullets streaming blood and gore exploded from his midsection, punctuated by a machine gun's steady rattle.

The shooter crumpled in on himself and the weapon fell silent. A voice crackled in James's earpiece. "You okay, Cal?"

"It hurts when I breathe, but at least I'm breathing," James replied.

"Might want to start moving if you want to stay that way."

"Rafe, man, you're a tactical genius. Hey, is that a chopper I hear?"

"It is. And it's not one of ours. Damn, it's firing on David. I gotta go."

"So, go. I'll catch up."

Despite stinging protests from his ribs, James climbed to his feet. The MP-5 had been slung around his neck, allowing him to keep hold of it even after he'd been shot. With quick movements, he reloaded the weapon, grinding his teeth as fiery pain seared his midsection.

He gave the battlefield a quick scan, looking for some sign of Hawkins, but saw none. Where the hell was that guy?

THE SECOND HUMMER swerved from the road and bore down upon Hawkins, ready to clip him with its front bumper. The warrior lunged from the vehicle's path, rolled and came up in a crouch, the barrel of his CAR-15 reflexively targeting the fleeing vehicle, which already had gained about ten yards.

The warrior didn't bother with bullets. He knew they'd be ineffective against the armored vehicle and he had no time to waste. He aimed the M-203, which was loaded with a high-explosive round, and triggered the weapon. The round landed several yards ahead of the vehicle, exploding in a sudden geyser of dirt, flame and thunder. The driver swerved to miss the round, corrected the vehicle's course and continued along the road. Hawkins reloaded, fired and, without waiting for the results, cut loose with a third round even as the roar of the previous one registered with him. The twin attack knocked the wheelman off course, forcing him to veer the vehicle left, then right as he tried to avoid the explosions erupting all around him.

He watched as the battered vehicle roared on, putting about fifty yards between itself and him. An instant later, taillights flared as the driver braked, slowing to take a bend in the road. Remaining in a crouch, he fell in behind the vehicle, but was in no hurry to catch up. He knew what was coming.

Thunder pealed, the intensity causing Hawkins to flinch involuntarily, even though he'd expected it. Flames tinged with black smoke billowed skyward like steam released from a covered pot. The Hummer rocketed skyward, rolling in midair before crashing to the ground with a grinding of metal and glass that set his teeth on edge. The soldier trotted toward the toppled vehicle, his assault rifle snug at his side, eyes scouring the killzone for signs of danger. At his flank, he heard the continued stuttering of autofire and an occasional explosion as his fellow warriors gave Markov's people hell.

As he neared the wreckage, Hawkins's nose wrinkled, assailed by a nauseating stench of burning rubber, plastic and flesh. Smoke wafted through the trees, stinging his eyes as he neared the downed vehicle. Approaching with caution, he heard the sounds of coughing, accompanied by muttered swearing and a groan.

Using nearby brush for cover, he scanned his surroundings and saw that the mangled vehicle had landed on its side. The land mines Manning had planted on the trail earlier had ripped through the Hummer's reinforced bottom, igniting its gas tank and causing a secondary explosion. The hulk's rear passenger's side door had been ripped from the hinges and thrown from the scene. A man, his upper body burned, lay on the ground, curled into a shuddering ball. A second man knelt over the first. An Uzi lay on the ground, easily within the kneeling man's reach.

Seeing the results of his handiwork, Hawkins felt nausea rack his insides for a moment before he swallowed it down. Like the other warriors of Stony Man, he took no pleasure in killing, but knew that blood, in their line of work, needed to be spilled. If Markov and his men had had their way, dozens, perhaps hundreds of people, would have been killed by VX gas in Liberia's capital.

He stepped into view, his motion snagging the kneeling thug's attention. His face contorting with fear and rage, the man's hand stabbed out for the Uzi. He never completed the grab. The CAR-15's muzzle flared. The volley drilled into the man's center mass, savaging flesh, nicking bone, before tearing jagged exit wounds in the man's back. The man's dead stare locked with Hawkins's own for an instant before he teetered over, his last moments marked by the mindless twitching of his ankle.

Hawkins switched his assault rifle to single-shot mode, turned toward the second man, whose groans had diminished to pitiful murmurs. The soldier raised the rifle to his shoulder and squeezed off a shot that crashed into the man's head, delivering the dying thug a brand of mercy he likely didn't deserve. Hawkins bent over the first man and sifted through his pockets. He found two spare 20-round magazines for the Uzi, which he promptly tossed into the brush along with the Israeli SMG. Next, he located a passport, a thick wad of American bills and an aluminum tin of breath mints. Stuffing the passport and cash into his own pocket, Hawkins returned to his full height. He gave the corpse at his feet a final glance and moved on to the second man. The search revealed a passport and money, both of which Hawkins confiscated.

He and the others could inspect the passports later, though he expected the items would yield little in the way of valuable intelligence. The passports likely were forged, the money untraceable. They'd try anyway.

Back at the compound, he heard the thrashing of a helicopter's rotor blades, followed a moment later by McCarter's voice on the headset.

"Look alive, mates," the Briton was saying. "We've got a chopper swooping in."

A heartbeat later, Hawkins heard the drumming of a heavy machine gun. Biting off a curse, he loaded another HE round into the M-203 and started back for the main compound.

A MAELSTROM OF 30 mm slugs tore into the ground behind McCarter as the Black Hawk's door gunner tried to get a bead on him. He crossed the field in a zigzag pattern, legs pumping like pistons as he worked to avoid the war bird's onslaught. The soldier's oxygen-starved lungs burned as he poured on the speed. The run itself was less than nothing for McCarter, who prided himself on his athletic prowess, despite his affinity for tobacco. No, what stole his breath this time was the realization that he had no visible means of cover and the gunner's aim seemed to be improving by the microsecond.

McCarter twisted at the waist and fired the FNC one-handed. The bullets sparked off the craft's skin, allowing it to continue its attack unabated. McCarter had expected as much. Still, he'd held out a slim hope that he'd hit close enough to the gunner to drive him to ground, even for an instant, thereby buying himself a precious bit of time. Nothing doing. Big-bore bullets continued to blister the air around him.

His foot struck something hard, causing him to fall forward. He hit the ground, his right elbow absorbing the impact, but somehow managed to keep his grip on the FNC. Rolling onto his back, he watched as the Black Hawk swooped in toward him. It turned and leveled out, allowing the door gunner a clear shot. A snarl of rage and fear escaped his lips, lost in the throb of the craft's engines, the whip of its rotor blades. McCarter cut loose with the FNC, emptying its clip at the door gunner. He knew it was the last action of a desperate man. If he had to go, he sure as hell didn't plan to do so peacefully.

The bullets sliced several inches past the airborne shooter. An instant later the FNC went dry. In the meantime, the guy remained cool under fire and readjusted his own aim, ready to savage McCarter with one final blast from the machine gun.

Something whipped by McCarter, flying at an upward angle toward the gunner, leaving a long, curving trail of white smoke in its wake. The projectile drilled through the chopper's open side door followed by a fiery tempest that erupted throughout the craft's interior, consuming it in flames. McCarter stared at the helicopter for an instant, transfixed as rolling flames burst through the its side door and out its windows. The craft shuddered and lurched, its rotors slowing visibly as multiple mechanical systems failed simultaneously.

Something in McCarter's head screamed, "Move!" He was on his feet and running, hoping to find sufficient cover before the Black Hawk exploded in a supernova of fire, steel and glass. Before he took his third step, a shock wave from the explosion crashed into his back, hurling him to the ground. Tucking himself into a ball, he rode out the explosion. A blistering wave of heat cascaded through the area. The helicopter plummeted to the ground like a stone, disintegrating upon contact, and unleashing a torrent of glass and metal shards that whizzed past McCarter.

The Briton stared for a moment at the mass of rent steel that lay burning in front of him.

A voice buzzed in his earpiece. "I do good work, don't I?" Manning said.

Turning, McCarter spotted his ruddy-faced companion approaching through the smoke, reloading his grenade launcher as he moved. "Bloody well about time you did something," McCarter said. "Other than sitting on your arse and watching the grown-ups fight."

Manning laughed. "I'll take that as a thank-you."

"You should. Now let's finish this up."

PAUSING FROM HIS WORK, Markov listened to the gunfire raging outside and felt his nerves fraying as the sound edged closer. The strike itself hadn't been unexpected, of course. But he'd hoped for more time before it occurred, that perhaps finding a dead end at his compound within Mogadishu might buy him a little breathing space before American forces descended upon him. It had been a gamble and he'd lost. But now it was time for him to salvage what success he could from the operation.

Standing inside the hangar, he stared once more at the pair of flying killers stationed in front of him. The unmanned fighters were fueled. He and his small army of technicians had completed a systems check on them both. They were ready to fly; they just needed the nuclear warheads loaded on board. After that, he'd launch them, fly them several miles away, where he could recover them once the attack concluded. He knew without a doubt that his own survival hinged on whether the vehicles were ready to fly, at Campbell's command, to China. Surviving the siege by these commandos would be a hollow victory, indeed, if he left without these weapons.

So he wouldn't.

A guard, his face and forearms smeared with dirt, approached. "The 707's ready for takeoff."

"What's the situation outside?"

"We've put down all the scientists," the guard said. "And our guys have hit these soldiers hard, but they keep on coming. Radar indicates that we also have enemy aircraft approaching our position."

"The Black Hawks," Markov said. "You've put them in the air?"

The guy nodded. "We lost one, but I gave the order a minute or so ago to put up the other three."

"Anything else?"

"We must evacuate soon."

Markov waved dismissively at the man. "I stay until we get these unmanned vehicles off the ground. Otherwise, Campbell will see all of us dead."

"Understood."

"Now get back out there and fight."

The guard's face reddened and his lips tightened into a bloodless line. Hesitating a moment, he nodded and walked away. For the first time, the notion that he might fail struck Markov, causing a cold sensation to plummet through his stomach. He turned to the technician at his right, a young woman dressed in combat fatigues, her green eyes riveted to the control board at which she sat.

"The missiles," he demanded. "Where are they?"

"Any minute," she said without looking at him.

"What's taking so long?"

"In case you can't tell, all hell's breaking loose out there," she said.

MANNING RACED through the compound gates and collided with a world of chaos. He'd heard several explosions from within the main structure, causing it to shudder as windows burst outward. Orange-yellow tongues of flame licked through the openings accompanied by boiling black smoke. He watched as the remaining Black Hawk helicopters climbed skyward and began circling the facility, apparently seeking targets. One of the craft loosed a Hellfire missile that punctured the building's main facade. An ear-splitting explosion followed an instant later.

Poised ten yards from a Quonset hut, Manning froze and covered his head as brick dust and small bits of masonry rained down on him. Obviously, Markov—if he still was here—had decided that he wanted to leave scorched earth as his legacy.

Fine. Manning and the others would be only too happy to oblige him.

Manning came around the corner and caught a pair of hardmen, each carrying an M-4 assault rifle, scurrying from the hut. The CAR-15 spewed a hail of hot lead that cut down both men. A third fighter, a grimy, muscle-bound monster toting an HK-11 machine gun, stepped into view. The weapon kicked to life, sputtering flames as the guy worked his way through the contents of a 20-round box magazine. Manning thrust himself back behind the building, but was immediately besieged by 7.62 mm slugs as they tunneled through his cover, forcing him to ground. When the weapon went dry, he peered around the building and saw that the shooter had disappeared. An instant later, the hard guy stepped out of the building, the HK-11 poised at waist level. Firing at an upward angle, Manning dealt the guy a decapitating burst from the CAR-15.

Slipping inside the hut, he grimaced as a stench registered with him. Beds turned on their sides or shoved against the walls told him the building normally served as a barracks. In the middle of the room, several corpses— men and women, all in civilian clothes—had been piled on the floor, a mess of tangled limbs. An overpowering smell of gasoline hung heavily in the air and clothes stained dark and matted against the bodies told Manning the corpses had been doused in gasoline.

"Gary?"

"Go," Manning said.

"Location?"

Manning gave it to him.

"We're coming up on you. It's best not to be inside any buildings at this point. The air cavalry should be here any moment."

"I'm coming out now," Manning said. "Try not to shoot me."

"I'll see what I can do."

Stepping outside, the Canadian found McCarter and the other men of Phoenix Force approaching. Manning nodded at the main building, the upper two floors of which had collapsed in on each other as the ruins continued to belch large plumes of smoke skyward. A white film of dust from the collapsed building was spreading throughout the compound, causing Manning to cough and squint against the haze enveloping the area around them.

"You find anything?" McCarter asked.

Manning told them about the gas-soaked bodies.

"Destroying the evidence," McCarter said.

"Looks like it," Manning replied.

"We'll need to get fingerprints," McCarter said. "And pictures. It'd be good to identify these people."

Manning nodded his agreement.

"Time to hit the airfield," James said, "before our friend Markov takes to the skies."

The group wound its way between buildings, pushing toward the airfield. Explosions from the Apache helicopters' laser-guided Hellfire missiles tore through a barracks, rending the air, drowning out the crackle of small-arms fire. One of Markov's choppers cut a line across the compound, heading for the commandos, its guns rattling through a flurry of 30 mm rounds. Before they could react, another Apache swooped in low and spit a missile at the approaching craft. The stricken gunship flashed like a sun going nova as boiling flames ripped through the interior. The steel carcass spun toward the ground, passing well over the heads of the assembled Phoenix Force warriors, drilling into the ground fifty yards behind them before exploding. Two more missiles hurled forth from the craft, crashing into the second guard tower, ripping off the tops with a fiery blast.

Markov's remaining men had fallen back, fortifying the airfield. Manning counted half a dozen or so crouched behind parked vehicles, their weapons trained on the soldiers. The hardmen spotted the Stony Man warriors and began unloading their weapons in their direction. Splitting apart, Manning and McCarter sprinted for an overturned truck, crouching behind it for cover while Hawkins and James thrust themselves into a drainage ditch that ran alongside a gravel road leading into the airfield.

Manning quick-fired a pair of fragmentation grenades from the M-203. The rounds hit the ground, exploded, dealing up murderous barrages of shrapnel. One of Markov's thugs popped up over the hood of a Jeep in the same microsecond in which the swarm of shrapnel sliced through the air seeking prey. His face, chest and arms torn open in a grotesque display, the man wheeled around staggered a few steps before his lifeless form crumpled to the ground.

Another fighter jumped up from behind a Jeep, his arm cocked, a grenade clutched in his hand. McCarter cut loose with his FNC, hosing the man down with a sustained burst.

In the meantime James and Hawkins began raking the vehicles with autofire, punching holes through steel, safety glass and tire rubber. The dual onslaught produced results as three more of the fighters were cut down under the blazing gunfire. Left alone, the sixth man broke cover and sprinted for the main hangar, occasionally firing his M-16 with one hand. The bullets flew wild.

Manning moved around the truck, brought the CAR-15 to his shoulder and sighted down the barrel at the running man. The assault rifle stuttered and bullets tunneled through vital organs, turning the runner's legs rubbery, felling him.

As they closed in on the hangar, a side door popped open and two thugs spilled forth, guns blazing. James took both out with a burst from his MP-5.

Stepping over the bodies, he crept through the doorway, the MP-5 poised to fire. Edging along the wall, he watched the flurry of activity in front of him. Computer workstations stood in two lines along the hangar wall, all occupied by men and women in camouflage fatigues. Two guards stood next to a small man who was waving his arms and shouting at the others. The main hangar door stood open and an aircraft stood in front of it. Although he didn't recognize the specific design, James was certain the craft was an unmanned combat vehicle of some sort.

Training his SMG on the guards, he took several more steps forward. McCarter and Manning fanned out behind him, each man sweeping his weapon over the area as he sought a new target. Encizo and Hawkins had remained outside, guarding the group's flank.

One of the guards, obviously already on edge, heard the movement and spun toward the intruders. James already had him solidly in his sights and triggered his weapon, striking the man in the chest. Raking the weapon to the right, he took out the second guard before the man could react. He slammed a fresh clip into the SMG, while the others waded into the group of technicians.

McCarter made a beeline for the small man, who James recognized as Markov. The Russian reached behind his back, apparently seeking a weapon. The FNC spit out several rounds, chewing into the concrete at his feet. The scientist stopped, raised his hands and glared at the Briton.

Grabbing the guy by his shoulder, McCarter spun him and marched him over to the UCAV parked in the doorway. From his vantage point, the commando also saw a second, identical vehicle parked on the tarmac. He patted down the Russian, the search producing a Walther PPK/S, chambered for .32-caliber ammunition, and two spare clips.

McCarter waved the weapon in the guy's face. "Nice piece, lad. You think you're on Her Majesty's Secret Service or something? I mean, who brings a lady's gun like this into the bleeding desert, for pity's sake?"

"Get your hands off me," Markov snapped.

"Gladly," McCarter said, pocketing the Walther. A glance over his shoulder told him that the others were herding the technicians, hands on their heads, fingers intertwined, away from their workstations. "In the meantime, say goodbye to your little aircraft over there. "We'll be shipping those back to the United States. And we're going to bomb this place into rubble."

CHAPTER SEVENTEEN

Ling's rage seared her insides. The bastard's smile, lop-sided, smug, only heightened her anger.

"Ellis White," she said. "I thought you were dead."

"Darlin'," White said, his eyes rolling over her from head to toe, "you still look great."

"I thought you were dead," she repeated, as though saying it again might make it true.

"As Mark Twain said—"

"Spare me the cliché," Ling said, cutting him off.

She saw something flicker in his eyes for a moment before they went flat. White, decked out in a pair of khaki pants and a black turtleneck, was seated on a metal folding chair. Uncoiling from the chair, he strode across the room toward her.

Ling's stomach lurched in fear as he moved within inches of her, her nose wrinkling unconsciously at the foul stench of cigarettes. She looked sideways, eyes locked on a smudge on the wall. She felt the first two fingers of his hand press under her chin, as if to raise her head toward him. She shook her head violently to avoid his touch, tried to take a step back, but was held in place by the pair of thugs who stood on either side of her, each holding an arm.

"No reason to get shitty," White said. "I just wanted to get a good look at you."

"Go to hell."

A derisive laugh burst from White's mouth. He stared past her at the men holding her arms. "Sit her down and get the hell out of here."

Nodding, the men did as they were told, shoving Ling into a couch. She felt broken springs pushing into her buttocks. He paced for a moment and Ling used the break to take in her surroundings. The room was Spartan. From what she could tell, she'd been brought to a large building, one with concrete block walls and oil-soaked concrete floors. Was it a warehouse? Possibly. She'd smelled diesel exhaust and brushed against stacked boxes as she'd been led through the building, eyesight obscured by the hood that now lay discarded on the floor near the door.

She stared at him, her insides alternately burning with anger and quivering with terror. She hadn't known White when he'd broken into her house that night all those years ago. Even Blancanales had all but forgotten the bastard, from what he'd told her later. But she'd done everything she could ever since to learn what she could about the bastard.

She knew all she needed to know about White, the man who'd violated her, shattered her sense of security. The man who'd left with scars she still carried today, the kind that yanked a person from a sound sleep, that caused them to jump at the slightest noise when they were alone.

When White turned and looked into her eyes, he apparently saw the hate simmering there. He grinned. "What's your problem, honey? You're not still pissed off about our romantic encounter, are you? Let it go, woman."

More bitter laughter exploded from his mouth, every reverberation grating against Ling's nerves, stoking the anger inside her. He fell silent, shaking his head as he stalked the room. Ling noticed almost immediately that the man's movements were a contrast to his boisterous personality. His footsteps were nearly inaudible scuffles, his arms locked in at his sides, as though any extraneous movements were forbidden.

Moving to his desk, White leaned his rear against the outer edge and stared at the woman, letting his gaze linger over her body. Ling sensed immediately where his mind was going and she wanted to take his mind away from there.

"I thought you were dead," she said.

"Wishful thinking, darling,'" he said. "I'm as alive as you."

"I figured that much out."

His grin widened, but still didn't reach his flat, hazel eyes.

"What the hell?" he said. "I worked for the government. When they heard that I tried to even an old score by getting cozy with you, they had to make me go away. If I got arrested, it would have raised all kinds of nasty questions. I mean, what the hell, right? I'd been busted in the Army for war crimes, thanks largely to Blancanales and his big damn mouth. Now I was working with the government. That'd look like shit. So my superiors were more than happy to fake my death, to kill any possibility of any investigation. They're pretty image conscious, the U.S. government, and I definitely made it clear that I'd do everything I could to soil their image."

"What agency were you working for? CIA?"

He shook his head. "Forget it. You've never heard of them. Most people haven't. I'm a secret agent man, like Blancanales."

"You're nothing like Pol."

The skin of his neck reddened. When he spoke again, his voice had lost some of its volume and adopted a harder edge. "Bet your ass I'm not. He's a simpleton. Very predictable. Very moral. That puts him at a disadvantage. See, I know he'll come looking for you. When it comes to doing the right thing, he's like a salmon swimming upriver. He just can't help it. As a matter of fact, I'm planning on it. I switched out all the guys' wiped-down magazines for trainings clips they'd handled a few days earlier. All the shell casings have fingerprints on them. Harter, the guy you blasted, he and I go way back. If Blancanales picks up that lead, and I believe he will, he'll find us."

An image of the man Ling had killed flashed through her mind and she felt sick. In the shock of seeing White for the first time in years, she'd forgotten that she'd taken a life.

Swallowing hard, she turned her attention back to White. "If Pol finds you, he'll kill you."

Pushing himself off the desk, he crossed the room and dropped next to her on the couch. She felt her breath constrict as he got so close.

"I don't think he'll kill me," White was saying. "See, I've been waiting a long time for this. All of it. You know why I did what I did when I was in the Army?"

Ling wasn't sure she wanted to know. But she did want to keep the bastard talking. "No," she said.

He shrugged. "Because I could. I could do whatever I

wanted to do, whenever I wanted. Then your boy comes along and opens his mouth, screws everything up. All because he had to be a damn Boy Scout. He couldn't just leave well enough alone, turn and look the other way."

"He did the right thing."

"Shit, he did nothing. It's not like I stopped having my fun. I just got more careful, learned not to get caught. And my handlers with the government, they didn't care what I did. So all he did was bring a bunch of grief on himself and you."

Ling felt her face flush hot. "You bastard."

White sat back, amused. He stared at her for a moment, as though contemplating something. Then he reached out and grabbed her by the arm, squeezed it hard, causing Ling to cry out, and dragged her to him. She spit in his face. Wiping it away, he raised the soiled hand to slap her. Before he could, a knock came at the door.

His smile faded. He called over his shoulder, "Come in."

A guard stepped inside.

"You're wanted in the videoconferencing room," the man said. "Something's happened and Campbell wants to speak with you immediately."

He rose to his feet, brushing his fingers along her cheek as he did. "We'll pick this up later," he said.

He turned and started for the door. As he did, he reached into his pocket, withdrew something from it and handed the objects to the man. "Put her out," he said before leaving.

"Yes, sir."

As White exited the room, the guard took the plastic-wrapped object and removed a syringe. He filled the syringe with a clear liquid from a small glass vial and walked

over to Ling. Her mouth went dry and she felt her heart
slam against her rib cage as he approached. She lashed out
with a kick, trying to knock the syringe from the guard's
hand. He'd apparently been anticipating such an attack
and sidestepped it easily. A moment later he was on top of
her. She felt a small prick in her neck followed by a burning sensation. The man stepped away and tossed the syringe into a nearby trash can. He turned and left the room,
shutting the door behind him.

She was alone, finally. She came to her feet and started
for the desk. She needed to free her hands from the plastic handcuffs. She hoped she could find some sort of sharp
object that she could use to slash the bonds. Within a few
feet, she felt her knees become wobbly and, by the time
she reached the desk, her legs felt like the trunks of oak
trees. She scanned the desktop but saw nothing of use.
Rounding the desk, she backed into the lap drawer, bent
at the knees and grasped under its lip with both hands and
pulled it open. Turning, she almost lost her balance, as her
head had begun to feel light, as though disconnected from
her body. The she saw it, a plastic letter opener, one outfitted with a razor blade. This was it, she thought. She
could use the exposed edge of the razor to sever her bonds,
and even use the blade as weapon, if it came to that.

She dipped her hands into the desk drawer, fingers
scrambling for the implement. As she did, her eyelids became heavy and a sense of vertigo began to overtake her.
No! I can't let this happen. I can't go down and I can't let
Pol come searching for me. I won't let this happen.

Frantic fingers found the opener, but her fingertips had
begun to feel swollen, numb. She willed them to close
around it, but found the motion as hard as walking into a

strong headwind. Her eyes slammed shut, even as she fought to keep them open. She felt herself swaying and leaned against the desk for support. Within a couple more seconds, her thoughts slowed and standing no longer seemed as important. After another few seconds, her worries about Blancanales, about herself, seemed miles away. Her knees buckled underneath her and she blacked out before she struck the floor.

WHITE HURRIED to the videoconferencing center, a cold sensation in his belly betraying the undercurrent of fear he felt. Campbell wasn't supposed to contact him for another two hours. The man was compulsively punctual, obsessed with schedules and plans. For him to place an unexpected call wasn't a positive sign, and White knew it.

White moved through the corridor, the smell of dust and grease cloying at his nostrils as he walked. He came to an old freight elevator, stepped inside, pulled a lattice-work steel screen closed behind him and mashed the second-floor button. The big car lurched to life, taking him up, his dread increasing with every inch of altitude he gained.

White wasn't a man given to fear. As a rule, he instilled fear in others, used it as a tool to get what he wanted, the same way he used his superior athletic prowess and the skills borne of years of combat training that allowed him to kill with deadly efficiency. Few people scared him; Campbell was one of them. The man was as crazy as hell, but not in a ranting, violent sort of way. There was a coldness about him, as though every nerve ending, every emotion, had been cauterized. The guy had a single purpose in life, ending what he believed to be the Communist threat still at work in the world, and White had witnessed the cold savagery heaped upon those who tried to derail his plans.

That White had taken a hostage, with the expressed intent of drawing a government operative to him, wouldn't sit well with Campbell. If he knew. White couldn't dismiss such a notion out of hand because he'd known Campbell too many years. He realized that very little escaped the man's attention. Under normal circumstances, White never would have attempted this. But with all hell about to break loose, and Campbell on the run, White figured now was the best time to try. If there was a time when he could pull this off, dish out a little payback, now was it.

At least he hoped so. The elevator shuddered to a halt and White disembarked. He passed a group of his warriors, all dressed in camouflage fatigues, a few of whom gave him sharp salutes, which he absently returned.

Stepping between a pair of guards, he entered the conference room, shut the door behind him. From the corner of his eye, he saw Campbell's image staring at him from the screen, and he knew a dozen or so cameras, positioned throughout the room, beamed his image back to the other man. He avoided looking directly at the screen for as long as he could while he collected his thoughts.

"Ellis," Campbell said, his voice cold.

White looked at the screen, saluted. "Sir."

"Sit." White moved to the nearest chair and sat.

"What the hell were you thinking, Ellis?"

"Sir?"

"The woman. What the hell were you thinking?"

"She's nothing to worry about. I have the situation well in hand."

"I think," Campbell said, "you don't. Do you realize

how much attention you're going to get us, murdering a pair of marshals in a safehouse. What the hell were you thinking?"

"More attention than seizing the U.S. embassy or bombing a crowded mall?"

Campbell's voice grew quieter and White had to strain to hear it. "You know what I meant. Those attacks were well orchestrated and conducted through proxies. No one should have been able to trace them back to us. Unfortunately, our people got sloppy and now someone seems to be backtracking toward us, putting the larger mission in jeopardy. And, on top of it all, you draw even more attention to us. That's inexcusable."

"Now wait a minute—" White began.

"Shut up. What you've done is incredibly reckless. You've endangered this whole operation and drawn attention to us. What were you thinking?"

White clenched his jaw as he rode out Campbell's dressing-down. It wasn't completely unexpected, and it wasn't without risks. But, to hell with it, even if the bastard didn't like what White had done, it was too late in the game to sideline.

At least White hoped so.

"Sir, the woman and I have a history."

Campbell balled his hands into fists and leaned forward. "I'm well aware of your history. I'm the one who pulled the strings necessary to fake your death and make you disappear, remember? I know the whole sordid story, and I'm suddenly wondering why I ever bothered."

"I believe in what you're doing. I've shed a lot of blood for this cause, and will continue to do so."

"If I let you."

"The woman is important to us."

Campbell's eyebrows arched in disbelief. "She's a reporter. What does she know that could help us, especially when things have reached this stage?"

"It's not what she knows, but who she knows."

"Explain."

"Rosario Blancanales, the man I tried to kill, is close to her. He, also, was among the men who shot up the penthouse in San Diego. And he helped stage the hostage rescue at the Freedom Center. That makes him very dangerous for us."

Campbell seemed unconvinced, but willing to hear more.

"So far, not only have commandos fouled things up in both Africa and California, but they've started systematically backtracking through the weapons suppliers. I saw your dispatch earlier today. They talked to the Iraqi."

"Who's now dead."

"But they talked to him."

Campbell nodded in agreement, reluctantly so it seemed. "And he knew about Markov, who knew about us. I see where you're going."

"They may not know about us yet," White said. "But, if they do, these commandos are the ones most likely to find the connection. If that happens, everything you've worked for goes down the damn toilet."

"And the woman helps us prevent this how?"

"I know Blancanales. He'll come after her. The guy's a moron. A bleeding heart. And he's got hard-on for me, too. Wants to see me dead. So he won't be able to resist."

"That's what you think."

"I have no doubt," White said. "The guy won't sit on

his ass while I kill this woman. He isn't capable of that. You'll see. Maybe he'll bring his buddies with him, maybe not. Regardless, we'll take him out of the running."

"Leaving the rest of the federal government gunning for us. If it wasn't so damn late in the game, I'd probably fly out there, strangle you myself, drape your corpse from a flagpole so others could see what happens to people who derail my plans."

"I didn't—"

"Shut up. You've opened a huge chink in our armor, one that could result in mortal wounding. This operation isn't about us, don't you see? It's about the future. We can't let our country focus on terrorists, not when communism is alive and well in the world. It's suicide to do that. We have a sacred mission here and we need to carry it out with all our strength. This is bigger than any of us. You see that, don't you, Ellis?"

White had heard it all before but nodded patiently. "Sure, I see it. But I know Blancanales. The guy is trouble and, if anyone can screw things up, it's him. He was a hell of a soldier. And, judging from what I saw on those tapes, he still is. Don't shortchange him."

"And don't shortchange me, or my resolve. Your personal vendetta ends here and now."

White nodded. "Understood. But if he comes hunting for you, she might give you some leverage."

"If he comes hunting for me."

"It's a better than fifty percent chance."

Campbell glared at White for a full thirty seconds. "All right, damn it. Bring her here, to the platform. I need you here. And you're right. She might help us."

"We'll leave within the hour."

"BARB, COME HERE quick," said "Hunt" Wethers, a member of Kurtzman's cybernetics team. "There's something here you ought to see."

Price, who'd been working the phones, tapping old contacts in the intelligence community, crossed the room, stopping next to Wethers's workstation. Wethers, a tall, well-built black man and former cybernetics professor, leaned back from his terminal, allowing her full view of the monitor.

"The *Washington Register* has posted a breaking-news story on its Web site accusing the Chinese of supplying weapons to the Arm of God terrorists," Wethers said. "It's only a few paragraphs, but it attributes an unidentified State Department official."

Price read the story, which was short on specifics but explosive in its premise. It troubled her not only for its geopolitical ramifications, but also because so few people in the federal government knew the possible connection between the Chinese and the terrorists. Fewer still were inclined to buy the whole notion that China would take such a foolhardy action, especially when it faced its own threats within its borders and wanted American support for its battle against Xinjiang separatists. Not to mention the billions of dollars in trade and other ties the two countries shared.

"This doesn't add up," Price said. "But it says that America's ambassador to China plans to meet with high-ranking U.S. officials later today. Hopefully something can be sorted out at that level."

"Hopefully," Wethers replied, sounding anything but hopeful.

Price set a hand on Wethers's shoulder. "Get me a bio

on this reporter and see if you can track down any other information on our State Department leak. In the meantime, I'll contact Hal."

BLANCANALES STOOD in Stephens's kitchen, next to a scarred wooden table. Schwarz had positioned himself nearby, leaning against a wall and drinking water from a clear plastic bottle. A satellite phone, switched to speaker mode, rested in the middle of the table, linking them to Stony Man Farm. Outside, members of a Justice Department cleanup team were milling around the grounds, questioning the hostages and searching for weapons. The group had found half a dozen cylinders, all unmarked, but similar to those found at the mall. In addition, they'd located a cache of assault rifles, handguns and LAW rockets, all stored in crates and marked for delivery to military bases.

Price was briefing the group on the raid at the safehouse. While he listened, Blancanales crossed his arms over his chest and, balling his hands into fists, tapped the knuckle of his left index finger against his chin while he waited for the mission controller to finish.

Once she'd shared the basics, he asked, "There's no sign of Donna Ling?"

"None. I'm sorry, Pol."

"I thought this was a secure location," he said.

"It was supposed to be. Hal has his people from Justice tracking leads. With two federal agents dead, obviously everyone wants to nail these guys. The kidnapping's only a piece of a much larger, much uglier picture. We have reason to believe this goes a lot higher than a revenge strike by Hakim and his handlers."

"How so?" Schwarz asked.

"Only a handful of people knew about the safehouse, Hal and I among them. For someone to get that kind of information, they'd need a top-rate security clearance, something Hakim's people likely didn't have."

"What if they hacked their way in?"

"Possible, but not probable. I mean, if they had that kind of ability, why not use it for a bigger target? No offense, Pol, but if they could hack into the Justice Department's computer system, they could do a lot worse to our country than kill a couple of marshals and kidnap a reporter."

"Understood," Blancanales replied. "So they must have someone on the inside. Someone highly placed."

"That's how we see it."

"Any clues?"

"One," Price said. She told them about Campbell, the Cadre and Campbell's links to Stephens. "His group easily could have hacked its way into the system. And they've gone rogue so it's not out of the question that they'd do it."

"Do it why?" Schwarz asked.

"Perhaps to cover their tracks," Price said. "If they're linked with Campbell, who apparently is tied in a roundabout way to Stephens and Hakim, then maybe she turned up something in her reporting that made them nervous."

"Maybe. But it still doesn't explain why they didn't just kill her at the house. I mean, if they wanted to shut her up, why actually take her out of there instead of killing her on the spot? It makes no sense."

"If she knew something," Price stated. "That could include them grilling her to find out who'd busted up Hakim's operation. My guess is these guys aren't going to take it very well. And, unfortunately in this case, she actually does know who you are. At least, in Pol's case, she does."

Blancanales nodded slowly. "Cal and Gadgets used false names with her, so their identities are secure. But that would explain the kidnapping. What do we know about the people who hit the safehouse?"

"They're still processing the scene, but we did get a break. All the gunshots—especially in that neighborhood—didn't go unnoticed. Within a few minutes, a dozen squad cars were on their way, putting a squeeze on the shooters, forcing them to leave behind one of their own people."

"Alive or dead?" Blancanales asked.

"Dead, but easily identifiable. His name's Nick Harter. We ran his records and found that he has some assault charges dating back a decade or more ago. He was in the Army and was a real hell-raiser for a while after he got out. But he's been pretty quiet for the past several years. But what raised a red flag with us was his current employment."

"And that would be?"

"Campbell Aerospace. He worked for them as a security guard. We checked his IRS, credit and the state bureau of motor vehicle records. He seems to lead a pretty prosperous life for a security guard making $34,000 a year. He owns a big house, a Lexus, a Cadillac and two boats."

"Maybe he clips coupons," Schwarz said. Grinning at his own joke, he swigged from his water.

"We checked through his financial records and found out he's gotten some pretty substantial money transfers over the past couple of years, all from the same sources as Stephens. At least twice a year, he also has been traveling to Virginia where there's a private security school. We checked with the Man and he told us that it's the same place where Campbell trains his elite troops for the Cadre."

"Well, if Campbell's dropped out of sight, what's the next link in the chain?"

"Give us an hour to do some digging and I'll send some names. What else have you learned on your end?"

"The scientists here definitely were working on the Skyfire project, or at least bits and pieces of it. They say there's another facility somewhere else, though none of them seemed to know any solid details. It was all based on rumors they heard during their time here. I'm guessing the Justice Department agents will quiz them further about that."

"They will."

"In the meantime, we need to move out."

"Right. Did Stephens have anything important to say?"

"Ironman's having a heart-to-heart with him right now."

"God help him."

TWENTY MINUTES LATER Lyons joined the others in the house. When he entered the kitchen, he clapped Blancanales on the shoulder, nodded toward a chair.

"Sit," he said.

"I don't need to sit," Blancanales said.

"I'm not asking, damn it. Just sit."

The man dropped into a straight-backed wooden chair, one of three ringing the table. Lyons stared grimly at Blancanales for a moment before speaking.

"Ellis White, the guy you told us about in San Diego," Lyons said, "is still alive."

Blancanales tensed visibly at the news. "Bullshit," he said.

Lyons shook his head. "Wrong. According to Stephens, the guy's alive and kicking. He's mixed up in something called the Cadre Project, or some crap like that."

"I thought he was dead."

"That was the idea," Lyons stated. "Everyone was supposed to think he was dead, for two reasons. One, he was important to the project. And, two, everyone figured that he'd tell everything he knew about the Cadre if they put him on trial."

"So where the hell is he?" Blancanales asked. "Where's Donna?"

Lyons shook his head again. "He doesn't know. And trust me, if he had known, he'd have told me. I put enough pressure on him to turn coal into a diamond. He wasn't trying any heroics. He knew the score if he didn't give up the information."

Blancanales pounded his right fist into his left palm. "Damn it, if he's got Donna, she's as good as dead."

"Unless he's using her to get at you."

Blancanales's expression was skeptical. "It's possible," he said. "But how would he know I was anywhere near him?"

Lyons shrugged. "Who knows? Maybe we were caught on video footage at Hakim's office or at the Freedom Center. Or he had spotters at one of those places and they shot photos of us. Or maybe Donna told him after she was captured. At this point, those questions really don't matter a whole lot."

"We just need to find her."

Lyons face went stony. "Maybe we have to find her," he said. "There's a hell of a lot more to this than we thought."

"Meaning what?" Schwarz asked.

"Meaning that, according to our boy Stephens, the terrorist strikes were a dodge."

"You mean, something worse is coming?"

"Yeah, something like that. Armageddon. All within a few hours."

CHAPTER EIGHTEEN

Five hours later Blancanales guided the Corvette through the tree-lined streets of the suburban Los Angeles neighborhood. Dressed in a summer-weight suit, the sports car's air conditioner blasting him with cold air, he scanned the numbers on the houses situated on either side of the road. The neighborhood was lined with big houses, most topped with red Spanish tiles and fronted by lush green lawns. It was dusk and lawn sprinklers sprayed out silvery lines of water with programmed precision.

Blancanales noticed all of it, but pushed most of it from his mind almost immediately. He wasn't here to admire the architecture or the driveways stuffed with all manner of Lexus, BMW and Mercedes luxury cars. He'd come here looking for information and he planned to get some, one way or the other.

He thought for a moment of Ling, wondered what sort of hell she might be going through. She was a tough lady, sure. But White was a psycho, a man without remorse or empathy. He'd inflict pain on her just because he could, just to fulfill some sick power fantasy. Or maybe he'd killed her outright. After all, Blancanales knew he was the one that White wanted. If the other guy believed that he'd already lured Blancanales into looking for him, then, hell, she was of little use to White.

Blancanales couldn't help but feel guilty. Ling hadn't wanted to go into protective custody, but he had forced the issue. He hadn't wanted her to end up in the line of fire, at least that's what he'd told himself at the time. It was a partial truth at best. He'd wanted to protect her, to do that which he'd failed to do so many years ago.

He'd failed again.

Nice work, hombre.

He exhaled deeply, and about that time he saw the house number he'd been hunting. He rolled the car up to the curb and parked it. Killing the engine, he stepped from the vehicle, pocketed the keys and eyed the house. Lyons's voice crackled from the handheld radio in Blancanales's grip.

"What's the word, Pol?"

Blancanales raised the radio to his lips. "The eagle has landed."

"What? What the hell does that mean?"

"It means I'm at the house."

"Oh. You sure you want to go this one alone?"

"Yeah. This guy's the security chief for Campbell Aerospace. There's no way he's going to give me attitude, at least none that I can't handle. Besides, you and Gadgets have plenty to handle on your end."

"Clear."

Blancanales climbed the driveway, which was built on a slight incline, and navigated his way around a pair of children's bikes lying on their sides on the concrete. He thought fleetingly of the twin Beretta 93-Rs riding in a dual shoulder rig under his suit coat. He felt a twinge of concern, knowing that if there were kids in the house, the guns would stay put, unless he was left with absolutely no other alternative.

As he negotiated a circular sidewalk leading to the front porch, he reached inside his pocket and withdrew a leather case containing his fake Justice Department credentials. He kept them in his left hand, along with his radio. Standing to one side of the door, he reached over, rang the bell and listened as it incited dogs into barking. An adult's voice, definitely male, sounded from within, yelling for quiet, the dogs rewarding his shouts with more noise.

Blancanales heard the click of dress shoes hitting the floor, growing louder with each step. The footsteps stopped, followed by a pause as Blancanales assumed the guy was staring at him through the peephole. The Stony Man warrior flipped open his credentials and held them in plain view of the peephole. The door swung inward and a man with a sunburned face scowled at Blancanales. The guy had the top button of his dress shirt undone, his tie hanging down several inches from his neck and his sleeves rolled up to the middle of his forearms.

"Yeah?"

"You Dexter Block?" Blancanales asked.

"Yeah."

"I'm agent Gonzalez with the FBI."

"Yeah."

"I need to speak with you. May I come inside?"

"Okay." The guy stepped aside, allowing Blancanales to enter. The Hispanic took a quick glance at the only two rooms visible, the living room and dining room, noticing that both were modestly furnished. Gunshots blasted from a television in the basement and a hip-hop tune thundered from a stereo on the second floor, spewing a string of four-letter words that impressed Blancanales. A dog frustrated by a door somewhere in the house continued to bark and scratch. The guy, who'd probably been home from work a grand total of forty-five minutes, already smelled like a brewery.

"One of your people was involved in something, a crime, and I need to ask you a few questions," Blancanales said.

The guy shrugged. "Sure. C'mon."

Two words, Blancanales thought. Now we're getting somewhere. Block turned his back on Blancanales and headed into the house. The pair wound its way through a short corridor that spilled into the kitchen, where Blancanales noticed a pizza box fanned open on the kitchen table. A stray mushroom, a few blobs of cheese and some grease spots provided the only evidence that the box had once contained a pizza.

They exited through a sliding-glass door, stepping onto a wooden deck. Bug zappers crackled intermittently, and Blancanales heard the occasional yell of children playing in another yard.

The guy flopped into a well-worn chair. Reaching over the side, he grabbed his beer from the ground, set it in his lap and seemed to relax visibly. Blancanales noticed a cooler just within the man's reach. The guy snatched a half-burned cigar from an ashtray and placed it between his lips, gnawing at the end but leaving it unlit.

"Sit," the guy said.

"I'll stand."

"Suit yourself." Block shrugged. "What's the crime?"

"One of your employees, Nick Harter, got in some trouble. You know anything about it?"

The man shook his head.

"Nothing?"

Another shake.

"So you didn't know that he was involved in a murder-kidnapping in San Diego?"

The guy was either paralyzed from the neck up or able to play off his surprise, Blancanales decided. His face betrayed nothing,

"Bullshit," Block said finally.

Blancanales reached inside his jacket, withdrew a couple of photos and tossed them on the deck at Block's feet. After shooting Blancanales a nasty look, Block reluctantly set down his beer and retrieved the photos. He fanned them open like a handful of cards and scrutinized them.

"Who're the stiffs?"

"U.S. Marshals."

"The guy in the mask?" It was a photo of Harter's corpse taken from the security camera footage.

"Harter."

"Bullshit."

"No real shit. We've got fingerprints to prove it."

"Wow."

"Well said."

Block plucked at the tab on the top of his beer can, causing it to make an irritating twanging noise.

"You guys served together in the Army, didn't you? Military police, if I recall."

"Yeah."

"Any reason you can think of for our friend Mr. Harter to run around shooting federal officers?"

His eyes narrowed, the guy regarded Blancanales. "Hell, no. If I'd known the bastard was this crazy or stupid or whatever, I'd have canned his ass. I was a cop myself, you know."

"L.A.P.D. Right?"

"Gang squad. How'd you know?"

"I'm FBI, remember? I get paid to know these things."

"Look—"

"Your buddy Harter, he had a drug conviction, a federal drug conviction. Seems like a bad candidate for security."

"He did a good job. I was giving an old buddy a break. When he came back from Nam, well, he had some problems."

"Problems?"

The tapped his right temple with the index finger of the same hand. "You know, problems. You not getting me?"

"I got you. So he got into drugs?"

"Not using or selling. Guy would never put that shit into his body. He was a freak about his body. He ran. Lifted weights. All that crap. He just didn't want to work, you know. He figured someone owed him something, so he decided he didn't want to work."

"Which means?"

The guy rolled his eyes, as though he were suffering a fool. When he spoke again, he did so slowly. "It means he went into the drug business for a while. He never sold the junk, not that I know of, anyway. He just was hired muscle for the dealer, part of his personal security team."

The guy finished his beer, crumpled the can and tossed it, grunting with the effort. He popped open the cooler, reached inside and sloshed around until he'd found another one. Popping it open, he swigged some, swirled it around his mouth like mouthwash and swallowed audibly.

He laughed. "He wasn't too good a bodyguard, though. Stupid bastard he was working for got waxed in a car wreck or something."

"That'd be Ellis White."

Block shrugged. "Maybe. They're all scum to me. You know what I'm saying?"

"Sure."

"Truth be told, I'd never have hired Harter in the first place if I hadn't known him. But I did and I felt like we owed each other something, us serving together in the Army and all."

"We searched his apartment, found it empty. Any idea why that might be?"

The guy studied Blancanales over the rim of his beer for a second. Tightening his grip on the can, he extended his index finger at Blancanales. "Look, Agent Gomez—"

"Gonzalez."

"Whatever. I hired the guy. I handled his paperwork and his evaluations and all that administrative crap that I do so I can make a lot of money and put this high-priced roof over the heads of two bratty kids and a bitchy wife. I've got 150 guards working for me. I do the same thing for all of them. I tried to do right by this guy, and he flamed out anyway. That's not my fault. And what he did during his off hours was none of my business. I wasn't his damn babysitter or his mother. Got it?"

Blancanales felt his face color with anger, but he kept his voice even. "Sure," he said.

"I don't know why he killed those two marshals. I don't know who was with him. Understood?"

"I guess that explains why your cell phone records indicate that you two talked at least twice a day for the last month or so." Blancanales's pager vibrated on his belt. Absently he reached down and thumbed the button that acknowledged the page, never taking his eyes from Block.

Something flickered in the guy's eyes for a moment. He blinked, as though coming out of a trance, and fixed a hard stare on Blancanales. "I don't know what the hell you're talking about."

Blancanales cocked an eyebrow at the guy. "Really? You willing to tell that to a judge?"

"Go to hell. I want a lawyer."

Smiling, Blancanales slid a hand inside his jacket and withdrew several sheets of folded paper. He took a step forward and tossed them at the guy's feet. "Make sure you show your lawyer these. They're copies of the phone records. I've got the originals in my office. And don't get up. I'll let myself out."

A MINUTE LATER Blancanales slid behind the wheel of the Corvette, backed it out of the driveway and drove away. Taking the car less than half a mile from Block's home, he pulled into a cul-de-sac and parked the sports car at the curb. Gripping the handheld radio, he brought it to his mouth. "Gadgets, this dumb bastard should be reaching out and touching someone any minute now. You get those bugs planted?"

"Right. He's already dialing from what I can tell," Schwarz said. "Did you put the fear of God in him or what?"

"I'm not Ironman, but I get the job done," Blancanales replied.

A whisper came over the line. "Damn straight you're no Ironman," Lyons stated. "I'd have stuck his head in a food processor and gotten some answers, quick."

A grim smile played on Blancanales's lips. "The kids see you in the house?" he asked.

"House is empty. Other than a golden retriever. I took care of him, though."

"Aw, Carl, you didn't—" Schwarz said.

Lyons sounded almost hurt. Almost. "Hell, no, I fed him some pizza. Practically had to pry the damn thing off me with a crowbar. But the wife and kids are out, whether for a little bit or the whole night, I can't tell."

"Maybe he left the television and radio blaring for company," Blancanales mused.

"Or to keep up appearances," Schwarz said. "He was a cop. He had to expect that someone would contact him about the shooting. Whoa! The phone call's gone through and is ringing. I'll patch it through the radios."

"—do you mean Harter's weapon had prints on it?" Block was saying. "We made sure all the guns were clean. And, besides, his prints should have been purged from all the federal databases. That was the plan."

"Relax." Blancanales immediately recognized the voice as White's. The sound, after all these years, still set his teeth on edge, stirred up feelings of blind rage that burned like a pool of molten steel in his belly.

Block continued, "Don't tell me to relax. We were supposed to be covered on this. This was supposed to be an easy hit. Now Harter's on a slab and the FBI's breathing down my neck."

"I said relax," White said. "In a few hours, none of this will matter. The FBI will be answering to Campbell, and the rest of us will be sitting high and mighty. So why you worrying about one stinking FBI agent? Have another beer and relax."

"He knew I'd been talking to Harter. He has the phone records to prove it. I told you this hit was too dangerous, that we'd get caught."

"You afraid of the FBI?"

"Hell, no," Block replied. "I'm afraid of Campbell. If he gets word of this, he'll skewer us. And since he's going to be the big man by tomorrow, that scares me."

"I've got Campbell under control."

"Bull. No one has Campbell under control."

"Look, just stick with the plan and everything will be fine. Okay?"

"Okay."

"I need you to come in. There was some stuff that Harter needed to handle. With him gone, I need you to step in. You understand?"

"I understand."

"Good. I need you to meet Taylor and Lawson at the old warehouse. Pack your gear. We're moving out to Washington, tonight. We do this as we planned, by the numbers."

"Got it," said Block, the tautness of his voice evident.

"And watch your back. We don't need anyone following us."

THE PHONE WENT DEAD in Block's hand and he threw it across the room. Watch your back? What the hell kind of a chump did White take him for? Block had half a mind to drop a coin on the son of a bitch, call Campbell directly and tell him that his second in command was chasing his own vendetta on the eve of something so much more important.

Running a hand through his hair, Block admitted to himself that he wouldn't tell Campbell anything. It wasn't because he had any particular loyalty to White. The bastard was arrogant and reckless, more than worthy of Campbell's wrath. But Block knew Campbell well enough to realize that the crazy bastard wouldn't be satisfied just punishing White. He'd make an example of every last one of them, make damn sure anyone else crazy enough to betray him would think twice before undertaking such a fool's errand.

Sighing deeply, he lifted the beer can to his mouth, drained its contents with a loud gulp and threw the can's crumpled remains into the sink.

"I am so fucked," he said.

A voice from behind replied, "Damn straight you are."

LYONS WATCHED for a stretched second as Block, his body tense, hesitated, likely weighing his next move. An instant later the security guy lunged forward, hands scrambling for a knife that lay on the counter. The silenced Beretta in Lyons's grip chugged out a single subsonic round that smashed into the knife, sending it skittering across the counter like a billiard ball.

The guy raised his hands and turned toward Lyons, who kept the Beretta trained on the guy.

"I won't even touch the whole bringing-a-knife-to-a-gunfight thing," Lyons said. "C'mon. Up against the wall so I can frisk you. Then we're going for a little ride."

THREE MINUTES LATER Blancanales watched from the passenger's seat of a telephone company van as Block's Cadillac SUV backed out of the garage, down the driveway and into the street. He had abandoned the Vette back in the cul-de-sac, leaving it for the FBI to pick up later, and joined Gadgets in the van. They had rolled up on the house as

Block had finished his phone call, positioning themselves for a fast response should Lyons need backup.

The Cadillac kicked into gear, its headlights firing up as it approached.

Blancanales clicked the talk button on his radio. "Ironman, you in there?"

A hand, middle finger extended, popped into view in the rear driver's-side door.

Schwarz turned to Blancanales, smiled. "He's in there."

FIFTEEN MINUTES LATER Lyons felt the SUV slow. When it turned, he poked his head up from behind the seat and scanned his surroundings. Block had turned his vehicle into a driveway wide enough to accommodate at least three cars. He sat motionless, sweat beading on his forehead, as the vehicle idled. The headlights illuminated the area in front of them, creating a whitish glare as they reflected off a For Sale sign affixed to the gate. The word Sold had been stenciled over the sign.

Beyond the gate, Lyons saw a three-story warehouse with its windows boarded up. The wind whipped the flagpole's tether line around, creating an awful racket. A Lincoln Town Car was parked in front of the building, its silver skin dully reflecting the single overhead light illuminating the parking lot. Tinted windows made it difficult for Lyons to discern whether the vehicle was empty.

With a touch, he activated his throat mike. "We've already got company."

"Numbers?" Blancanales asked.

"Negative. One car that I can see. No people in sight. And my friend here swears he doesn't know how many people are inside. What's your ETA?"

"Going EVA even as we speak." Lyons heard doors bang shut in the background as Blancanales spoke. "We're parked around back and about two blocks east. Give us thirty seconds and we'll be there to cover your six."

"Clear." Block looked expectantly at Lyons, who nodded. The security chief touched a small black button on his sun visor and the gate lurched open.

Lyons took the silenced Beretta and jammed the muzzle under Block's chin, causing him to tilt his head at an angle. Lyons caught a glimpse of Block's right eye, narrowed, brow arched, in the rearview mirror. "You're looking cranky, Block. And guilty. Anything you'd like to share?"

"Screw you," the guy replied. "I told you before. They said two guys will be here to pick me up. Two guys. I don't know anything else."

"For your sake, I hope you're not lying."

Block laughed, but the tautness of his voice betrayed his fear. "What? Are you going to kill me? Man, I got kids."

"I'll send flowers," Lyons replied. "Drive. Now."

The gate slid to a stop. Block gunned the engine and the SUV lurched forward, passing through the entrance. When the vehicle rolled inside, the gate pulled closed behind them. "There's a pressure plate in the ground," Block explained. "Once the car passes over it, the gate automatically closes."

"Park behind the Lincoln," Lyons said. "I want your door to kiss its back bumper."

Block guided the vehicle as Lyons directed. He slammed the gear selector into Park. He turned to say something to Lyons, but before he could complete the motion, Lyons smacked him in the temple with the butt of the

Beretta. The guy grunted and slumped forward, his safety belt suspending him in place. The Able Team leader cast a quick glance over his shoulder, watching the warehouse for any threats. As he did, he gathered Block's hands behind his back and bound them with plastic handcuffs. With that completed, he unfastened the man's safety belt and dragged him over the driver's seat backrest, depositing him on the SUV's floor.

"We're over the fence, Ironman," Blancanales said.

"You got a back door?"

"Roger that."

Lyons studied the building again. "No lights. Going through the doors is asking to get pegged."

"Suggestions?"

"Let me create a diversion. You guys ready for some noise?"

"Shit, Carl."

Gunning the engine, he slammed the vehicle into Reverse, felt it catch for an instant before it lurched into motion, tires squealing. Lyons glanced over his shoulder. He guided the vehicle back a dozen or so yards, cutting the wheel in a violent J-turn, bringing the grille and headlights in line with the warehouse's large bay doors.

Shifting into drive, Lyons stomped the accelerator. The vehicle surged forward. For an instant, the headlight glare grew larger, more intense, as the Cadillac closed in on the bay doors. The SUV's front end collided with the wooden barrier, splintering it, sending shards of wood sailing through the air.

The Cadillac surged through the door.

At the rear of the building, muzzle-flashes exploded in the darkness. Slugs punched through the front end, drilling into the engine block, shattering the right headlight. Stray rounds sparked off nearby concrete support pillars.

Lyons stomped the brakes, cut the wheel into a hard left. The Caddy swerved, tires squealing, as its rear end fishtailed, throwing the vehicle into a sideways skid as it came to a stop.

Bullets continued to pierce the vehicle, lancing through the interior, a few whistling within inches of Lyons's face.

Suitably angered, Lyons put the vehicle in Reverse, bringing its front end on line with his attackers, his headlights illuminating them, causing them to scatter like cockroaches.

Over the engine's growl, Lyons heard the chatter of submachine guns as the thugs unloaded their weapons in his direction. Picking the nearest one, a man positioned about fifteen yards away, the Able Team warrior stomped the accelerator, filling the vehicle with the engine's roar, and took off after the man. Caught in the headlights, the guy raised his SMG, the weapon spitting fire, and raked it over the Caddy's front end. Bullets drummed against the vehicle, like rain striking a tin roof, and pierced the windshield's safety glass, causing a line of spiderweb-like cracks to line the glass. On the fringes of his attention, Lyons identified the smell of antifreeze and greasy smoke, as the vehicle began to falter. Lyons ducked farther below the steering wheel, using the dashboard for additional protection as he closed in on the shooter.

At the last instant the guy dived from the Caddy's path, losing his weapon in the process. Lyons stomped the brake, sending the car into a wild spin that carried it over the oil-stained concrete floor and into an exterior wall. Lyons struggled to maintain some control of the vehicle, but he had too little time, too little distance to right it before impact. The Caddy shook as it slammed into the wall. Shards of glass rained into the passengers' seats. The chassis rasped against brick, causing it to bow inward. The Caddy shuddered again as the battered engine block broke loose from its mounts and crashed to the ground. The force of the impact thrust Block's unconscious form from the backseat and hurled his crumpled body into the windshield. The glass disintegrated as he sailed through the window, his body bouncing along the hood until he dropped out of sight.

The seat belt held Lyons in place, preventing him from smacking his head against the steering wheel. Still disoriented, the warrior unhooked the belt, popped open the door and set his left foot to the floor. From the corner of his eye, he saw someone approaching. Turning his head, he spotted the same shooter he'd nearly hit a few minutes ago walking toward him. The man's right hand was extended at the shoulder, a pistol tracking on Lyons.

Acting on instinct, the big ex-cop lunged from the vehicle, hand clawing inside his jacket for his Beretta. He struck the ground, rolled. His opponent squeezed off a pair of shots from his pistol that thudded against the SUV's hide. Lyons brought up the Beretta, aimed it quickly at the man's chest and loosed a trio of shots. He staggered back, his body quickly going limp before collapsing to the ground. An instant later, Lyons set out to find his teammates.

STATIONED NEXT to one of the building's two rear doors, Blancanales heard a loud crash followed by the clatter of boards skittering over concrete and the scream of an engine.

He glanced at Schwarz, who grinned and gave him a thumbs-up. Nodding, Blancanales raised his Ithaca 37 shotgun—modified with a pistol grip and short barrel—and fired it into the lock. The blast briefly illuminated his face and the shotgun slug tore into the lock, causing the door to swing inward on its hinges.

Schwarz moved through the door in a walking crouch. Blancanales fell in right behind him, sweeping the shotgun's barrel over his field of fire, the echo of screeching tires, the cacophony of gunfire setting his teeth on edge. His night-vision goggles cast the room, its features and its occupants in green. He saw at least one man pinned in the vehicle's headlights for a brief instant before the guy sprinted away, with Lyons hot on his tail. The muzzle of the man's weapon flared yellow as it chugged through its store of ammunition.

Blancanales counted muzzle-flashes from four weapons as a quartet of shooters unloaded on the Cadillac from various positions. Almost immediately, however, his shotgun blast caught the attention from at least two shooters, one to his right, the other straight ahead. Both men began unloading chatterguns at Blancanales, the withering hail of fire forcing him to drop into a crouch while he drew down on the shooter in front of him. The shotgun roared once, its thunderous report reverberating off the walls. The slug sliced just past his target. The guy held his ground, but his brush with death threw off his aim, buying Blancanales a precious microsecond to pump out the spent round, readjust his aim and discharge the Ithaca once more. The slug rammed into the man's thigh bone, eliciting a wrenching scream and knocking him to the ground.

Blancanales jacked the slide back, ejecting the spent shell.

Suddenly he felt something thud hard against his side, the force stealing his breath, shoving him onto his side. He'd been shot enough times to recognize the vicious pain as the blunt impact of a bullet striking his ballistic vest. Dropping the Ithaca, which had just one round left, he rolled away, simultaneously stripping a pair of Glock 19s from his dual shoulder holster.

The Glocks cracked almost in unison, spitting fire and lead. Blancanales's first shots flew wild, but drilled close enough to his attacker to force the guy onto the defensive, prompting him to dart between several stacks of wooden crates positioned along the structure's back wall.

Blancanales came to his feet and sprinted for the wooden containers. His opponent came back into view, wrapping himself around the corner of one of the crates, swinging his pistol into target acquisition. Before the man squeezed off a shot, and without losing stride, Blancanales centered the sights of the Glock in his right hand on the man and fired a double tap that drilled into the man's skull. The man stiffened, staggered back, his body still responding to commands sent by his ravaged brain. The man folded into a boneless heap. Vaulting over the body, Blancanales slipped between the stacked crates, flattened against the ones at his back and took a moment to evaluate the battleground.

Autofire crackled to his right.

Whipping his head in that direction, bringing up his pistol in the same instant, he spotted Schwarz taking fire from a shooter who'd holed up in an office that overlooked the bay. The shooter had shattered a rectangular window that looked out into the cavernous area. He'd jammed the muzzle of a long weapon through the window and was spraying the room with autofire.

Schwarz had ducked behind a concrete pillar. His opponent's unrelenting fusillade struck the Able Team warrior's cover, sparking off the concrete and angling off into the darkness, seemingly pinning him down.

"I got your back, Gadgets," Blancanales said into his mike.

"Negative," Schwarz said with emphasis. "Fire in the hole."

"Clear."

FROM WHAT Schwarz could tell, a pair of shooters had snuck into the office, a ten-foot-by-ten-foot box that in the building's former life probably had housed administrative staff or midlevel officers. They'd caught sight of his approach and directed a relentless barrage of autofire at him. Schwarz had hoped to catch a lull in the shooting, a moment when the men emptied their guns, so he could counter their attack. It hadn't happened. They seemed to be taking turns, one attacking while the other reloaded.

Over the din of the relentless gunfire, Schwarz heard the wail of sirens. Wonderful, he thought. He respected the police, but their intervention would create a distraction that Able Team didn't need.

They needed to clamp down, and now.

Schwarz grabbed a stun grenade from his satchel, pulled the pin, but left the spoon in place. From what he could tell, the shooting had paused for a heartbeat while the gunners switched out. The slugs pounded into the side of the pillar behind his right shoulder, stitching out a line across the support column. The guys had been smart to a point, by keeping on the pressure. But they also were predictable, which was the kiss of death in battle. As the gunfire moved toward Schwarz's left, he whipped around the column's right side and lobbed the grenade with an underhanded toss. The weapon sailed through the window, blowing the blinds inward for a moment as it dropped past them and struck the floor. The shooting ceased for a second as the men inside the office fully realized the turn the battle had taken. A moment later, a thunderous peal and a white flash erupted inside the enclosure.

Coming up in a crouch, Schwarz rounded the pillar, his FNC in front of him. Moving quickly, but cautiously, eyes trained on the shattered window, he moved to the door, opened it and slipped inside. One of the men sat on the floor, his gun just out of reach, his hands clamped over his ears as he rode out the effects of the stun device. The second man, an MP-5 in his grip, was bringing the weapon up, ready to deal out death. In the microsecond Schwarz had to react, it was hard to tell whether the man had been trained to fight through the effects of a stun grenade. Or whether he just planned to employ the spray-and-pray method on anyone within shooting range. But he promised himself that he'd ask the guy in the afterlife, provided they ended up in the same place.

The FNC spit a short burst that pounded the man's upper chest. The guy jerked in place for a moment, as though being struck by a half dozen invisible fists. Rubbery legs gave out from under him and he fell to the ground in a boneless heap.

Schwarz turned his attention to his second opponent. The man seemed to be quickly regaining his senses and was clawing for hardware carried in a shoulder rig.

Schwarz drove a booted foot into the guy's head, the force of the blow whipping the man's head to the side. The thug grunted and blood sprayed from his lips. But the kick halted his desperate play, giving Schwarz a moment to drop his full weight on the guy. Grabbing the man's wrist, Schwarz pinned the guy's hand to his chest, preventing him from gaining the pistol. The guy struggled for a moment, until Schwarz waved the FNC's barrel an inch or so from his face. "I give, man. I give," the guy said.

"Good choice."

Schwarz cautiously came to his feet, the FNC still locked on the other man's face. Ordering the man onto his belly, Schwarz secured the man's hands behind his back. Relieving him of a 10 mm Glock, the Able Team commando unloaded the pistol. He tossed the ammunition across the room and the empty weapon through the shattered window.

Blancanales appeared in the door. His expression almost immediately morphed from concern to relief as he saw his comrade was okay. He gave Schwarz a grim smile, nodded at the prisoner.

"Friend of yours?" he asked.

"We just met, but I have a feeling he's going to talk my leg off really soon."

Blancanales nodded. "I want to find Donna."

"I know."

"I don't care who I have to burn through to get her. You understand that, don't you?"

"Understood."

Blancanales turned to the other guy, locked eyes with him. The guy was relatively young, probably early twenties. He had a rangy build, a lean, angular face and hooded green eyes. He returned Blancanales's stare, a sneer curling at his lips.

"What about you, son?" Blancanales asked, his voice soft. "You understand what I'm saying? You can do the tough guy act, if you want. You can swear you won't talk. Believe me, you will. I'll break you. And enjoy it. I was breaking people while you were a gleam in your father's eye. You'll snap easy, and I won't feel the least bit bad."

The gunner swallowed hard, but his face betrayed no emotion. He studied Blancanales's face for a moment, apparently gauging his resolve to drop the hammer.

"What do you want to know?"

"White, where is he?"

"He's with Campbell."

"Which doesn't tell me shit."

"Campbell has an oil rig off the coast of Mexico. I don't know exactly where it is. But that's where White is. If Campbell called him out there, it means he's about to pull the trigger on something big."

"The woman, did he take her with him?"

"Yeah. He knew the Feds would come for her. He figured she might be valuable if they did."

"Where did they fly out of?"

"A little airport in the suburbs."

"I want a name."

The guy gave it. "Campbell has private jets and helicopters all over the place. My guess is White flew to Mexico and caught a chopper out to the oil platform. That's what he's done in the past."

"You know what's about to go down? With the satellites and all that?"

The guy nodded, cracked a smile. "Hell, yeah. Campbell's been planning this for months. He's got it planned down to the letter. When all this comes down, it's going to change everything."

CHAPTER NINETEEN

Alexandria, Virginia

Charlie Stewart hurried down the stairs of his three-story brownstone, whistling.

Reaching the sidewalk, the State Department official shrugged the tweed jacket over his rawboned frame and started for the black Lexus coupe parked alongside the curb. Fishing in his jacket pocket, he found his keys and curled his fingers around them, pulling them out.

Walking alongside the sleek vehicle, he ran his fingers along its smooth surface and stared at the face grinning back at him. At forty-two, he still looked young. Sure, a few character lines were etched into his skin at the corners of his eyes and occasional gray hairs streaked his otherwise jet-black hair. Regardless, he didn't look that much different than he had when he'd arrived in Washington, D.C., more than a decade ago as a congressional staffer. He preferred it that way. As far as he was concerned, people in Wonderland respected age, but not people who looked old.

And he wanted respect. Hell, he'd earned it. He was a deputy to the secretary of state, something he'd worked his ass off to get. And he felt as though he was finally getting his due on the job.

Pressing a button on the key fob, he heard the car emit a small chirp and a click as the locks released. Leaning inside the car, he set his briefcase on the passenger's side floor, making sure the locks faced upward.

"Charlie!" a woman's voice called.

Smiling, he pulled himself out of the car, stared over its roof and spotted Linda Cox running across the sidewalk toward him. Just home from a twelve-hour day at her law firm, she still wore her navy-blue pantsuit, still had her long blond hair tied up in a ponytail, her high-heeled shoes clicking loudly against the sidewalk. He felt his body warm with desire the minute he saw his girlfriend.

He leaned against the car, crossed his arms over his chest and gave her his best lopsided grin. She stepped up to him and they exchanged a kiss, brief enough to be publicly acceptable in this upscale neighborhood, lingering enough to make Stewart wish he wasn't going to spend the night locked in a bunker with a bunch of bureaucrats.

She let the palm of her hand trail down his chest and over his forearm, which she lightly wrapped her fingers around.

With her other hand, she held up his cell phone.

"You forgot this."

He shook his head. "Thanks, but I can't take it. No personal cell phones or pagers. Only the secure stuff they give us."

She scowled. "But what if I need to reach you? Like in an emergency?"

"Dial the call center. I left the number on the counter, under the cat's dish. They'll know how to get hold of me."

She pouted. "I'd rather call direct. You're going to be gone for twenty-four hours and I know I'll miss you." Her pout turned into a mischievous grin. She leaned a little closer. He felt the firmness of her breasts pushing into his chest. "I might have something to tell you. You know, something for your ears only? Like just how much I'm missing you. And what we'd be doing if you weren't hiding out in an undisclosed location somewhere."

Stewart smiled as a pleasurable heat pulsed through his stomach and groin.

"You fight dirty," he said.

"I do a lot of things dirty. I think you'd testify to that."

Stewart decided to change the subject before he gave in to his baser instincts, hung around home too long and missed his flight. "Honey, I can't take the phone. If I do, they'll just seize it and throw it away. They're serious about this stuff. That means I have to be, too."

She shifted back to her pout. "I know. I just hate it when you're gone for a day and I can't reach you. It just bothers me, not being able to talk to you. I'm sorry. I must sound like some needy idiot going on like this."

"Forget it. You sound just great. Look, when I get back, I'll make it up to you."

An excited glint came to her eyes and she smiled. "How?"

He paused. "It's a surprise."

Crossing her arms over her chest, she gave him an exaggerated scowl and furrowed her brows. "Meaning," she replied, "that you still have to think of something."

He laughed again. "Guilty as charged, Counselor. Now I have to get going."

They kissed once more and Stewart slipped inside the Lexus. Pulling the car into traffic, he scanned the rearview mirror once more, saw her standing along the curb, waving.

One hell of a lady that one, he thought, grinning. Pretty, well educated and a tigress in the sack. She definitely had him thinking of something more permanent. Maybe not marriage. Not yet, anyway. He'd already been down that road—twice—and was in no hurry to see if the third time was, indeed, the charm. But he definitely wanted something more permanent.

But first he had to spend the night in a damn bunker.

LINDA COX WATCHED Stewart's Lexus crest the hill, the ruby brake lights gleaming for an instant before the car turned and disappeared down another road.

Slipping her hand into her purse, she traded his cell phone for her own. She tapped out a few buttons and the phone dialed a programmed number. She heard the phone click as the call passed through a series of cutouts. The phone rang and she waited for someone to answer.

She ran the back of her hand across her lips, wiping away the taste of Stewart. Although she wanted to wallow in self-disgust for her performance as the clingy girlfriend, she instead congratulated herself on a good job. She was, after all, not herself. She was Linda Cox, hardworking, intelligent, but ultimately manipulative and needy. She'd played her part to the hilt and, though she didn't like it, she'd done what was necessary for the cause.

After the third ring, a gruff voice answered, "Yes."

"He's on his way."

"Did he take the phone?"

"No. He refused, as I told you he would."

A pause. "Fine, we'll deal with him."

The disappointment in his voice wasn't lost on her. "I tried to give it to him, but he wouldn't take it."

"I said we'll deal with him."

"I can help."

"Let it go. Tomorrow is a new day."

"The dawn of a new era."

"Precisely," he replied before hanging up.

BY THE TIME Stewart reached Interstate 395 north heading toward the capital, a light rain had begun to fall, the drops pebbling his windshield.

He checked the dashboard clock and, seeing the time, swore under his breath. He had ninety minutes to get to the helipad before the chopper took off without him. And he still needed to contend with the uniformed Secret Service agents at the White House gates before he could get to the helipad.

He sucked in a deep breath, let it out slowly. Relax, he told himself. Unless he hit a traffic snarl—always a possibility in Washington, D.C.—he could make the flight in plenty of time.

If not... He'd rather not think about that.

Under the current White House administration, Stewart had become a rising star within the State Department. With bachelor's and master's degrees from Yale, and his father's connections as a Fortune 500 CEO, he'd enjoyed a leg up on the competition in trying to make it in the dog-eat-dog world of national politics. It hadn't been easy by any stretch. But the clout his parents carried definitely had lessened the uphill climb he'd faced.

Stewart's position with the State Department, though,

had carried with it an extra perk. He was now part of the continuance of government team, meaning that he'd been hand-selected to help run the government in the event of a decapitating strike on the government.

Before September 11, he'd heard rumors of such a program, but had considered it little more than a cold war relic, a hangover from spending the last several decades waiting for another superpower to nuke you into extinction. His attitude had changed after the terrorist attacks on New York and Virginia, with that horrific day galvanizing his belief that the country needed a fail-safe in place should something happen to the federal government.

Half an hour later Stewart wheeled the Lexus off the interstate, his mind consumed with getting to the White House on time. The orders had been explicit, the implications of failure thinly veiled. If he arrived too late, the chopper would leave without him, ferrying the others to a secure location where they could wait out the president's speech to Congress. If he missed the flight, he might as well go home and begin surfing the want ads on the Internet.

He only vaguely noticed the traffic light ahead had turned red, and then only when brake lights winked at him through the windshield. He pumped his own brakes, brought the car to a halt. The rush-hour traffic had largely dispersed for the evening, but he still had cars on all sides. Absently, he cast a glance up at his rearview mirror and caught a pair of headlights bearing down on him.

Before he could react, the car smashed into the Lexus, shoving it into the car ahead of him. With a loud pop, the air bag deployed, swelling out of the steering wheel and flattening him against the backrest, doubling his confusion.

For a moment, the stench of the air bag's accelerant burned Stewart's nostrils, filled his mouth with an acrid flavor as he gasped for air. The bag almost immediately began to deflate, easing the pressure on his chest and allowing him to begin to regain his senses.

Movement to his left caught his attention, prompting him to turn. He saw a pair of jeans-clad legs and the bottom of a leather jacket in the side-view mirror. Releasing the automatic door locks, he reached for the seat belt.

Before he could release the clasp, the door flew open. He turned to look up at the person who'd opened it, saw a big man with a clean-shaven head standing in the doorway. The man was yelling, "Oh, my God, are you okay? Are you okay?"

Stewart thought the man's concern was over the top, considering that it had been a minor fender bender. He'd been about to say that when the man leaned inside the doorway, his left arm leading the way. Stewart felt a small pricking sensation, followed by a burn in his neck, near the carotid artery.

"What the hell?" he said.

The guy pulled back his arm and Stewart caught a glimpse of the man stowing something in his jacket pocket. The State Department executive again started to release his seat belt, noticing almost immediately that his arms felt heavier than usual. He fumbled with the buckle for a few moments before his fingers finally found and pressed the release button.

By this time, the man in the doorway had withdrawn and turned his back on Stewart. He could hear the man yelling, his words becoming increasingly garbled.

"—police officer," he heard the man shouting. "This man's having a seizure. Everyone get back!"

A seizure? Stewart thought. He didn't have seizures. He tried to raise an arm to grab the guy, tried to open his mouth to speak, but found his muscles didn't respond to his commands. He could still hear the man—his assailant—yelling. But it was becoming increasingly difficult to make out the words. He stared up at the car's upholstered ceiling, realized with horror that his lungs were straining for breath. He struggled to catch his breath, heard the faint croaking coming from his mouth as the sounds around him sounded increasingly distant, garbled, like a recording played at half speed.

He felt someone grabbing his shirt, shaking him. "Hang on!" they shouted. Was it Linda? Was she here to help? Maybe she had followed him, hoping to convince him to take the phone with him. She'd miss him so much overnight. She'd told him so. He heard someone wheezing and felt himself spiral into a panic. His vision dimmed, replaced by an oppressive blackness, as though someone had pulled a blanket over his head. Maybe it was Linda, trying to cover him up, trying to take care of him, he thought just before he stopped thinking at all.

THE STOCKY MAN with the clean-shaven head—an assassin named Clay Robbins—pressed his fingertips gently against his target's wrist, under his thumb, checking for a pulse. Finding nothing, he released his grip, letting the hand fall. He began to back out of the car's doorway. Before he'd taken his third step, he felt a hand on his shoulder, fingers digging into his shoulder muscle.

Tensing, he whipped around. A woman, short, stout, dressed in blue hospital scrubs took a step back, startled at his sudden motion.

"I'm a doctor," she said. "Can I help?"

Robbins shook his head. "I think he's gone."

Scowling, the woman brushed past him and leaned into the Lexus. Robbins backed away from her, letting the crowd flow around him as onlookers vied for a peek at the dead man. He continued to distance himself from the scene, first stepping out of the street and onto the curb, then walking briskly away, trying to keep an eye on the accident scene as he went. In the distance, he heard sirens wailing and knew he needed to get away before the authorities came and complicated things.

Grabbing his mobile phone from inside his jacket, he placed it to his ear and stared at the accident. The few onlookers who noticed that he was walking away, probably assumed he was calling for help and turned their attention back to spectacle unfolding before them.

A few blocks later, he was home free. Walking three blocks east, he stepped between a pair of marble buildings where he found a black Chevrolet sedan, windows tinted, engine running, waiting for him. Sliding into the front passenger's seat, he gave the driver a curt nod and dialed a number on his phone.

His right foot tapping out a manic beat, he waited for the call to pass through a series of cutouts. When Campbell answered, the assassin kept it brief. "Target eliminated."

"Good," Campbell replied before ending the call.

STANDING IN THE CONTROL room, Campbell clipped the mobile phone to his belt and ran a mental tally of the dead.

Nationwide, his operatives had killed twenty-five government employees—each one a part of America's conti-

nuity of government program—within the last week. Most
of the deaths had looked like accidents, but the killers had
occasionally used other causes—an apparent heart attack
in Ohio, a home invasion in Los Angeles, a mugging in
New York—to prevent a pattern from forming. Of those
killed Stewart had held the highest rank; the deaths of the
others, a host of midlevel bureaucrats, barely would make
a ripple, especially since no two had worked for the same
agency.

With all the very real threats facing the United States
within the past twenty-four hours, Campbell was willing
to bet that no one within the government would have the
time or inclination to piece together twenty-five seemingly unrelated deaths. He checked his watch and realized
that the numbers had begun to fall, that he now was just a
few hours from bringing the country back from the brink
of its madness, setting it back on course so it could return
to its true fight, its sole calling.

Scanning the control room, he saw his people positioned at their workstations, each handling some critical
piece of the mission. A tickle of excitement registered in
his stomach as he realized just how close he was now. It
was just a matter of hours. He thought of his grandfather,
his father, and wished both men could be there to see him
now. This was, after all, their moment of glory, not his.
They'd fought the good fight for decades, steeling the
country—hell, the world—from communism. They'd sac-
rificed everything for their country—family, friends, social standing—and now that same country wanted to steal
all that away. Dismantle his family's legacy, leave the
country vulnerable to communism's creeping threat.

Campbell crossed his arms over his massive chest. They

all could go to hell, the nonbelievers. He'd save the damn country from itself, restore it to its former glory.

Almost like a tidal wave slamming into him, the visions returned, this time with staggering clarity. Fields of fire in Chicago, New York, Los Angeles. Flashes of white, like a storm of supernovas exploding across the country, swallowing everything in their path, transforming flesh into wisps of charred, tattered paper a microsecond before bone disintegrated into air choked with radiation and smoke.

These were the visions that had been passed down to him. His father, his grandfather, both had made sure he understood the consequences of allowing Communists to overrun the earth, like vermin, infecting everything they touched.

These unholy bastards lived only to deal nuclear death upon others. This much he knew because his elders had assured him of all of this, day in, day out. They'd hammered it into him from the age of five, that one day he'd be the only thing standing between the free world and utter annihilation. He'd known since childhood that it'd come down to this, spilling blood to preserve even more.

A lesser man might have caved under the pressure, have considered the visions a harbinger of insanity.

Campbell welcomed them, in some ways considering them an uncomfortable ally. They drove him to operate on an hour's sleep, pushed him to plan and plan, propelled him to train his body and mind, rendering them flexible, sharp, deadly. He'd trained all his life for this day, often praying long into the night that it never would come, but always knowing it would.

The visions would have it no other way. If he were to snuff out the raging fires, the agonized screams thundering in his head, then he needed to unleash a hellish rain on Washington, one powerful enough to wash away the indifference toward the world's real evil. Doing so also would bring him another step closer to exorcising the horrific images that raged through his mind, which, though a powerful ally, also haunted him mercilessly. He reasoned that, after today, they would have served their purpose and he'd be free to move on without them.

"Sir?"

Campbell blinked, turned toward the speaker. Stephen Preston, one of his aides, stood to his right, arm cocked in a salute.

"Yes?" Campbell asked.

"We have the Marauder in the appropriate orbit. It should be over Washington at the appointed time."

Campbell nodded. "Fine." The man didn't budge. Campbell studied his face, saw his lips drawn tight, forehead wrinkled as though he were contemplating something, weighing his words carefully.

"You have something else to say?" Campbell asked, irritated. "Spit it out."

"It's Block, sir, your security chief. He came up missing. Now we're catching reports of a shootout at the warehouse in Los Angeles."

Campbell muttered an oath. "Who took him?"

"We don't know. Not precisely, anyway. We'd been listening in on his phone calls, as you'd instructed. A federal agent came to his house, asked him about the kidnapped woman and the dead marshals."

"And?"

"White told him to head to the warehouse. Wanted him to help remove any last signs of our operation there. We followed his car on GPS. He went to the warehouse. Shortly after that, the police radios went crazy with calls about a shooting. The place likely will be crawling with police within minutes."

"How many of ours are there?"

The guy shook his head. "Not sure."

"Could any of them know about this place?"

Campbell watched as the man licked his lips, using the motion to buy time. "Yes."

"So we could get hit soon."

"Yes."

"How long until White gets here?"

"Twenty minutes, maybe longer. Your orders, sir?"

"Mobilize our people. I want them ready for any strikes that might come. I want whoever attacks us to encounter seven kinds of hell when they get here."

"Yes, sir!" The man saluted crisply, turned on his heel and went to deliver the order.

CHAPTER TWENTY

Hal Brognola stood in the control room, watching his people labor over their computers.

Akira Tokaido, the youngest member of Stony Man Farm's cyberteam, whistled, grabbing the big Fed's attention. The young man stared at his screen for a second, tapped a few keys, drummed his thumbs against the desktop, apparently pantomiming a drumbeat playing on the portable CD player hooked to his belt. A moment later, he stopped drumming, whistled and slid off his earphones.

"What've you got, Akira?" Brognola asked.

The young man turned to him. "You know the list of government employees the Man gave us? The folks who'd step in to form an interim government should something happen to the president, his cabinet and most of Congress?"

"Of course," Brognola said, nodding.

"I took the names and cross-checked them against a bunch of databases. It was more of a fishing expedition. I wanted to see whether any of them had any connection with Campbell, be it business or political. I checked the usual criminal and counterterrorism databases, of course.

But I also cross-checked the names with a lot of others, everything from the Securities and Exchange Commission to the Agriculture Department, whatever I could find. Even the commercial news databases."

"Got it," Brognola said. "So?"

"What would you say if I told you fifteen of those people have died, across the country, in the past hour."

"I'd say, 'uh-oh.'"

"That's what I'm saying," Tokaido replied. "It's all happened so fast, across such a wide geographic area, that most people wouldn't have a chance to piece it together. And the deaths run the gamut—car accidents, medical ailments, even a murder. No one would piece it together unless they were looking for it, which I wasn't."

Price had walked up beside Brognola during the conversation. "Campbell's eliminating the competition," she said. "He wants the Cadre to be able to step into the slot immediately, should something happen to the president and the others."

Brognola heaved a big sigh. "Contact the FBI," he told Price. "Send them the list and tell them they need to start rounding up the rest of these people, if they can. Tell them to activate every field agent necessary to find anyone on the list not already under wraps. If they give you any grief, drop my name."

Price nodded. "Consider it done. What else?"

Brognola thought about it. "Contact the Pentagon. Tell them to double or triple the security at Andrews Air Force Base. If I remember my cold war lore, that's where the vice president and selected cabinet members hop a jet and take to the skies so that someone's in the air if a nuke falls on Washington."

"Drop your name again?"

"Like a sledgehammer. Not that I carry a lot of weight there. But enough people know me well enough to know I don't cry wolf."

"We don't want them to scramble those jets," Price said.

Brognola gave her a quizzical look. "Why?"

"If Campbell's people have shoulder-fired rockets or some other ordnance, they potentially could take out the plane without much problem."

Tokaido interjected, "Considering that Campbell's group is supposed to be a damn shadow government, it's pretty safe to assume they have access to heavy firepower. For all we know, he has combat aircraft and the like available for his own use."

"Make the call," Brognola said. "In a perfect world, we'd scramble Phoenix Force, Able Team or Striker to protect these VIPs. But, as thin as we're spread, that's not an option. So contact the military and lay it on the line for them. If they get a heads-up, we know they'll move heaven and earth to protect these folks. In the meantime, I'll call the president. He doesn't know it yet, but he has a speech to cancel. And I'm the lucky bastard elected to tell him. In fact, I may end up suggesting that he evacuate every square inch of the Capitol before it's all said and done."

Aboard the U.S.S. Pendleton

SCOWLING, LYONS LEANED against the wall of the officers' wardroom, his arms crossed over his chest. He stood behind Schwarz and Blancanales, both of whom were seated at a table, across from Oliver Kresge, commander of the nuclear submarine propelling them through the Pacific

Ocean, two hundred miles from the shores of Mexico. Three Navy SEAL commandos and the ship's lieutenant commander also were present.

Kresge spread a series of photos over the tabletop, arranging them in two neat rows of three. "The oil platform is 175 miles off Mexico's coastline. According to these satellite photos, we count at least a couple dozen people on the decks at any given time. The place is bristling with satellite dishes. Although we couldn't see any weapons in the open, these photos reveal a dozen or so doors, possibly hydraulic doors like those on this ship's missile batteries. I can only assume that the tower has the sonar capabilities necessary to pick us out of the water."

"Making an approach potentially deadly," Lyons said.

"I'd feel better if I had two or three more submarines going along for the ride," the commander admitted.

Lyons shook his head. "Too risky. I'm antsy using even one. If I'd have thought we could have made it under our own steam without this submarine, I'd have done it."

"Understood. Like I said, the ship's at your disposal. We'll drop you off, and then the clock starts ticking. You folks have one hour. On the sixty-first minute, we drop the Tomahawk missiles on that platform. Those aren't my orders. They come straight from Washington. I'm sorry."

"Right," Lyons said. He knew the commander spoke the truth. In addition to Able Team, a missile strike would slaughter a hostage and the three Navy commandos helping with the op. No officer wanted to bear that burden, though Lyons trusted Kresge would carry out his orders with efficiency.

"We play this by the numbers," Blancanales said. "When we get the hostage, we'll activate the beacons on our radios and set off red smoke grenades. If you get one or the other, instead of both, the mission's fallen apart." He turned toward the three Navy commandos. "If that happens, you guys get your butts off the platform, stat. No heroics. If I had my way, I'd do this damn op solo. I already had this discussion with these two hardheaded bastards, but they won't listen to me."

The SEAL commander, Lt. Jake Bombeck, a short, barrel-chested man with a scar snaking down his left cheek, shook his head. "'Preciate the sentiment, sir. But my men and I stand down when I decide, and not a moment before. We want hard proof that the lady's okay, or that she's out of the picture entirely, before we hit the water. Understood?"

"Understood," Blancanales said. "Thanks."

Schwarz cleared his throat and hit a button on his laptop. A three-dimensional drawing of a shaft extending from the underside of the platform filled a screen on the far wall. The drawing, green lines set against a black background, indicated a tube-shaped chamber with two hatches.

"This is our entry point," Schwarz said. "From every bit of intel we can find, the platform's design is similar to that of a commercial platform manufactured by a subsidiary of Campbell Industries. This shaft has a pair of hatches, one opening into the water, a second leading into the platform."

"Like the escape trunks on this sub?" Blancanales asked.

"Right. The problem is, the chamber only accommodates three people at a time. So a few of us will have to wait while the others board the platform."

"We can go first," Bombeck said. "Secure the entry point."

"Negative," Lyons said. "No offense, Lieutenant, but we take the lead on this play."

Bombeck's lips formed a bloodless line. Exhaling, he said, "Your call, sir."

Lyons turned to Schwarz, nodded. Schwarz pressed a series of keys and, moments later, a close-up of the oil platform's top deck came into view. A pair of Sea Hawk helicopters, each coated in flat black paint interrupted only by white tail numbers, stood within thirty yards of each other.

"I'll need one of you to get topside to secure these helicopters," Lyons said. "There's two reasons for this. One, I don't think the lady is trained for deep-sea diving. And, if she's injured, I'm not subjecting her to cold water and pressure unless absolutely necessary. Two, these craft likely are outfitted with torpedos and sono buoys, so if a pilot takes them in the air—"

"He could knock us out," Kresge said.

"Right."

Bombeck gestured with a thumb at one of his commandos, a slight man with swarthy features. Lyons remembered him from the introductions as Tony Haddad. "We'll put him on the choppers," Bombeck said. "He can shoot the balls off a fly at a hundred yards. And he's a hell of a pilot. Can fly anything with rotors or wings. So he can airlift the lady out, once you find her."

"You read my mind. And just to clear up any other misconceptions you guys might have about this mission, listen up. These people are not American soldiers. They worked for the American government. Some are former military, but these are the die-hards. They know what David Campbell plans to do to our country, and they've elected to throw in with him. Whether it's for ideals, or money, I don't care. They've killed people and, left on their own, they'll kill more. What I'm saying is, don't feel squeamish about putting them down. Clear?"

The members of the SEAL team nodded.

"Good," Lyons said. "Then let's hit it."

THE WATER PRESSED HARD against Blancanales's face, sucking away the heat from the exposed skin of his cheeks, chin and lips as he sat in the rear of the Swimmer Delivery Vehicle. Lyons and Schwarz were seated next to him, all three men hooked into the vehicle's closed-circuit breathing system. A fourth man, Tony Haddad, the SEAL commando, also was situated with them in the rear of the vehicle. Bombeck and the third Navy commando, a lanky Texan named Johnny Emmett, were operating the vehicle.

Blancanales had checked his gear three times before the departure, but patted himself down again, making sure everything was positioned properly, running over his mental checklist as he did. His lead weapon on this mission was the M-16 A-1 outfitted with the M-203 grenade launcher. He also had fitted the weapon with the Aimpoint Comp-M sight, which imposed a red dot on targets, increasing accuracy in close-quarters combat, and a vertical broom handle on the underside of the muzzle. A pair of SIG-Sauer P228s, loaded with 9 mm HydraShok cartridges, rode in thigh holsters. Like the others, he also carried a speargun. In his belt pouch, he carried the smaller SIG-Sauer P239 loaded with a 10-round magazine. He planned to hand this weapon over to Donna Ling if he found her.

Scratch that. *When* he found her.

He'd consider no other alternatives.

It was, after all, his fault that she was in this situation.

Ling was a tough lady. Strong, confident, independent. But against a guy like White, and his boss, Campbell, she was in over her head. In over her head and possibly drowning. Blancanales knew the stakes were much bigger than helping her. He realized that if Campbell had his way, America would suffer its darkest day. So Blancanales had no illusions about what was at stake here. But he also realized that Brognola had stuck his neck out, buying them an hour in which to pull off the rescue. He knew Lyons and Schwarz and these SEALs were putting themselves in harm's way, in part to help him. He could never thank any of them adequately enough for that. Except by doing what he'd come here to do. So he'd damn well do it. Or die trying.

BOMBECK'S VOICE BUZZED in the SDV's radio. "We're at thirty-five feet," he said. "Get ready to switch to the Draegers." Blancanales switched to his Draeger Mark V bubbleless diving rig and saw his comrades doing the same.

Blancanales estimated they were about 250 yards northwest from the platform when he and the others began disembarking from the craft. He adjusted his buoyancy vest to compensate not only for his own weight, but also that of his weapons and gear. Taking his attack board in his hand, he began heading toward the platform, using the board's built-in compass to help guide him. Schwarz fell in with him, as Lyons and the other divers split off and swam at the platform from another angle. The final SEAL remained with the SDV, where he would wait for the group to give him an all-clear signal. Once he received the signal, he would travel to the platform and tether the SDV to it.

Using powerful kicks to propel himself forward, Blancanales glided through the water. Occasionally he'd lift his gaze from the dive board, scan the bluish-green field of water for threats. Although he saw nothing, he still could feel his pulse thud in his throat as he neared Campbell's stronghold. He knew that Campbell would have trained combat divers among his crew and, like Blancanales, they also would have the rebreathers, making them virtually undetectable, except by sight.

Casting a sideways glance, he checked to make sure Schwarz remained close by. His fellow commando flashed him a thumbs-up, which he returned before continuing on. Schwarz carried a speargun and was swimming in a heads-up position, following Blancanales who was navigating with the attack board. Blancanales slipped a combat knife from his belt scabbard and clutched it tightly in his right fist as he again focused on the compass.

After about two hundred yards, Blancanales slowed his pace and scanned the area again. This time, he felt his combat sense nagging at him, though he still couldn't see anything. He looked over at Schwarz who continued sweeping his own gaze over the horizon. Several yards later, Blancanales spotted bluish-white flashes in the near distance, prompting him to stop. Schwarz did likewise and both men stared ahead, straining their eyes to identify the source of the lights.

Moving more cautiously now, they closed in on the platform, gliding through another twenty yards or so. The light grew brighter with each kick forward until Blancanales finally identified the source. A welder was working on one of the support struts, the torch's glow illuminating his front, with two other divers hovering nearby. Blancanales knew it was only a matter of time before the men spotted him and Schwarz.

He looked at his partner, an implied question in the gesture. Schwarz nodded and dived downward at a forty-five-degree angle, as Blancanales angled upward, slow, powerful kicks propelling him forward. Flattening out his approach, Blancanales hung suspended in the water for a moment, watching Schwarz cut through the water below, like a shadow. He prayed that the men kept their attention on the repair job for another moment or two while his friend moved into position.

Sunlight streamed through the water at Blancanales's back and he noticed almost too late that it had caused him to cast a shadow, slight, nearly imperceptible, but enough to catch the attention of the diver to his left.

The diver whipped around, raising his speargun as he did. The motion caught the second diver's attention and prompted him to turn even as the first triggered his weapon in a hastily placed bid to end Blancanales's life.

Acting on instinct, the Able Team warrior kicked hard to get off the firing line, his body suspended for a moment as he tried to get his weight moving. Almost too late, he slipped off target, the trident-tipped spear cleaving through the water just in front of his face, driving him backward. Even as he recovered, he saw the second man acquire him as a target with his own weapon. Before Blancanales could react, though, a black shaft lanced upward from the depths and caught the man under his chin, driving forward through his mouth and into the uppermost parts of his skull. A dark crimson immediately streamed from under the man's chin as his body went slack, and he released his hold on his weapon.

Blancanales immediately spotted Schwarz rocketing up from the depths. He'd let the empty speargun fall loose on its strap and was fisting a combat knife as he closed in on the welder. The man turned, a column of fire spitting from the torch. Schwarz brought the knife around in a vicious arc, the blade biting deep into the man's flesh. The welder's mouth opened and his regulator slipped from between his lips. Before his victim could react further, Schwarz had ripped the knife from the man's leg and shoved it into his abdomen.

Suddenly outnumbered, the final diver whipped around, ready to fire his reloaded speargun in Schwarz's direction. Blancanales surged forward. He fisted his own speargun, snap-aiming it and firing on the move. The shaft caught the man in the arm, prompting him to release his weapon and whirl toward his adversary. The Able Team commando actually had been aiming for the man's chest, but, under the circumstances, was willing to take what he could get.

As Blancanales closed in, the man ripped a knife from his scabbard and kicked backward, allowing him to face off against both commandos. Moving cautiously, the Hispanic closed in on the other man. Like Schwarz, he'd let the speargun hang on its strap and instead clutched the long combat knife he carried on his belt. The inflated buoyancy vest, combined with the slowing effects of the water, made him feel as though he were pushing his way through a wall of frozen tree sap.

Outnumbered, the guy apparently had decided to go for broke. Planting his feet against the steel support column, coiling his legs, he sprang forward, the knife slashing out a path toward Blancanales. The soldier feinted to the right, letting the man's momentum propel him forward. The enemy passed within a few inches of Blancanales's shoulder, but corrected his course by arcing back toward the Stony Man fighter. Blancanales whipped around at the waist and brought up the blade, burying it in the man's gut, twisting it, dragging it horizontally across his adversary's midsection. A moment of shock registered on the man's face as his mouth gaped open and he spit out his regulator. He writhed like a speared fish for a moment. His left hand stabbed out wildly as he grabbed for his opponent's face mask, the last act of a desperate man. Blancanales ripped the blade from the man's gut and stabbed again, driving it between the man's ribs. He drove the flat of his palm into the man's chest, shoving him away as he yanked the knife free. A small line of silvery bubbles escaped from between the man's lips, tracing the length of his cheek. His eyes closed and his corpse sank into the cloudy depths.

With his buoyancy device punctured, the hard guy began to sink, striking against the steel support structure before slipping away into the cloudy depths of the gulf. Blancanales kicked his way toward Schwarz, and both men continued for the air lock. As they closed in, they saw that Lyons and the SEALs already had gathered around the door. A pair of shadows circled overhead, grabbing Blancanales's attention. He glanced up, saw two more divers, their chests torn open, leaking blood, floating above them. Apparently the other team also had encountered its own difficulties along the way, Blancanales thought.

Bombeck, the SEAL team leader, was using a security card to open the door. Blancanales assumed the man had stolen it from one of the dead guards. A light on top of the locking mechanism switched from red to green, and a moment later, he was opening the heavy steel door.

Bombeck gestured toward the opening. With a nod, Blancanales moved through the door with Lyons and Schwarz right behind him. The room was cylindrical, probably about eight feet in diameter and nearly that tall. Blancanales spotted a camera. Kicking his way toward it, he used the knife blade to slash away at the wires leading from the camera into the wall. In the meantime Schwarz had closed the door behind them and latched it shut with a metallic click.

A control panel stood on the wall next to the damaged camera. Schwarz's fingers glided over the panel, selecting a series of buttons. Blancanales continued to check out their surroundings. A steel ladder attached to the far wall led up to the overhead hatch. Lyons, who'd shed his flippers, climbed the ladder, clutching a Glock in his right hand. Blancanales knew the durable pistol could be submerged in water or mud and still fire dependably.

Blancanales followed behind Lyons. Taking the M-16 from his shoulder, he stood on a ledge that jutted about two feet from the wall and ran the circumference of the room. He left in place the condom he'd wrapped over the muzzle to prevent water leaks. Jets hummed from within the walls as they began to expel water from within the sealed chamber. Shortly, a one-foot gap had opened between the ceiling and the water's surface. Lyons spit out his regulator, yanked the mask from his face, leaving it looped around his neck.

He jabbed his trigger finger into a green button on a small panel situated next to the ladder. The door stood fast. He swore through clenched teeth, then spotted a yellow lever behind glass. With a wicked grin at his lips, he shot out his hand, driving the pistol butt through the small pane of glass, shattering it. Reaching through the small portal, he gripped the lever and yanked it down. The overhead hatch jerked into motion, sliding into a recessed area in the ceiling.

Alarm bells also reverberated through the small chamber.

Wincing, he looked back at Blancanales who stood on the ladder just behind him, scowling.

"Nice, Ironman," Blancanales said into his throat mike.

"Kiss my ass while you're back there," Lyons replied.

When the steel door had slid away enough to accommodate his bulky frame, Lyons surged forward, his head cresting the portal's rim. Scanning the room, he spotted a pair of men, both togged in camouflage fatigues, moving through door. They split in separate directions as each raised a weapon in Lyons's direction. The Able Team leader bracketed the guy scrambling to his right in his sights and fired a double tap of .40-caliber rounds that pounded into the guy's chest, slamming him back into the wall as his assault rifle slipped from nerveless fingers.

The Glock leading the way, Lyons spun and found the second guy locking him in the sights of his assault rifle. The rifle rattled through a quick burst of fire. The bullets sizzled the air around Lyons, forcing him to drop back through the portal. Holstering the Glock, he grabbed a stun grenade from his belt pouch, activated it and tossed it up through the hole. A white flash pierced the room above. As he scrambled back up the ladder, Lyons fisted the Joint Service Combat Shotgun by its pistol grip.

As he surged through the hatch, Lyons caught the guard, still blinded, hands scrambling to unleather a pistol in a shoulder holster. A roar rent the air as the Benelli-made shotgun hurtled a 12-gauge slug into the man's center mass, savaging his torso and thrusting him into a nearby wall. The guy slid to the ground, head lolling to one side, foot twitching in a final death spasm. Clambering up the ladder, Lyons slipped through the portal and swept the weapon over the room. His ears rang from the exposure to the shotgun blast in such a confined area. He spotted the toe of a boot-clad foot protruding from behind an upright locker, the door ajar, diving tanks and other gear visible from within.

"Behind the locker," Lyons yelled. "Step out now, or we take you out on a slab."

The foot remained still.

"I'm going to count to two," Lyons said. "Then I fire."

Another pause.

"One," Lyons said.

The Benelli roared once in his arms. The blast hammered against the open door, ripping it from the hinges, sending it bouncing away.

A guy stepped into view, hands up, face bloodless. "Prick," he said.

"Get out here. Drop on your knees. Now!"

The guy complied. He even went the extra step of lacing his fingers together and clasping them behind his head. Lyons was out of the portal and stepping onto the deck. Blancanales followed right behind, the M-16 held at waist level. Stepping behind the guy, Lyons drove a foot into the man's back, knocking him facedown onto the deck. An instant later, Blancanales was on the guy, relieving him of a 9 mm pistol and binding his hands with plastic cuffs.

Lyons activated his throat mike. "Gadgets, what's your status?"

"I'm ready to let the rest of the party in. What you got upstairs?"

"Couple of corpses, thanks to yours truly. One hostage."

"I need two minutes. Can you get me that?"

"Bet your ass."

Loading fresh shells into the shotgun, Lyons turned and saw Blancanales rising to his feet. He had the M-16 aimed at his captive's back.

"A woman was brought here several hours ago," Blancanales said. "She would have come with Ellis White. Where is she now?"

The guy hesitated and Blancanales drove a booted foot into his ribs, causing an audible crack. The sheer savagery of the attack, the glint of rage in Blancanales's eyes surprised Lyons. He'd seen his old friend keep his cool against terrorists, drug dealers and crime kingpins, exuding a range of personas from quietly detached to outright charming. Whatever the mission required. But something in Blancanales's posture, the hardness of his voice, told Lyons his friend was ready to deal death, not with the detachment of a professional soldier, but to quell some inner rage.

"The woman," Blancanales said.

"Second level," the guy replied. "Officers' quarters are up there."

"You want to tell me which room?"

The guy did.

Blancanales nodded. "Good choice."

He looked at Lyons. "I'm going," he said.

"Bullshit. Wait until Gadgets brings the other guys in here. You can take a couple of the SEALs with you."

Blancanales shook his head. "Wrong. This is personal. I appreciate the help, but this I do on my own. You guys just take out Campbell and the satellites."

Scowling, Lyons regarded his friend for a moment. After a few seconds he exhaled audibly, nodded toward the door. "Go," Lyons said. "Give the lady my regards. It'll brighten her day. I think she was hot for me."

Blancanales allowed himself his first grin in several hours. "Aren't they all, amigo?"

"SIR," THE CORPORAL SAID, "they've breached the entry shaft."

"Strength?" Campbell asked, scowling.

"Six."

"Casualties?

"Seven."

"Ratio?"

"All ours."

Campbell's frown deepened in tandem with the creases lining his forehead. The corded muscles sheathing his arms, shoulders and legs seemed to buzz with electricity as rage coursed through him, energizing him, threatening to immolate him if he didn't strike out at someone or something, release the rage roiling within.

Pinning the corporal under his gaze, he took a moment to weigh the situation. He was so close at this point that he couldn't afford to lose focus, no matter how much he wanted to do so. There simply was too much riding on this for him to give in to his baser emotions. He tried to size up the situation, and decide on a corrective course of action. They'd already lost their operation in Somalia, losing one of only two control boards capable of handling the

Marauder satellite. Glancing over his right shoulder, he saw a team of technicians seated at the remaining control board, putting the Marauder in position to fire its deadly payload.

"Time until launch?" he asked.

"Fifteen minutes, sir."

"Unacceptable," he yelled. "Un-fucking-acceptable."

"But, sir," one of the technicians said, "we can't accelerate the firing sequence without endangering the satellite. If we do that, the missiles might fire prematurely and destroy the Marauder."

Campbell felt his face and neck burn hot with rage. He let his right hand settle on the butt of Beretta holstered on his right hip. "Accelerate the sequence," he said. "Get that thing in flight as fast as you can."

The technician stared at Campbell for a stretched second, swallowed and turned toward the control panel. "Yes, sir."

Campbell switched his glance to a bank of television monitors affixed to a far wall. All were tuned in to various news channels, each broadcasting coverage of the president's address to Congress. The president already had taken the podium and stood silent while the legislators showered him with a thunderous applause. Disgust welled up inside Campbell as he watched the man, the alleged leader of the free world, bask in such adulation. The way Campbell saw it, the man was a farce. He defanged true patriots such as Campbell and other members of his family who'd served the country with such selfless loyalty, by befriending Russia and China, coddling the savage hordes in North Korea. Campbell knew his first act as president would be to send a clear message to the world, one that would reverberate for generations.

By God, he'd do what should have been done long ago.

He'd unilaterally withdraw troops from South Korea and let missiles rain down on Pyongyang, North Korea, turning it into a nuclear wasteland. China, Japan, South Korea, even Russia and Europe, of course, would protest mightily. To hell with them. Let them posture and protest publicly. Privately, they'd fear him and the United States, they'd know with a certainty that to cross him would invite wholesale destruction, particularly now that he'd claimed strategic superiority with satellites.

The thought of North Korea, its massive army decimated, its citizens vaporized, its land, water and air irradiated for generations, caused his lips to twist into a satisfied smile. He exhaled deeply, felt the tension drain from his shoulders and neck, knowing that within hours he'd right the wrongs perpetuated by the government.

The other governments, even so-called major countries such as Russia and China, would back down. And his ancestors would smile down upon him, praising him for doing even what they could not do.

A voice interrupted his thoughts. "Sir?"

He turned toward the corporal.

"Your orders?"

"Kill them, of course."

ELLIS WHITE HAD SWITCHED into a black, SWAT-style blacksuit. He slipped on a load-bearing harness covered with ammo pouches and a heavy Bowie-style fighting knife. A Glock 19 hung in shoulder leather and a micro-Uzi ran counterpoint, slung in the opposite armpit. Alarms blared throughout the oil platform's interior. He heard boot soles slamming outside his quarters as his men mobilized to root out the intruders.

He stared at the image frozen on the security monitor in his room, spotted a man he knew all too well. He stood less than six feet tall, but he had a bulky, powerful upper body, like a bull. The face was painted black with combat cosmetics, but White recognized Blancanales in an instant.

A grim smile played on White's lips. The guy was so damn predictable. White knew he'd come looking for Donna Ling. He'd want what he considered justice in that deluded, idealistic mind of his. Hell, he probably felt some sort of guilt for her capture, some responsibility for her situation. White couldn't fathom such loyalty and certainly couldn't respect it. But he was more than happy to exploit it.

An H&K MP-5 filled with Black Talon 9 mm rounds lay on the table next to White. He grabbed the weapon, switched it to full-auto and started for the door. He didn't have to contemplate Blancanales's next move. He knew the guy would head directly for Ling, making her safety a priority over his own. He'd do it, White knew, because he was predictable, little more than an automaton, unable to stop himself from doing the right thing.

It'd be the death of him, White thought. He'd already arranged things so that Blancanales would likely learn the woman's location. He might—might—even get to her.

But he'd never get out, that much White knew. The knowledge filled him with a joy he'd never felt before. By this time tomorrow, White, discredited soldier, would be the chairman of the Joint Chiefs of Staff under Campbell. And he'd do it in a world without Blancanales.

Slipping through the doorway, he headed down the corridor, ready to destroy the man who'd tried to destroy him.

BLANCANALES SWEPT alongside the wall, the M-16 held at hip level. The scream of alarms filled the corridor, handicapping one of his most critical combat senses. About ten yards distant, he saw the passageway end, splitting into a T-shape. Scanning his memory for details from the floor plans, he recalled that the elevator lay to the left.

He'd ditched his mask, fins and tanks in the dive chamber's control room. The blacksuit clung tightly to his skin, wet, but not restrictive. Rubber-soled dive boots gave him the sensation of almost walking barefoot along the smooth, steel decks. His heartbeat thudded in his ears, competing with the wailing alarms.

He checked his chronometer. The group had used up fifteen minutes getting this far. He had less than forty-five minutes to grab Ling and get her topside before the *Pendleton* started raining Tomahawk missiles on the platform.

Just before he reached the corridor's end, he caught subtle movement. Shadows! A glance forward told him he'd betrayed his own progress the same way.

Flattening against the wall, he felt his breath deepen and accelerate. Nice moves, Blancanales, he thought. He forced his breath to become artificially shallow and slow until he brought his body under control. Dropping into a crouch, he held his ground, deciding to let them tip their hands first rather than bulling ahead into an ambush.

The first man came into view, wrapping himself around the wall, his pistol's snout homing in on where he'd expected to find Blancanales. In the instant it took the man to adjust his aim, the Able Team commando stroked the trigger of his own weapon, lashing the man with a burst of autofire that savaged his arm and shoulder.

The man reeled back, stepping from cover as pain drove him into view. Blancanales pressed the advantage, pummeling the stumbling man with a fresh volley of 5.56 mm slugs. As the first man crumpled to the ground, the Able Team warrior considered tossing a frag grenade around the corner, but immediately nixed the idea. With Ling somewhere on the craft, he had no intention of unleashing wholesale destruction.

At least not until he could see his targets. After that, all bets were off.

Anticipating a renewed attack, he did the unexpected and threw himself into the middle of the fray. He dived forward, rolled and came up with the M-16 ready to deal death. His targets—a man and a woman—both togged similarly to other fighters he'd encountered, reacted to the move surging in separate directions, each bringing assault rifles to bear on him.

The M-16 chugged in Blancanales's hands, spitting a blistering onslaught of tumblers. He drew the chattering weapon across his midsection, acrid white smoke fouling the air and stinging his eyes as spent brass spilled on the floor. The pair of soldiers jerked under the volley of slugs, death overtaking them as bullets rent their flesh.

Blancanales got to his feet, reloading his weapon as he did. He looked at the dead fighters and felt his lips tighten into a grim line. At one time, these people likely had been real soldiers, ready to fight and die for their country. But for one reason or another, they'd thrown in with a madman and the decision had cost them their lives.

Blancanales muttered a curse. Some days, he hated this damn job.

THE BENELLI SHOTGUN poised in front of him, Lyons slipped up the stairs leading to the third floor. Schwarz was two steps behind, an MP-5 steady and sure in his grip. The control center was on the fourth and final level of the platform. It was Lyons and Schwarz's destination.

The pair continued on up the stairs as the SEAL commandos split off, slipping through a doorway leading into the third floor, where they believed the barracks were located.

As the men disappeared through the stairwell door, Lyons heard Bombeck's voice buzz in his earpiece. "We've got your back."

"Raise a little hell, Bombeck," Lyons replied.

"Always."

Lyons and Schwarz ascended the last flight of stairs. Crouching on the landing, Schwarz poked the flexible camera lens underneath the door and stared into the viewer. Lyons stood at the ready, his combat shotgun pointed back down the stairs in case they got a surprise attack on their six.

"Clear," Schwarz whispered. Lyons watched as his partner gathered up the viewer's tubular lens and stuffed the apparatus into a belt pouch. Schwarz took up the MP-5 again.

Grasping the door handle, Schwarz nodded toward the door. "You want to do the honors, Shotgun?"

"Never send a boy in to do a man's job," Lyons replied, grinning.

"Ouch," Schwarz replied.

Schwarz popped open the door and wrapped himself around the jamb, the MP-5's muzzle searching out adversaries. "Clear," he said.

Lyons went through the door low, sweeping the shotgun barrel over the short corridor. Seeing nothing, he nodded to Schwarz who came in behind him. The men continued down the corridor, Lyons taking the lead. The small hallway spilled into a much larger corridor lined on both sides with doors. Fluorescent lights shone down on the polished floors, creating intermittent islands of white that bisected the length of the corridor.

The muffled sound of gunfire crackled from below. Lyons spoke into his throat mike. "Bombeck. Sitrep, now!"

"Hit a small pocket of them waiting for us," Bombeck said. Gunfire was audible in the background.

"Casualties?" Lyons asked.

"Negative. There's five or six of them hunkered down in the barracks, emptying their weapons at us. Nothing unexpected. Already took out two."

"You got it under control?"

"Stupid question."

Lyons grinned. "I'm full of them. If it gets too hot, don't be afraid to call the pros."

"Clear."

He turned and saw Schwarz holding a small device of his own design dubbed the Zapper, a handheld device capable of firing a concentrated burst of microwave radiation and melting a surveillance camera's insides.

"In the old days, we used to just shoot the things," Lyons groused.

"Welcome to the twenty-first century," Schwarz said, grinning.

"More like, same shit, different century," Lyons replied.

"Same Carl," Schwarz said, disappearing around the corner. Lyons knew his friend was going to disable the other cameras. It was no secret that the security people knew they'd boarded the platform, and probably realized that the fourth floor had been breached. But at least disabling the cameras would make it harder for the security guards to track their movements.

Lyons hoped so, anyway. He followed Schwarz into the main corridor, keeping the Benelli snug against his shoulder as they made their way toward the control room. As they neared the entrance, Lyons felt the small hairs on the back of his neck rise. A cold fist of anticipation buried itself in his gut, spurring him into action.

His hand snaked out, fingers grabbing the left shoulder strap of Schwarz's combat harness. He dropped to the floor, yanking Schwarz with him, whipping the Benelli's barrel around toward his rear. He spotted a pair of hardmen stepping into view, weapons trained on them. Lyons was barely aware of colliding with the floor as he locked the weapon's muzzle on his opponents. Tracking fire scythed through the air, carving out a path toward the Able Team warriors, pressing down upon them like a pendulum's blade.

The Benelli roared in Lyons's hands. The slug slammed into the man's knee, cut his leg in two, sent him crashing to the floor in a screaming heap. The second shooter abandoned his buddy and darted right, apparently trying to take cover behind the nearest wall. Lyons swung the Benelli, squeezed the trigger. The slug zipped just past the man's head as his return fire blistered the air just above Lyons and Schwarz. Before Lyons could readjust his aim, autofire chattered from behind him. Schwarz's MP-5 rattled out a murderous burst that caught the man midstride, tearing away part of his head in a bloody spray.

The man with the shattered leg lay in a pool of blood, breath coming in shallow gasps as he slipped into shock. Schwarz knelt next to the man, stripped the man's belt from his waist and used it to tie a tourniquet around his leg to staunch the bleeding. Wiping his bloodied hands on the man's shirt, Schwarz took up his MP-5 and returned to his feet.

Lyons, in the meantime, cast a wary glance around the corridor while he thumbed fresh shells into the Benelli.

"Command center," he said.

Schwarz nodded. Before Lyons could take another step forward, thunder pealed on the floor below, causing him to wince involuntarily. Even as the shattering noise dissipated, gunshots sounded below, crackling like a dozen bonfires. Shit! "Bombeck, sitrep," he said into his mike.

Nothing.

"Bombeck!" Lyons repeated.

Lyons clenched his jaw so hard it throbbed, even as his mouth went dry.

"Bombeck!" he said.

He felt a hand on his shoulder. Turning, he saw Schwarz staring at him, his mouth tightened in a grim line. "Ironman, we gotta go."

Lyons nodded.

Blancanales's voice sounded in his headset. "Ironman, report."

"We're okay," Lyons said. "I think we lost Bombeck and his team, though. Sounds like they got fragged."

Blancanales cursed. "Sorry," he said. "If you and Gadgets—"

"Don't go there. Get her and get her out of here. We're going to go save the world."

"Thanks."

"Don't get all weepy. Just do your job."

He heard a smile in Blancanales's voice. "Damn teddy bear is what you are."

"It's my curse."

Turning to Schwarz, Lyons gestured down the hallway with his gun barrel. He and Schwarz split apart and began moving. As they came within ten steps of the steel door leading into the control room, Lyons's scowl deepened. Here they were closing in on the nerve center of this psycho's operation and there were no guards to be found. What the hell was going on?

A light scratching noise caught his attention. He glanced over his shoulder, looked at a window that stared out over the broad expanse of blue ocean surrounding the platform. Concern etching his features, he stepped forward, the Benelli coming up, ready to meet any threat. An instant later shapes appeared in the windows. The shotgun belted out a full-throated roar as it thrust a slug through the glass pane and pounded into a soldier rappelling from the roof. Uttering an anguished cry, the man flipped backward and tumbled out of sight. Three hardmen, all brandishing assault rifles, came into view, their weapons rattling a single deadly refrain. Bullets lanced through the air at the commandos, forcing them to dart in separate directions as each returned fire in a desperate play to stay alive. In the next instant, motion to Lyons's right caught his attention. A ragged line of three more gunners came into view, their weapons spitting flame.

No doubt. They were outgunned.

He just hoped they weren't outclassed.

LING HEARD GUNSHOTS exploding outside her room, felt conflicting emotions of fear and relief. The shooting, she hoped, heralded a rescue attempt. But, unarmed, her hands bound by plastic handcuffs, she knew she was in no condition to fight or assist her rescuers.

But she planned to change that.

She had no intention of doing the helpless female routine. She had hesitated to make any moves toward escape, knowing full damn well that to do so was a suicide play. One unarmed person trying to plow through a small army would have been foolish, and she was no one's fool, period. And, even in the unlikely event that she'd managed to elude her armed captors, where would she have gone? She couldn't fly a helicopter, and the notion of trying to navigate a lifeboat through hundreds of miles of ocean was only slightly less attractive an option than taking a bullet in the heart.

But now? Just like at the so-called safehouse, she couldn't sit around and let others do her fighting for her. Couldn't let people take a bullet so that she could live. She needed to act.

Swinging her legs over the edge of the bed, she sat up. A swimmy feeling came over her and her stomach lurched. It's just the aftereffects of the tranquilizer, she told herself. Get off your tail and get to work. She got to her feet, unsteady at first, temples throbbing, throat and mouth parched.

Go!

She began to move, her strides becoming surer with each step, the motion purging the toxins from her system. She scanned the room, searching for a weapon or sharp object of some sort to cut her bonds.

Nothing. A bed, a chair, a table and an overhead light. She moved into the bathroom and felt hope swell within her. A small rectangular mirror was hung over the sink. She stared at it for a moment. Frustration almost immediately washed through her, drowning out the small flicker of hope. With her hands secured behind her back, she couldn't use them to crack the glass. Barely eighteen inches stood between the edge of the sink and the wall, robbing her of the space necessary to launch a good strong kick against the glass.

Stepping sideways, she brought up her leg and fired a kick at the glass. She misjudged the force necessary to break the mirror, and the toe of her tennis shoe bounced off the glass. Damn it! Her legs were strong from hours of jogging and yoga. But she wasn't a martial artist. She fell forward, coming flush with the wall. Pressing her chin against the wall, angling her back to place her weight behind her, she rocked herself back onto the soles of her feet.

Frustration welled up inside her, causing her throat to throb, her eyes to brim over with angry tears. An image of Ellis White on top of her filled her mind. The memory of his mocking smile, the glint in his eyes loomed large in her mind's eye.

Damn him for what he'd done. Damn Rosario for having brought this hell upon them in the first place.

And damn her for having been too weak to prevent it, she thought.

White had compounded her pain by putting her in a situation where she'd been forced to take a life. Morally, legally, she knew she'd done the right thing. But the thug's look of surprise and pain was seared on her mind, her soul, one more image she'd never be freed from.

Now White wanted to use her as bait, use her to draw Blancanales so he could kill again.

She'd see him in hell first.

She kicked again, her foot striking against the mirror's edge. The impact rocked the mirror, but didn't cause it to break. Another kick split the glass, but the frame held it intact. Two more strikes knocked it from its moorings, causing it to fall against the sink and shatter, littering the floor with silvery shards of glass. Kneeling, she gripped one of the shards, felt its edges cut into the soft flesh of her palms.

Ignoring the pain, she stroked the glass along the edge of her bonds. When the bonds held, she moved the glass across them in a furious sawing motion. As they snapped open, she heard the door latch click, followed by the heavy slap of footsteps against the floor as they entered the room.

WHITE MADE HIS WAY through the doorway leading into the room housing Ling. A quick look around the cramped quarters revealed that she was nowhere in sight. He crossed the room in quick strides, heading straight for the darkened bathroom.

Sweeping his gaze over the room, he noticed that a lamp was missing from a table. A grim smile played over his lips. The woman was nothing if not predictable.

He knew there were only two places the little bitch could be hiding, under the bed or in the bathroom. He brushed past the bed and headed for the bathroom. If he knelt next to the bed first to look for her, he risked getting hit from behind. It'd hurt, but not enough to knock him unconscious or to kill him.

He just didn't want her to get the best of him again. For

a moment, he swore he could feel the scarred skin, puckered and wrinkled, where she'd sliced him with a lamp all those years ago. He cared little about the scars themselves; it just pissed him off that anyone—especially a woman—had sliced him open and lived to tell about it. And, with Blancanales here on the rig, she'd outlived her usefulness.

Maybe.

Reaching the door, he rounded the jamb. Something glinted as it dropped toward him. Acting on reflex, he batted aside the lamp as it arced toward his head, the MP-5's cold steel shattering the light. Ling stepped forward from the shadows of the darkened bathroom, her full lips pulled back slightly, teeth clenched with rage and exertion. Her other arm stabbed forth. Pain seared White's forearm.

White bulled forward, threw his weight into the woman, pinning her up against the wall. He heard breath explode from her lungs. A bloodied hand clutching a shattered piece of the mirror, her hand slashing wildly at him. Clamping down on her wrist, he drove the muzzle of his weapon under her chin, pushed back her head at an excruciating angle.

"Stop," he whispered.

She struggled another moment before she went still.

"Drop it."

She hesitated. He stared at her, saw eyes, angry, narrow, searching his own.

"Don't test me," he said. "You won't like it."

Injured fingers unfurled stiffly. The weapon dropped to the floor. Seeing that she'd fashioned a makeshift hilt by wrapping a washcloth around it, he guessed she had to have cut her palms earlier, probably when she'd sawed through her bonds. Whatever. He knew a few superficial cuts were the least of her worries.

"Good choice, sweetie," he said. Easing his weight from her, he shoved her roughly through the door. She whirled toward him. Clutching her injured hand to her breast, her face framed by long tendrils of black hair, she smiled at him.

"He's here, isn't he?"

"Screw you. Let's go."

"Pol's here. Isn't he?"

"Yeah."

"You're scared."

"Keep talking crazy and I'll blow your damn head off."

She raised her chin defiantly, but he detected a hint of fear in her eyes. "Do it," she said.

He let out a short, derisive laugh. "Honey, if you'd wanted to die, I mean really wanted it, you'd have pushed me back there." He nodded over his shoulder at the bathroom. "You didn't. So spare me the bullshit."

The light scuff of a boot sole against the floor caused White to whirl toward the door. Centering the SMG on the door, he appraised the threat. One of his men, weapon raised, poked an arm and a sliver of his face around the doorjamb.

The guy's gaze lighted on White. He looked relieved.

"'Bout time you people got here," White said. "Watch this floor. You're about to have some company."

"Yes, sir."

"We're going to the first floor. You understand me? The first floor."

Both men nodded.

He reached out for Ling, but she yanked her arm away. "I'll go, damn it," she said. "Just don't touch me."

Grinning, he nodded toward the door. They exited her

quarters. White gestured toward the elevator with the MP-5's muzzle. Ling started toward it, walking a couple of steps ahead. An elevator ride later and they were on the first floor, wending their way through the corridor that led to the outer deck. He swiped his card through the reader and the door hissed open, allowing them access to the main deck. He gestured with the SMG and Ling walked through.

The sun hit square-on, warming his skin, the breeze brushing over his face. Donning a pair of wraparound sunglasses, he reached out, grabbed Ling by the arm and led her away.

The pair walked several paces over the deck. They reached an iron tool locker, a rectangular box that stood waist high and measured seven or eight feet in length. He led the woman around to the other side and, with a hand on her shoulder, forced her to kneel behind it. Coming down next to her, he rested his weapon on top of the locker, aimed it toward the doorway, ready to blast anyone stupid enough to walk through it.

Taking in a deep pull of the briny air, he exhaled loudly. He loved moments like this, when all hell was breaking loose around him. The carnage brought his senses to life. Sounds became more vivid. Same with smells. Some might consider it an odd paradox, but he never felt more alive than when he was killing someone. And White knew that killing Rosario Blancanales would make him feel damn good.

CHAPTER TWENTY-ONE

Blancanales slipped through the stairwell door and onto the second floor. He slung his rifle and stripped the SIG-Sauer handguns from his shoulder rigs, preferring the sound-suppressed weapons to the M-16 as he closed in on Ling's position.

His belly burned with anger, mostly at himself, as he edged along the wall, pistols raised, eyes scanning for threats. Though the SEALs knew the dangers they faced, he couldn't help but feel partially responsible for their deaths. He had insisted on making one last try at extricating Ling before they decimated Campbell's stronghold with a shower of Tomahawk missiles. His comrades on Able Team and at Stony Man Farm had supported the move, had insisted on helping him. Had Phoenix Force been close enough geographically, they likely would have stormed the platform with Able Team.

Campbell would answer for the deaths, Blancanales vowed. Whether by his own hand or someone else's remained to be seen. But the guy was going out on a slab.

Soon enough.

He smelled cigarette smoke and stopped just before rounding a bend in the short hallway. Muffled voices reached his ears and he strained to listen.

"Put that thing out, man. What the hell's the matter with you?"

"Nervous."

"Campbell's going to kick your ass."

"Screw that crazy bastard. He's not out here on the line, waiting to get shot."

"Chickenshit."

"Screw you, too."

The owner of the first voice laughed. Blancanales peered around the corner and sized up the men. Two soldiers on opposite sides of the corridor. The smoker leaned against the wall, his assault rifle hanging from his shoulder, his shooting hand busy fiddling with his cigarette. The second hardman stood upright, CAR-15 assault rifle cradled in his arms. Fidgeting, the guy stared at the end of the hallway opposite Blancanales.

Blancanales stretched the SIG-Sauer in his left hand around the corner and fired at double tap at Smoky. In the same instant, the guy opened his mouth to speak, but was interrupted by a pair of 9 mm rounds piercing his temple and cheek. As his comrade stiffened, head disappearing in a crimson haze, the second guard reacted. In a single fluid motion, he surged from his position and raised his CAR-15. Muzzle-flashes blossomed from the weapon and a swarm of bullets sizzled around Blancanales.

Dropping into a crouch, the warrior gritted his teeth as bullets punched through the wall, cutting a vertical line toward him. He thrust himself from cover, sliding across the floor, the SIG-Sauers chugged out half a dozen shots. Bullets slammed into the man's legs, rending flesh, causing blood to geyser upward. The man plummeted to his knees, his weapon slipping from his grip, skidding across the floor.

The man clawed for a pistol hanging in a shoulder holster. Blancanales fired the dual pistols again. The rounds ripped through the man's arm, hammered hard against his body armor, the blunt force knocking him backward. Blancanales rocketed to his feet and closed the distance between himself and the fallen soldier. Kicking the CAR-15 out of the man's reach, he knelt next to the man, jammed a pistol against his temple. Blancanales kept his gaze cold, sending the guy an unmistakable message.

No mercy.

"The woman," Blancanales said, "where is she?"

"Gone. White took her."

"Where?"

The guy licked his lips, swallowed hard. "Don't know. They went down. Maybe to the deck."

Blancanales nodded. Coming to his feet, he crossed the hall, found a door hanging open. The SIG-Sauers leading the way, he went through the door, searching for targets. He found no threats, but what he did see caused his stomach to clench.

Blood droplets—some the circumference of quarters, others larger—lay on the floor, etching a trail from the bathroom to the door. A glance into the hallway revealed the blood trail continued. He'd missed it before, obscured by the heat of combat, the life fluids spilled by the fallen fighters in the corridor.

A curse exploded from between clenched teeth. Anger surged through him. He allowed himself the momentary luxury of letting blind rage course through him, anesthetizing him to the overwhelming realization that he'd again failed Ling. Swallowing hard, he drove the blind rage into a dark corner in his soul, felt his body go numb.

He rounded the doorjamb and surprised a pair of hardmen, probably dispatched to investigate the shooting. The men split apart. The one to Blancanales's left triggered an MP-5 submachine gun, filling the hallway with tracking fire that chewed its way toward the Able Team commando. The other man was bringing up his own weapon, an Uzi, ready to cut Blancanales down.

Flame erupted from Blancanales's twin pistols. The guy with the MP-5 suddenly seized up as a trio of red holes opened across his chest. The second shooter caught two rounds in the face, stiffening as they drilled through his nose and forehead. Even as the men folded to the ground, Blancanales was stepping over them. A third soldier who stepped out of the stairwell went down in a similar manner, after a pair of Black Talon rounds lanced through his throat.

Blancanales passed by that man, too, appraising him with the cool precision of a soldier, making sure the guy really was dead, but otherwise forgetting the expression of shock etched in the man's features. At the moment, Blancanales felt like a man split in two. One part dealt death coldly, the other watched, divorced from the actions he witnessed.

Reloading his pistols, he started down the stairs, his mind locked on his target like a heat-seeking missile locked on a fighter jet's exhaust nozzles.

SCHWARZ AIMED the MP-5 toward the soldiers at the window. One wrapped a leg over the window ledge and laid down a sweeping barrage of autofire that sent Schwarz diving left. A second man was trying to hook his leg over the ledge so he could get some stability. Schwarz leaned on the MP-5's trigger, swept the SMG over the window. Rounds sparked, careened off the metal frame before stabbing through it. Hot lead ripped through flesh, chewing through Campbell's soldiers before they could correct their own aim and retaliate.

SLIDING HIS RIGHT LEG out straight, resting most of his weight on a bended left knee, Lyons emptied the Benelli in the direction of the approaching hardmen. One of the slugs hammered into the middle guy's face, causing his head to evaporate in a red mist. The other flew wild.

The sight of their suddenly decapitated comrade caused the other men to scatter. Tossing aside the spent shotgun, he fisted the Glock and the Colt Python. The guy to his right had flattened against the wall and had Lyons caught dead to rights. The second guy disappeared through a doorway.

Lyons fired a double tap from the Glock at the guy, a shot winging past the man's face, while the second grazed his cheek. The shooter twitched, as though stung by an insect, even as his assault rifle stuttered out several rounds. The shots buzzed harmlessly overhead. Centering the Glock's and Colt's respective barrels on the man's chest, Lyons squeezed off multiple shots from both weapons. The rounds tunneled through the man's chest, stealing his footing, ripping large holes in his back.

Instinct told Lyons to move and he complied. Uncoiling from the floor, he moved to the wall, flattened himself against it. In the same instant, the shooter came around the doorjamb, squeezed off a short burst from his CAR-15 before disappearing back under cover.

To hell with this, Lyons decided. Stepping away from the wall, he aimed both weapons at the point closest to the door and began unloading them into the wall. Bullets drilled through plasterboard, leaving gaping holes in their wake. A shrill cry sounded from within the room as Lyons emptied both weapons, the Colt clicking dry quickly. A heartbeat later, the Glock was empty. He holstered both weapons, fisted the Uzi and glanced inside the room. He spotted the shooter, his sprawled form riddled with bullets.

He turned to Schwarz, who was reloading his MP-5. Schwarz shot him a questioning look.

"Dead," Lyons said.

"That your professional assessment?"

"Bet your—"

"Yeah, I know. My ass. Bet my ass."

"Right."

"Next?"

"The big guy."

"Rock and roll."

CHAPTER TWENTY-TWO

Watching the pandemonium unfold on the security monitors, Campbell bit off a curse. Casualty reports were filtering in from all over the damn place. Making matters worse, White had disappeared. He stared at the technicians huddled over the controls of the Marauder, felt his rage edge up another notch.

"Sergeant!" he yelled.

The lead technician, the armpits and collar of his T-shirt darkened by sweat, whirled toward Campbell. The man's face was a mixture of fear and anger. "Sir?"

"Launch time?"

"We accelerated the sequence, chopped it down to three minutes."

"Not fast enough!"

"Sir—"

Couldn't they see how critical this was? Couldn't they see the tongues of flame raging through his mind, the visions tormenting him, driving him to fight this fight? If they couldn't see it, then by God, he'd show them.

His hand a blur, Campbell stripped his Beretta 92 from

a hip holster, leveled it at his men. The weapon cracked and a shot passed a foot or so over the technicians' heads, tunneling into a wall, drawing all eyes to him. "This isn't a debate. I've issued an order. Do it!"

"Sir! Yes, sir!" the technician said. He and the others turned back toward the control boards, the bank of monitors. Their hands glided over buttons and switches with renewed urgency. Holstering the pistol, Campbell glanced at the monitor again. Gunshots sounded outside the command center, muffled only slightly by the reinforced doors.

They were coming, facing less resistance with each second. They could be here any second, ready to take him out. Destroy everything when he was so damn close, literally seconds from realizing a multigenerational dream of a new world order, one without communism, one unwilling to suffer the fools, murderers and savages populating the world. If he failed, the visions remained behind to torment him.

Snapping up an M-4 rifle, he moved to the lead technician. "Continue the launch," he said. "If anything goes wrong, I'll hold you personally responsible."

Swallowing, the technician nodded. "Yes, sir."

Gesturing to two of his guards, he exited the control room and went in search of the commandos. The armed men followed him through the door, ready to hunt down and kill the intruders.

SURROUNDED BY WISPS of gun smoke and scattered corpses, Lyons popped out the Colt Python's cylinder, emptied the spent brass on the floor. Using a speed loader, he recharged the weapon. The Benelli, now loaded with double-aught buckshot, was slung over his shoulder. He heard Schwarz ram a fresh clip into the MP-5 and chamber a round.

Lyons expected reinforcements to arrive at any moment. They had, after all, raised enough noise to wake the dead.

Let them come, he decided.

He was ready.

Edging along the wall with a silence that belied his hulking frame, the warrior traded the Python for the Benelli, knowing this was no place for surgically precise shooting. His heart hammered in his chest. The stakes, he knew, were enormous. Taking out the platform, in and of itself, was a simple task, one that could be accomplished by a few well-placed missiles. But doing his part to make sure his comrades left the platform alive, mission accomplished, was Lyons's definition of winning.

So it was time to win.

Peering around a corner, he spotted three men exiting the control room, immediately recognized one. Campbell! Stepping from behind the wall, Lyons sprinted for the trio of men, bringing up the Benelli as he did. He stroked the trigger and thunder pealed in the corridor's narrow confines. Even as the weapon discharged, one of the hardmen flanking Campbell reacted, shoving the man roughly from the path of the shotgun's assault.

The MP-5 coughed to Lyons's right as Schwarz raked the SMG over the guy.

In the meantime Lyons tried to readjust his aim, but Campbell darted from his field of fire, disappearing down another corridor. The shooter remained behind, muzzle-flashes blossoming from his CAR-15. Lyons dropped to one knee, allowing the tumblers to whiz overhead. Moving the Benelli in target acquisition, he triggered the weapon, squeezing off three shots in rapid succession. The first struck his opponent in the belly, shoving him backward, nearly eviscerating him in the process. The second and third shots also struck the man, but did little more than rip through already dead flesh.

Lyons turned to Schwarz. "Control room."

Schwarz gave a curt nod and headed for it.

Lyons passed the fallen hardmen and picked up Campbell's trail, moving down the same hallway that had swallowed up the madman seconds ago. Windows lined the passageway and about halfway down Lyons saw glass spread over the floor, the M-4 discarded and lying on the floor.

Moving cautiously toward it, Lyons heard the rumble of the gulf waters swirling below, smelled the salt clinging to the air. Closing in on the window, he saw that it had been shattered, the Gulf's white-crested waters swirling below.

Campbell, a jumper? Bullshit.

Lyons combat senses screamed for him to turn. He wheeled, caught sight of Campbell, eyes narrowed with rage, cheeks colored an angry scarlet. The Benelli rumbled twice, both shots hammering into Campbell's torso, shredding flesh and fabric, nearly tearing the man in two. Like a leaf caught in a gale, Campbell sailed back into the room behind him. Lyons gave the guy's remains one last look and headed for the control center.

SCHWARZ WRAPPED C-4 plastic explosives around the control-room door's locking mechanism. Clutching the detonator in his hand, he took several steps back, slipped into an alcove for shelter from the impending blast. He'd overdone the amount of explosives, but didn't care. He hoped that the ensuing blast would send shock waves reverberating throughout the room, knocking Campbell's people on their asses, giving him the advantage.

He thumbed the button on the detonator. A bright yellow flash filled the hallway, accompanied by a thunderous crack and boiling smoke. Even as the blast's report died down, he sprinted for the control room. He came through the door low, the MP-5 seeking targets as he scanned the room for threats.

The blast had floored two of the men. One lay on his back, hands cupped over his ears as he groaned in pain. The other was on all fours, apparently trying to collect his senses. The MP-5 stuttered two short bursts, taking out each man. A bullet burned just past Schwarz's nose, originating from his right. Whirling, he caught the shooter, a young woman. She was already readjusting her Glock to take another shot. The MP-5 stuttered once more, bullets pounding into her torso, killing her.

Another man, apparently still stunned by the blast, sat on the floor, his back propped against a table leg. A half dozen or so other people—possibly technicians—stood up from their workstations, raised their hands.

"Who's in charge here?" Schwarz bellowed. When no one answered, he pointed the MP-5 at the man closest to him, startling the guy. "You hear what I said?"

The man, his moon-shaped face made all the more ridiculous by a pair of horn-rimmed glasses, pointed toward another guy, a man in a T-shirt, his face and torso wringing with sweat.

"Him," Moon Face said.

"You got a launch in progress?"

The guy avoided Schwarz's gaze. He stared up at the

ceiling, spoke. "Saddler, Charles. Sergeant. Serial number—"

A shotgun boomed from behind, causing Schwarz and the man named Saddler to flinch in unison. The blood drained from the guy's face as he and the others in the room stared over Schwarz's shoulder.

From the corner of his eye, Schwarz saw Lyons enter the room. "Awfully hard to play hero without a head, Saddler," the electronics genius said. "If you don't want to play ball with us, fine. But we'll burn you down like a damn field of sugarcane. Prisoners are optional with us."

The guy stared at Schwarz and Lyons for a moment, his face pale but otherwise inscrutable. An instant later, his body sagged and he looked at the floor.

"What do you want to know?"

"The Marauder," Schwarz said. "Where's it at in the launch sequence?"

"Five minutes and counting."

"Shit. You need to stop it."

The guy shook his head. "Can't. I need a code to stop it."

"Who has the code?"

"Campbell."

"Uh-oh," Lyons said.

Schwarz felt his mouth go dry. He turned to look at his comrade. "Does that mean what I think it does?"

Lyons nodded. "He's fish food."

Schwarz cursed under his breath. "Can you destroy the satellite remotely?"

The guy hesitated. Schwarz snapped off a burst from the MP-5. The bullets passed inches over the guy's head, causing him to duck, yelling as he did. "What the—"

"Can you destroy it remotely?" Schwarz repeated.

The guy nodded.

"Then do it," Schwarz said.

Nodding, the guy turned and walked to his workstation, Schwarz following a few steps behind. When the technician sat, Schwarz shoved the MP-5's muzzle against his temple. The guy began tapping on the keyboard. Moments later, Schwarz saw the words Launch Sequence Aborted flash across the screen.

He turned to Lyons. "It's over," he said.

Lyons nodded.

CHAPTER TWENTY-THREE

Crouched next to White, Ling stared at her captor as he all but ignored her.

With slow, deliberate movements, she reached inside her pants' pocket, wrapped her fingers around the chunk of broken glass she'd stowed there before confronting him. The piece was hardly an ideal weapon, only about three inches in length, the tip slightly rounded, likely to hang up on clothing if she tried to jam it into him. But it was something. She'd use it when the opportunity presented itself.

In the meantime she had other weapons at her disposal.

"Maybe he's not coming," she said.

"Shut the hell up," he said, his gaze never wavering from the doors leading onto the decks. "He'll come."

"Don't be so sure," she said. "Campbell's the real threat here. For all you know, if they get Campbell, Rosario and the others will leave."

He shook his head. "Never happen. He'll come for you. He'll come for me."

"What makes you so sure?"

"Unfinished business."

He looked at her, eyes narrowed, not in anger, but in the cold confidence of a hawk winging its way toward prey.

"This time around I'll kill you, too. And I'll enjoy it."

A cold sensation darted down Ling's spine. Her breath stopped momentarily, but returned when the sensation of glass cutting her palm registered with her mind. Her face must have betrayed the pain because White's expression changed from cocksure arrogance to anger.

"What the hell?" Reaching out, he grabbed her shoulder, fingers pressing hard into her flesh. Before he could make another move, the chatter of gunfire grabbed their attention.

Ling turned in time to watch as glass windows pounded by bullets disintegrated. The sweeping barrage ripped through a line of soldiers, rending flesh, killing them before any could squeeze off a shot.

White dismissed Ling with a rough shove. For an instant, through the swirling gun smoke, she spotted Blancanales, his black eyes staring out onto the deck. She heard White growl, only to have it drowned out an instant later as his MP-5 came to life, tongues of flame darting out of the muzzle.

BLANCANALES DARTED AWAY from the window, heading for the main door. Peering around its jamb, he spotted a pair of Campbell's warriors, walking about ten feet apart from each other but headed toward him, their weapons churning out twin streams of death. Rounds lanced through the doorway, striking the walls behind him.

Reaching inside a satchel on his web gear, Blancanales palmed a fragmentation grenade. Pulling the pin, he let the spoon fly from the weapon as he tossed it through the door. Thunder pealed, drowning out the small-arms fire, and a flurry of shrapnel whizzed through the doorway, burying itself into walls and the floor.

The din subsided and Blancanales chanced a glance outside. He saw no other soldiers immediately in view. However a second later, bullets dug into the walls at his back, driving him inside.

He rode out the barrage, trying to determine whether it came from one or more sources. From what he could tell, only a single gunner was firing at him. But that didn't mean only one shooter, possibly White, remained on the outside deck.

"Pol, sitrep," Lyons demanded through the headset.

"I've got shooters pinned down on the deck," Blancanales said. "One. Maybe more. Too hard to tell."

"I'm on my way up."

"Got it, Ironman. You take care of Campbell."

"Already waxed him," Lyons replied.

"Good. What about the satellite?"

"Out of commission."

"Clear."

"You stay put. I'll be up there to cover your six in a second. No heroics. You read?"

"Roger."

Sorry, Carl, Blancanales thought. I just can't do that.

Ending the call, Blancanales rose up into a combat crouch and slipped through the doorway. He was rewarded for his efforts by a fresh fusillade of gunfire winging its way toward him. Surging left, he took cover behind a forklift. He saw the source, a shooter hunkered down behind a large steel box about fifteen yards away. He recognized White's face in an instant, especially the thick, arched eyebrows that had been etched into his memory years ago.

Blancanales figured that he had a better than fifty percent chance that Ling was with White. Not wanting to endanger her, he unslung the M-16 and switched it to single shot, waiting for the gunfire to die down so he could draw a bead on the guy.

He probably should have heard his attacker sooner, but his ears continued to ring from sustained exposure to gunfire, dulling that critical sense. At the last moment he heard the scuff of a shoe sole against the ground. Whirling, he had a microsecond to process what he faced, an attacker driving a rifle butt at his face.

Blancanales tried to avoid the strike altogether, but only succeeded in rolling with the blow. The impact of the rifle butt against his chin sent him reeling, throwing him to the ground, driving him from cover. He'd lost his grip on the M-16 and found himself empty-handed against an armed opponent.

The coppery taste of blood filled his mouth and he found it hard to focus. The guy raised his weapon again, ready to deliver another buttstroke. Blancanales, powerful leg muscles coiling, uncoiling, sprang forth. He struck the guy's stomach, drove a meaty shoulder into it. He was rewarded with the whooshing sound of breath exploding through clenched teeth. He and the other man struck the ground hard, with Blancanales on top, his fist raised to deliver another blow. The guy brought his legs up, wrapped his ankles around his adversary's neck and yanked back on his head, until it felt as though Blancanales's spine might snap.

Grabbing the man's feet, Blancanales, his muscles surging with adrenaline, pried them apart, freeing his head. The guy tried to catch his opponent with the move again, but

Blancanales knew better this time. Reaching out, he grabbed a handful of the man's hair, yanked his head forward and slammed it against the oil platform's steel-plated floor. The guy took a swing at Blancanales, while also bucking like a steer to throw him off. The Able Team commando threw out his forearm, blocking the guy's right hook and continued his own assault.

Two more strikes against the platform and the guy's body went slack as life left him.

Stripping one of the SIG-Sauers from his shoulder harness, Blancanales crawled off the dead man.

Lyons's voice crackled in his earpiece. "I hear gunshots. What the hell's happening?"

"Got it in hand, Ironman."

"Damn it."

"See you soon."

Blancanales darted out from behind the forklift, drawing fire from White. Bullets struck steel plating, sparking and whining. Turning at the waist, Blancanales fired a double tap at White. The bullets whizzed past the man, missing him by more than a foot, but forcing him to seek cover. Blancanales fired three more shots into the steel barrier protecting White. As expected, the bullets careened off steel, but forced his adversary to remain under cover.

LING WATCHED as White grabbed a fresh magazine from his satchel. Ejecting the old one, he prepared to reload the weapon.

Now! Ling's mind screamed.

Pulling her hand from her pocket, the mirror shard clutched between bloodied fingers, her hand shot out. The point carved out a path toward his temple. Sensing the movement, White wheeled, batted her hand away with the empty MP-5.

The broken glass flew from outstretched fingers, landing somewhere out of sight. Out of reach.

Ling thrust herself forward, wrapping her arms around White's waist and knocking him flat onto his back.

"Fucking bitch," he said. Balling her hands into fists, she began striking him about the face and shoulders, felt her own fists, unaccustomed to colliding with bone, go numb. She stared down at his face, saw it was contorted with rage.

Then a smile.

Pain seared her side. Suddenly her throat felt constricted, her chest crushed under an unmovable weight.

White pulled back a hand and showed her a knife covered in blood.

Her blood.

His hand shot forward, a flat palm striking her in the middle of the chest, knocking her backward. She lay for a moment, struggling to regain her breath, quiet her racing mind as it struggled to make sense of the overwhelming pain. White came at her again, the knife arcing down at her. Throwing up her hands to protect herself, she felt the blade bite through more flesh. Heard someone screaming.

Her screaming.

"Stop," she heard someone say. "It's you and me now."

Pol, she thought as consciousness slipped away. It's Pol.

BLANCANALES ROUNDED the steel locker, the SIG-Sauer pointed in a two-handed grip. In the same instant, White surged up from the ground, went in low at Blancanales's midsection. The SIG-Sauer coughed once, the round whizzing just past White's face as he closed in. Before Blancanales could readjust his aim, White came in close, his knife hand slashing up, slicing through the flesh of his adversary's wrist. Blancanales grunted, dropped the pistol.

White pressed the attack, whipping the knife blade across his body in wide sweeps, forcing Blancanales back, separating him from the fallen pistol.

Fists clenched in front of him, the Able Team warrior stepped back three paces, the knife cutting less than an inch from his face each time. On the third cut, Blancanales stepped to his left. White dragged the blade in a horizontal swath, exposing his ribs. Powering the punch with his hips, Blancanales drove a fist into the other man's torso. It felt like hitting a bag of cement mix, hard, unyielding.

White spun away, firing a kick at Blancanales's lower leg. The kick probably was meant for his knee, but was sloppy, glancing off his shin instead. Bolts of pain almost immediately began stabbing through flesh and bone. Blancanales sucked in a deep breath, heard his heartbeat thunder in his ears. The two men circled each other for about ten seconds before White's right hand rocketed forward, the knife blade gleaming as it cut toward Blancanales's left shoulder.

Instinctively, the Hispanic threw up a hand to block the attack. White's right foot fired out for the other man's groin. Blancanales twisted at the waist, inserting his upper thigh into the path of the kick. The blow shoved him back, made it painful to put his weight on that leg.

White was unrelenting. The blade lanced forward. Blancanales stepped aside, robbing the sharpened steel point of its intended target. The knife's edge slid across the Kevlar vest, but didn't pierce it.

The sudden movement saved the man's life but stole his balance, causing him to crash down on one knee. White fired another kick that cracked Blancanales in the face, breaking his nose, and thrust him on his back.

Immediately blood spurted from the point of impact, draining into his mouth and trailing from nostrils, saturating his face and neck. Blancanales tried to stand up, but a spinning kick delivered to his head knocked him off his already faltering balance.

"Good moves," White said. "Just not good enough."

Too late, Blancanales caught the impression of a boot sole lashing out at him. It struck his temple, the edge of a heel tearing open his skin. Grinding his teeth, he rolled with the blow, allowed the force to carry him from his opponent. Staring at White's face through a haze of blood and pain, his lip curled in a snarl.

"When I'm finished with you, I'll party with your ex-girlfriend."

Eyes narrowing, Blancanales spit a watery mixture of saliva and blood onto the deck. "Should've stayed dead," he said.

His foot surging forward, its edge collided with White's knee, snapping it like dried kindling. White teetered, his face contorting with rage and pain, before crashing to the deck.

Blancanales came to his feet. His movements fueled by rage and adrenaline, he closed the distance between them, fired off a side snap-kick that landed squarely in the center of White's face, knocking him back.

Blancanales knelt next to the other man. Gripping White's head in his hands, he snapped the guy's neck with a violent twist, released his hold and let the body fall to the deck.

"That had to hurt." Blancanales spun, saw Lyons standing there.

"Him more than me," the Able Team commando said, managing a smile. He looked down at his injured wrist, saw his sleeve matted to his skin, shiny with blood. Feeling unsteady on his feet from the blood loss, exertion and physical punishment, he wanted to sit on the deck.

Ling.

Making his way to her, he found her sitting up, her palm pressing against an open wound on her chest below her right shoulder. Dropping heavily next to her, he pulled a compress from inside a pocket in a thigh pocket on his pants. Ripping open the plastic sheathing with his teeth, he took the compress from the package. Gently removing her hand from the wound, he pressed the compress against it.

She gave him a weak smile. "Thanks."

He nodded at the deck. "Lie down."

"I'm not that grateful," she said, wincing.

"Smart lady."

She allowed Lyons to help her lie flat on the deck.

"The *Pendleton*'s sending a second SEAL team, with a medic," Lyons said, his voice sounding farther away. "You've lost a lot of blood. Let me have a look at the arm."

"I'm okay," Blancanales said. A moment later, everything went black.

EPILOGUE

Virginia Beach, Virginia

Blancanales sat on the balcony of his hotel room, watching the sun, a creamy orange-red orb as it rose over the Atlantic Ocean. A copy of the *Virginian-Pilot* newspaper was fanned out across his lap, a cup of coffee situated on the floor at his right heel. A pair of lights burned behind him, illuminating the balcony as he waited for the sun to come up.

From behind him, the screen door slid open. He turned and saw Ling, wrapped in a white terry-cloth robe, stepping from the darkened hotel room. Sliding the door closed, she flashed him a tight smile, brushed past him and positioned herself in front of the chair next to his. Gripping the armrests, she gingerly lowered herself into it, wincing as she put weight on her injured shoulder.

"You okay?" Blancanales asked.

Staring out at the ocean, she nodded. "Not bad for someone who's been beaten, stabbed, stuffed in a trunk and exposed to a couple dozen corpses."

"I know how to show a lady a good time," Blancanales said, grinning.

"You have an interesting job. Care to tell me who you work for?"

"No."

"Bastard," she said, smiling. "How are you?"

He held up the forearm, still heavily bandaged, and smiled. "Just a flesh wound. I've had worse."

Folding her arms over her chest, she hugged herself, warding off the cool, morning air. "I mean, about things."

Blancanales felt his stomach plummet. Cocking an eyebrow, he searched her face for a clue as to where she was going with the conversation. "You mean us?" he asked finally.

"There is no 'us.'"

Exhaling, he felt his shoulders sag, relieved. "Good. I mean, nothing personal, but I'm not looking for anything permanent. My career doesn't exactly lend itself to white picket fences and homes in the suburbs."

"Darn, and I so wanted to wash the bloodstains from your fatigues when you came home at night," she said. "I love you, Rosario, but not like that. When it came to commitment, there always seemed to be something missing."

"Like, maybe, commitment?" Blancanales asked, his smile deepening.

"Precisely," she said, returning the smile. "We have a connection from the past, and I treasure what we had. But I don't think either one of us ever considered walking down the aisle. Not with each other, anyway."

Nodding, Ling stretched out her legs. Crossing them at the ankles, she studied her red-lacquered toes as she contemplated something. "You're a good man, Rosario. You always were."

"Thanks, but I'm like a magnet for violence, and so are most of the guys I work with. I tried to go back to a normal life after the Army. You remember that. I worked at the VA. But the real world just didn't fit anymore. Not after the war."

"You need the fight."

"Not for the sake of fighting. But because what we do—me and my friends—needs doing. Some people in the world don't want to negotiate. Won't negotiate. They kill people to further their own objectives. They cloak it in idealism, but when it gets right down to it, it's still the same thing—murder. I can't sit by and let that happen. Never could."

"We came pretty close. The country, I mean," Ling said.

He nodded. "Too close."

"Is it over?"

"He had a few people scattered here and there. But tracking them down was easy enough, once we hacked through all his records. I'd say everyone left behind is in prison by now."

She gave him a skeptical look. "Prison?"

"Or something."

"Like a body bag?"

"I prefer," he said, "the term 'zippered tuxedo.'"

She laughed again and Blancanales realized it sounded good. Turning to face him, she brushed a few strands of raven hair from her face, tucked them behind her right ear. "I leave tomorrow," she said. "I have to go back to California. To the real world."

"I guess that means we're hitting the outlet malls today."

"I might have a better idea," she said, a slight husk creeping into her voice.

Rising from the chair, she faced Blancanales, untied the robe's belt, let the fabric part. Blancanales took in her nakedness, felt a stirring inside as he did. Brushing past him, her fingertips grazing his shoulder as she passed, she slipped through the door and was gone. He stared after her. Standing inside, glancing over a shoulder at him, she let the robe fall from her shoulders, pool around her feet before she disappeared inside the suite.

Crumpling the paper, Blancanales tossed it aside, stood and followed her inside. If she was heading back to the West Coast the next day, he knew it was only proper to give her the appropriate send-off.

DEATH LANDS®

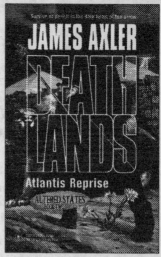

Atlantis Reprise

GRIM UNITY

In the forested coastal region of the eastern seaboard, near the Pine Barrens of what was New Jersey, Ryan and his companions encounter a group of rebels. Having broken away from the strange, isolated community known as Atlantis, and led by the obscene and paranoid Odyssey, this small group desires to live in peace. But in a chill or be-chilled world, freedom can only be won by spilled blood. Ryan and company are willing to come to the aid of these freedom fighters, ready to wage a war against the twisted tyranny that permeates Deathlands.

In the Deathlands, even the fittest may not survive.

Available December 2005 at your favorite retailer.